# the king of good intentions

BY THE SAME AUTHOR

*the knucklehead chronicles*

# the king of good intentions

*john andrew fredrick*

VERSE CHORUS PRESS
PORTLAND ✪ MELBOURNE ✪ LONDON

Published by Verse Chorus Press
PO Box 14806, Portland, Oregon 97293. www.versechorus.com

Cover and book design by Rachel Gutek for guppyart.com
Cover drawings by Steven Schayer
Author photograph by Steve Keros

Library of Congress Cataloging-in-Publication Data

Fredrick, John Andrew.
The King of Good Intentions / John Andrew Fredrick.
pages cm
ISBN 978-1-891241-10-9 (pbk.) -- ISBN 978-1-891241-93-2 (ebook)
I. Title.
PS3606.R4367K56 2013
813'.6--dc23

2012043157

"All novels are, in a sense, fairy tales."
—Vladimir Nabokov, *Lectures on Literature*

"I record these speculations not for their subtlety, certainly not for their generosity of feeling, but to emphasize the difficulty in understanding, even remotely, why people behave as they do."
—Anthony Powell, *At Lady Molly's*

"The poor King looked puzzled and unhappy, and struggled with the pencil for some time without saying anything; but Alice was too strong for him, and at last he panted out 'My dear! I really *must* get a thinner pencil. I can't manage this one a bit: it writes all manner of things that I don't intend—'"
—Lewis Carroll, *Through the Looking-Glass, and What Alice Found There*

"Madam, I say strange things, but mean no harm."
—Dr. Johnson in Boswell's *Life of Johnson*

*"She had to leave . . . Los Angeles."*
—X

# VERSE

## the house she used to live in

Los Angeles. Pale orange light coming from one of the double-cruciform upper windows and the sound of a piano low and plaintive. The sound of a passage most likely classical, gone over again and again, painstakingly and with method and too-beautiful too: the notes then swooping up and up and prettily trilling and then stretching out like weary sleepers eager for a bed and a blanket and a very dark room. Or so they struck me. It could have been, the sound, a record skipping, but doubtful. Outside the hot, boxy practice shed we were taking a break and smoking a hundred cigarettes apiece (well, Rob and I were; Walter hated smokers smoking), thankful for the relative cool, the night, with no clouds to tear the sky and maximum stars and a winking half-moon. For this was a time in La-La Land when tremulous stars could still be seen; when the firmament was firm, as it were, and unquenchable light-pollution did not yet hold sway over our glorious metropolis. Maybe I'm romanticizing, but at least it seemed that way—that there were heaps of stars that night. And isn't that—often—good enough? Or very good enough—a phrase we used jocosely when we'd flogged a song, over and over, till it sounded not exactly *very good* but very good *enough*.

The shed itself was a smallish wooden edifice rigged up inside with crapulous mingy orange carpet on the walls to keep the sounds down and the neighbors from positively freaking; a not-great midsized public address system with microphones and a gallimaufry of all our gear—drums, guitars, bass, chords, amps, a tape deck for taping rehearsals and random ideas, lyric sheets, stray strings, etc.—and the detritus of junk food and cardboard six-pack caddies. Plus tattered posters of Echo and the Bunnymen, Sonic Youth, My Bloody Valentine and the Beatles: all the heroes who buoyed us in our mad quest, well, to become a band. And one that *mattered.*

A small hot wind there was as well, an early fall unbreezy breeze thickening the air with night-blooming jasmine, palms canting in the distance and plosive jacaranda and purple bougainvillea everywhere you looked, in the starlight, in the moonlight. The house we were looking up at was Walter's, owned outright. Not bad for a drummer/trendoid menswear clerk with a trustful he, smartly, didn't dare allude to too often. Of course he'd inherited it, the house, an expansive, pretentious, pastel Victorian folly (castle blue, if there is such a color, with seasick-green trim and windows done in off-off-white)—a five-bedroom bastion of über-bohemianism he shared with a revolving cast of roommates and his diminutive, shrill goth girlfriend: a full-grown woman with the body of a little girl. A girl with charcoal hair and strange/beautiful non-Occidental grey-green eyes and too much makeup who came at you in a black plastic punk-rock miniskirt and a too-small top (perhaps to match her super-dinky mind). Pretty in a "she's *quite* photogenic" way—in other words, someone you could handle in Polaroid or celluloid (how Walt loved to roll out his/their Super 8 home movies; and how Nasty every time unfailingly said "Oh Walter not again—*please* don't," and the next thing you knew, another twenty precious minutes of your life was *gone*; just you try and wriggle out of watching someone's domestic flick when they quaintly propose just a little, hey-we-don't-have-to-watch-all-of-it, screening: sooner sit there blinking or shrugging when they say their dear old favorite ancient apple-cheeked granny's just kicked, or their baby's caught cancer or advanced leukemia or something, I'm not kidding you), but not in the fleshy flesh. Not at all, at all.

Name: Nastasha; Natasha; Nasti; Nasha or Nashi.

What she went by most oft, as far as I could tell, was Nasha: short for nauseous, basically. Which is what she made anyone with any taste, I always thought. I mean, not being able to specify what you're supposed to be *called* or anything? What's up with *that*? To be less than terrifically particular about what your particular nomenclature or even cognomen fucking *is*, as long as it starts with an "N" sound and ends in something mushy and faintly-fairly Russianish? I mean, come *on.*

But at that time in Los Angeles and especially Hollywood her kind, Natasha's, wasn't terribly uncommon or anything: you were *always* scraping acquaintance with or being hastily/insincerely introduced to people named Jayle or Paintpot or Psycho or Jordache; Keg or Krishnia or Krash or Snooshi; Quark or Quaalude or Mike-o or Mooki. And who, in the fat chance that you'd ever run into them again, say, a month later, might go: "Oh. Hey. Um, I'm not called, like, *Slush*, anymore, man, like, okay? I went back to Johnzo. That's what you can call me now, old sport. Only, like, you can't *call* me 'cause I don't have a phone right now—which is a drag. They won't let me have a jack at the Storage World storage space I just moved into, if you can believe it. Anyway, cool to see you."

Like, *seriously*, dude. Totally.

Out she came just then, actually, Nasha, just as Robert and I were putting out our flagging fags and wheeling back to the practiced shed. Onto the pale-blue-and-scuffed-black-checked porch, the ripped screen door singing like a monk or yak in pain, Natasha came and I (also like a monk or yak in pain) said:

"Hi, Natasha."

I didn't like her. You might have already gathered that. I didn't like seeing her; I didn't like hearing her; I didn't like smelling her; I didn't like talking to her. She brought out the old misanthrope in me, all right. Well, nearly *everyone* brings out the old misanthrope in me but Nasty, like, really ringmistressed him around and wound him up and got him jiving and ranting and slavering and shucking for the rabid, panting crowd, if you know what I mean. I had to watch myself around her; I really did. But the broken notes in my salutation—I know—betrayed me. I'm not the kind who conceals what he thinks of people. Not at all. You'll see.

A big plane blinked across the sky, headed anywhere, its colored lights a momentarily mesmerizing presence.

"Oh, hello," Natasha said back vacantly. Then, seeing her boyfriend emerging from the shed, added: "Do you guys want beers?"

"That's a silly question, darling," Walter singsonged. "Hi, baby."

Uxorious boy.

"Of course we do, babe—don't we everyone? Robert?" Walt went on.

"I know *Rob*ert does," Nasty tittered, then kind of lisped like someone pretending to be drunk. "He's such a *lush*. Aren't you, Robert? Walter's bass players always are. "

"Oh thanks a *lot*, " Rob said like the good sport he was.

*Walter's* bass players, I thought: you're joking me.

"Come on in then, you guys, " Natasha urged us. "It must be hot in the shed 'cause it's hot here, you know? It's time to stop anyway. I don't want the neighbors to . . ."

"Um, " I said. "We sort of have to kind of go over another song. We just have to tape one more new one, okay, you guys?"

Nasha gave me that schoolmarmy look she did so well—as if to say "You are absolutely *not* bashing away at any more indie rock songs tonight. This is *my* house and *my* shed and what I say *goes*. *Got* it?"

"I don't think so, John," she said. "It's past ten and you guys have to quit now, okay? All right? *Now!*"

Rude shrew.

Talk about your ice queens. I mean, fuck you and the popsicle stick you rode in on.

But I wasn't looking for a struggle of wills just then, a tussle I could not win. Boy was she ever a real nail-in-the-tire, that Nasty. Just a human headache, irremediable. If you quote-unquote got into it with her you might never quote-unquote get out of it. Or hear the end of it. So instead of coming up with a comeback—not that I wasn't fucking tempted, mind you—I contemptuously crushed out the involuntary ciggie I'd involuntarily lit and kind of screwed up my eyes and asked: "Hey, who's that playing?" and pointed in a quasi-conspiratorial way to the window we'd aforementionedly been gazing up at.

"The piano?" Natasha said.

"No, the *tuba*, baby," Walter sweetly sarcastically said.

They had that kind of relationship: the kind in which even their very lame jabs at one another smacked of cloying intimacy.

Positively vomitous.

"That's our new roommate Jenny," Natasha said. "She plays the piano. Teaches too."

"Really," I said.

"Uh-huh. She just moved in. Over the weekend."

"Huh," I said.

"The piano," Walter said, drawling it out like he was Jimmy Fucking Stewart in *Rear Window* talking to Grace Fucking Kelly or something. They were such a perfect match: I mean, Walter stomp-tromped on my nerves almost as much as Nastasha goddam did. What are you gonna do, though? Nothing, that's what. I was thinking of splitting right there and then but something told me not to. Something called my penis. Maybe this Jenny girl would be supercute or something, sexy *and* talented. And besides, I had a beer in my immediate future. A sure thing, beerwise. An import maybe. Drummers, I thought-huffed to myself—*and* their girlfriends. You could write a book about them. *You* could. *I* wouldn't. Go right ahead. Have fun.

What I *said* was:

"What's her story? Is that what she does—just give lessons? I mean, she sounds like she's really good."

"What you mean, John," Natasha interjected as the music stopped, "is 'Is she pretty?'"

All coy and stuff. Like she was on to me. Which she was, I reckon. I had known her, Walter's inexpressibly petulant peevish controlling bellicose obnoxious little girlfriend, the four months we'd had this yet-to-be-named band (Walt drove me mental from time to time by referring to us as a *project*), and had been practicing just outside their domicile all this time and in that time I suppose she'd seen enough of me to note well that I was positively *not* the kind to trust around her friends of the female persuasion. Seriously though: all I'd done was try to make nicey-nice with the various girl-ghosts (they were all of them goths) she'd introduced me to at the two or so soirees they'd thrown since I'd known them. The semi-fetching ones, I mean; that is, girls with glabrous alabaster skin, platinum or tar hair (teased out to tomorrow or cut short and blunt or electrically spiky), and impasto-ed purple eye shadow with bright pink or garish lavender lipstick smudged well beyond the lines of their for the most part invariably unfashionable thin lips. Every one of them in perpetual obligatory black—black tops, black tights, black bell-like skirts, black jackets, black stockings (torn, of course), black leggings, black gloves (torn-er, even more torn), black handbags and purses, black scarves, hats, belts, boots, bows. Black, black, black.

I hadn't even tried to scrog any of them, Nasty's girly gothfriends, but that was probably the rub: the fact that I hadn't probably made me even more suspect: like I wasn't planning on trying to bed any of them till later, after I'd maybe pissed them off by not trying to fuck them or something. Girls are weird. They definitely sense your worst intentions. Even if you haven't thunk them up yet. I'm not kidding. So don't kid yourself. Ever. (I'm kidding.)

When at last we single-filed inside, through the horror-film-screech screen door, with me Chevy Chasing on one of the moaning almost-kindling false-steps and nearly eating it, there was this girl at the obese, buff-colored refrigerator, bending into it. The light was really bright—shockingly so, like an apricot on fire—on account of Walt having inexplicably installed these interrogation-issue strip lights of maximum glaringness. And there was Jenny, presumably, opening a yoghurt. She seemed a little startled as we shambled through the laundry room and into the kitchen proper. Like she'd been listening to our fascinating goddam conversation or something. But maybe I was imagining things. I'm always imagining things, it seems. For instance, say you are a really spectacular-looking girl who is reading this book right now. Wow! *Are* you? Well guess what: I just wondered what you looked like in just a nice bra and great-fitting/flattering panties. Red, frilly, lacey—or maybe black, satin, naughty. Quaint toy bow in the *milieu* of the brassiere. Boyshorts, thong or slut-cut. In the ballpark, am I?

Okay: it's a *joke*, all right? Don't get all huffy. Don't get all mad. I don't care what you look like, in dishabille or otherwise. But Jenny—I don't know why it popped to mind this way—seemed like the kind of girl you'd never, once you got to know her of course (otherwise too lewd), picture in a peignoir or lingerie; rather, she seemed the sort you'd imagine in your softest light blue button-down, barelegged and heartbreakingly so. As I said, I don't know why. I don't.

Anyway, Natasha kinda semi-vixenishly or at the least cloyingly said: "Oh, *there's* Jenny. Hi, Jenny. Hey. Come meet Walter's band!"

*Walter's* band, I thought. The *nerve* of her. What nerve! And the cutesy way she said the former stuff ensured Jenny'd at least sense and maybe fully twig we were just talking/asking about her. What a blunderbuss, that Natasha. Honest. She put the *wonder* in blunder, that's for sure. You just stared sometimes, I'm telling you.

"Hello, 'the band,'" the Jenny girl said cutely/flippantly and Nastasha initiated introductions. Ponderously, naturally—her voice going all phony and like she was performing something egregious like "I'm a Little Teapot" ("*This* is *Rob*ert—*he's* a *Can*cer. *Works* at a *man*agement company. *Plays* the *bass* . . . This is *John*—he's a . . . I for*got* what he is . . . Oh yeah—yikes!—*Virgo* . . . Lives in Santa *Mon*ica or somewhere *beach*y like that . . . works at a . . . anyway . . . Plays gui*tar* . . ."), or like someone'd shoved a conductor's baton in her right paw or something and told her to talk in waltz-time, or like someone'd plunked down a class of extra-slow first graders in front of her and . . . you get the idea.

This is what she looked like, Jenny: cherry-hued hair, great, straight and to the shoulder, in thick streams like it was a little dirty, with long bangs but not too long; very watery-dreamy large round brown-as-mulligatawny eyes, bright and doe-like, sad-beautiful, inconsolable somehow; that had seen things, maybe. Things that had made her perhaps reluctantly lose her innocence. I don't know: I'm probably reading too much into it, her physiognomy. Oval, Pre-Raphaelite face with great cheeks and raspberry lips that would've been too big, too full, too luxuriant had she had normal teeth. Which she did not. They—the teeth, that is—were quite white but on the just-oversized side of somewhat acceptable. A slow, sly smile that somehow jarred with the ready-if-not-eager-to-please demeanor. Sheer white peasant dress with folds and muted flounces and enticing drawstrings half-undrawn and somewhat décolletage-y on account presumably of the stultifying Indian summer heat. Ample breastals. Very ample. Semi-pendulous. Braless. Incomprehensible breasts, come to think of it: yes. On the sternum red skin from sunburn. Adorably barefoot. Not-lithe, almost matronly upper arms. Torso on the—how can I say this?—plump side. The pleasantly, naturally. A tad zaftig. Very pretty, beautiful, even, actually, but decidedly reassuringly not my type. Not my type at all.

"It's nice to meet you," I said. "Was that you playing?"

"Oh no," Jenny said. "Not at all. One of my students. Amber."

"Oh, so you teach," I said.

Total stupid fucking cretin.

You have to mumble something, though, don't you? You can't just stand there and gander.

Well you can if you're the smoldering type, the full-on James Bond kind or whatnot. The kinda guy who thinks "She doesn't know it yet, but she *digs* me" whenever he clocks a nice-looking girl. Even a married one. Or one who's just turned eighteen. You know the sort I'm talking about; you may even *be* him for all I know.

"Yes," Jenny laughed and I furtively noted her trembling breasts as she chuckled. "I'd better get back to her, in fact. Nice meeting you guys."

"Hey," Rob said. "Have a beer with us."

"Oh, no thank you," Jenny said. "I can't and besides Amber's not quite finished yet. That's nice of you but I really have to get back upstairs."

"How 'bout now?" Rob joked, kinda flirtatiously, I thought, and everyone—me included—cracked up.

"No thanks, really. I'm kind of a wine girl anyway."

"Maybe *she'd* like a beer," Rob quipped and gestured with his eyes upstairs, above the kitchen, to where Amber was presumably waiting patiently for her maestro, and everyone laughed again, the pneumatic girl especially.

"Her mom would love that!" Jenny said. "She's twelve. See you guys, then."

"Rob!" Nastasha remonstrated. "What kind of person are you?! Offering alcohol to a twelve-year-old girl. See: I told you guys he was a lush!"

A to say the least awkward pause as Jenny made it half out of the kitchen and towards the stairwell. Nasty's quivering attempts at flummery (or irony, for that matter) always ended in something eyebrow-ascension-inducing. Always.

"Listen," I said before she could get completely away. I was inwardly weighing up whether to proto-intimately stick her name into my question. "I don't know whether you would be into something like this or not, uh, Jenny, but we have a few songs that, well, keyboards would be perfect on, I think. I mean, I don't know what you're into or anything but . . ."

"Oh?" Jenny said, canting back a bit into the kitchen. "Okay. I dunno. I guess I might be able to come up with something. Sounds good, I guess. I really don't know though: I've never played with a rock band before. Do you guys have a tape or something I could listen to?"

"Really? I said, trying unsuccessfully to hide my excitement. "You could? That'd be great. Really."

"Sure," she shrugged, "why not? You guys know where I live."

Then she added "basically" and everyone (and Walter of course too muchly, totally honkingly) laughed again.

"That's great," I said. "I'll get you one—just some rough stuff we've done on a boom box but you'll get the gist of it."

"Okay then," Jenny said. "I'll just be right upstairs; Amber's got one more Chopin piece to do and then I'm done."

"Great," I smiled, and away she sailed at last. We could hear her quick-quick footsteps as upstairs she flew.

So out I went to the pisshouse/outhouse of a rehearsal space I was telling you about, my newish Doc Martens scything through the sparse long grass of the unkempt backyard, and ticked open the lock and found the corner of Walter's toolbox with my bare shin (I wear shorts rain or shine—or at least a lot of the time). Fuck, that hurt. I must've looked like some kind of whooping fucking, er, Native American (the hyper-politically-correct era's just dawning—it's the early Nineties, okay?) as I hopped up and down going "fuck fuck fuck fuck" and balancing on the unscraped leg as I reached blindly for the string that depended from the long light bulb in the fucking perilous place. I found it at last and light didn't exactly flood the room or anything but at least now I could see. I rewound the tape in the deck we had and limped/marched back through the kitchen—only to encounter Walter and Nashy slumped against each other at the sink and practically swallowing each other's heads. Or at least noses.

Clearing my throat I said: "Uh. Sorry. Rob left, I guess?"

"Mmmhmmmm," Walt "said," not disengaging or even looking at me.

"See you Saturday, right?"

"Ermhmmmm," they moaned in tandem, too romantically entwined to gargle anything more comprehensible, obviously.

That's one thing that totally puzzles me about certain so-called very close couples: how do they do it, keep up the affection, the emotional Watusi, the everloving Grind? Innumerable must've been the times Walter's had his Gene Simmonsesque tongue scouring round the tonsils of that freakish Lilliputian girl, and he's still not sick of it? They'd been going out for nine or ten goddam high school sweetheart years (they maybe had ten junior college credits between them, *may*be) apparently, and there they were, making out like first-time teens at the sock hop or drive-in. Truly amazing. Especially as they could have just as easily been gnawing at each other's hot throats like rabid Rottweilers. I'd seen them going at it; you know I had. If you were heavy into *Schadenfreude* they put on a pretty good show, those two: screaming in public and Nastasha's voice going up, up, and away into the stratosphere of the higher registers of soprano and mad with relentless ire. And poor Walt just sitting there squirming, with this fucked look on his vulpine face, pleading her name a hundred and sixty different ways in order to stave off a meltdown, until finally, spent with restraint, he'd absolutely detonate, his whole head going rancorously redder than red, like you wanted to go dash tap water over him or something but you were too stunned that anyone not on daytime television would fight like that in front of others. I mean, his long, black, gothy backcombed *hair* seemed to catch fire when she'd pushed him too far. Have a band with some people and they'll let their guard way too down around you—like you and the guard, as it were, aren't even there. "I want a divorce!" he'd shriek. Which was risible as they weren't married. Or maybe they secretly were. I'd bet they were *related* somehow. Ha! That they were clandestine second or even first cousins and clandestined greedily to inbreed every single night till they met their clandestiny and death did them part. I know that sounds catty as hell, and morbid too, but if you ever met them you'd know what I'm talking about. It was like they were the same person (different sex, natch).

So anyway, up the dark polished stairs I went to look for Jenny's room and of course hearing the music coming from it I waited till there was a break in it before rapping lightly on the door.

"Come in," Jenny's voice kinda fluted and I gentled the knob.

"Hi," I whispered. "Here you go."

"Thanks," she said, throwing an I thought apologetic look back at Amber, and continued: "Is there a number where you can be reached?"

And of course I wrote it down and asked for hers in exchange and got it.

Good.

*

Do I have to lecture you, reading reader, on the unambiguous elations a guy feels when he gets the telephone number of a girl he thinks is really pretty? A girl who's obviously supertalented as well, and seems almost too nice, and just might jam with his band? My God: the whole world, for a while at least, changes. Colors brighten. Rows of roses, daisies, violets, poppies explode from golden clouds. Trees grow green flags and the air tastes like apples dappled with summer raindrops. The universe burns like cinnamon incense and, er, I guess I'm getting a little carried away here, lily-gilding. Let's just say it feels real good, okay?

Okay.

*

When I got home that night my roommate Jaz was there, Buddha-ed on the couch as per usual and palpably stoned, reading the *Times* and drinking luxuriantly from a bottle of imported beer. My imported beer probably, but no matter. What is one import between friends? Twelve ounces, that's what. Unless it's the *last* imported glug. I hoped it wasn't. Boy did I hope that.

"Heya, John," Jaz said. "How it goes?"

"Great," I said. "Unless that's the last glug, my lazy, thirsty chum."

"Super. Hey! I got another unreal idea for a script. You're gonna like it, believe me. Have you ever wondered or has it ever occurred to you that . . ."

"Answer the question implied, Jaz, please," I expostulated.

"You don't wanna hear it, my idea!?"

"Of course I do, Jazbo; but first I wanna know if I or perhaps *you* have to pop down to the glug store," I said by way of a gambit.

"Jeez, Johnny," Jaz said. "I'm beginning to think you don't have any respect for me as an artist."

"I don't think you have any respect for me as a *thirstist*," I opined.

"Nice one."

"Is it? Just say."

"I don't know that you have any respect whatsoever. Admit it!"

"What? That you are very extra high?" I said a little more truculently than I'd perhaps intended.

There was a mini-hiatus. I mean, the bong, still kinda smoking, was right there on the toy coffee table. Jaz gave me a look like he'd been transmogrified into the caterpillar with the hookah in *Alice*—one, well he knew, that got me every time. Plus I was having a hard time being miffed at him on account of being in such a skyey mood and all. And Jaz in his stoney state must've sensed it.

"Okay," he said, his normally twinkly eyes even more asparkle. "Uncle. *Mea culpa*. There are indeed no *stupefacients* in the fridge."

"No *what*?" I laughed.

Jaz went to his desk, an ancient, almost toy or at least junior student's thing, painted an unidentifiable color that made you fairly queasy, and plucked up a piece of paper and handed it to me like it was my ticket to success, or his straight "A" report card from fifth grade.

I read the square bit of paper from his *365 New Words a Day Calender*.

"Huh."

"Pretty good, right? 'Libations or potations with the capacity to intoxicate or inebriate.' Awesome! Sometimes they have pretty good ones. Ones you can relate to. (I hope I am pronouncing it right!) And yes we need indeed indeed to go to the store. Sorry, bud. I am in violation of Maxim 10 unquestionably and unconscionably (I got that one the other day from the calender—hope I pronounced it right).

"You did. You don't always, but this time you did."

"Good. And speaking of bud, do you wanna get stoned first? I think you do. You should have a little hit of this."

He indicated the budledge and the bong.

"It is *quite* superior. Got it from a Jamaican chess player I met in Venice."

"I'll be the judge of that," I said. "Did you play him?'

"At chess?"

"No, paddleball. What do you think?"

"In that case, yep."

" Did you *beat* him?"

"Nope."

"Got your queen in five moves or something?"

"Six, actually. Seven, tops. God he was good. What he got me *afterwards* was stoned as hell! Ha! Least he could do, the fucker: I lost ten bucks to him. Five bucks a throw."

"After he put his ridiculous skills on display, you played him *again*? You should learn better, Jaz."

"I know but you know what? The thing is, I never do. I *never* do. Normally those guys elongate the first game so that you think you think you have a chance. They all must've majored in Psych at Berkeley or something. But this guy—he just had this bloodlust for conquest right off the bat . . . or the pawn or whatever. He was so good I had to lose another five bucks to him just to watch him whomp me one more time."

"You never took Logic in college, either, did you?"

"Nope. Nor was I good enough for the chess team. Or any college team, for that matter. Who wants to be on a team in college anyway, huh? Who would do that?"

"Guys who are good enough, I guess."

"Right you are again. Hey!"

"What?"

Jaz indicated the budledge and the bong once more.

After we had a lung-ballooning/eye-watering/cough-and-get-off hit of sticky pot apiece and yet another good hearty roommately laugh, Jaz put on his polo shirt and tackily shoelaceless tennies and out we went from the apartment and down the treacherously steep slick pale blue stairs and towards the corner liquor store—our very favorite place in the whole wide world, run by this incredibly deadpan family of Sikhs called Singh. We played this game each time (if we went together) to see if either one of us could get even the faintest smile, smirk, or even shirk from one of the Singhs—the winner would get a six pack for a smile, and a twelve pack for a laugh, for just one laugh. In the four or so months I had roomed with Jaz neither one of us had come close—despite the fact that we considered ourselves pretty amusing fellows. I thought it was a sort of mini-triumph that Jaz had got the taller of three brothers to go "Hmm" one time when a really pretty girl, just come from the beach, had sashayed into the store and Jaz had made this noise of approbation like he was gargling custard or treacle and the Singh in question, I could swear, had almost semi-grinned and, like I said, gone "Hmm"—even if just barely audibly. No wonder they say the Sikhs are warrior types—they don't think anything's funny; they're not horsing around one bit, I'm telling you.

Out the door we went and it was a good thing Jaz put on a shirt this time (he didn't always or even all that much— you know beach people— and the store was really super close anyway) because without one he is positively frightful—as hirsute a person you will find who is not currently encaged in a zoo somewhere. A tumbleweed on wheels, an abominable snowman-at-large. Tersely put: he is one very hairy *hombre*. The sort of wooly mammoth of a guy whose tanning process at the beach might at any time be interrupted by someone going: "Hey, dude—aren't you kind of hot in that *sweater*?" Ha!

I should talk, though. Lately I've noticed that hair epaulets are becoming more and more implacably attached to my fucking shoulders; and a horrid dark patch of the fluff stuff is quietly, relentlessly encroaching in a menacing triangle just above my fucking butt crack. Not pretty. And not that I want you to think of me and my crevice *derrière*. Indeed it is very disconcerting, this startling new growth. It's a real existential wake-up call when you realize you might be one of those guys who has *back hair*. Yow! Extra—how d'ye call it?—*unwanted* hair don't help. Don't help at all. Chicks don't dig it. You *really* don't (over)hear a lot of girls these days who go: "Ooh: what I really want, the kind of guy who really turns me *on*, is a man with hair *every*where—on his shoulders, his forehead, his protuberant football of a fucking stomach, his back, his neck, his prick in fact. *Just* what I'm lookin' for."

No: you don't hear that all that much these days, do you? Or even ever in the entire history of history, probably.

Of course bald don't help either. Which is what Jaz, who has more hair than a Hollywood wig shop or downtown barber's floor, thinks he's going. He's always yanking back this lank dark-blonde thin mass of shaggy bangs he has in order to check to see if there's been a recent recession or something in his follicle-economics. The guy's *gonna* go bald any day now from worrying whether or not he's gonna lose his hair; I'll bet you any money.

He has a right to be paranoid, I reckon: anyone knows that, when it comes to getting girls, bald, as I just mentioned, don't help. Girls don't trust guys who are bald, man. I mean, they figure if a guy can't maintain a consistent *hair*line how's he going to maintain a lasting re*la*tionship? Sorry but they really do think that; they do. They don't wake up many mornings, pining terribly, pining prayerfully, their soft fine hands aclasp, going, "Oh my stars, how I wonder if I will ever ever meet the tall, bald and mysterious guy of my dreams? Oh, Baldby, Baldington, or Baldersberry, where *are* you?"

(And to all you Balderdashes who might get miffed at this, have a sense of humor, why don't ya? Lighten up a little. I'm only joking you. The other day I showed this section of the narrative to one of my tetchy buddies who never doesn't wear *some* kind of hat or cap or goddam scarf (if you know what I'm saying) and he was ready to tear out *my* hair for making such, ahem, bald statements. N.B. There are loads of chrome domes who, by being extra-charming, extra-talented and compassionate, and having extra spending money—if you really want the cynical truth—have gotten girls most of us would die for, would kill for.)

Anyway, on our merry way to the glug store we ran into two of our neighbors. One was the insane maniac of a possibly septuagenarian woman who inhabited the pink apartment directly below us and who I swear to God seemed to keep herself irreversibly alive just to torture Jaz and me at all hours of the night playing the collected works of Richard Wagner full blast.

Name: Marie.

Nationality: German.

Description: one woman, very round, of hideous aspect; a turtle-colored human leather beanbag with legs, who dressed perpetually in what looked like (you couldn't look too close) a brown bib and brown diapers.

Ostensible comestibles: pungent meats of Teutonic origin, presumably, acridly fried; unsavory cabbages, malodorously boiled, bits of which are sometimes obliviously worn on the chin(s) after feeding-time; beets; sauerkraut (youch, one's *nose*!); red wines (identified by pointillist stains on aforesaid brown bib).

In short: a harridan.

Jaz sometimes attempted (I've no idea why) to engage her in conversation. In my opinion he was either an immense humanitarian or very extremely bored. The only thing *I* would have liked to engage her in would be a contest where I would be very heavily armed with a quantity of sharp, lethal, preferably nasty medieval-type weapons, and she would (obviously) not be. Such was the huge rage I felt towards her for having spoiled so many of my dreams that I regularly pictured her wearing a harpoon between her juddering udders (they were a shelf of much massiveness, you might have already twigged), blood fountaining from the unbarbed end of the projectile.

That sounds fully harsh, I realize, but you just try sleeping with "March of the Valkyries" or whatever it's called blaring up at you at four in the morning. You won't like it, I guarantee it. We had the police on speed-dial on Jaz's home phone, believe me; not that they ever turned up. The only "weapons" we could wield against her operatic onslaughts were broom-ends, bookshelf bricks, and a blender (against the floor), and pillows and palms (against our ears). It sucked beyond sucking living above her—she was barking fucking mad bonkers *crazy*—but the rent was crazy cheap. Sometimes you'd bound downstairs and there Marie'd be, berating the flowers in her admittedly formidable front garden: giant hyssop, pink marguerite daisies, sweet William and Johnny-jump-ups; hollyhocks and columbine; butterfly miikweed, milkwort, begonias and marigolds. Once I overheard her mantra-ing her hatred for roses: "Naughty, naughty, naughty roses. Bad, bad, bad. Naughty, naughty, naughty roses. Bad, bad. Bad." It was a good idea to avoid her whenever possible.

The other neighbor we had lived next door and was outside in her backyard. We watched her for a bit through the chain link fence that fenced in a strange arrangement of haphazard bamboo and palm shrubs. She never seemed to mind—even, if not especially, when we stared and clucked at her and called (almost always ineffectually) to her.

Name: Heidi.

Nationality: Australian.

Description: Six feet tall with tiny, hispid head; thin legs that are very long, exceedingly disproportionate to body; totally large-buttocked (she outbummed Marie, even), with heavy-lidded brown eyes big as a professional photographer's most puissant camera lens.

Comestibles: leaves, grasses, sugarcane (one surmised, but didn't know for sure).

In short: an emu.

Now Heidi I *definitely* attempted to engage in conversation, especially in conditions stonified. And as I was high as hell right then, I said "Hey, Heidi, hello there, girl" as Jaz and I made our way out to the alley.

Nothing.

"She's not talking to me," I told Jaz. "She won't tell me what's wrong!"

"I don't wanna sound cynical," Jaz retorted, "but is she not a female of the species?"

"Don't start," I said.

Past caroling bums driving shopping carts and bums like bears tipping themselves into rubbish bins and bums self-sentried on the glittering still-warm pavement we walked the litterstrewn indigo alleyway to Wilshire and went in to the glug store. There was yet another bum huddled to himself right outside it, lecturing to no one and gesturing semi-wildly.

"Heineken or Becks?" Jaz asked as we loped in, nodding to the unsmiling be-turbanned clerk.

"Becks," I said as Jazz set down some sand-caked, crumpled ones and quarters, counting them out grandiloquently before the glug store clerk.

Shockingly, there was change. Jaz handed it to the homeless man as we made our way out with suds in hand.

Four pennies, one nickel, one dime.

On the way home (another, longer route this time, past a public park with a tennis complex, a frou-frou coffee shop, a print shop, a pie shop, an importer of British militaria where Michael Jackson was rumored to browse), Jaz, before I could stop him, told me his latest loopy idea for a movie. It was this: *Othello* meets *2001: A Space Odyssey*.

"What?!" I said, trying not to guffaw.

"Hear me out. Here's the deal," Jaz enthused, making a camera of his hands, Panavisioning slowly. "Takes place in outer space, natch. Okay. And instead of strangling Desdemona Othello rips off her oxygen supply and the last we see of her is an exact replica, er, replication of the shot in the Kubrick masterpiece where Dave's co-spaceman is cut off by Hal and floating to infinity . . . Whaddaya think of *that*?!"

"Spectacular," I said. "Let's open a couple of those beers and celebrate your impending Directors Guild Award."

"Negative," Jaz said. "Unless you're, like, fully homeless they will put you in jail for having an open container on the street, the spoilsports. Besides, I don't think you quite appreciate my latest idea. I really don't. Hey! Have you ever wondered about, like, if they, like, *reject* someone from jail? Ever wonder that? Like if they find out somehow that you've gone and got yourself arrested just for free room and board and stuff? I wonder about that sometimes."

"I wonder about *you* sometimes, Jaz, I really do."

"Me do too. Seriously though: what about my idea? And another thing I was thinking about. Have you ever wondered why . . ."

"I think it's about the most dubious idea for a film I have ever heard," I said, cutting to the proverbial chase, to use a movie cliché. "So dubious that it might just get made, Jaz! You never know."

"That dubiosity," Jaz riffed, took a deep breath to puff himself up in a mock-showoff way, and laughed huskily, "is just what I am counting on."

*

On the way back up to the apartment we passed Marie deeply engrossed in berating a flowerbed at uncharacteristically low volume. This time, however, Jaz didn't try conversing with her. She was way too far gone. It wasn't the first time we'd heard her chastising her promiscuously growing roses, jonquils, tulips, sweet William, Johnny-jump-ups and forget-me-nots, etc., and you didn't get the feeling that interrupting her interrogations was the most Phi Beta Kappa thing you could do. She looked like a superannuated, exploded basketball crossed with a Roman soldier who'd got the worst of a swordfight. Because she was rarely out of the sun, she was as brown as the in-shreds dress she wore almost every day: this way-too-short-for-her-ovoid-person get-up that appeared to be a series of hoary brown belts wrapped haphazardly round her.

Something else Marie did that tripped you out, aside from having talks with flowers, was to rap with the around twenty-seven and a half cats she kept in an apartment the same size ours was—in other words, the size of a baseball dugout. You know how young women who like cats, live by themselves, and currently don't have a steady or even remotely sober boyfriend have this secret fear that they're going to end up as the Crazy Cat Lady That Lives Downstairs? Well Marie *was* that woman. The one they were afraid of becoming. Plus she never seemed to leave. Just hung around in her garden collecting more neighborhood strays and ferals and conversing with her flowers and smelling (I *knew*—I got downwind of her a couple of times) like a high school varsity locker room (the section sectioned off for the wrestling team).

When we got upstairs Jaz and I had a brewski apiece and went about our separate lives. The apartment: a tiny one-bedroom of shabby appearance, six blocks from the beach, and hence—without rent control—one thousand hundred million sixty two dollars a month. Fortunately we had rent control, though. We were unreally lucky. That way, at least. The living room (where Jaz crashed): magazines everywhere, newspapers, bleeding pens, cans, milk cartons, ripe socks, exhausted shirts and towels, a telephone and answering machine, books, more newspapers (Jaz was a journalism fiend), shoes, swim fins (well, one), dishes, plates, marijuana paraphernalia, wiffle balls and wiffle bats, and lots of other stuff on the floor; on the walls notebook-page-sized Van Goghs, Monets, Pollocks, de Koonings, Diebenkorns (prints, of course, except for the one original Vermeer we kept behind glass—ha! yeah right!); on the kitchen walls dried spaghetti sauce and grime, scuffmarks from whizzing Nerf balls, marks from old scotch tape.

And the way it smelled, our abode, in case you were wondering? Who can say? Only people who didn't live there—not Jaz and I. For all the world your own place renders you practically anosmic: you don't know what your own home smells like 'cause you nose it all the time. I could *guess*: the sweet taint of ghostly, lingering hits of pot, of course, and tennis shoes and socks (not *too* dirty ones—laundry got done more often than you imagine), and air freshener and "pine" (on account of we did rinse the hell out of the bathroom, refusing to live in a place where a girl might go "Pubic Palace!"—and then go straight home; for well we knew that there was no greater etiolater of feminine desire than filth, dirt, grease, and grime—unless it was bugs).

The place must also have smelt of the sea on account of we were no more nor less than three blocks from the beach.

The place was aclutter, admittedly, with too much *stuff*, but it wasn't a sinkhole, it wasn't a hellhole, it wasn't, as the French say, *sale*. (Okay, it was pretty messy.)

On the fridge a list, imperfectly typed, of Jaz's and my co-credited, cannabis-inspired maxims/rules for two people living in a space hardly big enough even for one. They were as follows:

1. Don't be the sort of person who makes lists of any sort; lists suggest an untidy mind yearning for the broom; they are never or at least rarely followed, lists; avoid them; list-making is for people who thrive on kidding themselves about their hopes for accomplishment.
2. When or if (a big "if") one of us "gets lucky" and hauls by the hair or an available appendage a female of the species back to this domicile, we must remember to shout a warning out to counterpart/roommate, something along the lines of "Don't come in just yet!" or "Please go away! I have [insert name like Bridget, Kathy, Liz or Lisa here—those are names cute girls have] in here and she doesn't want you to see her topless unless you *really* want to!" Yeah: something along those lines.
3. Do dishes immediately after eating.
4. Or at least do dishes by following day, especially if #2 is in process.
5. Keep quiet hours when either of us is writing or reading. Quiet hours contingent on Marie's outrageous proclivities, naturally, but this is an Artist House, whatever that means, and we must needs respect the almighty elusive creative spirit at all times, especially when it seems to have absconded, which in many cases is often.
6. Masturbation is to take place *only* in the shower—an extra hot

shower, making sure no traces of . . . well, um, enough said.

7. Indoor Nerf wiffle ball play is to be encouraged at all times when boredom overtakes. It is a great reliever of the many stresses of big city life, and if one of us really wants to play and the other doesn't, the one who doesn't should pull himself together for the sake of Sportsmanship and Roommatemanship and play to oblige and humor the other.
8. Can't think of anything for "8" 'cause really stoned right now and the number "8" looks weird.
9. Same deal.
10. Try not to leave notes or harbor resentments too much when familiarity (and in this case proximity—way proximity) breeds contempt, as it will do in cramped, impecunious situations like these; bring things up, in other words, shortly after they happen, or try to, and be nice to each other and don't drink roommate's beer unless you have to (i.e. you have had a bad day, you have a guest, or you are about to go to the liquor store or any store that has libations on offer).

Furniture: a pale blue desk, a daybed (a Jaz bed, that is), a tatterdemalion beach chair, one sad lamp, a TV the size of an oversized paperback. The bedroom (where I kipped): a purple futon bed, three electric guitars (one vintage Rickenbacker, one Gibson ES 335, one Fender Telecaster), one acoustic (Martin D28), a box of unpacked paperbacks, clothes, towels, shoes, notebooks, crumpled-up pages like inscribed paper flowers, pennies, nickels (no dimes or quarters—those were worth *money*), pens, pencils, a sleeping bag for a blanket, a parka for a pillow, a telephone and answering machine.

It was to the telephone that I turned my half-baked attention then. I plucked it up and dialed the number in my top pocket.

"Hello?" she said.

"Jenny?" I said. "It's John."

". . ."

"From your roommate Walter's unnamed band."

"Oh, hi," she said. "I'm so so sorry! I didn't expect to talk to you so *soon*. Ha! Funny, huh? And I was engrossed in something. Your tape, actually."

"Really?!"

She giggled in a way that made me really happy.

"Yeah, I was. I actually like it."

"'Actually,' huh?"

"Oh I didn't mean it that way. I hate it when people say 'actually' . . . actually."

"I know what you mean. As in: 'Actually, you are not such a cretin' or something like that. A poltroon."

"I love that word. I call my brother it all the time."

"My little brother's a total poltroon."

"They probably know each other."

"They're in a poltroonish club together, I bet."

"Totally."

"Anyway, Jenny . . . hey—what is that in the background? It's doesn't sound like our tape, I don't think."

"Oh, let me see . . . The Smithereens, I think. They're kind of poppy and silly and Beatles and stuff but I kind of like them. Guilty pleasure."

"'This is the house she used to live in,'" I sang. "Great stuff. Yeah, I like that song a lot. It's hard not to, sort of."

Reprobate and liar!

But you can't start out by telling some girl you just met that some dumb song by some dumb band she likes *sucks* now, can you? Even though they totally suck, the Smithereens. Wow are they sucky. Like, the *suckiest.*

"Anyway," Jenny said. "Yeah, you guys have good songs, I think."

"Thank you!"

"What are you up to, anyway?"

"Oh nothing. Just calling to say hey. Avoiding hanging out with my roommate—who's my good friend, actually, but our flat's too small for us not to be on each other's cases from time to time, you know. It's not like the sitch you have at Walter and Nasty's."

"I am really glad to have a room upstairs away from it all, let me tell you."

"I bet. What are you up to?"

"Nothing. Getting ready for bed. Natasha was just up here, actually. She said you live right on the beach or something."

"Pretty close."

"Must be nice."

"I grew up right by it in Santa Barbara—I'm kinda sick of it, truth be told."

"I never tire of it, me. Hey! What's that in the background—it sounds like opera."

"Opera? Oh my God: it's Wagner!"

"Wagner? Wow."

"It's a story, actually, and not a happy one. This crazy lady downstairs plays it all and any hours of the night or day. Totally insane. I'll tell you about her some other time."

"Okay," she laughed.

"I'll let you go, then."

"Okay."

But then I said: "Listen, Jenny. Would you maybe be interested in rehearsing with us on Saturday or something? That's when we rehearse next."

"Okay. All right. I'm pretty sure I'm free. I'll let you know if something comes up. Otherwise, okay! I have a few ideas already for a couple of the songs, actually."

"You say 'actually' a lot."

"I do."

"Anyway, see you Saturday, then. Great!"

"You say 'great' a lot."

"I do? Pretty articulate, huh? Great vocabulary."

"I heard you throw around some thesaurus words."

"You *did*? When?"

"Not telling."

"Not fair! And besides, that's my roommate who's sesquipedalian, not *me*."

"Ha!" she laughed. "Okay, bedtime. I'll will see you guys Saturday, then, okay?"

"Excellent," I vamped.

That got her. She laughed.

"Bye!"

"Bye," I said and hung up the phone and hopped around a bit, danced around the room, dancing my Johnny-dance. Yeah. Not even minding that Marie's caterwauling stereo had gone to "eleven."

*

A few months later Jenny told me that after we hung up nosy Nastasha actually came back into her room and started quizzing her about our conversation, probing her like the veteran meddler she truly was.

"So," Nasty apparently said. "What do you think of him?"

"John?" Jenny'd said. "He's intriguing and funny and *tall* and all. But not my type, really. Not my type at all."

## yes we're going to a party party

The next night Jaz came home from work around 11:45 p.m. (he worked the graveyard shift, proofreading and editing at a downtown financial magazine) and flopped onto the daybed just as I was putting the *White Album* on the turntable in order to counter the aural barrage—I think it was Rachmaninoff this time—coming from Marie's.

"John!" he said. "I just remembered! Do you want to go to a party? I *hope* not, 'cause I am completely exhausted."

"I do," I said. "Let's go. Whose is it? Can you rally?"

He canted forward and stuffed some hairy-sticky green fresh bud into the bongo: "I think so. I have to warn you, though."

"What?"

"Movie people."

## oh you've got green eyes

Bright red Tiki lights danced above the heads of the maybe three-hundred-strong throng. The backyard of the Hollywood Hills mansion Jaz and I found ourselves in was a phosphorescent football field festooned with luminous balloons, of the festive Chinese type mostly, and a matrix of pellucid streamers. The pulsating lights shooting forth from the bottom of the huge swimming pool made heaving amoebas on the surface of the water, and the tall shrubs and snowy flowerbeds, makeshift bars, and cabanas were like psychedelic cartoon characters, jumping with ever-shifting light, obscuring the stars above, blotting out the constellations.

The dance mix of a New Order song I couldn't recall the title of poured into my head and made me think of discotheques and washing machines and the ineluctable katzenjammer that was going to be mine-all-mine tomorrow morning. The vast punch bowl on the dining room table inside the house was an vertiginous, alcoholic mini-Jacuzzi, the kegs a row of suits of armor. The cigars and ciggies in the hands of the various hipsters surrounding us seemed like censors or wands or detachable phalluses on fire. The words I spoke or overheard waltzed in extra slow motion and echolalia-ed surreally. People went in Pixelvision in and out of my periphery and all the pretty girls in their pretty best cocktail dresses and tight jeans looked incredibly edible. Or at least like an arrangement of bright paper flowers—perfect yet oh-so fake.

Was I drunk and high or what?

It occurred to me in a (rare) moment of personal prudence that I ought to find something to eat in order to counterbalance the insane amount I'd had to drink (a veritable cocktail of beers, vodka tonics, *gin* and tonics—for fuck's sake, what was I? eleven or something?—double margaritas, whiskey tonics, and even more beers encore), so I mingled through to a room just off the kitchen where an Everest of fat prawns winked pinkly at me. There was a small hill of guacamole too, and a vat of chips and salsa, piles of canapés and spinach dip, sushi and sashimi plumped yea-high, and a grand plate of viscid cheeses and crackers. The whole room was awash in cold gold light from chintzy chandeliers on the ceilings and fake sizzling electric candelabra on the walls, and there were silver mirrors and silver salvers and silver candlesticks like so many silver soldiers sentineled on the tables, on whose crisp white tablecloths perched explosions of white flowers (lilies, roses, carnations, orchids)—all above a sea of Olympic white carpet that, to walk through, was like trudging drunkenly through new snow. I was in the by-now—after too many drinkies drunk—comically laborious process of taking two black plastic plates too many and a black napkin and at-this-point superfluous plastic fork when a dark-haired pretty sidled up and, her nicely husky voice lifting (lifted?) above the thump thump thump of hiccupping disco, asked if I had a cigarette by any chance?

"By all means," I replied, trying not to slur my words too badly and of course in the attempt slurring them very.

Without being too too obvious I tried to get as good a look at her as

I could and found that she was quite cute in a not-average way. Medium tallish, borderline slenderish and maybe on the verge of flirting. With me, that is. I put down the food-laden plate(s) and produced a Marlboro and lit it for her as we stepped outside the vast sliding glass doors to smoke. Yes.

"I'm Samantha," she said. "*Thank* you. Who do you know here? My friend Lacey I came with and I don't know anyone. We're crashing."

Her accentless English made her even cuter somehow.

"Well," I said, "now you know me, at least: John. Even though I live right next door, I don't know anyone here either. Thought I'd come over and meet my neighbor whom I've never met and introduce myself and everything. Nice place, though, isn't it? There must be fifteen bedrooms at least."

Of course I said all this in my best Great Gatsby voice. Gatsby smashed on mint juleps or sloe gin fizzies, natch. Or "fizz" (champagne).

"You live next *door*? Really? Get out!" she said.

I started to go, taking two theatrical steps.

Irremediable comedian.

"I didn't mean *that*, Sean!"

"John."

"Right." (She was as drunk as I was, I'd bet; had to be; didn't know for sure, but she seemed, like, *quashed*. Toasted. Walloped. Squished. Blinkered. *Fucking legless*, as my Irish and English friends from college sometimes said—the one that cracked me up unfailingly every fucking time I heard it.) Yeah: she *had* to be gonzo.

"I only live there during the summers, though, you know? The rest of the time I spend in Italy—at my Italian villa in the south of France. Unless I'm skiing Australia or trekking the west of Tibet. *You* know how it is."

Thoroughgoing liar!

"*Which* house?" she said, screwing up her eyes, as we sauntered back to the backyard. "Left or right?"

"That one," I pointed, gulping.

"That big blue and white one?"

"That's right."

"That's *my* house, silly," she said.

"We must be roommates, then!" I laughed. "It's so big, our place, that we could've gone on like this for *yonks*."

"What's 'yonks'?" she said.

"Years."

"Oh. You're funny. Weird, kinda. The way you talk."

"I know," I said.

"'Skiing the west of Tibet!'" she laughed.

"I think I said 'trekking,'" I laughed back. "Making stuff up comes in handy at parties like these—not that I go to parties like these. I mean, I do *now* and everything but, well, this isn't, er, my sort of crowd. Not really."

"Guess not," Samantha said.

"Make love to me. Let's go back to your place and make the most mad, passionate love of our lives. I want you so badly, Sam. My desire for you is a monster," I breathed out breathlessly.

Ha!

Had you fooled there for a sec, though, didn't I? Wouldn't it be amazing if you *could* say stuff like that, though? Just blurt it out brazenly? Well, I suppose people do spew stuff like that sometimes, but it's likely that just afterwards they're wearing someone's drink or spittle or knuckleblood on their faces.

What I really said was:

"So, what are you up to these days, Samantha?"

"You mean what do I do for a job? Everyone in L.A. asks that, I noticed. Almost everyone."

"I didn't mean to be an instant cliché, if that's what you mean. I normally wait a beat or two to haul out the old platitudinous inquiries."

"Huh?"

"Nothing. What do you do, then? Sorry."

"I'm an assistant at a place that does psychology research."

"Oh," I said and took a sip of the drink I was holding, whatever drink, whatever it was, hoping there wasn't a cigarette floating in it, at least.

"On patients who are substance abusers. Drug addicts."

"That's interesting. What made you choose that line of work?"

You could see the answer coming from a mile:

"I am a former user myself, actually."

"User of which substance, may I ask?"

"Marijuana," she mused aloud—it seemed kinda wistfully. "Pot. Coke too. Speed sometimes. Okay, a *lot*. Heroin. But never shooting it, only smoking. But mostly dope, yeah. I was mostly just, like, a major pothead. For reals. A couple of times—oh yeah, I forgot—crystal meth. And peyote when I could get it. Which was never, almost. Plus all the downs and the ups, you know: Darvon, Vicodin, Percocet, that shit. I love drugs. Or used to, you know. Hey: wanna hear a funny story?"

"Shoot."

I was completely smitten by now—smitten as fuck. At her mercy completely. Notwithstanding the fact that she had this utterly nauseating tic that loads of elocution-challenged moderns of both sexes seem to have: turning every single bloody statement/observation into a question. Plus of course the heinous habit of incessantly interjecting "like" and "you know" every third or fourth word—an awful thing that half the half-wits and especially anyone under thirty in Angelenoland are guilty of. She was really pretty and fun in, of course, a very dumb way. Stupid girls always have a chance with me. Those and really smart girls. They got a shot too.

Nevertheless, this Sam girl was so comely I didn't mind her verbal butcheries at all. Not at all. I'm one of the most deeply shallow guys you'll ever know—I own up to it, okay? I know it. Plus, if you'd seen her you'd forgive me. Trust me. Even though you shouldn't.

"Well," she giggled, "when I went for my first interview they asked me if I would, like, have a problem taking a drug test if I made it through the interview process and I said I would have no problem taking a drug test, it's *passing* one that I might, like, have a problem with! Ha-ha! Isn't that, like, funny? I know. It *is*, huh. Totally."

I was laughing too. Overlaughing, probably. Till, mercury-quick, she got really serious, pushing back on her cute nose the equally cute wire-rims she was wearing, this sudden unmistakable frown on her fantastically pretty face (she really was getting cuter by the minute).

"Yes," she said really earnest-like, "I had a lot of problems. But the worst problem, believe it or not, was with pot. There's a real reason—for reals—why they call it 'wasted,' believe me."

"That's a great story," I lied. "And coincidentally, I am 'on' that very substance as we speak. Did you, as a result of your vast experience and current job situation, detect that and decide to do an impromptu experiment on me?"

"Sorry? Oh. No. I didn't know you were high. I asked you for a cigarette because I thought you were cute."

Oh my God: I am not making this up this time. I'm not joshing. Do women ever say anything even remotely like that to me? To anyone? In the movies, maybe. The movies that ruin you for all and ever. But not in real life as we know it now. No way.

"Wow. Thank you," I said, moving in, as it were. "I am going to be very flustered thusly flattered, Sam. I don't know what to say except that you are totally adorable. Can I get you a drink? Or do you not drink as well?"

"No. I drink. I just don't smoke."

And here she made this queer funny face at the second cigarette I'd given her, the one in her hand and that she was fairly fucking *wolfing*. God this girl was hilarious as hell: I was having the greatest time; the party had gone from sucky to wondrous in no time. In Samantha time.

"A gin and tonic, please," she said. "That's sweet of you. Have them make it strong, okay?"

"Don't go anywhere, okay? Don't move. I'll be right back."

She said okay and effortfully I made my way through the now even-bigger crowd to one of the bars at the edge of the long patio, occasionally encountering the bowl-me-over odor of some big shot fuck's cologne or aftershave or the hauteur-filled gaze of a girl who looked at me to see if I was a Somebody and looked precipitately away. What a great but fucked up party! The *worst*, these movie people! It reeked, this fête, of the movies, let me tell you. Just the worst bits. You couldn't swing a proverbial dead cat without pelting wannabes of every flavor—agents, directors, actors, production assistants, makeup people, writers, producers—boasting their meager achievements and vain dreams in straining voices, yakking on about who they know or who they'd seen or succeeded in meeting, who they'd witnessed behaving badly on set or appallingly "on location," or who'd just had advanced plastic surgery on their butts, noses, chins, tits, eyes or tummies. The gossip and palaver of deals and roles and auditions and how much the cast of some unconscionably unfunny sitcom gets per episode. Money this and money that, with actors and actresses the absolute *worst*—narcissistic vainglorious logorrheic bundles of nerve peppering their speech with Intro French and dropping so many goddam names you needed a *broom* to sweep up after them. There was practically no one there you couldn't picture barking into a walkie-talkie, dressing down someone in a high-pitched voice or urging them to do something faster, faster, now, now, *now*.

When I'd first moved here, five months earlier, Jaz told me he had just three bits of advice to offer me about Los Angeles: 1) Don't get bummed out in traffic—it happens all the time and there is nothing you can do; 2) Don't date actresses; And 3) Don't date actresses.

Wanna hear a joke? What's the difference between an actress and a sperm? A sperm has a one-in-a-million chance of becoming a human being.

*

The epileptic lights continued to light up the partygoers and I made my way to fetch Sam a drink. To my left as I got there were these two girls and one of them (a Drew Barrymore clone, but taller, older, prettier and way more made-up) was going:

"Oh, *my* acting teacher—excuse me, coach—is just simply *brill*iant. Totally and completely. I mean, the things he does in class are so just . . . brilliant . . . you know? . . . sorry? Oh I don't know . . . It's just so hard to put into words, you know? So hard to explain . . . what he does and stuff. I can't even begin to tell you how much, I mean, I have, like, learned? Like, about myself, mostly. So so much; believe me. Like, I am this whole different person . . . He only takes, like, three new people a year. I mean, I am so lucky to have gotten in! So lucky! And then to have underwent this . . . undergone, I mean . . . this total tranformeration? I mean, *wow*."

Wow indeed, I thought. Kind of just ahead of me in the queue was a halfway pretty girl (lovely eyes, but with a disconcerting unibrow planed too low and right above them) spewing to this other chick in a leopard-skin/Mrs. Robinson kinda coat that had to be too hot for the evening. Had to be. She had perfect hair and perfect skin and a perfect smile and a perfect retroussé nose and a perfect body and perfect teeth and she was perfectly banally *perfect*, the hilt of uninteresting.

"Oh my God!" she was saying. "New York is just not the sort of place I could, like, live without, like, a *lot* of money. A *lot* of money . . . Oh I know! They are just obsessed with us! Obsessed, I'm telling you. New Yorkers are totally obsessed with telling you what the difference between us and them are! Amazing! This one guy, from Brooklyn, *he* was just going on and on last night at Bar Bar. Or was I at Bar One? Can't remember. Doesn't matter. Anyway, he was going on and on about it and I am just like "Whatever!"—buy me a Manhattan and shut the fuck up, buster!

Hahahahaha! Suck my left one, okay? Hahahaha . . . My tit . . . Oh I *know*. San Franciscans are just as bad—worse, even. They *hate* us! And we don't even think about them! We could care less, huh? Hahahaha. 'The City!' What a *laugh*. It's like some pretty boy that you are just so over going out with 'cause even though he's beautiful and everything he's just, like, so boring and shallow! That's San Francisco in a nutshell, right? Right? Wanna know something? Every time I go there I call it 'Frisco' on purpose! Drives them fucking crazy! Buncha idiots, if you ask me . . . Me? I don't *know*, you know? *May*be. We'll see. I miss New York, though. I really do. I will prolly move back there next year sometime, I just dunno when. Hey: get this: Jared just last week told me I was starting to become a Hollywood cliché. *Ja*red, of all people . . . Yeah, *him*. I know, I know. If anyone's a walking fucking Hollywood cliché, it's Jared. It's him, believe me Why do I keep picking psychotic men, do you think? Why *is* that? Adam? My last boyfriend? He held up a fucking 7-Eleven with a fucking *blow*torch! I am not kidding you. A blow torch. You didn't hear about that? I never told you? He was up for this role in a Gregg Araki picture and he didn't get it—of course, he's an *id*iot, right? There is just no way he is getting that part—and he just, like, *freaked*. No kidding. They never caught him, either. That's the funny thing. He got away with it. This town is crazy. Everyone's *nuts*. I love it here. Why would I *ever* wanna go back to New Jersey? Er, New York, I mean . . . There's just no way. But hey listen, Kathy? You don't think I'm, like, a Hollywood cliché, do you? I mean, I'm *not*, right? . . ."

"Hey!" this guy in a slick shiny vest (no less) and collarless shirt—what a thespian!—who was standing next to me trying to get a drink too, said super-conspiratorially: "Who's that chick you're talking to?"

"Oh, someone I just met," I said.

"Fucking-A, she's pretty, dude."

"Uh-huh. I know."

"I would fuck her like a trucker."

"Sorry?"

"I would fuck her like a trucker. I would hoist her like an *o*yster, dude. Trim her like an Olympic swimmer. You know, like, Plow her like a meteor shower. I would put my *dick* in that, is what I'm saying, bro."

"Two gin-and-tonics, please," I yelped, making it at last to the bar, got them, said thanks and got the fuck away.

Not fast enough, it seemed, as vest-oaf yelled after me: "I would do her like a sewer. Rape her like a taper. Hey, bro! Try and fuck her (he was practically bullhorning now), buddy—you know *I* would!"

Jesus fuck—these *people*. Me, I was Sisyphus with a couple of drinks instead of a rock in my hand. That's who I was. And oh, I know, thank you very much, that Sisyphus didn't have a rock in his *hand*—it was a boulder—so don't go showing me the way back to Prep School Mythology Class, okay? I can find the way myself—or tomorrow I can; tonight I am lost and have eyes like a spirograph in the hands of a child on methamphetamine and am utterly out of my head on good drugs and bad alcohol.

As you or I or anyone might've expected, Sam was gone from the spot where I'd left her. Three guys were standing huggermuggering where she'd stood so I just kinda milled around and hoped. They were, the guys, so loud you couldn't help being an incorrigible eavesdropper.

"What is up, bros?" the largest, most Type-A type was burbling-bellowing amidst the kaleidoscopic echolalia of the big backyard. He had on an unreally brash red mesh jersey instead of a shirt, like he'd dyed a tennis net and donned it, and a shiny-slick black blazer that looked four and three quarters sizes too big for him, even though he was just humongous to begin with, a real super-linebacker or champion shotputter or German Women's Swim Team Captain. "Are you guys *wasted?* " he was inquiring facetiously of a cluster of other fuckers. " Are you guys fucking totally shel*lack*ed, or what? All *right*. I hope you are, is what I am saying. I hope in fact you guys get *wrecked* tonight man—blotto. B-L-Oh-Double T-Oh, okay? Not *in* a wreck but fully fucking hammied, okay? Like, *right?!* Awesome. Totally. Help yourselves to anything, alcohol-wise, okay? Anything you want. And did you see the *talent* here tonight, my men? Jesus! Jesus *Christ*! Jesus Crispies, man. There are some *pretty* girls here tonight, no? Some sweet fucking *honeys*. Look at that shit over there, wouldya? Just look at that rack. Look at it. Them. Her. Whatever. Holy *Moly*! Whew! The one with the fantastic tits. Real, too. I bet they are. Hey! What am I *saying*? *I* fucked that. I *know*. Those pups *are* real, man. No lie. Julia Something, is her name. Janet. No: Juliette. Something with a "J." One of those names. Anyway, I know I sound like a sports announcer or something but . . . *Ladies and gentlemen, those are some fine looking bazoombas*! Hahaha! God she was good. Hot to fucking trot, if I recall—and I gotta pretty good memory, if you know what I mean. As your host, I think I will personally greet her later on, if you know what I mean. She'd better remember me, is all I'm saying. I certainly remember *her*. Hell: I almost cast her in my next thing. The project we got going now. She'd better remember me. Ha!"

Those of you who are having a hard time believing people actually talk like this—well, you've never been to California in general and to the City of Angels in specific, have you? Thought not. And movie people aren't people, anyway; they're *movie people*. It was making me sick to think I was wasting my life (at even more than the usual wasteful wasted rate I wasted it at) amidst these so-called beautiful people. I couldn't help thinking the whole party (Jaz, Sam and me accepted of course) was just this bunch of human *whatevers*, these walking nothings, these minus-zeros, an inflorescence of them.

But maybe, I also thought, I shouldn't be so brutal, be so harsh, such a snob, so judgmental. At the time, now I think of it, I was actually kinda feeling a tiny bit magnanimous. No kidding. For one thing, cannabis, that great attenuator of self- and other hatred, was coursing through my corpuscles, and a pretty girl with hair the color of plum jam and sporting spectacles (I have a glasses fetish like no one I know—I ought to just chuck all this art yen for good and all and become a fricking optometrist, I really ought to) might come back and accept the drink I was sent on a mission to fetch for her. There are worse things in life. (And things *would* get worse—just wait. You have no idea.)

I'd downed half of the drink I neither wanted nor needed when I saw Samantha at last emerge from the house where she'd presumably gone to use the loo or have a trite chat with someone new.

Thing was, there was a guy with her. *That* put a crimp in continuing our colloquy. *There*'s an obstacle-task for ya, Mr. Hercules. Nine feet tall, sparse, short, brown, goo-spiked hair, and a freshly pressed button-down buttoned all the way up to his thick I-am-going-to-crush-you-now neck, there he was chatting up the chick I hoped to go home with. A guy whose body language consisted of just one word: shark. Hammerhead shark. The kind of shark who would hammer her over the head and sweep her right away from me and this ridiculous shindig. Fuck! What to do? Was it her *boy*friend? Her bodyguard? Please let him be her big gay friend! Her big, super-macho-looking, gay or eunuchy friend who—who was I kidding?—was going to have the wonderfully meaningless sex with her tonight that *I* was supposed to meaninglessly wonderfully have. It was like this: guy's on a desert island, hallucinating like anything, wasting away and on his last half-coconut and can barely remember his own name, and a boat floats miraculously into his astonished ken and he reaches out his famished hands and the other guy, the guy all smiley on the boat, goes: "Hey, Shipwreck! Yah, you! What's *up*? *Ahoy*, boy! Oi! You look like you could use a ham sandwich or something! Hahahaha! Well I got one for ya, actually, mate!" And the guy jets out of the skiff or whatever it is, triple-jumping through the waves and the blazing wet sand, and he's about to give the poor starving guy this downtown New York-sized ham stack that is just dripping with piggy deliciousness—homemade honey mustard and perfectly mouthwateringly melted non-imitation Swiss on bread baked by a real live from-France French fucker—and a seagull the size of a mature pterodactyl, like, out of *no*where fucking swoops down and makes away with the desert-island guy's miraculous lunch, flapping triumphantly into the sorry sky. That's kinda like what I thought was about to happen. With me the hapless fuck of course and the giant guy the seagull.

"Here's your drink," I said to Samantha. "Hey there," I said to the hulk.

"This is Brendon?" Sam said.

"Brandon," the guy said as he set about mangling around fourteen of my fingers. "How it goes, bro?"

"Fine," I said. "How are *you*?"

The way he said "How it goes, bro?" made you imagine he would practically pummel you if you said it was going anything other than fine. That it would take a union of free safeties or cornerbacks to restrain him from quote-unquote correcting you for responding incorrectly. His as I said *way* thick neck bullfrogged over the too-tight collar. Several too-visible veins blued forth from his ultra-tanned forehead. Talking to this guy, the way you had to look up to look at him (to make sure he wasn't about to reach out and choke you for fun or just for something to do), was like running late to the movies and being urgently ushered down to the front row—the worst seat in the house. My neck was waxing fucked just from talking to him for two minutes; I was going to need a world class chiropractor or at least a champion neck brace in about four more minutes, I'm telling you. I needed to think fast while there was still some blood in my head.

"Great party," he said.

"For sure," I said.

"*Great* party. A lot of important people here, I'd say," he said. "Some real cool cats."

*Voila*! An actor! And if there is anything I hate more than the things I hate more than other things, it's when people—musicians especially, not just actors—refer to people as felines. God I can't stand that. The other moniker thing I hate is when people call you "man."

"Oh I know, man," I said. "I just met someone's casting director just a minute ago, actually. Whose *was* it? Wait: Quentin Tarantino's?—that's whose it was! He was right over there. Short little guy. That guy," I said and pointed to a hapless-looking Woody Allen-ish kinda homunculus sort of a fellow in a paisley shirt and white jeans, who was standing alone by the bar I'd just braved and sort of craning his neck in a fake way of faking looking for someone who was expecting him or something. He looked in fact just like a kid who you know has just lost his mummy and daddy in the mouth-breathing crowd at Disneyland or fucking Disneyworld or somewhere and is about to lose it big time.

"Really nice guy," I continued unconscionably. "Super friendly. He looks a bit like Woody Allen, doesn't he? Kinda uncanny. I thought he said something about looking for some specific-heighted guy to play a . . . oh forget it—I can't remember exactly."

"Nice to have met you guys," the über-tall guy waved to neither Sam nor me specifically and, probably anticipating immediate stellification, made a beeline for the unfriended guy I'd indicated—who was now following someone's dropkick dog towards the far end of the humungous backyard.

"There's another bar, I saw, on the balcony upstairs," I told Sam and tipped my head thataway.

"Sure," she said, then kind of smirked: "Nice work, by the way."

"Thank you, my lady," I laughed and took her by the hand.

## whoa whoa whoa she's a lady

It's not what you think, okay? I'm not gonna painstakingly describe some movie-like seduction scenario and then spring some scriptish cliché on you like: "*Pulling Samantha gently toward me I noticed a slight embulgement in her growing groinal area: 'Oh my God,' I ejaculated, 'you're a MAN!'"*

No: it was nothing like that. She was definitely a femme. Definitely.

Here's what occurred. When we got upstairs and went to the ornate wrought iron railing and looked down on the mayhem below, Tom Jones came on the sound system and Sam came on to me, pulling me towards her with her eyes and saying this:

"I don't really live next door, you know. I made that up."

"Oh yeah?" I managed to say before her tongue went butterflying around in my open mouth.

"Uh-huh," she said as we took a break from, then went back to, kissing. "But I actually did come here with my friend Lacey. She's probably looking for me by now."

"How come?" I breathed out.

"Probably because she knows I'm such a slut."

"You are not a slut," I said, trying to convince me.

"Am so," she said. "Can't help it."

And we kissed deliciously once more.

"If you say so, Sam," I said.

You have to understand: the way she moved her lips, her mouth, her tongue was more scrumptious than any homemade, icing-thick/flaky pastry dessert you care to fling at someone who's been on a strict diet for two whole days or something. She was so that good at kissing. A champion busser, the Wayne Gretsky of tonsil hockey. It was very hard to listen actively to anything she was telling me. She might have insisted that a SWAT team of angry ninjas was gonna waste me if I didn't get out of there that instant and I would not have budged, yeah. Not an iota.

But then I heard her say that we shouldn't be doing this.

"Oh I don't know," I said and tried to French her again—but she turned away.

"I'm serious."

"Okay," I said but of course the note of disappointment in my now-gruff and worked-up voice couldn't be more clear.

"Lacey's probably looking for me."

"You said that."

"I know. "

"She's *fine*. Maybe she's with my friend Jaz."

"A guy?"

"Uh-huh."

"Doubt it. Hey: you never told me what you do. I told you, but you didn't tell me. So tell me."

"Me? I'm in a band."

"For reals?"

"For *real*," I said. "Singular. Real."

Sentenious pedant.

" I'm also a sub," I continued. " Just for a while, though. You know. Till we go on tour with Sonic Youth or the Rolling Stones, of course."

"You're a teacher? And a band guy too? Wow. Everyone here seems to do two things. I mean in L.A. and all."

"So you're not from Los Angeles?"

"No. Tucson. Tucson, Arizona."

"Oh, that Tucson."

"Shut up. Listen, though: I only just moved here three weeks ago and it's, like, weird. Everyone's just so weird, you know? Like they're all from somewhere else other than here, I mean. Like, no one's, like, from here. But they're still, like, here, you know? Well, it's really true—what they say—isn't it?"

"What is?" I asked.

"Oh, that everything happens for a reason. Do you believe that too? I totally do."

"Oh, for sure," I lied. "Totally."

It's funny how we exonerate the brutally stupid when they're totally hot; and I am telling you that this girl, with her perfectly plump lips and wild-beautiful eyes and expensive, ideal hair was *stupid hot.* Stupidly so. I don't even like to use that term—I think it's so lame—but when you're hot, as they say, you're . . . oh I don't wanna say it again. (But she *was.*) And even more amazing was the fact that I was still standing talking to this girl after she'd said the thing that drives me most mad of all: the bit about how everything happens for a reason. I hate people who say that. I can't tell you how little respect I have for them; but it seems that suffices for a "philosophy" amidst most oafs these days, you know? Like they think that is an actual ethos. And no mistake. That's all the thinking they have to do about life and its meaning, a way to rationalize anything, and never think about the fact that there are zillions of things that happen for no reason whatsoever, that happen because the universe is essentially, on the contrary, chaotic and fucking inexplicable. God I hate the "Everything Happens" People. What morons! What twaddle! What was I even doing continuing this farcical roundelay of lust and the chase? I wish had a picture of this gal; I'd show you; she had the kind of face you could forgive anything for. There's all the quote-unquote reason you need, pal. That's *it*. Kierkegaard or Wittgenstein or R.P. Blackmur—I can't remember which—used to moan on and on, apparently, about how sorry he felt for people who merely "lived for the sake of gathering experiences." But Kierkegaard or Wittgenstein or Blackmur hadn't seen *this* girl: they would've wanted to quote-unquote experience her, that's for sure—even if they were gay or asexual or had lost their penis in a trench in a war or something, I'll bet. That's how cute she was.

"I just moved here too," I said. "From Summerland. Summerland, California. Do you know where that is?"

"By San Diego?"

"No," I laughed, "it's up north. On the coast."

"Oh okay. It's supposed to be pretty."

"It is," I said, "but it's boring—a yawn-by-the-sea. No one has any ambition but to go surfing and then have some Coronas and tacos while watching the game."

"What game?"

"Never mind. Do you mind if we resume locking lips a few more hundred times? I really like kissing you, Samantha."

"All right," she said and we tangoed away a little further from the front of the balcony railing and towards the wall and glass doors.

Kissing me relentlessly she whispered: "You aren't going to fuck me tonight, by the way, John."

"I'm not?"

"No. Maybe I will let you go down on me, but we aren't going to fuck—you get it?"

"Um, okay," I gulped.

If there was a loop, I was being thrown for it for sure.

"How do you like my breasts?" she asked and glanced down at the arched top of her swelling, um, top, shimmery purple and tight as anything. She looked like she was about to dust them off or hoist them up to me. "Do you like them? *Really*? Don't lie to me."

"Very nice," I said. "Spectacular, even. They're great."

"Everyone here has fake tits," she said I thought kinda bitterly. She was even more drunk, I now twigged, than the drunk I thought she was. "*I* don't. Mine aren't. Fake. These are mine. They *are* . . . One hundred percentage. Do you really like them, Brandon?"

"*John.*"

"Oh sorry. I fucked up. That was the other guy."

"Yeah."

I mean, who the heck did she think she was, anyway—Marilyn Monroe or something?

"Will you be my boyfriend—just for tonight, okay?"

"Okay," I said.

Then she gently meniscused my tumescent cockshaft with her right hand.

". . . John," she added and batted her vast eyes at me.

"Samantha!" I said. What she'd done was sort of *sobering*, actually. I was reeling: a little shocked.

"Let's have another cigarette," she said.

She let go of me then and I got two smokes out and sparked them in turn. Her glasses were now sliding down her nose, I noticed, and she was getting sort of slumpy.

"So you're from Arizona. I love it there. The sky's amazing."

"Oh I know," she said. "I loved it there. I was working in a vintage clothes shop and bartending at Hotel Congress—the coolest bar ever."

"That sounds grand. So: why did you move here then?"

"Because I had to," she said, and it sounded like she was perturbed, and just then a girl, short, all nose, with weird angular unabundant yellow hair and ping-pong paddles for ears came up from behind and was ominously beside us. In her wife-beater tank top and with her innumerable tattoos, she didn't look too happy. You wouldn't be too happy either if you looked like her. *Quel* gargoyle, I thought. She looked like a young, pony version of old Queen Victoria, a hip-hop Queen Victoria: the too-big head, goggle eyes, distressed teeth, and a savage air of glaring glaringness.

"Samantha!" the chick remonstrated instantly. "Let's *go*, okay? Time to go, all *right*?"

"Nice to have meet you, " Sam said and dropped her ciggie. "John."

She index-fingered her glasses back up. God, she was pretty. God, her "friend" was not.

"You must be Lacey," I ventured. Then I looked back at Sam: "I suppose I am fully tilting at windmills here, but do you wanna give me your number or something? I mean . . ."

The short-haired/arsed potentially truculent Lacey girl gave a horrified look like someone had just unflinchingly issued a stentorian flatus (wet) right at her. Then, risibly, she stamped out her girlfriend's still-burning smoke and I choked back a snort-laugh. For a second there I thought there'd be a stupendous (or little) row. There wasn't. No contest. I wasn't even a contestant in this. Not close.

"I guess not," I said as I met Sam's forbidding, forlorn (at least it seemed so) look. "Nice to have met you as well."

I felt like someone had poured a fresh mug of piss-warm saltwater down my forced-open throat, being careful not to spill a single drop. Like I'd actually consumed an entire domestic or budget international airline meal.

"Good night," Samantha said extra-formally—she almost fucking curtseyed—and downstairs they went, hand-in-hand, and *exeunt* right out of my ludic life.

## turn and face the strange changes

All right. So what? I had been flagitiously used. Used flagitiously. Cockteased unimaginably. Imponderably. Prodigiously. Big wow. But now I had to find Jaz, whom I hadn't clocked for hours, it seemed (though the aforesaid encounter had probably lasted at most forty-five minutes). It was imperative I find Jaz: he'd driven. And, one hoped, had not driven away, assuming I had hooked up with a hot chick and wouldn't need a ride. He wouldn't do something like that, I thought. Jaz wasn't the sort of guy who'd strand you. He'd find you and tell you he was leaving, he would. Definitely. He'd never strand me.

"I think he left," a girl named Celestine (the Jaz acquaintance who'd invited him) slurred-yelled over David Bowie when I asked her if she'd seen him.

"Seriously?" I said. "He split?"

"Haven't seen him for a long time. I think he was looking for you before he did, though. I dunno. Been enjoying yourself?"

"Immensely," I said. "It's been grand."

She looked at me askance (of course): "I can't tell whether you are being sarcastic or not."

"Everybody says that."

"Whatever."

"Everybody says that too."

"Good luck, then," she fluted, all snarky. "Can't help ya."

I didn't say what I might have, like, "Bite *off*!" or "Fuck *you*!" or "*See* ya, ya stupid bitchy cunty cunt!" or something clever and cutting like that. I rose above it. I snubbed snubbing the super-bitch. What I said instead was: "Well, thanks all the same, Celestine. Take care."

She turned her back and resumed, one assumed, some ultra-banal confab, probably. People at Hollywood parties, boy—they never wanna help you out unless it gets them a pilot or a commercial or an agent that actually calls them back or tells them when their suckass audition for a first-time student director for a student film fucking *sucked* or something.

Where the fucking fuck was the fucking fucker? This was potentially fucking *fucked*. I didn't know a soul there except that wicked witch I just told you about. This was not good. I toreadored my way through other assorted harlequinades of hipsters in the backyard, the pool room, the kitchen, the side yard, the balcony again, and all the unlocked bedrooms and the seven-car garage and still no Jaz. Really not good. I was ten miles from home and *sans* the money for a cab—even if you could get one. A cab? An impossibility. There are no cabs to be had on weekend or day nights in Los Angeles. There are no such things. They don't allow them. Where the goddam was he?

## spare us the cutter

Keep in mind that I was still quite polluted. Quite quashed. On top of too many mixed drinks I had glugged three draft glugs in the wake of my intense, "I'm stranded! I had better try and drink my way out of this!" panic. Moreover, you may recall, I had been blueballed to the supermax. By a lesbian, no less. A girl from the Isle. The Isle of Lesbos. Get it? Good.

And quite the accomplishment, don't you think—getting an Isle Girl to torture me thusly? I was not pleased. And can you blame me? I don't think so. Not if you'd gone through what I'd gone through. And I wish it *had* been you instead of me, quite frankly. Sincerely I do. When people say "I wouldn't have wished it on anyone" what they *really* mean is "I would so jesus goddam rather it had been anybody *but* me, thank you very much." Because if bad things happen in life—and they invariably *do*—it is always better for them to happen to others than to oneself. That, I believe, is what ancient stoic philosophers like Aristotle or Darwin or Deepak Chopra meant when they were writing all the profound shit they were writing, whatever it was, that shit. The wise shit they wrote and shit. You know? No? Well, that's what they *meant*, even if they never said it. I'm quite sure. When bad things, in other words, happen to other people, they're not so bad, are they? Huh. Never thought about it like that. There may be a song lyric in there somewhere. Have to think about it more when I am not thinking about all the ways I am going to kill Jaz if I don't find him. I will hope, in fact, that he is dead; then I will spare myself the sorrow of having to slay him, my dear abandoning friend and *artiste confrère* whom I hate with the hate of I-don't-know-what-'cause-I-can't-think-straight.

The funny thing was, as happens in so many ridiculous situations in ridiculous circumstances and ridiculous settings, something went ridiculous in my ludicrous mind and I thought about this one time in college when a bunch of my absurd friends and my best friend Bradley and I were sitting round getting stoned (this was somewhere provincial in Merrie Olde England where I went to university) on hash-and-tobacco hand-rolled superspliffs and we played this game where you had to say "Farmer Brown" and "girthy stump" in the longest, dirtiest sentence you could and the winner, if I recall correctly, was: "Farmer Brown nightly plumped his girthy stump into the earthy rump of his next door neighbor's neighing daughter, retarded and beautiful and who moreover loved it (she never frowned) when Farmer Brown would 'go downtown'."

Preposterous, I know. Out of control. And I will leave you to guess whether it was me who came up with such stuff or someone else. (Okay, you win; it was me.) I mean to say, that's the dumb kinda stuff you occupy yourself with, as it were, when you are: a) in college in a mostly cold foreign country and/or; b) young and idiotic and delirious and going crazy horny 'cause there are only around five attractive girls available and two of *those* are Irish and the rest exclusively date the rugby team.

I started laughing like mad to myself—like a quiet madman, one who has hatched an escape plot or mapped out a perfect murder of someone who has never done him a footling bit of harm—till I noticed someone or other or maybe even two people taking note (in a not-good way) of me and sort of moving quickly away. Then, only a smidge nonplussed, I started thinking how in England all the Irish guys said the English girls were the loosest and the English guys said the Irish girls and the Welsh guys said the Scottish girls and the Scottish guys said . . . well, the Scottish guys said lots of things but you couldn't understand a fucking word they fecking said. Never. And I *speak* Scottish, am ancestrally *from* Scotland. So there.

Anyway, after this little spell of comically uncomic just-to-myself relief I thought I had better take a serious whiz before I starting in on really starting in earnest to panic completely. (And N.B. and for the record: I didn't really *truly* hate Jaz for having left without me—not that I would do that to *him*, though.) I had better find, I thought, a loo, and soon. I didn't want to compound matters by pissing my pants. Many of you, I imagine, advance the same policy whithersoever you roam. I had visions of trying to blag a ride from people I didn't know, smelling of freshly beery, tequilaish and gin-and-tonicish urine and walking up sideways like a track star in warm-ups doing those twisty exercises—we on the old prep school Varsity teams used to called them Caryokies, though I haven't a clue why—so as to try to hide the unavoidable stain. An unseemly, malodorous Hula Hoop-shaped spot of wetness was not, well I knew, an asset in the can-I-bum-a-lift department. There was only one bathroom open, the one on the second floor, but a queue Eschered ten deep down the winding stairs. No go. Therefore I decided to seek out an accommodative shrub. I went out the front door and found a bush with my name on it. Piss thickly streamed out and on to the roots and leaf-fall of a towering eucalyptus. Thus happily disburthened and sighing with temporary relief, I spotted out of the corner of my eye someone who had nearly encroached upon my territory, as it were—someone pissing next to me and humming a Bunnymen song I faintly recognized. Blearily I recognized this person. Sterling! Sterling, a.k.a. "the Scather"—former amphetamine merchant, ex-altar boy, rival indie-rock songwriter, *raconteur par excellence*, and (very) part-time clerk at everyone's favorite record store, Finyl Vinyl: a shoppe so hip, so cool, so trendy *beyond* that sometimes the "associates" would not let you buy a record you ported to the counter. Not if they're weren't in the right mood, or if you didn't strike them as worthy enough, cool enough to buy it. Honest.

Sterling Somerset Severin Smith. The Third, no less. Easily one of the most impishly scathing outrageous brilliant and irreverent personages in unsung Modern American History and in rock and roll.

"Scather!" I said, startled but oh-so-happy to see him. "What are *you* doing here?!"

"Juan! . . . Getting bombed for free—what else! I saw you as I was leaving. Are you as gone as I am? This party has been so unbelievably, goringly boring that there's been nothing to do but get pro*fuse*ly bombed. How are ya, Juanny?"

"Terrible. I came with Jaz and apparently he got so blitzed that he forgot he brought me. Can you . . .?"

"Arrrghhhh! All the way to Santa Monica? You know I am going the other longitude."

"Please, Sterling?"

He narrowed his eyes in the half-dark.

"You'll owe me."

"I know."

"Okay. Let's get the bejesus outta here. The cops are on their way, anyway."

"What?" I said. "How do you know?"

It didn't seem likely the police would show up now that people were leaving in mini-droves, anyway, the drunken females crazyleggedly clacking down the walkway driveway in high high heels with the males of the species weave-lagging after them, blazers shouldered like tired capes, everyone talking at once, or silently, determinedly plodding towards the cars they'd drunk-drive away in.

"How do I *know?*" Sterling said and laughed his fulgurating laugh. "Because I called them myself, my dear friend Juan. Hahaha!"

"Are you kidding? That's brilliant."

"Someone," Sterling insisted, "had to report these people for throwing a party of epically boring proportions—goes without saying. I take boring parties rather personally, I do. I asked someone—and I hope it was the host himself—if I could use the telephone and I summarily called the cops. Why are you looking so dubiously at me? You don't think I did?!"

"Oh, I believe you. I just don't be*lieve* you. That's hilarious. Was it some big fuck in a red mesh shirt?"

"Maybe. I don't noticed so-called "people," especially if they are atrociously attired, as that personage seems, as per your report, to have been. I say, let's get out of here before the authorities show up; though, knowing them, they won't be here for another hour."

"'I've never been happier to see you, Sterl," I beamed.

"You want a ride home, don't you, Juan-Juan?"

"Yes," I said, with an "and so?" tone in my voice.

"Then spare me your obvious obsequiousness, and help me find my car."

Sterling! The flamboyant effrontery he was capable of! Immense!

One time we, me and Sterl, were at this party and this chick got a little miffed at Sterling's waspish ways, the way in which he could say the *most* cutting things right to people's unsuspecting fucking faces; sometimes he *did* cross over the line, you must understand. The girl—Faye Dunaway pretty, with emerald almond eyes, sour lips in a perpetual turned-down frown, and a very jaded mien—was the frontperson for a fledgling band that he was putting down right in front of her. The Monks, they were called.

And Sterling goes: "The Monks! I saw you guys at the Roxy last month! You guys are simply *ter*rible. A ga*la*vious [he often made up words just to see if anyone would call him out on them] abomination! The *worst*, you guys are! Monks? Why don't you live up to your name *and take a vow of silence or something!* Hahaha! The *Monks*!"

The chick had gotten, as you might expect, way upset and well huffy and said "How can you *say* that to a person? I mean, my *God!*" and Sterling had, like a dandy adjusting his cufflinks, all impenitent and cucumber-cool and stuff, gone: "Well, Deidra, I don't really actually con*sid*er you a person, come to think of it. I don't consider you a person at *all*."

That was when I started calling him the Scather.

He almost always pretended that he was kidding but we all knew he wasn't. He really meant the horrid, hilarious things he said. He didn't, however, really want to hurt anyone's feelings, curiously enough. Honestly. And I truly believed him when he said it was all in fun, that he was just trying to amuse himself in a torridly boring world. It was just that these outlandishly clever and ripping things came to him and he just couldn't resist saying them—it was like he was possessed by some cut-down devil or avatar of the ghosts of Oscar Wilde, James Whistler, fucking *Shake*speare, John Gielgud in *Arthur,* and/or the immortal Dorothy Parker all at once. He really couldn't help it; that's just how he was. He always maintained he didn't have a choice and you kinda believed him. Sooner tell Marilyn to turn off the sexy; Cary Grant the charm; Groucho the funny; and Chaplin the adorability..

The ride back to my place was uneventful—Sterling chain-smoked the whole way and sang along at the top of his capacious lungs with every song, whether it was something cool or something by Foreigner or Boston. As we bounced into my alleyway (Sterling had a seemingly shockless and unaccountably powerful VW; cruising with him was like a ride at Disneyland or Magic Mountain), I remembered I was going to tell him about Jenny. Despite the fact that Sterl had the most exclusive taste in music, he really rooted for his friends who had bands. He'd kinda given up on music himself but that didn't mean he was going to go crushing *your* dreams; in fact, he encouraged them greatly.

"I forgot to tell you!" I said. "We met this female keyboard player and she's amazing. Very cool. She's meant to jam with us tomorrow, actually."

"What's she like? Would I approve, do you think?"

"She's great. Funny too."

He narrowed his big, expressive eyes once more: "What's she look like?"

He was one of the few people—so bright—who saw right through me, who were onto me *completely* and, thank fuck, only lorded or queened it over me occasionally.

"She's pretty, I'd say, in a very Pre-Raphaelite way, but not my type, really." I was trying to act all nonchalant.

"John," the Scather said, all avuncular like he often got when he used my given name, with another of his irrepressible laughs.

"Yes, Sterling?"

"If she's *breathing*, she's your type. No matter *what* period she's from!"

# VERSE

## being for the benefit of Mr Kite

In the morning I woke up tragically early.

Please, someone—pretty please *remove this stake from my eye*, I thought, feebly massaging my sore, sore head, matting my already Rastafarianed hair into, I imagined, an even more horrendous hair-beret. I decided to go down to the beach to have a look at the ocean's sky blue splendor before it turned the dull silver-dappled green it always turned by mid-morning. At least I didn't have to go to the trouble of getting dressed: I already was. Even Converse kicks still on feet.

It takes a lot of man to fall asleep dead drunk in your tennis shoes.

But what a katzenjammer this man had. Wowsome. Like someone playing the Beatles' most immortally psychedelic song jet-engine loud, and sometimes—though one could not predict when—*backwards*, a record number of times till someone else went irreversibly crackers.

I lurched towards the loo and, careful not to look in the mirror (a horror mirror, potentially, a bad trip to end all trips), baptized myself in the glowering sink and realized I was still drunk. I had heard of such a thing—sleeping then waking up still plowed—but even in college, one's king drinking days, when one is most, er, and in libation-imbibing fighting fitness, so to say, I'd never experienced it. Huh. So that's what it's like. It's fucked 'cause you are drunk and hungover *at the same time*—like your liver and head can't make up their respective minds. I divested myself of my gross clothes, ran the shower extra cold for penance, took the Guinness Book's record shortest wash-off, and found some not too dirt-stiff shorts and a T-shirt and my yellow thongs. Flip-flops, I mean. *Thongs* have not only not been invented yet (I mean the terrific girl underwear—the panty that for minimum cloth-coverage gives a girl maximum attractiveness), but I also would not wear them—not even as a gag, unless it was on my head and I was sure to get a laugh out of it from a girl with a good sense of humor—ever. But you knew that. I think you did. I think I'm having a kinda *déjà vu* hangover here. I do beg your pardon, and if you would be so kind as to bear with me I will try to get on with the telling of this, thank you ever so kindly and so very much, thanks.

Jaz hadn't been home (though he might've been sleeping in the bushes outside or in the laundry room cubbyhole below stairs or spooning next door with Heidi, for all I knew—or even Marie, ghastly thought . . . he *easily* could have been that blitzed, had he drunk even half of what I'd seemed to have fucking quaffed) when I got in the night before, but as I made my way through the sitcom set-thin door that separated our "rooms," there he was on the daybed, a postmodern beachy Pieta or surfer version of a Civil War soldier dead at Gettysburg, arms all pinned beneath him (like a walrus sleeps?) and legs fully pretzeled. You aren't going to believe this unless you were in a frat in college or at least a major stoner, but he had a half-eaten hamburger in his mouth. Not kidding. I nearly vomited. I kind of laugh-vomited, if there *is* such a thing—and there is, I know, 'cause I did it. Then I vomited for real, and jackknifed myself back towards the bathroom in order to do it—the thing I had hoped against hope not to have to do. I hate throwing up. You inveterate bulimics out there won't understand, I realize, but it's really no fun at all. A bilious *etouffé* of shrimp, guac, beer, chips, cheese, vodka, gin, beer, tonic, more vodka, more gin, more chips, and beer swirled in the startled toilet. "Yuck," I retched and spasmed and spat and spat.

"Practicing your Arabic, Johnny boy?" I heard Jaz's voice go. Then I heard it nearer and there he was, large as life and utterly starkers, offering me the hamburger half.

"You have got to be kidding me!" I managed to say. "Get out of here!"

"Thought you might be hungry. I'll give you two—no, *three*—whole bucks, not even in couch change, if you can down this right now. Three bucks cash money."

"You're fucking heartless," I laughed. "You *fuck*."

Then I turned round and grabbed the thing out of his hand and stuffed it into my mouth.

Are you *kidding*? Of course I did no such thing. (When are you gonna learn not to trust me?)

What I really did was groan Shakespeareanly, which made Jaz laugh more than he was already laughing. It did serve me right for being such a wasteoid last night.

"If you are just about finished, I would love it if you vacated the old water closet as I am anticipating yakking myself pretty soon here, okay? The technicolor yawn cometh on, I fear."

I rammed our common toothpaste tube into my mouth and injected a mess of it, then went for the stash of one of the six or sex bottles of plaque-remover mouthwash (I'll explain later) we normally stashed under the sink and, staggering into the living room, announced: "Okay, Jaz. I am out of here for the beach. You should put on a towel, at least. Jesus fuck. I won't ask you to come, seeing as we are decidedly unfriends right now, okay? Not happy with the Jazster! What the fuck *happened* to you last night, anyway? Luckily the Scather turned up. Luckily he was at that party or I'd have been stranded, you know?"

"Sterling was there?" Jaz said. "No way. I *love* that guy. Never get to hang with him, ever. Or hardly ever. How is he, anyway? That guy's hilarious. How'd he find out about the party, anyway? Sterling. I tell ya; he's a riot."

"Jaz."

"Okay, okay. All right. If you will deign to take my deposition, I will explain to you the logic of why I left. I don't feel so hot right now . . . And to be perfectly honest, you don't wanna know what happened to *me*, believe me," Jaz said. "Simply put, it looked like you were 'in there,' by the looks of it. I saw you with that total babe. Right?! I thought *for sure* you were going to go home with her—and *of course* then I looked for you to *tell* you I was splitting but I couldn't find you! I thought *you* left! With *her*."

"Lesbian," I said.

Jaz hummed-shouted his incredulity: "Seriously?" Then corrected himself, realizing we were both insanely hungover and super-sensitive to blasts of noise of any sort, and said more quietly: "Seriously, John? I really thought you were gonna pull that. She was pretty cute too. *Very* cute."

"Not even."

"I mean, *les*bian lesbian? Or just, like, lesbian as in the definition of any-girl-you-strike-out-with lesbian?"

"Lesbian lesbian," I said. "Her live-in probably girlfriend came up and rescued her and the whole motif."

"No shit," Jaz said and tucked a hank of his dusky blonde surfer's mop behind one ear. "A rug-munching cockblocker. Now I've heard everything. Hey! Have you noticed that since the advent of rap *music* no one says 'rapped' as in 'talked with' anymore? I mean, have you? No one ever says anymore, like, 'So there I was rapping with this really fine looking girl when I noticed she was checking out other chicks!' I was just thinking . . . I was just thinking that . . . I was just . . ." Then, just as he'd predicted, it was his turn to lurch toward the loo-bowl and the next sound I heard as I scurried to the front door was him pre-horking, kind of a spit without saliva spitting sort of sound, then of course I heard him salaaming majorly to the john.

"Bye!" I said.

"Yaaahhkkkkkkawwwowgrrrrohahhaha," he replied, horking megaly now.

"Sorry, John," I heard him say before he ralphed again.

And I knew he was, 'cause we were longtime buds and he wouldn't have split unless he was way too drunk to think straight or unless he was really sure I was going home with someone.

*

The ocean was a very cerulean thing, a shimmering salver, so beautiful it hurt to look at it—the morning light making twinkling arabesques on the translucent waves and salt-white foam-crests.

I closed my eyes. Opened them. Closed them again. No change. My head was pounding like a big wave at low tide but the beach felt velvety and nicely warm. Scuffing the thin sand near the shorebreak I walked a ways towards the pier, noting the red, yellow, orange, and blue isosceles flags and the dormant Ferris wheel and a couple of lonesome, Prufrockian types going fishing, hanging over the railings in the distance. Nearer, a kid, all crazy-legged, was fighting to get his kite up in the thin breeze; but then the onshore wind kicked up and the thing jerked twice and swam into the air, royal blue with a heraldic yellow dragon and white tail worming behind it, the sky a Neapolitan ice cream backdrop of oblong mauve and cream, cumulus clouds all white with geometrical stretches of beautiful blue.

And I too would live, would fly, as it were, another day. After of course thirteen more cups of acerbic, budget coffee and a tin of generic aspirins taken like mint candies. I waved to him, my kite-flyer, and smiling shyly-proudly he waved back.

I headed back, nearer the water now, and sallied forth across the hard, wet, gray sand and through the mini-dunes and up the steep winding sand-slippery ramp past a not-populous parade of the totally insane: scattershot ambitious blue-hairs jogging; mothers with strollers chirruping; the odd Neptune of a homelessmeister with a grand crown of seaweed and a sad, mad, faraway gaze; couples in dopey matching or almost-matching hats; obvious tourists, pale and beaming or taking pictures of everything indiscriminately—that stranded starfish or this movie star lookalike, those stunted Santa Monica skyscrapers or that fugitive Frisbee, a he-man with a parrot on his shoulder or a bleached-out banal bathing-beauty lying on her stomach with her bikini top unstrung.

Los Angeles, boy: it's weird here.

*

His Hairiness was face down on the couch again: the hamburger was nowhere. Good. Maybe he'd eaten the rest of it, an after-yakking snack. Maybe he'd used the bun for a face towel and flung the rest of it out the window for Heidi to munch on. (But emus must be vegetarians, surely?) Perhaps he'd tooth-fairyed it beneath my pillow or left it floating in the toilet, a memento of the night before.

What was I doing thinking about it? If I thought about it any longer I might risk a reprise of the chuck I'd had earlier. I had some fair number of hours to kill before rehearsal so I made that pot of really viscous coffee and mechanically drank it all, black, cup after cup, sticking to the kitchen, leaning against the counter, trying to be as quiet as I could so I wouldn't wake Jaz. The thing is, he was talking in his sleep, all gruff and stuff. He's a sleeptalker, sometimes, Jaz is: it's fun to ask him quiet questions when he does it: he sometimes answers, and it's invariably an hilarious *non sequitur*. One time when he was murmuring in his sleep I asked him where the shampoo was and he said "Napoleon never made it there" and—just fucking with him, of course—another time I asked him which Beatle made the best post-Beatle albums and he said "Bingo!" Hilarious. Anyway, I heard him go: "What if . . . just for something thing to do . . . see if you could do it . . . you decided to like all the things . . . like all the things you don't like . . . like cauliflower, French, French people, people from San Francisco, the 49ers, the Eagles, Scientol . . . cauliflower . . . zzzzzzz . . ."

*You just can't make this stuff up*, I thought to myself; not if you took a grad class in it; no one would believe you. Then I tiptoed through the living room and went back to sleep, blissful sleep.

*

The bockity-bock clucking of a banjo was coming from the living room as I woke up and recognized a song by Neil Young: *A man needs a maid, indeed*, I thought, looking around my room in a post-nap haze—a maid with one of those backpack leaf-blowers the professional gardeners use. Really, my room was in need of a serious swabbing, a hurricane of tidying up. Any moment a battalion of Democrats waving social programs and pushing Hoovers could be expected to burst through my door. Were I ever to lure either a not-blind or anosmic girl back to it, my "space"—even a chick with the most lax notions of order and hygiene and asepsis—it was gonna take hours ungodly to get it organized. These were the least of my many worries, however; I had to get ready for rehearsal; I had to get going. Put boots or regulation-issue rock 'n' roll Converse Chuck Taylors (black, low tops, of course) on the right feet (yes, I chose those for today's rehearsal) and scrape the now-formidable stubble from my sweat-caked face. The heat from outside was bullying its way in through my screenless windows and several flies darned the air. I lay there on my mingy purple futon a while longer, dreamily torpid and trying to psych myself up to get up, get up, get up. *Get the fuck up, John*, I internally cheerleadered—*it's time*.

## isn't she pretty in pink

No one was answering the freakishly gargantuan Addams Family-esque door at Walter and Natasha's so I quote-unquote set a spell, as Midwesterners say, on the front porch and had my first cigarette of the day. I could leaf through the *Times* which hadn't been picked up from the walkway (being careful not to get caught by Walter, who, I'd learned the hard way, wanted his paper—the only thing I'd ever seen him read aside from cereal boxes or street parking signs—fresh and unread and unrumpled), or lean back and dream at the October sky—marshmallow clouds and Prussian blue air and discernible ugly smog hovering in the distance, hot wind-play in the penchant poplars, sycamores, oaks, palms and eucalyptuses, the sparkle of fallen leaves like talking hands in burnt tangerine and warm gold and quite deep brown; and on both sides of the big old front lawn unweeded little fields of flowers, yellow, blue and purple-white. I stuck three pungent sticks of Juicy Fruit into my mouth and made a sort of automatic menthol of my next cigarette, thinking I should leave off smoking anyway, go cold turkey or to acupuncture. Get the patch. Get several patches. Become bepatched like the young Russian in *Heart of Darkness*. Patch up my biceps, lower back—make a headband of one, haha. Like the headband on some sort of demented vet, some nicotine-fiend Bruce Springsteen. (I can't stand Bruce Springsteen.) The thing is, it'd take a patch the size of a snow jacket to curtail my pack-a-day/pack-and-change-if-I-am-drinking habit. Ha! Not good. Lately some of the vile boluses of gunk I'd hacked up could be mounted by art students—avant-garde ones, of course—and passed off as sculptures.

I stabbed out the cigarette and zoned on the old-timey lamp posts and parked cars and two- or three-story house fronts and the quite pleasant Saturday east-of-mid-Wilshire scene and thunk my thoughts and waited. It really was a beautiful, stately old neighborhood—the houses replete with cream cake facades and languid verandas, long dry lawns and balconies or cupolas, spires, even, weird old Victorian follies (like Walter and Nasty's, as I illustrated earlier) and ramshackle Tudorish monstrosities—on the border of much badness. As are so many like *vecinos* in Los Angeles: ganglands a not-long jaunt away, where broad-daylight burglaries and pistol whippings were a real ho-hum. Nights, summer nights especially, helicopters whirred and were your lullaby; they vroomed above Crenshaw, near Walter's, all the bloody time, their searchlights trained on suspects like spray on bugs from a can of Raid. The report of a gun, now nebulous, now like a howitzer, was often to be heard, "At least twice a week!" I remember Walter noting one time; "More than that! More!" Natasha interjecting. Nightly sirens for sure from cop cars and ambulances and fire trucks.

After not too much time Jenny and a girl I didn't know came riding up on a couple of nice bicycles. They looked flushed and happy (already, at 10:30, the sun was well hot), their hair in thick bands across their sun-touched faces. Which (their errant hair) they touched away reflexively upon seeing a grinning, hopeful male now standing up to meet them, regarding them from the front porch step. Beaming, beadily perspiring Jenny had on a loose pink lemonade sleeveless top that exposed a bit of sexy black bra as she dismounted and bent down to pull the probably bothersome shoestring out of one of her shoes. Some white shorts, tennis shoes with no socks. And yes, I was a little flustered by the bra-sighting, the peak sneaked sneakily.

Ladies, most guys are. Distracted, that is. Even a hundred-and-twenty-year-old guy with stage five Alzheimer's gets nonplussed at the sight of a bra strap and some cup action. Especially a black one. Or a red (or a white). Lacey, especially. Or any color, come to think of it. In a police lineup most men couldn't pick out their own moms even if they were promised record-setting lottery winnings, but get a couple of Victoria's Secret or even just sports bras up there and they'll identify the right one every single time. "That's the one, officer!" they'd say. "The silky little chartreuse job with the dainty little bow in front and crenellated décolleté? There's your man right there!"

Even guys like me who aren't especially boob guys are always—I'm talking always—into bras.

It all goes back to the immortal Sears catalog.

Nearly every American male child who grew up in the 60s and 70s was initiated into the realm of sexuality by the Sears, Roebuck & Co. catalog. Or maybe the Spiegel (Chicago 60609). Say a boy kid is sitting minding his own business and maybe scribbling out the serial numbers of the air gun or bi-plane model kit he wants for Christmas or for his tenth or eleventh birthday. Say he gets up suddenly to answer the telephone or answer the doorbell or torture the cat or pound on his horrid bratty little sister and he *just so happens* to knock the pages of the catalogue around so that they go to—I dunno—page thirty-two or forty-something. Kaboom. *Sexy sex.* Pages and pages of brassiere-ed breasts of all sizes and breast-shapes. Perky, pretty junior misses in training bras. More-than-attractive girl- or mom-next-door types in A cups, B cups, C cups, D. There's all the ABCs a kid needs right there, a veritable 101 of Undergarment Education. *Lingerie.* The very name! Its liltingness! It just *smacks* of lust, doesn't it. Underwire, full figure, padded, strapless, seamless, everyday and front-hooking; athletic, even—form-fitting, demi-cup, balconette and convertible. Racerback, surely (but—heaven forefend!—not training or nursing: no, no, *no!*) Cross-your-heart . . . and hope to die and go to bra nirvana. And the glorious push-up not even invented yet! Think of it!

Pretty soon Junior's got the old catalogue stashed under his bed full time, full stop. And his mom, in a minor nit over not being able to find it in order to order some Teflon pots and pans or those new plaid flannel sheets she's been eyeing, goes a-quizzing him: "Junior, dear? Have you seen the Sears catalog anywhere? I thought you were looking at it last." "No, mom," Junior lies, cold sweat breaking out in pores he never even knew he had. "I think I saw it in [insert kid sister's name here]'s room. Sorry." "That's okay, honey," Junior's mom says. "I think Aunt Hephsiba said the new one just came out. I'll call them tomorrow. That reminds me in fact that J.C. Penny has a new one too! I'll get that as well. Oh by the way: we're having leftover meatloaf and yams for dinner tonight, and succotash with cauliflower and broccoli. And for dessert: frozen Brussels sprouts!" "Sounds great, mom," Junior says, dreamily, insouciant. "Uh, *okay*, honey," Mrs. Junior's mom, puzzled that her normally savvy son didn't get her joke, says perplexedly, "Do you want your door closed or open?" "Closed," Junior says and sighs extravagantly when she leaves.

For now, he's off the hook.

A week later, a new catalogue with new models comes in the mail. *Two* new catalogues come. Destiny plunked on the doorstep. More bras, more, *more*. Bras everywhere. Bras, bras, bras. And panties—let's not forget them, though they're somehow sexless, not as enthralling. Junior's interest in sticking together those model ships, planes and tanks has waned greatly; they languish on his desktop, in his toychest, the darkest recesses of his closet, docked and hangered and demobbed forevermore. By now his parents are way confuckingcerned. He hasn't touched a baseball glove or plastic Yank, Reb, Jerry or Tommy in over a month. Isn't even all that interested in—gasp!—television anymore. Something's going *on* here. His marks are slipping. Slipping and falling. Math test scores are way way down. More down than the usual down they usually are. Kick the can, hide and seek, smear the queer, and pass the trash are an obsolescence. He's not leading any patrols against the Afrika Korps anymore; he's not up at dawn and out in the street with his friends, arguing over who gets to be Johnny Unitas and who Bart Starr; the last two Saturdays he's bowed out of his Cub Scout meetings, feigning chest pains. Sometimes he looks more wan, pallid, clammy and haunted than any Keats, Shelley, Chatterton, or Clare. And speaking of reading, Junior doesn't seem to haul down, dust off and prop up any of the poetry, history, and mythology hardbacks he normally devours. What is up? *Some*thing's up. Something's up with him.

The cycle continues. More catalogues disappear. His twin bed is practically pumped to bunk elevation by now. It looks like a life raft. A stage prop for a Beckett or Pinter play.

He's hooked. Hooked on phonics? No, bra-nics.

Junior high comes round for Junior. His dad psyches himself up to have the quote-unquote chat with him. Does he already know about sex? Does he? his mom and dad wonder together, whispering in their veritable echo chamber of a master bedroom, the one that intercoms everything all over the house. He's never even mentioned liking girls. None of his friends have ever mentioned girls. Not that we know of. There was that one time he had both hands stuffed down his pants while he was watching *Gilligan's Island*, but that was shortly after we got him the tapered cotton boxer shorts he begged for and maybe he was just adjusting them. Let's see: he was pen pals with a pretty little freckle-faced blonde girl from Scotland or Ireland or somewhere back in fifth grade but he stopped writing to her after she sent him a picture of herself doing the Mashed Potato or the Locomotion or one of those dance crazes with her drama teacher. (Stopping correspondence with her was probably a good thing.) Still: what does he know? What? *What?* What should we *do?* What? What? *What?* Is there an afterschool program we can enroll him in? Thrust an informative, illustrated pamphlet into his adolescent trembling hands? Perhaps we could see how much of *Portnoy's Complaint* or *Catch-22* his just-teen mind can wrap its, er, mind around. Check the *Boy Scout Handbook*—now that he's a Boy Scout: we're so proud of him, really; he got to Second Class from Tenderfoot so fast!—to see if there's a chapter he can summarize or merit badge he can earn. There must be something we can do. What can we do?

Perhaps the glee club teacher or our pastor can meet with him! Oh, none of this is any help, any good. None of it is any good at all. Junior quit the glee club when his voice changed; and the darn pastor is in a coma as result of a picnic-misfortune involving an errant lawn dart. That was the most horrible Ice Cream Social *ever*, wasn't it, dear? Terrible. And anyway, the glee club teacher, whose first name is Bruce, is, suspiciously, a *very* high soprano, sports lemon ascots and sunburnt-flesh-colored dickies, and once resided in San Francisco. Or so we heard.

How about the scoutmaster?! There's an idea. But Junior says the scoutmaster is always hugging the boys, even when they chop down a living tree or get caught stealing things from 7-Elevens on patrol meeting days, *and* he calls them "Tiger" and often encourages them to compare the sizes of their Swiss Army or regulation Boy Scout pocketknives. Junior says that once the scoutmaster even drooled on him. What does *that* mean? What does *that* say? My goodness, the world is odd. Is our son the sort of person who's going to be hit by people's spittle plus ignorant about sex for the rest of his life? That would be far too much. The Scoutmaster's name is Mr. Jewitt-Hewitt, for crying out loud; and even though, like Sir Somebody Baden-Powell, the starter of Scouting and author of *Scouting for Boys*, he's *British*, Mr. Jewitt-Hewitt is, you can't really trust someone whose very name seemingly can't make up its mind.

What should we do here? What to do?

"You've simply got to talk to him," Junior's mom says at last. "There's just no way around it, dear."

"I suppose you're right, my love," Junior's dad says, sighs. "First thing tomorrow, I most certainly will."

"Well, you *could* wait till then," Mrs. Junior's mom says sweetly, all June Cleaverishly, her words crisp aural gingham or nicely iced gingerbread, her eyes watery-lovely. "But don't you think, as the saying goes, you shouldn't put off till tomorrow what you can do today? He's up in his room studying right now, John. Tell him about the birds and bees, et cetera, won't you, darling? Then you can both come down and have some rhubarb pie—if you both promise not to let it spoil your appetite 'cause I am making yesterday's Salisbury steak and instant mashed potatoes into a sort of special shepherds pie and I think we have enough packages of lima beans to beat the band!"

"Okey-doke, honey," Junior Sr. says, "but I don't know exactly just what to say. Hmm. I'm trying to think what my dad told me, and, gosh, I can't remember one durned thing. Just nothing doing."

"You'll do fine, dear, just fine," Mrs. Junior's mom opines; "I know for a fact you will. You assistant- coached his Little League team to sixth place in the Southwest Division "B" bracket, didn't you? Yep. You taught him how to take care of a purebred German Shepherd puppy, didn't you? *Two* puppies on account of what happened to the *first* Kaiser, no? Yep. You sat with him as he built so many model airplanes and boats that I thought I'd never see the two of you again? Well, I saw you both of course—what I mean is I thought I'd never see the two of you stand up again?! Yep. (That was funny, wasn't it, hon?) And you even taught him how to do algebra or one of those other difficult subjects. Yessiree. This should be no different. After dinner we'll take the kids down to Thriftys to get triple-chocolate chocolate-chip ice-cream cones and Rocky Road—your favorite—for you, okay? You can do it, dear; I know you can."

"You're too right, honey," Junior's dad says, his resolve leavening, the pluck he showed in the Pacific theater as an ensign on an aircraft carrier that one time almost left port shining through. "Here I go."

"I'm very proud of you, my dear," the Mrs. says and pecks her valiant husband on his impeccably shaved cheek.

"Well, here goes nothin'," says he.

The knock comes. The door opens. Mellow yellow music wafts through the air. Junior's lying daydreaming on his junior high school bed, his hands clasped behind his mooning junior high school head. His Introductory Biology text is turtled on the bedspread next to him. Sellotaped color pictures of baseball/football/basketball stars from *Sports Illustrated* have curled and yellowed on his walls. There are unjacketed phonograph records fanned out everywhere, LPs and 45s he incessantly feeds his voracious Victorola. They are by groups with obscure, confusing names like the Strawberry Alarm Clock, Paul Revere and the Raiders, the Jimi Hendrix Experience, the Lovin' Spoonful, Love, Vanilla Fudge, the Troggs, the Seeds, the Hermits of Herman, Moby Grape, the 13th Floor somebodies, Creedence Revival something or other, the Who, the Kinkys, the Doors and Byrdies and Yardbirds and Buffalo Springtime.

"Hmmzzz," Junior's dad thinks, using a sort of unconscious onomatopoeic device to remind himself of his purpose in being here, in his son's room, about to discuss the aforementioned birds, bees, etc. "No clues in any of these phonograph recordings, apparently. Maybe the one that is playing now can lend some insight. Some of the lyrics are in French, I see."

"Oh hi, son," he says headscratchingly.

"Hi, Dad."

"Whatcha doin'?"

"Listening to a record."

"Oh? What record's that?"

"Donovan."

"Who's it *by*, I mean."

"Donovan."

"Oh."

". . ."

"Whatcha thinkin' about, son?"

"Me, Dad?"

"Uh huh."

"I was thinking about how nice it would be to gently scrape off Mary Beth Johnson's soft cotton panties."

"Excuse me, son? I didn't quite catch that. Can we turn the stereo down, please?"

"I said: 'Not much, Dad. Is dinner almost ready?'"

"Oh. Almost, Junior, almost. Your mother's cooking up something special tonight, actually. Hey, *Jun*ior? I've been meaning to talk to you about something for some time now. Something that's . . . very important and, um . . . very important indeed. Your mother and I, we . . . You see, the thing is . . ."

"Dad!" Junior, startled as all get-out, cries out. "Dad, I'm *sorry*. I know I got a 'C' in one subject last semester and I promise—I *swear*—it'll never happen again. I hate Math, Dad. I hate it. I just can't *do* it! Even with help from my friend Brad I just can't seem to . . . I mean, every time I . . ."

"Son! That's not what I came up here to discuss with you. That's not it at all," Junior Sr. says, practically pantomiming washing the hell out of his russet crew cut. "It's not your scholastics—far from it. You're an excellent student; we know that. That 'C' you got was the only one you've ever gotten, we know. Don't we know it. And you know we are very very proud of you. Absolutely so. You know that, don't you, Junior? We wouldn't give you spending money for all those A's if we didn't think you were getting good grades and really smart and so disciplined! No: this isn't about anything you've *done*, son, or, er, haven't done—it's about what you might, ah, *know*. Or know *about*. You see, it's like this: when your mother and I met we . . . when a man and a woman, that is, want to . . . when two *people* care for each other and want to express that caring in a way that's loving they, er . . . Let me put it this way: you know how when you are looking at the Sears catalog and you get to page thirty or so? . . ."

*

"Hi!" Jenny said and leaned her bike against the house and threaded round one ear a hank of hair. "How are you? This is my friend Sandy. Sandy, this is John."

"Hi," I said. "Nice to meet you. How was your ride?"

"Long. We went all over Hancock Park," Jenny said. Her friend just smiled a cute but I thought kinda odd smile—even though I'd never seen her smile, that is. It just seemed . . . I don't know.

"And it was great?"

Jenny laughed. "Uh-huh. So pretty."

"I'll see you tomorrow, Jen," the Sandy girl said and re-mounted and wheeled back up the driveway.

"Okay. Thanks for coming with me!" Jenny said. "We work together."

"Bye, John," Sandy said.

I told her take care and Jenny invited me in, her nice big friendly teeth showing: "I need to take a quick shower and then give a lesson—just a half hour—at twelve thirty? Amber has to cram for a recital and her mom asked me for a favor to help her get ready today, so I will just be a bit late for rehearsing with you guys—is that all right? Do you mind? I will come right down and won't go one half minute over the half hour I promised, okay?"

She was so at ease and she said all this so sweetly how could I say anything other than no problem, take your time, it doesn't matter, seriously though.

Then she bit her nice plump lower lip and said: "Wanna take a shower with me?"

I *wish*! Of course she said no such thing.

What she really said was "I'll see you in a bit," and not so adroitly ported her bike upstairs before I could grab it from her and all gallantly carry it for her. I watched her ass move like two beautiful I-don't-know-whats up the stairs, ivorine thighs quivering nicely (you could tell she was leery of the sun, or just that she spent all her time indoors practicing).

My heart kind of leapt out of my chest right then.

## just get an electric guitar

An hour later Walter, Rob and I were flogging a new song for the twelveteenth time in a row when the shed door swung open and searing daylight banded symbolically in, and so did Jenny—tentatively, with apologies, blah blah blah. Walt stopped hammering on his toms and Rob and I turned round.

"Hi, you guys—sorry I'm late."

"Hi, Jenny," I said. "Walter set up keyboards for you. We don't have a keyboard amp, but you can go through the P.A."

"Just don't turn it up too high, okay?" Walter said. "It cost me two hundred dollars used, almost. Try not to blow it up."

"I'll blow *you* up," Rob kidded, "if you don't get this middle bit right."

"Yeah right," Walt said. "Hey, Jen."

"We're working on a new song," I explained.

"Okay, cool. I didn't mention it, I don't think," Jenny said, "but I play a little guitar too—if you want me to. I have an acoustic upstairs so I worked out a couple of songs from the tape on guitar as well."

"You're kidding!" I said. "That's amazing."

"Wait till you hear me," Jenny said all demurely.

We had a second electric guitar—my backup hollow body, another cheaper double cutaway—and I got it out and plugged it in to a spare amp Rob brought and made the strap smaller for her and handed her a cool red tweed guitar lead so that she could try it out.

"Yeah, baby," Walter quipped, "plug her in, J-baby! Ooh, *ba*by!"

I gave him a nothing less than censorious look but everyone, even me, ended up laughing their most nervously relieved laughs and the proverbial ice went *crack* and we settled down to work and Rob futzed around with the mixer for a bit and got Jenny some appropriate volume and appropriate reverb for her mike (she even said she could sing!—she would just try it out to see if we liked it) and she droned some notes on the guitar first, then honked out a couple of bar chords that sounded kinda *rock* and chopped some notes and chords out on the keyboard and it all sounded a touch ratchety but okay enough. I suggested we start with a song called "Field Day," the first one on the practice tape, and Jenny went "la la la la?" to sort of sing the melody in order to make sure that that was the one we wanted. I said "That's it!" and thought, this girl's a fucking genius, she knows our songs already, even though she'd form chords and go "What's this one?" and it'd be the most rudimentary "D" or "G" chord and she wouldn't know it! And then she'd make up the weirdest chord-formations, things I'd never dreamed of in all my from-a-child years of playing guitar and later, when we got to working on a few other songs, they would sound so cool over our progressions, really melodic yet dissonant at the same time (just what we were, without knowing it, perhaps aiming for) and there were these two-chord/seesaw sort of back-and-forths she would play on the first song, "Field Day," like I told you, and on the sad-toned verses and a chorus that built and built she put these long sweet lines over them like the Cure or the Smiths in Johnny Marr's simpler moments play—just simple two-string plinkings moving contrapuntally and languorously over the fuzyy-poppy pop song I'd taught the band the first time we ever practiced.

We made it through the whole song with only around twenty-seven fuck-ups and as you might imagine I was wowed on account of notwithstanding all the "clams" (not even Jenny's especially, but everybody—mostly Walter, spacing out, or trying out ill-advised fills and baroque beats that just didn't work—messing up from time to time) it sounded like an actual indie rock band playing an actual indie rock song. A song! (What Walter to my eternal consternation often and just to piss me off, I suspected, called a "tune"—I *hate* that word; I'd rather you called it a "turd"—another word I hate and *never* say: it's like it's onomatopoeic or something: I can *see* it.)

"That was pretty good!" I said, nodding emphatically. "All right, you guys. Let's try it again."

"Was that along the lines of what you wanted?" Jenny asked me. "I have something else I came up with I can try—just on keyboards this time."

"I bet there's *lots* of things you wanna try," Walt, clicking his sticks for punctuation, as it were, innuendoed and he-he-he'd his snickerish

Walter laugh, and winked at her dramatically.

"Very funny," Jenny said and smiled—not a bit miffed, it seemed, being one of the guys, embracing it, laughing along, not taking herself too very.

"I like that tune, actually," Walter said.

"Song!" I said.

"Whatever," Walt said.

"Okay," I said, ignoring Walt. "Ready? One-two-three-four! . . ."

## very superstitious

"Here are menus, you guys; you can sit wherever," the cheerleaderish waitress in her cheerleaderish outfit said.

"Thanks," I said and turned to Jenny. "Do you want to sit at the counter or in a booth?"

"Booth, I think."

We found one and I told Jen what fun I'd had—we all'd had—and how great it was that she could play guitar as well.

"Not very well, though."

"Very good enough, though," I said (we'd initiated her into our world via that cliqueish expression, plus a couple of others we had going, though they seem to change from week to week).

Jenny laughed as if to say thanks but mostly I was not good at all, that we weren't exactly *tight*. Or at least that's how I interpreted it.

"It was fun, though. I've never played rock—in a rock band—before, you know. And I like the songs a lot; I really do. They remind me of the Church or, well, the Beatles of course, that's obvious—the psychedelic Beatles more than when they were cute and not so hairy!"

I laughed. "You know the *Church*?! That's one of my favorite bands! That is so . . ."

"Wait . . . 'great'? Is that what you were going to say?" she kidded me and laughed generously.

It was the sort of laugh that I was hoping, without being too calculating about it, to get out of her; there's a laugh you look for, when you are kickstarting a crush on someone, that you look for—there really is.

"Well, I did go to college, you know, and listen to college radio. Yeah: I like them a lot, especially a record called *Heyday* that I used to play incessantly. My roommates hated me and hid it from me once, I am not kidding! Let's see: R.E.M. and U2 and all of that. Of course them. You know: it's not all just Chopin and Rachmaninoff and herbal tea and turtlenecks and candlesticks. I like the Jackson 5 and Stevie Wonder [and here, because "Superstition" had come on the jukebox, she nodded towards the music, if you can do such a thing] more than *any*thing. I like to have fun. I really do. It doesn't always *show*, but I do. Honestly."

"Uh-huh."

"You don't believe me?!"

"Oh, I'm sure you do," I said.

Before I could continue this line of flirtation the ridiculously pretty waitress—black hair somewhat dreadlocked, little gold nose ring, crazy-pretty dark blue eyes, impossible lips, button down shirt oh so tight and undone to her bellybutton ring, practically, *had* to be an actress or the frontwoman of a goth band—sidled up with a supersmile like she'd just rounded off a triple cartwheel or double half-gainer plus and plié and a jeté too. Not that I noticed her, the server, or anything.

"Do you guys need another minute? Something to drink?"

"Hot tea, please," Jenny said.

I ordered a lemonade, trying so hard not to check out (how I hate that phrase, by the way; people aren't library books; I hate the term "hot" too; it's idiotic; people aren't sides of beef either, and anyway during the period in which this takes place no one said "She's hot!" or "What a hot dude!"—the lame term hadn't, thank God, been invented yet ) the waitress as she strutted away that it must've been obvious I was making a pretty strenuous gentlemanly effort, and Jenny said: "Anyway, I was going to say the songs remind me of another of my favorite bands, the Psychedelic Furs. Something about the lyrics—though I don't really pay attention to lyrics—reminded me of them."

"*I* don't pay attention to lyrics either," I joked.

"Oh sure," she said. "Well I know I should and everything but it's always the melodies that hook me."

"Me, too. Listen, Jenny: what do are you doing for a living anyway? What do you do? Do you live off of giving lessons or . . ."

"Oh, I work in a law office. This law firm downtown. I take care of two lawyers in a big firm, Johnson and Johnson. It's . . ."

"Boring?"

"Very. And not exactly what I thought I would be doing with my stupendous liberal arts college education. Everyone I know in the arts is in the same situation, though. Almost. The ones I know are. It's really tough."

"My roommate Jaz works at a law firm too—Thompson and Thompson. He's a proofreader. He will *never* pay back his student loans—until he sells a script, he says."

"I'm glad I don't have that hanging over my head. My gosh. I was really lucky: I got a scholarship, which was really nice for my parents, for sure. What do *you* do, by the way? Natasha said you're a teacher?"

"I sub," I said. "High school, and *junior* high when I am really lucky."

"That must be . . ."

"Awful? It is. But it's easy, at least. I have a lot of time to write songs, for sure."

"My dad thinks I should teach. He's always telling me what I should be, actually. Don't you like it at all?"

"It's okay sometimes, I reckon. I don't really ever get to teach anything, really. Mostly I get paid a hundred and twenty some-odd bucks a day to have brats throw things at me. They have these "Sub" uniforms for us with bulls-eyes on them so the kids can have some goals to achieve while their regular teachers are out, you know? Ha! I mean, talk about wasting a perfectly great education? Now I am helping waste the educations of a buncha *kids*! Ha! Three, sometimes four, days a week."

Her laugh was sort of revving now, and she remarked how she remembered how the kids in her primary school tortured substitutes and how she felt so sorry for them.

"It's really not so bad," I said. "What's torture, actually, are the other teachers—the ones that try to strike up a conversation with you during lunch breaks. You're sort of trapped with them 'cause the playgrounds are crazy and staying in a classroom is simply sad. They're unbelievable."

"Why?"

"Well, if they are subs too they're almost always singers or actors or swordswallowers or something, and they wanna tell you all about some third-rate play they got a two-bit part in, you know? And if they are regular teachers they wanna drill you or rather grill you on what kind of life you have, on account of theirs are so incredibly boring and samey. Occasionally I won't be able to take it and I go out and risk grievous bodily harm by playing basketball with the kids. It's cool 'cause I work on my bad Spanish and pick up more cuss words that come in handy once the bell rings. It's not all that bad except . . ."

"Except what?" Jenny said.

I took a deep breath. "It's kind of nerve-wracking sometimes. The kids can get really out of control and from time to time you sort of lose it on them, even though you are trying so hard not to and know you shouldn't and that you will never win. But when a kid won't shut up or won't sit down and has lobbed a wad of bubblegum into your hair, it's way hard not to . . ."

"Lose it?"

"Exactly."

"I mean, it sounds . . ."

"It's like going to the dentist *every day*," I said.

"I like the dentist."

"I bet."

"What?"

"I mean, er, I can see why you might?"

"What do you mean? 'Cause my teeth are a little oversized, is that it?"

"Oh no: I just meant . . ."

"That's kind of mean," Jenny said.

"I didn't mean . . ."

"Yes you did; it's okay."

"Look," I said; I was in hot water now: "I don't know if you can tell by the way I have been looking at you, and flirting I would say pretty heavily with you that I think you are extraordinarily pretty, an extraordinarily pretty girl. Really beautiful, quite beautiful, in a very *different* way . . . unique, I mean."

"Well," she said, blushing a bit now, "that's nice; you didn't have to say that."

"I know. Have you ever worn glasses, by the way?"

"You probably feel sorry for me 'cause I have to spend so much on *tooth*paste. Glasses? No. Why?"

"No reason. And . . . Jenny! That was really funny—you're kinda hilarious too. Toothpaste."

She gave me a look like I wasn't so cheaply going to be let off the hook but just then . . .

"Here we go," the stunning punk rock Snow White waitress said as she came up and unwittingly bailed me out and slid down our drinks and asked what we wanted to order to eat. Now, I thought, Jenny thinks I'm a dick. Mean. Girls often think that. Why? Cause I *am* one, I imagine; it's only a matter of time before I say something dickish that gets them thinking what an asshole this dick that is me is. Whether it's five or five hundred sentences into an acquaintance, or fifteen seconds into it, it comes out sooner or later: I'm a fucking dick. I realize it. I say assholish, dickish, unthinking things. I'm not trying to be that way; it just comes out like that; I don't do it on *pur*pose: I'm not *that* much of a fuck.

But you see, the thing is, when it comes right down to it, it doesn't really matter. Girls kind of *like* it when you are a dickhole or at least not too lollipop/saltwater taffy sweet to them. I don't think it's in the least a misogynistic thing to say, so don't go calling your life coach or your "sister" with the butch haircut and one side shaved into the shape of an eternal female symbol, that dealie with the circle and cross, or anything, okay, lady readers and guys who are kind of pussified vagina-types? Girls, women, what*ever* want you to be a *man*. A man who is, on occasion, special occasions, that is, every once in a while, kind of a cunt to them. They want that; they do. So fuck *you*.

And it's a good job that naturally, without getting all self-conscious about it or conniving, I *am* a cunt once in a while. (How did "dick" become "cunt" here, anyway, huh? Well, they're kind of interchangeable and you know what I mean. Ha! Nice pun! Interchangeable! Well, sort of a pun, I guess. Dumb. Silly. Sorry.)

Conversely, we do not ever want you guys (chicks, that is) to be bitches to *us*. Strong, open and forceful of opinion (with logic and evidence to back them, your opinions, up), and with the ability to stand up to us and put us in our place when we get out of line—yes, that, absolutely. But bitchy? Never.

Anyway, Jenny like a total bitch ordered a salad with Italian (I'm *kidding*, okay? the bitch allusion was just my way of messing with you! People always say "I never know when you are kidding and when you are serious!" so here's a tip: if I am saying something *mean*, it's just a *joke*, all right?; if it's *nice*, I fucking *mean* it. Got it?) on the side and I got a roasted honey turkey breast on wheat with provolone and boot cut fries and a side salad with ranch and I asked her if she wanted fries and she said she shouldn't so of course I took that to mean yes and thus I went ahead and ordered them for her and she gave me a look like thanks but you didn't have to do that/I really shouldn't/for such a jerk you are a pretty sensitive caring considerate/you-know-I-want French-fries kind of guy.

The waitress walked away again, her navy pleated just-too-short skirt aswish, and I only flashed a look her way and quickly told Jenny I was really glad she liked the songs and I hoped she'd liked playing with us less-than-virtuosos and she told me we weren't *so* non-virtuoso and we both cracked up and then I said: "How come you aren't doing recitals or in a philharmonic or anything—or are you?"

Jenny snorted: "Do you have any idea how competitive that world is? Oh my goodness."

"You're telling me you're not good enough?"

"You have no idea," she said and gave out a different kind of laugh that's hard to describe.

"Seriously? I think you are being overmodest, I really do."

"I could do it," she sighed. "I could try. I thought I might when I first moved here but I got a pretty well-paying gig at Johnson and I was not in the mood to be too ambitious—not in that frame of mind at all . . . I mean, I would have to quit my job and practice six to eight hours a day just to even consider trying to get anything like that. And, if I am honest with me, with myself, I mean, I don't know that I have that sort of drive anymore. I *used* to. When I was a kid I did. Or, my dad had it for . . . *He* says I'm totally wasting my talent and all of that but I just can't seem to . . . I don't know . . . let's change the subject, okay?"

I looked at her for a little while, right into her big pretty mildly as I told you hurt-looking eyes till I risked saying *I* thought she was simply amazing—one of the most talented people I'd ever known. She seemed touched and then I asked her if, that said, she'd consider practicing with us again and—would you credit it?—she was so modest and deferential somehow that she asked if I really thought that was what Rob and Walt wanted too and I said "Are you *kidding* me?!" and she smiled and said she didn't see why not and right then—how can I put this into words?—I was so fucking happy I wanted to scream.

But of course I couldn't let her see that. Or not *too* much on account of I am the world's worst person at hiding anything concerning my emotions. Get me all elated and it's gonna show, I'm telling you; you have no idea.

"Okay, then," Jenny said. "I mean, I have always considered myself someone who got involved with good things. It sounds fun. I think I'll be pretty into it."

"Very good enough things," I laughed and the waitress came up just then with our food and I just smiled at her and thanked her and didn't even look at her twice.

## it seems like years since it's been here

I drove her back to Walter and Nasty's and said goodbye without trying to kiss her goodnight, making sure to tell her how much of a great time I'd had with her and how I was looking greatly forward to our next rehearsal. I really wanted to—kiss her, that is. I *really* wanted to. But no. No way. Not kissing someone's sometimes sexier, don't you think? *I* do. Throws most chicks off, for sure. "What's *with* this guy?" they invariably think when you don't make a move on them, when you don't nearly instantly try to get your tongue all the way down to their coccyx or sternum or liver or whatnot. "Doesn't he *like* me? Doesn't he think like all the other doggy doglike guys who are, like, dog-slobbering all over me day and night to try to get in my pants or at *least* to first base? What the fuck is this guy's fucking *deal*, anyway? Is he *high* or something? A heroin addict, or *may*be just missing a chromosome? Did he get wounded in a *war* or have his penis crushed by an avalanche or something? What's *up* with him? What's his goddam *prob*lem? I mean, *really*!"

It's not like—once again—you should overthink it and make it rote or some kind of policy or scheme or scam or whatever. Far from it. My rule is: if you feel like kissing her and you've only hung out with her two or three or even four times, *don't*. Don't do it. Hang back. Even if there are soft lights and a sort of oneiric propinquity and soft music and a softer breeze and the time seems right, like a scene out of the bloody movies—don't. Postponing kissing's at once more respectful (chicks dig that) and more suspenseful (chicks dig that too and so will you). It's like my infamous unknown theory about how little kids get a pre-sexual thrill out of being scared out of their little wits: they give these shrieks of pure pleasure that seem Freudian to say the least. They love it. I try to scare children every chance I get, boy. I don't mean coming at them in the night with a chainsaw and a clown mask kit like what you can buy at Target or Walmart, or showing up at their houses with a wrecking ball, a truncheon, and a monster mask made of green slime. Far from it. But jumping out of a closet at them (especially when they *know* you are lurking somewhere near and are about to *get* them) or coming chuntering into their rooms with a flashlight trained under your chin and making freaky ghost-noises? That's just good plain All-American scary-good *fun*. I love kids—especially when I have made them wet their pants from laughing or from being frightened half to death. It's what kids want. Give it to them. Chicks too: they want something, they should get it. And, ironically, what they want instantaneously is, ironically again, someone who is going to wait and to make *them* wait. It drives them *crazy*—in a good way.

On the drive home I flipped and tickled the radio dial till I found a song that really sent me; it took a while, sifting through disco and classical and salsa and heaps of godawful hard rock with the obligatory let's-see-if-I-can-break-a-few-hundred-windowpanes-on-this-next-note singer singing, but there it was: "Here Comes the Sun." That's my favorite Beatles song. I have one. I know it's ridiculous, just as it's ridiculous to think that you could pick a favorite Beatles album, but that's my favorite song by them. I'm different that way, I guess. Well, "Here Comes the Sun" and "Strawberry Fields Forever." Plus maybe "I'll Be Back" or "Hey Bulldog." Oh fuck looks like I'm just like everybody else, that way. Fuck a duck. Anyway, I cranked it up, the stereo, loud as it could go, the wind symphonying through the open windows of my trashcan-on-wheels, a boxy old tan Volvo (they don't make cars with such cool colors as that anymore) with much dents and cream-colored spongy seats and a cream-colored cracked dashboard and paneling. Even in normal circumstances Harrison's masterpiece, the one they say he wrote in twenty minutes in his backyard as the English sun came out, can make you feel *so* happy—even if your gran's just kicked or you didn't get in to San Diego State or West Fresno Polytechnic; your girlfriend's left you for a four-foot-eleven guy with unabashed halitosis or you are the last guy cut from the tennis team; you get grounded by mom and dad for no reason at all (well, you must've done *some*thing) or you find a condom (used, natch) in your wife's purse and you know she's on birth control (what the heck were you doing in her purse, anyway? What *are* you—a tampon?). But when you are—as you know I was—already elated and looking to get even higher, that song sends you and how. *It seems like years since we've been here*. What a great composition. Unreal. If I could write just one song half as good as that I'd die a happy death, I really would. Fuck the Beatles, my friend K.C. often says—and he's right: they at once ruined and *made* music with a capital M.

Home safe, I dragged my guitar and me (quietly past Marie's, careful not to make a peep and send her screaming towards her diabolical turntable) upstairs. Jaz was out. Out cold, not out having fun out. It wasn't that late, really. Maybe he'd exhausted himself writing or smoking from the hookah. I was looking forward to telling him about the rehearsal and Jenny and all.

"Jaz."

"Huh?" he sleep-snorted.

"Are you asleep?"

"Yes."

"Sorry," I said.

"Where you been?"

"Rehearsal, then dinner with Jenny, Walter's roommate who jammed with us today."

"How was it?"

"Really good. Excellent."

"Grand. I gotta go back to zzzzzzzzz . . ." Jaz said.

"Okay," I laughed and told him good night but he couldn't hear me.

I thought about cannibalizing/pirating some of his pot but I was already high enough on hope for the putative future —no need now for dope. So I went to my room and got undressed and read some good old Dr. Johnson for a spell and, though he is always interesting and always profound and always like reading a letter from an albeit orotund and somewhat sententious friend, pretty quickly I fell asleep and slept, it seemed, deliciously.

## sunday morning

As the Scather worked on Sundays at Finyl Vinyl on Melrose I usually drove down to the shop around thirteen o'clock in order to hang out with him, smoke beaucoup Marlboro Lights, and check out the week's new releases and let him load me down with a bunch of free twelve-inches when I split. Sometimes he gave me so many new records I looked like Bartholomew from the children's book *Bartholomew and the 500 Hats*. Only with albums and singles. Mostly imports. I'd halfheartedly leaf through the week's *Melody Maker* and *NME* and *Sounds* till I got well sick with envy and bewilderment (unless the bands the writers were writing about were really good and deserved the ink they got, which was rare); and I'd certainly amuse myself by listening to the myriad ways Sterling found to cut down the flibbertigibbet customers without their knowing they were being twitted: this ineffectual browser, that impossible bore (who thinks he can one-up the savvy record store clerk), those clueless wonders who haven't even heard of Orange Juice or Television or the Jazz Butcher, Felt or the Creation, the Verlaines or the Bodines (not the Bodeans—big big difference), the Jean Paul Sartre Experience (a recent favorite of mine) or the Clean. He'd try to make me like bands I would never, like, like, like Galaxie 500, the Gun Club, the Germs, or Buffalo Tom, no matter how hard I'd try to see what he saw in them, cocking my head like the iconic puzzled Victorola canine. And I *did* try, on account of Sterling was so sure about them and so knowledgeable about music in general, almost a Mandarin at it.

If you've never had the pleasure, Finyl Vinyl's this dusty, musty cavernous oblong shop on a prime spot of swank real estate on the trendiest street in the city. Or at least it was. Like most good Los Angeles things it's gone now. As are most record stores, which is fucking tragic.

Melrose then was the purlieu of Cure clones on parade, Siouxsies, Japanese tourists dressed to the nines, fierce-looking cholos wearing fifteen-pound neck chains and khaki trousers and immaculate white t-shirts twenty-four sizes too big, and of course supermodels *manqué* or actual, douchebags and douchebaguettes shopping their little acquisitive hearts out, identically dressed rockabilly boys and girls, plus daytrippers getting gaspingly overpriced angular-vogue haircuts or trendoid eyeglasses at the trendoid salons and vintage frameries, to coin a phrase, that abound there still. The models/actresses that maundered and sauntered down and around Melrose, in sheer, bellybutton-revealing silver-blue or tart lime blouses and short slit skirts in anthracite or black (or blinding white or dreamy cream) or in insane double-take skintight jeans, would make your heart melt or your dick thick. Or both. There were some really unreal girls there. Plus shirtless skate rats, imbecilic punk rock dorks, and boulevardiers of every stripe and make: rich bitches (boys and girls and especially boy-girls and girl-boys) on spending sprees and troikas of laughing gaylords in aviator sunglasses who'd just descended from speeding jeeps in search or cappuccinos or margaritas and conversation in any one of the innumerable *fabulous* outdoor bistros. Valley Girls with henna tattoos in five-foot fuck-me pumps; tanned cops with ultra-bright smiles and live-in-the-gym muscles; street people; shop girls loitering outside their workplace doorways, endlessly puffing accessory cigarettes and wearing looks that dared you, just dared you to enter and browse without buying.

The shops themselves: vintage rag rip-offs (though the occasional bargain "find" would sometimes descend on you like the visitation of a god and you'd come upon a Penguin shirt from the fifties that was marked down or a small-collar button-down plaid short-sleeved delight that you simply *had* to have, no matter what, even if you weren't especially a clotheshorse or fashion plate); overrated trattorias (and some good ones that you, or at least I, very couldn't afford); way expensive Mexican restaurants; torture chamber outlets (everything for today's most-knowing S & M'ers!); liquor stores that gouged you for a pack of mints, let alone smokes; scuzzy bars that beckoned in neon; ritzy ice creameries; hip hop haberdasheries; and immemorial high-dollar women's stores that showcased mannequins in dresses and poses so fucking fetching and arty that it made you fairly randy just to glimpse them intermittently.

And the *actual* girls on Melrose I mentioned? If you were a lecher of the first water or simply a run-of-the-mill horndog/quasi-obsessive about post-teenage libertinage you couldn't *find* a better place to go straight out of your fucking dirty *mind*. I mean there were girls—inter*na*tional girls—goddam everywhere: gorgeous Picasso-eyed Persians and Scandinavian specimens in cut-offs and tank tops, with lips like sugar, like raspberry icing, like bliss, and ice blue or gray eyes that looked your way—*may*be—long enough to hurt you with their you-can't-have-thisness. Hispanic babes in tight tops who simply slayed you, put you on the pavement, coated your tongue with gravel, made you marvel that anyone's skin could be so smooth-beautiful. Asian girls who made you so at once happy and sad to be alive you could easily imagine yourself *seppuku*-ing yourself right in front of them. Like, getting right down on your queasy, quavering knees right in front of them and going "Either you take me home to Koreatown or Westwood or Little Tokyo *right now*, or I stick this bleeding shiv into my belly, okay? No: better yet: *you* do it, Sachiko, Ayako, Grace or Daisy! You're killing me anyway. I'm dying for you."

Take that word *lecherous*, by the way. It comes from the French word for "lick": *leche*. In olde Chaucer's time a naughty boy was said to have a "likerous eye"—like he was *licking* you with it. It's the most intimate inside *and* outside thing you have, when you think about it, your tongue is. Isn't that something? Aren't words weird? And wonderful? A lecher: one who, like, licks you with his gaze. That's my surferish/wordsmith definition. Want someone to lick you?—the greatest feeling ever. A lick from one you don't like?—a super ew.

On the day I'm talking about, visiting Sterling for the manyth Sunday, plum clouds mottled the sky in the distant distance, auguring winter; it was one of those days when the day seemed to change seasons. I went inside and found him there, alone in the shop, the familiar sounds of our mutual friend, our favorite non-Beatles LP, *White Light/White Heat* by the Velvet Underground, assailing me at almost-full volume. Know that record? It's so dissonant and melodic at the same time that it's my preferred LP to go to sleep to. Try it one night. Sterl always maintained that there were two kinds of people—those who could make it through "Sister Ray" all the way (of course they were the chosen), and those who couldn't (the musical untouchables). I loved that.

"Sterling!" I shouted (he was looking down at some rag or other, reading; anyone USA could've come in and nicked the stock—lock, stock, and barrel).

He looked up, then turned down the stereo.

"Juan!"

"How are ya? Whatcha been doing, jefe?"

"Heroin," he jested. "Contributing to my favorite charity, my*self*.

Smoking like a *Symboliste. C'est magnifique, les cigarettes que j'adore. J'aime trop fumer beaucoup, c'est vrai. Et pour moi prochaine trompe l'oeil, je voudrais enflame un toute de suite maintenant!*"

"*Quel frommage que je n'ai pas des la mienne ici. Est-ce que je peux blager un de toi, si'l tu plait?*"

"*Certainement!*"

"Thank you," I said. "All this French—*très mauvais* on my part, *pour ma parte*, that is—is hurting my mouth."

"Soothe it with this," Sterling said and proffered me a Marlboro Light. "Delicious! Won't you have a sip! Hahaha!"

Then he told me what he'd been up to since I'd seen him last, since the ride home from the movie people party: "Reading—of course. My hobby horse, naturally: the Puritans [he was really, and weirdly, into all this early American literature shit—stuff I'd never even *heard* of: homilies and histories and hagiographies of the original monochromatic ones, the kooky kooks in black and white who founded this American mess]. What else? Listening to Love and the Bee Gees—the early stuff, of course. And Look Blue Go Purple—the greatest name ever, and a swell band of four Kiwi chicks, every one of them lovely. Drugs. *When* I can get them. Which is not often. Still. You could certainly do something about that?"

"Me?"

"Yes. Thrifting," he continued, "for the coolest shirts and cardigans. Not on Melrose, of course. But at my secret thrift stores in the Valley whose locations I will *never* reveal—not even for any money. Not even for "ready money" [he loved to quote *The Importance of Being Earnest*; it was a play we very had in common]. And of course handing out hassle sessions to the relentlessly clueless who come in here to ask if there is a new Bauhaus record out or something."

His voice was dripping with mock and not-mock contempt, you must understand. Like he was making fun of someone who was making fun of himself. Or a character who was imitating playing the character he played. He was what Sartre called, in reference to Jean Genet's *The Maids*, "a whirligig."

""What fools!' I said, throwing out my own quote from Wilde. "Do they ever learn?" I asked.

"The *fools*! The fools *I* have to suffer! Hahaha."

"One day a week! Must be pure fresh green Hell for you, Sterling!"

"Watch it, Juanny!" he gag-warned. "I'll bury you."

"I'm only joking you."

"Well, do tell: how was it, anyway?"

"Jamming with Jenny?"

He and I knew each other so well sometimes it wasn't funny, was uncanny.

"Of *course*. The one who's *not your type*."

"Well, it went well, actually: she's really talented—more than we knew. Plays guitar too."

"And?" he said, pruriently long, like the word was a hundred and six syllables.

"And she said she'd play with us again. That's a good sign, isn't it? I mean, we are not good. Not yet, we aren't. But we weren't so horrendous that an actual musician ran screaming from the room or anything."

"Come on," Sterling said. "I heard you practice once, you know. Your songs are really good, some great [I always played him things on my acoustic to see what he thought; he was always "positive"; he always saw the potential; he was like Jaz in that respect; he never let you down in the old encouragement department]. And you are a better guitarist than you think, John. Nowhere near *me*, of course. But still very solid."

"Of *course*," I laughed. the Scather teased you but he never really put you down—if you were his true friend, that is. If you weren't—as you've seen—look *out*. You had to pay him some obeisance. He wasn't wholly serious about it—but kind of. He was both making fun of someone so bumptious and being it at the same time. There wasn't anyone anywhere like him. You can't say that about many people. If you do, you're kind of an idiot and not very discerning or too accepting or trying to show off. But Sterling . . . definitely *different* with a difference. Back in college I had this Ivy League dropout "pub" friend called J.P. who, when people would pop off going "Oh you have *got* to meet this guy [or girl]; you've never met *an*yone *like* him [her]!" good old perpetual-Lacoste-shirt-and-shell-necklace-sporting J.P. would get this ineffably contemptuous and smug look on his face and kind of let his eyes go half-mast and say, "Yes I have," and it'd be one of those magic moments of perfect jadedness that are a kind of ecstasy of been-there-ed-ness, I swear. I loved that old J.P.—no idea what happened to him. He's probably still hanging at that college bar I always ran into him at, deflecting fuckers who think they can impress him with one of their *sui generis* friends, trading brilliant one-liners from classic movies, just like we used to do over a golden gleaming pitcher of pilsner, waiting for something epic to happen to him. I bet he's there right now, in fact. Have to go back sometime just for the hell of it. Ah but like that Steely Dan classic radio chestnut says, I'm never going back to *my* old school. It'd be sad—sad as seeing old J.P. who never even told you what J.P. was short for, come to think of it. Sad.

"That's right, sister," Sterling said. "Now: what's this girl's name again?"

"Jenny."

"Jenny what?"

"Dunno."

"Jenny Dunno . . . dunno her. Hahaha! Get it? Hey! Watch the till while I go in the back for a minute."

"Sure. Can I put on some Milk Amplifier?"

"No, em*phat*ically!"

He never let you listen to his old band. Not while he was around, anyway. I always asked; he always nixed me. It was a riff. One of them. Milk Amplifier had made one very good guitar pop record and split up acrimoniously, like so many bands do, everyone—once they'd had a bit of success—wanting different things, things to go their way. And Sterling, being as his given nomenclature suggested, a total purist and utterly uncompromising when it came to music, had called Milk Amplifier off, pulled the plug on it, left it sitting out on the counter till it curdled and spoiled. If the four-guys-against-the-world ideal of a band was gonna start all this internecine shit on *him*, fuck it, he was outta there. Music and especially playing music meant too much to him for it not to mean too much to him, if you know what I mean. I understood where he was coming from. But I couldn't go there: music meant everything to me too, but I was willing, I well knew (just think of Walter), to put up with a lot more stuff in order to feed my obsession with indie rock and living for it, living the dream, than most people were. I could (and did) take it.

Anyway, Sterling always asked about new people I brought up. Odds were he knew them: he knew everyone. But he didn't know Jenny. Not yet.

Just then some kids with jetty black bird-of-paradise hair came in. A boy and a girl, maybe sixteen or seventeen. With pointy pinched faces pale as any character in an Edward Gorey story. Of identical height. Tiny both. Like toy people or something. Cap-a-pe in black. Big smooth, like, riding boots. Goths! The monochrome folk. With obligatory crucifixes. Greatcoats too, despite the fact that it wasn't exactly cold outside, notwithstanding the plum clouds. I mean, they might as well have buttoned those coats up over their heads, they were so absurdly swaddled.

I smiled (goths *hate* smilers, smiling), gave them a friendly enough wink. Nothing. Don't you hate that? When you lather up a sort of smile or hello for a person or persons you'd never even think of eyes-smiling at or even grinning at, even if the goddam dentist was prying open your mouth with a megadose of laughing gas right in front of them, and they don't even faintly reciprocate?

"Need some help?" I smiled, even wider this time. I liked to pretend I was Sterling's assistant sometimes.

Goth boy mumbled out something that I interpreted as an inquiry as to whether "we" had any Depeche Mode.

(Of *course* Depeche Mode.)

Inveterate music snob.

Me, I mean.

"Sure. They were in the 'D's, last I checked," I told them.

Cruel pedant.

Goth girl gave me a very bad look like I was a very bad man. She should have known from the start I didn't really work there—what record store clerk-jerk wears Bermuda shorts and Sperry Top Siders?

Then I went too far I guess 'cause I said: "Hey, can you guys even name one of the Ramones? One? I'll give you a hint: none of them was called Jimmy or Bobby."

That did it. That got rid of them. You've never seen anybody who wasn't a king or queen shoplifter hightail it out of a store faster.

"Bye! Have a sad day!"

Sterling came back from the back just then: "Have you done paltering with the customers?"

"Paltering?"

"Trifling with. Bargaining insincerely. A brilliant word. I crave it. Who was in here?"

"Some goths, but I got rid of them."

"Good."

"Riddance!"

"Have you done pilfering the till?"

"Me, of course not—you know I only take records from you, not funds. That's *your* job, Sterling."

"Indubitably. There isn't much anyway: enough for two coffees and maybe a back-up pack of menthols so that you and every other cigarette-mendicant around here won't go bumming them from me. If you really wanna know, I buy regular Kings and put them in a menthol pack just so the oafs who are picky beggars won't bum them! "

"You are, just like everybody says, a genius," I said.

"Watch it, Juan—you are on not solid ground here! You are on probation, in fact! Let's see what the boss left here. Lately he's only been putting in around two bucks change. He must be on to me. He should be! He knows I am part Mexican—I'm kind of obliged by heritage to steal. It's a tradition."

"What a racistish thing to say!"

"Of course! Have you not heard black people running down 'niggers?' Or an Asian guy harshing on whatever Asian nationality he isn't—like, Chinese saying the Koreans are 'the dogs of Asia,' or Japanese people hating the Chinese more than they hate Whitey? Happens all the time. Or an Armenian in a tacky track suit smoking three Marlboro Reds at a time going on about how 'all these *new* Armenians are moving into East Hollywood?' An Armenian guy told me an Armenian guy joke the other day, in fact. I'm—where else?—in this bar in Hollywood and this Armenian guy goes 'Hey! What's the difference between an Armenian and a *gorilla*?' And of course I tell him I've never *met* a gorilla unless we count *him* and he laughs, he knows his brown brother's just kidding him, and goes '*Gorillas don't have pagers*.' Hahaha! '*Gorillas don't have pagers*.'"

"You're incorrigible. And you are only, like, one-fifteenth Mexican."
"Ha! I sure ain't paltering here," Sterling said and we both got a big chuckle out of it.

He handed me a five-spot, having ka-chinged open the register: "Go fetch us coffees, okay?"

"But that's stealing, Sterling."

"Stealing's just borrowing something without asking and assuming the answer is 'Yes.'"

"Now you *are* a genius—that's a good one, Sterl. I'm going to steal that for a lyric."

"It would serve me right. Now, mush! Get thee to a coffee-erie. Make mine black, medium blend, no sugar . . ."

"No cream. I got it," I said. "*This* mooch wants mocha. I'm kidding; it just sounds alliterative and assonant, *n'est-ce pas?*"

"*Vraiment.*"

When I got back I asked him what I always asked him, which was if there was anything new I really needed to hear, even though, unless it was from New Zealand, it cut no mustard with him. He was obsessed with Kiwi bands; everybody else, practically, could go fish. Or, as real New Zealanders quaintly say, *fush*. There were exceptions, of course—like the aforementioned handful of Sterling-approved bands I told you I tried to get into. He had the most exclusive, the most brutally narrow, taste imaginable: you could never predict what he'd dig and what he wouldn't. He *thought* he liked loads of things, though. In actuality he liked around seven or eight groups, ten tops—unless you counted punk bands (American only—English didn't figure, not even the Pistols) and jangly guitar bands from the freakout era of granny glasses and salad bowl haircuts. He was even critical of the Beatles. Gasp! He knew the Beatles even better than I did—no mean feat—but he only liked *two* records all the way through and he was one of the first people I ever encountered who said George was the best Beatle. George!

Sacrilegious miscreant!

And yet after fifteen minutes of listening to his rather granoblastic argument for George, and for *Rubber Soul* and *Help!* as the only real masterpieces ("What?!" I'd objected, "No *Revolver*, no *White Album*?! You must be quite insane."), he had me siding with him. Damn that Sterling: he could convince the Devil himself to come to Sunday School, a lady in white to buy a carton of ketchup popsicles, a claustrophobic to live in a ten-by-seven cargo crate, a . . . ah, fuck it—you get the picture.

When I returned bearing paper coffee cups, Sterling told me I had got to hear something by this band Able Tasmans. He put on side 1 and the strains of a jangly-poppy, bouncy but kind of darkish tune (there's that word again—but sometimes it applies) washed over us, very catchy and warm-and-fuzzy making.

"This is great! They're the Kiwi Beatles, huh?"

"I crave it," the Scather said ebulliently. "It's me best!"

Sterling was telling me boisterously his theory about alternative music and how either you knew *all* of it or you knew nothing—in other words, you sort of had to know it all, from Brian Eno's first solo records to the latest thing by the Sundays or whomever—when the bell that even when it rang never rang on account of the music was always or at least often really loud rang and in came Sarah, Sterling's closest friend besides me. Whose most salient characteristics were: 1) that she looked just like the ravishingly pretty, hyper-lissome and impossible-lipped chick in *Betty Blue*; and 2) that she hated me. I mean openly, evincing withering contempt kinda hated me. Cold as the just-discernible frosted aqua and milk-white streaks with which her deep, dark, rich, and perfectly cut hair was streaked.

Sarah did not like me and did not try to hide it, boy. Her disdain left me thinking sometimes: should I check myself in the mirror to see if I had inadvertently sprouted horns and a red, spadelike tail? Cloven hooves? Was I holding some sort of pitchfork that I didn't know about? What had I done? Anything? Where had I gone wrong? Why did she hate me so? How *come*? What had I done? Where had I gone wrong? Why didn't she like me? Why?

What had I said to her? A whole lot of nothing. I'd only met her twice: she, like me, like a lot of people, visited the Scather almost every Sunday, hung around and "helped" the customers, smoked and laughed and horsed around. She had to practice her diabolical scowl somewhere, I suppose. But why on me? I naturally preferred another satellite of Sterling's whose name changed every time I met her. Once he'd introduced her as Jane, another as Lisa. Then it was back to Jane, and a few Sundays later, on the phone, I'd heard him referring to someone called Lisette for around a half an hour before I realized it was the same chick. Usually she got there before I did. She'd be perched on the countertop, in fishnets and jackboots, a kilt and tight, orange or green cardigan, smiling prudishly (she was really nice, Lisette-Jane-Lisa was), never saying much at all. She gave the impression of being the prissiest thing in the universe, despite the very come-hither attire. I liked that a lot. Her I really dug. This other guy too, called Mike Fuck on account of fuck was the only thing he ever seemed to say. "You know Mike Fuck?" Sterling had asked and indicated this six-foot-six guy with long straight hair, like a conflation of Joni

Mitchell and Neil Young in their Laurel Canyon heyday, with braces (suspenders, that is) and 16-eye Doc Martens or whatever, who had the most shy smile, though he looked like he could kick your ass twelve ways from Sunday—and all he ever said was "Fuck" to whatever anyone else said and he just stood there smiling at Sterling who seemed to be just so amused by him. Just as he was by another Mike—Mike Jam—who even though the Jam had broken up, like, 400 years ago could only talk about the Jam, worked the Jam into every goddam conversation, started a the Jam Fan Club, couldn't shut up about it. One time when Mike Jam was in and had it seemed been hanging around for too long Sterling just said: "Mike Jam, that's *it*! That's all for you today! You're out!" And Mike Jam kinda shuffled off, still mumbling something about *Setting Sons* being just as good as *Sound Affects*.

But Sarah? No, no, no, no, no. She was just—I thought—a humongous phony. She dressed like an artist, occasional beret and all of that; she talked like an artist; she even smoked like one. But she wasn't an artist. She wasn't. The first thing she announced to anybody in her radius was "I'm not an artist, by the way." Like everyone would assume she was some Cindy Sherman or Susan Sontag or Patti Fucking Smith if she didn't let them know that she was, in some weird way, above being one, too cool to be an artist, for fuck's sake. By her deportment and stupendous air of impregnable ennui the whole world was supposed to just assume she was one. Unreal.

Pretentious twat.

I'd tried. I'd tried to befriend her, be cool, be nice. I'd even complimented her, grandiloquently, and pointed out admiringly her uncanny resemblance to, as I told you, the chick in *Betty Blue*. But Sarah-Who-Hated-Me got so offended! She didn't like that one bit.

"Hey, Sterling," she said dryly.

"Sarah! What's shaking?"

"Nothing. How are you?"

"Hi, Sarah," I said.

"Hello," she lied.

"Listen, Sterling, I have to go to the store—want anything?"

"Orange Crush! And another pack of Marlboros, please. You are the best!"

"Whatever."

"Get menthols, okay? That way I can put these in the menthol pack and no one will bum them."

Here he gave innocent me a meaningful look. But he laughed to show me he was only joking.

Sarah said she'd be right back. Her small, just-barely-at-the-tip aquiline nose went all scrunchy when she walked past me. Her full red sensuous lips seemed perpetually pursed—like she didn't even want to breathe the same air as you. As me, at least. The fully unquestionably glacial implication of her stating she'd be right back was "I will be right back—and *you* [meaning me] had better be gone when I do."

"*Hates* me," I singsonged to Sterling when she'd exited. "Totally hates me."

"Totally," Sterl confirmed.

"I'd better go."

"No! Don't yet. You haven't even heard *this* yet."

He held up a record by the Bats, another Kiwi thing.

"What's her deal, anyway? What did I do to her?"

"Who knows! I have no idea. I've known her forever and I still haven't figured what sets her off and what doesn't—or who does. Don't take her too seriously. *I* don't."

"But I mean . . . that chick fucking loathes me, for some reason. I mean, really fucking . . ."

"Like I said, don't pay it no nevermind . . . She probably just thinks . . ."

"Thinks what?"

"Oh forget it."

"No: what?"

"Well, one time she called you shallow."

Then he gave out his wicked impish laugh.

"Shallow?!"

"Uh-huh."

"Shallow!"

"Uh," he said in his best Valleyish voice, "yeah."

"She thinks I'm *shallow*. How can she think *that*? I've only said around twelve words total to her in my entire life! What twaddle."

"Like I said . . ."

"Seriously! Wow. Superficial, maybe. Facetious for sure. But *shallow*? You've got to be kidding me."

"Honestly, John. I really really wouldn't take her too seriously. Not in the least. I've known her since Catholic school practically and I wouldn't even venture to predict or speculate upon the judgments she makes on people. What can you expect from a nymphomaniac, anyway?"

"What?!"

"You didn't *know* that?

"No, I didn't know that. How could I know that? My God."

"Ha! Well, that's what she is, anyway. I thought it was obvious. I thought everyone knew."

"You're making this up, right?"

"Not at all, my good man. She is. Completely."

"Oh, that is just great: a nymphomaniac thinks *I'm* shallow. I better go. Wow."

"You just got here, though! Plus I wanna hear some more about your practice. When are you guys gonna do a show? Don't leave, Juan! It'll be too too boring if you split."

"A nymphomaniac's supposed to like men, though."

"Not necessarily. Think about it. Really, though: I wouldn't turn into a barbiturate over it, or anything. Like I said: I have no idea what her trip is. Why do you care?"

I started to walk out of the store and just sort of waved bye when Sterling said: "Juan, tell me about this keyboard-and-guitar chick. What's her name again?"

"Jenny."

"And she's pretty attractive too, you say?"

"Beautiful, actually."

"But . . ."

"Well, kind of . . ."

"Chunky."

"Oh you should talk—you don't look like you've been sparing yourself any beers these days!"

"Fuck off!" I laughed. "Beer, at least, really likes me back. Stop always being skinnier than everyone else, okay. Have another Diet Marlboro or something. I gotta go."

"Don't you want some records?"

"The one that's playing?"

"No way! That's mine. You can have the new House of Love, though.

And the new Ride EP you can *have*, if you know what I'm saying."

"You're kidding—Ride are awesome! It isn't any good?!"

"*I* don't crave it. You see what you think, though. To me, the Byrds did all that stuff they do *centuries* ago. Ride are just the Byrds with a passel of distortion boxes."

Passel was a word I'd come across and looked up a while back; Sterling and I had out-nerded each other lately trying to work it in to our super-sesquipedalian conversations. I had to laugh.

"Thanks," I said as I took the records off him, plus a couple of 7-inches I'd had my eye on, and two or three new cassettes.

"Now you owe me even more than you owed me from the ride home," Sterling announced.

"I know."

"Call me later. I'll tell you then," he said as three new record shoppers, plus Sarah-Who-Hated-Me came in. I squeezed past and sallied forth—without a look or a word of farewell from anyone.

# CHORUS

## my head is filled with things to say

I didn't feel like hanging around anymore anyway, not on Melrose at least, passing pungent, tempting restaurants—Indian joints and pizzerias were particularly egregious in terms of mercilessly pumping their savory smells straight at you—I could not afford. I drove up to La Brea, 'cause I was getting pretty hungry and thinking Pink's. But when I got there I spied this punk rock writer/poet chick queued up, nattering away with some lanky-tall Nick Cave-looking guy I didn't recognize, and not wanting the hassle of a one-way conversation about her and her work (her God-given name was, I swear to God, or at least *she* swore it was, Golden Sundrop), I decided I'd forego the famous chili cheese dog or greasy grease-burger and just go home and see what Jaz was up to, maybe hit a movie or make something to eat—find something to eat, more like.

Golden Sundrop's a nice girl and everything, a real sweetheart, and, on account of the fact that she used to be a model and was a scenester/fixture in the days of Black Flag and X and the Germs and all of that and has rad red or sometimes platinum blonde hair and cool/cute tattoos and a nose ring and a super cute face and a toothsome derrière, she gets a lot of people to her readings, packed house and everything; but if you *knew* her, you'd know why I bowed out of running into her. See, in Los Angeles there are jillions of "writers" as well as musicians and actors and directors and dancers and sword swallowers and whatnot. You guys in Brooklyn and Chiswick and Iowa City and especially San Fran Fucking Cisco think that where *you* live is where all the writers are, where all the writers come from, but you're wrong. We have just as many writers as you do. The thing is, they aren't *real* writers. The scribblers you meet here, or most of them anyway, are the sort of people who *write* but don't *read*; therefore, they are not real writers in my book. Not at fucking all. Many's the LA scribe who tells you how they *like* to write, love it, even: "Oh, I *love* writing," some guy or girl will tell you at the dinky bar at El Coyote or if you encounter them at 3 a.m. at Canters or at the "must-go" reading at Book Soup; "I just *love* it. That's all I'd do, like, all day long if I could—write. I really *mean* it. I totally love it!"

Barf.

Dear me, it's a sure sign that someone fucking sucks if they think that writing, real writing, is something even remotely enjoyable. Any real writer's gonna tell ya (probably *ad nauseam*) that it's fucking slow torture in slow fucking motion, writing is. Just a nightmare. A masochist's wet dream. And I just knew that Golden was gonna tell me all about her latest chapbook and her next reading and blabitty-blah-blah-blah and I just wasn't in the mood for it, not in the slightest.

Most of the quote-unquote writers (and I don't count *screen*writers at all—don't tell Jaz I said that, but I really don't; screenwriting's just a formula, *I* think: I could type you up a filmable *screen*play in four, maybe five, days *tops*; I have zilch respect for screenwriters, boy: absolutely zippo) I meet in Los Angeles like Bu*kow*ski, for Christ's sake. Old Charles. The pock-marked drunkie-flunky. Like, wow. I mean, I like him too, I really do, he's funny as hell and some of his poems actually really sing, but his precious, hipster-hallowed novels are kinda like *literature for people who don't really read*. I sorta have the same attitude about books that Sterling has about music (he actually has it about books as well—for a guy who dropped out of Catholic school in, like, maybe *third* grade he is astonishingly erudite and well-read). Either you know your Smollett and your Turgenev and your Brontës and your Chekhov—or you can *fuck* off; that's what I think. You'd better do your homework. You'd better know your lit shit. And Bukowski and John Fucking Fante and fucking Allen Ginsburg and Kerouac—all those beardos and pencil-butchers ain't cutting it, bud. You wanna be the next Faulkner or Fitzgerald?—you *read* them, fuck-o. And you read 'em again. Faulkner and Fitzgerald are, to me, writers that grown-ups outgrow anyway—it's kids' stuff, all their stuff. You're like me, a few maybe seven or eight years outta college, a responsible or at least semi-responsible member of society, you don't go near the shelves where Conrad and Hemingway and Mark Twain and Dickens are. You wanna *book*, pick up fucking

*Proust* or Mr. Henry Fucking *James* or goddam George or T.S. *Eliot* and shut the hell up, writer guy or girl! Tell me what you think about writing when you've done *Anna Karenina* at least twice and read *all* of Flaubert and *all* of Nabokov: come back for a little chat *then* and then I'll *maybe* show up to your poxy Monday Open Mic Night, you bloody fucking stupid fucking poetasting posing fucking fuckwad giggity *wannabe*! Ha! Fuck *you*.

*

Jaz was watching the day's football highlights on the diminutive TV, sitting at his little kinderdesk, tapping something out on the computer, when I got home.

I said hey and asked him if he'd eaten yet and he said yeah and so I solo-ed it in the kitchen and decided to Rube up some spaghetti or something. I mushed up a suicidal amount of garlic and put a little puddle of olive oil in a clean pan, crudely minced a dying half onion I found cowering, fainting away in a corner of the fridge, ripped apart a fresh (what a miracle!) red pepper and some succulent leftover roasted eggplant from an abandoned sandwich, and got the mixture winking and glimmering and sizzling. In another pan I sautéed ten or so waning mushrooms in a soup of butter, a finger-and-a-half of Zin and some more garlic. Got the water hopping with the aid of some margarita salt. Dumptrucked oregano into some bottled sauce and let it simmer with another pinch of salt, some crushed red pepper, a rumor of black pepper, and two errant bay leaves I found in a drawer. There was a bottle of Cab cached behind a box on top of the fridge neither of us had remembered, ostensibly, or of course it would've been glugged, so I spilled what was left in it into the sauce as well.

"You don't have any bread stashed anywhere, do you, Jaz?" I called to him.

"Don't interrupt me right now! I'm in the middle of this!" he said.

"Sorry."

"That smells pretty good, though!"

"There's easily enough—do you want some? There's enough angel hair for sure."

"Oh, all right; I guess I could eat again."

I liberated two pieces of frozen sourdough from the freezer and jammed them into the toaster. The water was roiling now, so I snapped in half enough angel hair for two and stirred it in.

"Screenplay?" I said as I poked my head in to the living/Jaz's room.

"Huh?"

"Are you writing your screenplay?"

"Yeah."

"And?"

"Don't know yet."

"Is this the one that re-invents *Othello*?"

"No. Let me finish this scene, okay?"

"Okay," I said.

When the pasta had thickened nicely and was good and foamy I strained it out on the sink's side (yeah, like we had a colander or anything!), got two plates and heaped the meal together, throwing the glistening mushrooms on last and frosting the separate helpings with the last of the parmesan. I put two pats of butter on each kinda burnt bread slice and put them on the plates.

"Awesome," Jaz said as I handed him his food.

We sat there inhaling, me on the beach chair (our only other chair) and Jaz at his desk, the full steam billowing off our plates.

"Is goot. *We*-we goot," Jaz breathed.

"Yeah, well, if you can only muster one meal a day, it had better be," I said.

"Whu'd you go?"

"Visiting Sterling at Finyl Vinyl."

"Yeah? How was that?"

"Very Melrose. I brought home some new records, though."

Jaz enjoined me to put one on and so I did. After a minute he asked who it was and I said "Ride" and he said "Cool" and I finished the last of my spaghetti and so did Jaz and I took the two plates and silverware to the kitchen and washed them easy-peasy up and percolated some coffee and when it was done I spiked it with vanilla powder and a sugar cube and a little drip of whipping cream: Jaz and I as you know are poor as hell but we splurge on stuff like condiments.

I gave him his cup and asked him if he wanted to work off the meal with a little Nerfball and he said the momentum on his writing was gone anyway so why not.

We moved the beach chair and Jaz's chair outside and the television stand to the kitchen, picked up some stray hardbacks from the floor, then Jaz got out the whiffle bat and Nerf ball and we started out with me pitching, like always. Jaz put one of the newly purloined records down for home plate and took a few burly practice cuts with the bat, then some tentative ones, the bat making that whooshing hollow comforting whistling sound you know so well from childhood.

Right away I got my curve/knuckleball/fastball/slider combo working for me and whiffed him on a count of one and two.

"You're pulling your head. Keep your head down," I said.

"Hey, just pitch, man. Are you sure you are standing back far enough? Step back a bit!"

"I'm right up against the wall, practically!"

"Okay-okay," he said.

"Aren't we supposed to get high first, though?"

"We're out of weed anyway," Jaz said. "And besides, I am trying not to get high so often, so that's good. Just make the rubber a tiny bit farther back."

I nodded okay and fired a fastball right down the middle; Jaz roped it past me and into the dinky hallway for a double."

"Nice one!" I said.

"Oh, yeah."

"That's the last hit you are getting today, though. No more hits for *you* unless we scrape the *bong*."

"Funny. Pitch!"

I wound up theatrically and threw a change-up at his ass, which unfortunately he read beautifully and the Nerf caromed off the left field wall for, *he* thought, a *triple*.

"Foul ball!" I called.

"No way, John! A double at least!"

I acquiesced and he said "One run in!" Then I got him out on a line drive so that was two down.

The Ride side one was done so, at Jaz's suggestion, I got out *Revolver* and put that on.

"That's more like it!" Jaz enthused. "This is music I can *hit* to!"

"Strike one!" I said as I got a screwball by him on the inside corner. "Hey, Jaz? Definition."

"What?"

"What would you say the difference is between someone who's shallow and someone superficial?"

"Well," he said, frowning as he fouled off my next pitch, "superficial is a choice, I guess—shallow would be something someone can't help, maybe. Some people just aren't by nature very deep?"

"Huh."

"Why do you ask, may I ask?"

"No reason," I said. "Strike two."

"Someone accuse you of being superficial?"

"No."

"What, then—shallow?"

"Yeah."

"Okay, your ups," Jaz said as he whiffed at the next pitch. "I like pitching almost as much as I like hitting. Isn't this the greatest game."

"It's pretty incredible."

"Who said you were shallow—Sterling?"

"God, no. This chick he's best friends with."

He opened with a curve which fooled me badly for strike one.

"Any cute?"

"Very, actually. But she fucking hates me. I don't know why. I never said "boo" to her. All I ever said was she looks like that chick in *Betty Blue*. Ball one."

"You said that?!"

"Yeah. Yes. One the outside corner for strike two. One and two."

Jaz got all excited now. He got super excited when he thought he'd caught you being a blunderbuss.

"Well, no wonder then."

"What?!" I said. "What are you talking about? Foul tip—still one and two. What do you mean?"

"*Betty Blue* is about the shallowest film you could've picked to compare a chick to—you should know that! It's just a lot of neurotic nonsense that leads to exciting, Frenchified sex, right? Some guy trying to make sense of a crazy, out-of-this-world-sexy-and-beautiful French chick who's, as I said, *crazy*."

We stopped playing.

"So? I didn't say I liked it. I just said . . ."

"Besides, anyone knows the French have no idea how to make a good movie . . ."

"You *are* high, Jaz. Renoir, Truffaut, fucking Godard, Bresson . . . What are you talking about? Even Eric Rohmer's stuff is really wicked sometimes!"

"Bah! What about their obsession with Jerry Lewis, eh? You tell a French guy he's an idiot for liking Jerry Lewis and he looks at you like you said something like 'Gosh, you know, fresh French bread from France just doesn't taste very *good* to me.' Or something. 'I don't know what the big deal is about French bread from France.' The French guy flips out. To him, *you* are the idiot, not him. *You* are."

"Oh my God—what's that got to do with *an*ything?!"

Jaz just kinda shrugged and we both laughed like we were stoned.

"The thing is, you blew it because—I don't know!—you should have compared her to Audrey Hepburn or someone."

"Audrey *Hep*burn? She doesn't look a *thing* like Audrey *Hep*burn."

"That seems kinda *shallow* of her."

"You are amazing."

"Furthermore, comparing this chick to the chick from *Betty Blue* was very eighties of you. Very eighties. You might have just gone ahead and told her she looked like Molly Ringwald."

"Oh give me a break," I said. "And besides, I *love* Molly Ringwald. Everyone does."

"Okay, I will explain—just this once, so listen well. If you absolutely have to, it is always always always safer and better to compare a chick to a *vin*tage chick—like Audrey Hepburn. Someone like that. Ingrid Bergman. Ava Gardner (though no chick was as sultry and beautiful as Ava Gardner, so that's kind of preposterous). Girls lap that vintage shit up, let me tell you. Grace Kelly—that's who you shoulda said she looked like, but with black hair. Except no girl except Grace Kelly in the history of the world has ever looked like Grace Kelly."

"Ha! That's the shallowest philosophy I have ever heard," I said.

"It might be—but it works. *Vin*tage, next time, John—I'm telling you."

"Don't you see, though, Jaz? I wasn't trying to work this girl at all. She's Sterling's friend—that's all. *C'est tout*. I was just being friendly. I'm not even remotely attracted to her . . ."

"Which always means . . ."

"Okay, I am attracted to her. I concede. She's pretty as hell. But not really. Actually, totally I'm not. Not at all. She's beautiful, in a try-to-ignore-this-scowl-and-focus-on-my-underlying-pulchritude way. But I was just trying to be friend-like, not even friend*ly*, I swear."

"Sure. But no wonder she said you were shallow: you weren't, to her, deep enough to know that you *should* be coming on to her—a *little* bit at least."

"What twaddle. You're suggesting it's *de rigueur* for me to come on to chicks I'm not even inspired to come on to, have zippo interest in?"

"Girls that cute expect that sort of thing. And when you don't give it to them, give them at least the oppor*tu*nity of shooting you down like a Spitfire that didn't notice the powerful Kraut howitzer cowering behind the French barn in the countryside? They *hate* you. Girls know when you generally aren't that into them. Guys never do. Guys are always 'God, she's really kinda into me' about some chick that thinks they're the most revolting male on earth. We've discussed this. It's uncanny. Believe me."

"Were you watching a WWII documentary earlier?"

"How did you know?"

"Huh," I said. "I never thought about that."

"Well, you heard it here first. I better get back to pretending to try to write."

"Hey, Jaz?"

"Shoot."

"How come you know so much about the psychology of chicks, anyway, huh?"

"Probably 'cause I haven't gone out on a date with one since, God, I don't know—college or something?" he said balefully.

"Six years?"

"Let's not talk about it. I can't seem to find anyone who lives up to my standards, I guess. Plus, it takes so much money to find an awesome chick in LA. They really are only into you if you have money, I swear."

"That's nonsense. You're only rationalizing and using that as an excuse! Look at me, for instance. I mean . . . And besides: you know what to do when you find your standards are too high, don't you? You told me this yourself one time!"

"What?"

"*Lower* them!"

# take them bowling

I lay down on the ol' futon and read for a little while (another *Rambler* by the Doctor), thought of giving Jenny a wee call, thought better of it, then realized I was supposed to call the Scather before he got off work. I tried him at home. I couldn't focus too well on Dr. J anyway; I kept thinking about Jenny, plus wondering how old Sam could be so incredibly brilliant and so prolix and Latinate and obviously purposefully difficult at the same time.

"Hello."

"Hey, sorry—I forgot to call you, Scathe."

"That's all right, Juan. I wanted to hang out with someone after work who'd help prevent me from calling my connection. That guy is a real menace to sobriety, if you know what I mean. And he knows I love drugs. What's up with you?"

"Sterling," I said sternly, "you are not doing speed again—tell me you're not."

"Well, let's just say I'm flirting with it, not exactly doing as in sleeping with it. Not that sleep is the point, anyway. I just miss the feeling of staying up for around three days in a row."

"Jesus. Just say 'No,'" I said with some little irony. "That's why you disappear sometimes and don't call me back for days on end, isn't it?"

"Well, duh. And besides anyone can just say no but mostly one ends up saying 'maybe.' Ah, it doesn't matter. Sarah and I went bowling after."

"Really? That sounds pretty fun. 'Take the skinheads bowling . . .'"

"'Take them bowling!' Yeah it was fun. I was terrible, and Sarah was even worse than terrible, but it was a blast."

"That's more like it—good clean fun," I said and returned to the topic of Sterling's avowed affection for amphetamines. "It's a bad program to be on, speed is. I have some real issues with that drug."

"Oh and what are you guys up to over there—smoking from the Hookah? You dirty filthy stoners!"

The Hookah was what Jaz and I had nicknamed the bong; pretty clever, no?

"No. In fact Jaz said he wasn't even interested in getting stupid before we played a little indoor baseball here."

"*Quelle accomplishment*!"

"Oh, I know. What was it you wanted to talk to me about?

"Tell you some other time, okay? Hey! You aren't still bumming about Sarah hating you, are you?"

"Nah."

"It's not exactly as though she's one-of-the-guys, you realize. She's not even one-of-the-*girls*, somehow! She loathes everyone even more than you or *I* do."

"That's comforting. I know. It's no big deal. But, I mean, I'm not exactly crazy about being treated like I'm a novel by Ralph Fucking Ellison and stuff."

"Ralph Ellison!" Sterling laughed. "That's a good one. You know what they say, though: no use crying over spilled blood. Gotta go. See you later, Invisible Man!"

"Okay," I said.

And took the phone by its super long cord back to the kitchen and thought about getting ready to crash but I turned back after a step or two and grabbed the phone again and tugged it into my room on account of I remembered that tomorrow was Monday, fucking Monday.

## monday morning you sure look fine

The above title is, of course, ironic. What it should be is, "Just another manic Monday." Monday mornings, a likely lad in terms of securing work. The terrible telephone normally detonates at about six fifteen, six thirty—a horrid screeching, searing, dream-crushing sound. A raw, carious tooth being drilled with a blunted corkscrew. By a gremlin or evil leprechaun who wants big time revenge. No matter how much sleep I've gotten, how early I've gone off to Dreamville, it's an unmitigated shock.

On the other end of the line is someone from the LA Unified downtown switchboard, ringing the subs to see who's feeling real masochistic this morning, who's up for some *hell*. The earlier they call, the more gruesome the assignment, seemingly. At least that's what I've found: they wanna get rid of the tough ones first, so they ring up the desperate—the subs with only one or two years under their respective belts, the ones who probably only get two, maybe if they are quote-unquote lucky, three days subbing in every two weeks. First to go are the junior high assignations. At that hour I have to try extra very hard not to employ, in answering the phoneski, a very soft but clearly articulated favorite expletive.

"Fffyello?" I go.

"Gawd mawning!" the voice on the other end drawls, boomingly schoolmarmish and overly friendly at the same time. "Ah you available fo' an assignment this morning Mr. [insert last name here—I'm not giving you *mine*]?"

"Oh, hello. I am . . . Yes, ma'am. But?"

"But what, sir?"

"*Please* don't send me to a junior high today, please? Please let me have a high school this morning. A high school would be . . ."

"I got a English and a P.E.—which'n you want, young man?"

"Where's the English, please?" I ask trepidatiously.

And she goes: "Which'n do you *want* this mawning, sir? I gots a lotta calls ta make this mawning. So if you jus' . . ."

"Oh, God. Door number three."

"'Scuse me?!"

"I said 'I'll take P.E.'"

"A'right. P.E. Itsa one day assignment—Arnold Junior. Teacher's name is . . ."

"Excuse me? Did I say 'P.E.?' I meant the English. I'll take the *English* assignment, please."

"Fine by me. You want t'English—that what you sayin'?"

"Yes, please," I go, helplessly.

"Ahkay: English. Less see . . . The teacher's name is Garoyan, Gargolyan—somefin like that. A *two*-day assignment—is that all right wich *you*?"

"Sure. Okay."

"A'right, sir. You have a *good* day."

"Thank you. Wait! You didn't say where it was!"

"Oh, sorry. Here it is. I'm lookin'. I'm lookin'. Here it is: Arnold Junior."

"Arnold Junior? The English one's there too?!"

"Thass right—B. Arnold Junior."

"Great."

"Bye, now."

"Are you sure you don't have . . ."

"Good*bye*, sir."

And click.

I kick up a fresh pair of boxers from the floor and take them with me to the bathroom. Run the shower scalding. Shave with the swashbuckling abandon of an Errol Flynn. Cut myself at least once, 'cause I shave in the shower, not in the mirror, feeling my (crest*fallen* but not out-for-the-count) face. Sometimes behead a mole. Don't care. Think of it as a metaphor for the psychological scars I'll incur during the longish, sometimes electrically terrifying, mostly prodigiously banal day. Lather up like a triathlete. Towel off on spin-dry cycle. Minuteman into the boxers, a pair of not too smudgy Gap or Gap-approximate trousers, not-too-maculate Oxford shirt. Sometimes socks. Only if they haven't been turned inside out already once or twice. Topsiders or low top Converse Chuck Taylors? Today the tennis shoes. I usually request P.E. though I am most qualified to teach English. Have no problem helping California's least accomplished, least ambitious adolescents further butcher French or Spanish. History I don't mind. Am, thankfully, never offered Science, Health or Math. God, the thought: Science? Yikes! Students already generously provisioned with things that might potentially explode? No thanks. Health? Me? Me the picture perfect spokesmodel for the chronically insalubrious? A late twenty-nothing malnourished, sleep-deprived, quasi-mentally unbalanced germ magnet on ice? Hardly. Math? I couldn't help *third* graders with Math—or what, Jesus Christicus, they call the *new* New Math—even if they put their junior revolvers or numchucks (I don't know how you spell it) or whatever they're packing that day straight to my temple, I couldn't. Music and Art I live in total mortal dread of, given that the students absolutely rage during those classes even when their regular teacher's teaching them.

I hunt down my keys, call for my wallet ("Where'd I put my goddam wallet? Where the fuck did I put that thing? Where the fucking fuck the fuck is it? In the wastebasket where it belongs, probably."), find it under a flayed paperback, try not to make too much of a racket on account of Jaz normally gets home from his graveyard shift right around seven and is sometimes up and peacefully reading the Sports or Calendar sections of the *Times* before he goes to sleep. Get the coffee pot rocking quickly. The sugar at the ready. Milk too. Can't eat, but scavenge something for later—a megacaloric granola bar or red or yellow apple with skin like your gran's after she's fallen asleep in the bath, face down, for around two days.

And am out the door.

These fine mornings, as I descend the stairs, the first thing I encounter is Heidi, whom I greet. My salutations are brief. I confide in her that today I will brave another junior high. I curse her way, conspiratorially. She doesn't seem to be all that amused, concerned, phased, surprised or bewildered, though I will, in the course of my work day, be three of the above at least.

"Heidi," I whisper, "see you later. Be a good emu today—the best emu you can be."

Then I get into my sorry car, the Volvo with much minor dents I told you about. A car of minimum velocity, maximum unsightliness: a car that keeps me in touch with the Holy Creator, for I call upon Him every time I turn the key. The series of noises that issue from it sometimes evokes a symphony by an avant garde composer in the final stages of syphilitic dementia; every so often an out-of-tune tuba burps from deep within the muffler and a scary angry chuntering ghost rattles a large chain from the bowels of the engine. A sadist tortures a small child or kitten underneath the dashboard, and the lime green steering wheel (it didn't start out in life as lime green, I shouldn't wonder) shakes like a broken tambourine. In the mornings the starter groans worse than I do talking to the switchboard ladies and then makes sounds like a record that can't get out of the last groove. A record by the Shaggs (the *worst*—and in a way *best*—band in the world, if you've never heard them). A record of fat, drunk, pill-addled Elvis doing the national anthem (there are bootlegs; you can find them; you and your dog won't believe your ears). Any platter by Kiss or Styx or Starship or Journey. (Sorry, mulletheads.) Okay, I'm stalling: time to drive to work. But one last thing: there are off-road motorcycles that are quieter than this car.

I mean, inexplicably the heater ticks on in the middle of the very hottest summer days, and smoke like a candle that's been sneezed on by a walrus snakes up from under the seats. And speaking of smoke, fire, and burnt stuff, if you happen to die one day and go to the lower depths of darkest Hell, I'll bet my car or one just like it will be awaiting you, to taxi you wherever you need to go.

Sleepy still (though the springs that spring up from the disemboweled leather seats poke me into constant consciousness), I'm flying down the 10 till traffic bunches around La Cienega. I flick on the radio talk shows, just to piss myself off and to drown out the dirdum of angry engines and tromboning honkings of the big rigs, sports cars, buses and jeeps that nervewrackingly tailgate me. Even people in pokey Yugos and those retired mail trucks you can buy from the government and paint unicorns or sunsets or Cher on are bummed to get stuck behind me. What can you do? What I do mostly is ignore them and twirl around the radio dial for something really obnoxious and distracting. The Christian Pop Psychology Gardening Show. Some Right-Wing Crackpot for Your Daily Morning Drive. I try not to make a miniature riptide of my coffee as I look around my trashcan-on-wheels for my toothbrush and toothpaste. Scrape the teeth. Rinse with what's left of the coffee. Try not to make mocha-colored whitewalls of the tires on the cars traffic-jammed to the left of me. They all have guns, large ones and loaded, the drivers. You don't wanna get them riled. Luxuriate, if I have one left, in a pre-prandial cigarette. Spark another if I have it. If I'm tapped I can always bum one from a custodian (or as they now call them Waste-Engineer Reduction Disbursement Specialists, or WERDS) or from one of the eighth-graders.

I remember Jaz's maxim/joke about not getting bummed out in traffic, get bummed anyway, worry if I will make it to first period on time. I hope I have first period off, veg out till I get to the gates of the school, i.e. the gates of this day's Hell.

There, in Hell, the fun begins. Not for *me*—no, no, no, no, no—but for the gods above who are, daily, doubling over at my ridiculous follies and pratfalls, pointing at me, a ridiculous object of ridiculous ridicule. "Look at yon Sub!" they a-ha-ha-ha; "what Monstrosities and Humiliations shall we afflict the Afflicted with To*day*, we wondereth? A freshly sharpened Pencil in the Eardrum, perhaps? An Eraser, greatly hardened by Non-Use, to the Forehead from close Range? A Compass boomeranged at his unsuspecting Cheekbone? Maybe we should have the Math Teacher here, a Mistress D'Ivision, that wizened old Goat with the flowing Gal-Goatee, corner him in the Teachers Lounge and make an accurate Grab for his Bone or Gonads?! Whom, you inquire? Why, she with the great continental Behind, of course, and splendidly bepimpled Bosom! Mark ye how the Teats, the very Dugs of her, Melonlike and extravagantly misshapen, are slung low as the Holsters on a long-armed Cowboy! We could have the Beldam threaten him with Sexual Harassment if he is unwilling to comply with her carnal Wishes . . . Would that not amuse us no End?! Hm. Perhaps, M'Lords, one of the exceedingly delicious and nubile Hoydens in hot pink Hot Pants—one of the Throng who, though but fourteen Years of Age look and act and dress twenty-two, could come on to him in the Hallway, lightly placing a long-nailed Hand upon his Cockstand just as the crypto-Feminist Principal is rounding a Corner with some Clipboard-carrying Visitors from the School Board? What say you? What *say* you, fellow Immortals? What shall we do this Day with our favorite Figure of Fun?"

Fun. And of course the fun begins for the kids themselves, who, from the moment I step into the classroom, will be more delighted to see me than any kindly grandmother or Midwesternly long-lost cousin ever could. If I go in all confident, all don't-even-think-of-fucking-with-me, they'll rabble-rouse and sabre-rattle to beat the band. If meek and hey-I-don't-like-this-any-better-than-you-do, they'll swoon with ecstatic glee and fond thoughts of mischief-making possibilities; their immediate futures are not something to give up on like their actual futures are. Their eyes widen. Their *nostrils* widen. Their mouths widen. For once in their lives, their minds widen: What can we do to torment this man? This trapped creature whom we have fifty minutes to toy with and fuck with. A sub! We've got a sub! Sub! Hey, *Sub!* How you doin'? We be doin' *you* now! Sub, sub, sub, sub, sub, sub, sub! Substitute! Subbarino! Subbarooski! Sub, subas, suba, subban, subbamos, subbabbamos, subby-sub-sub—yeah!

They yell, they scream, they freak fuckin' out. (Sub!) They whoop, they whistle, they throw themselves around the room (choose one):

a) like poltergeists.
b) like they are auditioning for roles in a dream/nightmare film by Fellini.
c) like they are being exorcised.
d) like the horrible Middle Schoolers they are.

e) all of the above.

The answer of course is e) all of the above.

It's like being stuck in a large stucco box filled with aggressively hectoring mondo-monomaniacal circumlocuting magpies, to coin a phrase. It's like that. You bleeding bleeding-heart social program fanners and people who majored in something silly like Sociology; you future teachers and child psychologists? Unless you have a serious sense of humor and take this all with a grain you ain't gonna like what I have to tell you. Nuh-uh.

Subbing: it's like a word problem, one of those things you totally hated in school:

*Juan-Carlos is an angry, impish student at an inner-city junior high school. If he has fifty-two minutes to irritate the hell out of the substitute teacher he has for that period, and he has seventeen (Pablo, Haik, Mariette, Aram, Grigor, Jung-Ho, LaTonisha, LaRonisha, LaKaiesha, Elbert, Egbert, Annabella, Olga, Frank, Tsing-Tao, Chester, and Hector) of the twenty-seven students in his class willing to "help" him, how long will it take J-C and his friends to get the already edgy teacher to the point where he will lose his cool and start yodeling fervent obscenities at the gob-smacked class? Bonus points: do an imitation of the innocent-acting John-Carlos when the Principal is called and he is standing before the Man, as it were—even if the Man is in this case a woman, say, a squat, no-nonsense, shelf-titted matron of mature years and then some, a real old-timey battleaxe or gal-longshoreman.*

Just in case you're curious, let me give you an idea of the sort of thing that can happen on any given lovely inner-city junior high school day. One time, after the bell had rung for third period (a shrill, air raid-like sound that made you want to dive under any available desk nearly every time it sounded), there were these three kids parked right outside my classroom, loitering and trading jejune information in the loudest voices. (And speaking of loudness, have you ever heard a four-foot-five barrel-chested seventh grader burp? It's like the mating or warning call of a *sea lion* sometimes. It's like they're possessed by a fucking I-don't-*know*-what; by a belch-demon or burp-Kraken or something. In Spanish, for instance, there's not even a *name* for a belch! In Armenian, the word for belch is a commonplace Christian name . . . Okay, I think I made that shit up: no offense meant if your name means "burp" in your precious native language. I just remember a couple of Latino and Armenian kids ripping one right in my face after snack time and I am still pissed about it, okay? Can still taste the fetid air bubbles of stinky stench-breath.) I waited, nevertheless, a few minutes to see if one of the counselors or armed security guards who patrolled the halls would come along and sweep them back to class with threats of write-ups, detention, expulsion, nightsticks, mace, pepper spray, handcuffs, or shotguns. No go.

"Hey!" I said sharply, my head floating just outside the door. We're tryna take a test in here!"

"Sorry, mister," one hood said with what I thought was genuine contrition and looked down at the linoleum. They didn't seem so bad. They didn't seem too evil, despite the fact that one of them had a Boston Celtics t-shirt on.

Sacrilegious twatface traitor.

"Get back to class, okay?!"

What I'm really trying to say, I guess, is that the way one or another of them sometimes sort of mock-groaned and gave out a quaint half-moon of a smirky smile made you see the real kid in them sometimes, the still-innocent residua. But then, nine times out of ten, they went ahead and performed some sort of advanced hijinks on you and quashed any feeling of humanity you had left.

One, a tall black kid, very handsome and aware of it, smiled just such a smile just then, in fact, and whinged comically, in a quasi-British accent that was clearly meant to take the mickey out of *my* tone: "Oh, do we positively *have* to, mister?"

"Go on now."

I backed back into my class, thinking that now for sure they'd disperse somewhat peaceably? Negative. When I went back inside I could hear them yelling-talking in the hallway even more loudly than before, each voice straining to rise above the others, like runaway helium balloons in a race to the clouds.

I went back out and confronted them; now I was gonna have to be something of a dick, somewhat of a something I didn't exactly like to have to be, but would be if forced, as the case in question necessitated, Your Honor.

"Hey!" I said again, my voice sharp and firm and coachlike and not at all mockable, I thought. "Don't you guys have somewhere to be right now? A class or something?"

Questions that are suggestions never work with kids. Contemplating a crummy sarky answer's just gonna give them more time to waste yours.

"Nope," a white kid with a scary Afro quipped, popping the "p" in his impertinent, saucy, dissy answer with a humongous bubblegum bubble.

"If you want to talk so badly, why don't you go to the library like everyone else?"

"Ha! You funny, mister," the tall kid said.

"Yeah-yeah. Scram!"

As I stood there, arms akimbo, waiting for them to heed my almighty warning and split, the one with the big hair took the wad of pink gum from his fat mouth and flung it, the gumwad, right at me. And before I could dodge it or catch it and huck it back at his ass, the chunk stuck in my hair. *Then*, of course, they beat it, fanning out in different directions down the corridors, their respective black, white and yellow windbreaker jackets flapping like the wings of the frightening flying monkeys in *The Wizard of Oz*.

Laughter. Riotous, trebly laughter. But not as fierce and mortifyingly horrid or heartless as the laughs that, once I went back into my class with a clump of Double Bubble the size of a seventh-grader's brain attached to the side of my head, issued forth from the kiddies in Room Thirty-Something. God did they laugh at that. They were already in a more-than–excitable mood: four or five of them had leprechauned from behind their desks and were javelining paper airplanes and pencils towards each other's heads and necks. One runt had the breasts of a hyper-developed girl with braces strangleheld in his hand-bra hands, in fact, but he set her and her boobs free when I gave him a stern scowl (that must also have been a look of incredulous, thus disgusted, wonderment).

I sat down at the teacher's desk and calmly, as they continued dashing around their seats, pointing at me like little Brueghelesque villagers in a harrowing fairy tale, took out a pair of *tijeras* and cut the offending confection out right in front of them.

That shut them up. I imagine I would have stunned them even more had I pushed the stupid hairy gumglob into my mouth just then; but I really wasn't willing to go that far in the realm of intimidation and personal scariness. Didn't need to: cutting my own hair was ballsy, tweaked, theatrical, unexpected and downright bizarre enough to get them to return to their seats and keep quiet for at least twenty minutes.

## take me to the other side

Here's the drill: when I first arrive at a school, I check in at Administration, give them my pastel blue LA Unified School District I.D. card, receive verification, get receipt, get room number, hustle over.

What do they think, though—that someone would voluntarily impersonate a substitute, just to be among schoolchildren of this ilk? What all subs *should* receive when they first turn up is extreme unction, or at least Excedrin.

Please! I could picture someone forging something or impersonating someone in order to get *out* of an LA school, but not to get into one. No, sir. Not even the true believer in *To Sir, With Love* or Edward James Almos's character in that film with him as a teacher/burger-slinger, the name of which I can't remember.

Dude! (A useless, offensive, sensibility-scraping, not-awesome word I *never* use!) No matter what school I report to—J. James Junior or G. Gilmore Senior or J. W. Gaby Middle—it seems I am quote-unquote welcomed straightaway by a woman who sports pink or pink 'n' blue cat's eyes. On her head it seems she's wearing a bushy Busby, size XL. I try real real hard to keep my jaw shut, to gulp down a *grande* laugh. Not at her, mind you, but at myself for getting so very carried away I envision giving her a coiffing with a chainsaw. I succeed in stifling that laugh, this snort-giggle, but I am sure my eyes, big as those swirly supersized lollies you buy at Disneyland, give me away. *You* buy at Disneyland, that is. Can you imagine me at Disneyland? The *un*happiest place on earth?

Lady Frontdesksby then hands me a note left by the regular teacher, and directs me vaguely to my classroom. Her voice evokes a shop-class table saw on overdrive. Her arms are bratwurst-colored jelly. She sounds like an actress who might have auditioned for the Nurse Ratched part in *One Flew over the Cuckoo's Nest* and was turned away for being too over the top. She's in that 45 to 50 range that doesn't look a day over 60.

Yes this is the lower circle of Hell itself, but Dante on his best day dreaming up the *Inferno* could never have foreglimpsed what awaits grimly pilgrimish *me*.

First, the teacher's note, in virtual cuneiform:

*Dear Substitute Teacher:*

*First of, I welcome you to Room 666! I have told the students' that you were going to be hear today, so they already have there assignment. Try to cover page 12-13. There are two stories of a pony. They may not know what that is so try and go ahead and tell them something from your own experience with ponies to tell them about. Most of, have a good day!*

*Signed, Mrs. Aurora Clotho*

*P.S. Most of the kids are behaved, but some are not so. If Juan-Carlos trys to stir up troublemaking, give him a Referral Slip and sent him to the counselloring office. One good student and nice is Julio, but he has been absent due to a broken arm, in three places.*

Christ-on-a-pony! After lunch, before the students come in from the playgrounds and lunchgrounds I carefully correct Mrs. Clotho's note with a spluttering red pen. At the bottom of the page, in my most fastidious hand, I scratch: "*Dear Mrs. C: Thank you for your helpful missive. Sincerely, Mr. Subkins P.S. I am going to try and have you fired. I compliment you on the superb hendiadys re: Julio, however—nice one. I hope you can* read *this.*"

And titter to myself.

Yes I titter, but that is about the only amusement I will have this, or any other, teeth-pulling, hair-grinding substituting day.

The junior high mornings are comparatively placid; the afternoons, unmitigated heinous pain, the fifth period, the one right after lunch, being the absolute worst. The boys and girls are all amped up on bolted lunches of sugar-and-starch and have been racing around the playground, so they're primed and ready to roar like high formula racing cars. They are Nitro. They are pistons. Perspirate urchins every one. The joys of littering, playing tag, defacing school property with knives, rocks, spray cans, magic markers, balls, bats, blowtorches, and cat o' nine tails, and generally gooning around have been too much for them. They cannot help it. Even the most docile, childlike, innocent-eyed milk-carton poster-child seventh or eighth-grader is, after a repast of chocolate-frosted mondo-pretzels, coke, corn chips, pizza, a candy bar, another coke and an ice-cream-free ice-cream sandwich, a hyperactive, pogoing dynamo.

And that's just the stuff they serve on the school-lunch program. If the kid opts for some extracurricular snacks—look out.

And oh the smells. In Oakland Raiders overcoats and mechanic jackets legions of them have disported themselves in the inner-city heat; woe to me, who sits downwind. Not to mention the overpowering barbecue flavoring on their breath, the brazen clouds of stentorian flatulence they trail. Even the torpid ones, the ones who at lunch merely toast themselves in the hot sun, the wheezebys and fatsos parked on orange benches, the metabolism-defiant beanburger eaters and chunky chocoholics, can pong like the dickens after thirty-five minutes of hyperactive inactivity.

I am olfactorily afflicted.

Every day I hope to exercise the patience of a Sadhu but end up displaying the temper of a Viking on a long, dark, merciless berserker. Maybe, I think, I should ask for History more often: I could use myself for show-and-tell! i am the crusader in the alien land, a lone Roman garrisoned in a fortress surrounded by menacing Scottish wilderness. I am the knight avenger, the irate revolutionary, the solo frontier guy in the fringy buckskins and boots and coonskin cap who jumps at every noise that comes from the sleepless, tenebrous forest. I am the last White Russian crouching behind a blasted cinderblock as the Bolshies crunch in drunken bunches over the dirty snow. I am the peeping-from-the-parapet French foreign legionnaire, expecting any second that his *tremoussant* kepi will be scimitared impeccably or rifle-shot right off. Am the twitchy corporal in filthy pith helmet, peering from behind a wind-huffed tent or warily around a Bodhi tree, his rifle describing figure-eights in the cruel blue Punjab sky, awaiting any moment a blue-painted horde of Jai-crying Hindus, ululating Mohammedans, or a peckish, springing tiger. I am I am I am I am the lice-laden, pistol-packing, Sam Browne–belted second lieutenant in the rotten, sodden trenches of western France, wetting the whistle in his mouth with minimal spittle, rat guts on his boot soles, smoke in his beard and his nostrils, quaking like anything before he sends the boys over the irrefragable top, his tin hat like an overboiled teapot, a knock-kneed nervous bleeding bloody bally wreck. I want to be like the "defeated" Emily Dickinson singularly referenced in her poems—the givers-up Boy Tolstoy and Shakey knew so well; I want to "sit upon the ground and tell sad stories of the death of kings"; I want to sit down on an LA roadside curbside, with the LA cars thundering by on their LA way to wherever and *weep*.

I want to be Proust in his cork-lined room.

I want to go back to Mommy's womb.

I want to lie down and sleep in a tomb.

I want to go home and sleep till noon.

If I were inclined to count the number of times I say "*Please* be quiet!" or "*Close* up that switchblade this *in*stant!" or "Please put away *all* Uzis!" I would probably need a calculator designed by NASA or JPL. Almost all day I look like someone has carefully cut up Munch's most famous painting, made a mask of it, and masking-taped it tourniquet-tight to my already fucking frantic face.

You think I'm kidding. I'm kind of not. I picture them, the children of the future, with halberds and mauls and flails, morning stars and quarterstaffs, cat-o'-nine-tails and maces and bludgeons and pitchforks; claymores, broadswords, and other medieval weapons I just looked up on Wikipedia.

The high school sitch is quite different, much more mellow—well, mostly. All the high school kids wanna know is if you are going to leave them alone to gossip, stare into space, braid, brush or dreadlock or play with one another's hair. They want never-ending passes to the bathroom so they can have a secret smoke or talk about boys or girls; they just wanna not be fucked with till it's time to go home. They want to put their heads down on their desks and go to sleep.

I can relate to them.

Right away they want to know if their regular teacher has had the beneficent foresight to schedule a video for them to watch. Usually the more violent the film the more tractable the class. But if the regular teach has left a VHS of, say, *Jude the Obscure* or *The Mayor of Casterbridge*—look round, mate! Look round for flying yardsticks and globes or zinging 9V batteries, jawbreakers, jellybeans, jellyrolls, jujubes, stones, fists, spitballs, javelins, radios, televisions, overhead projectors, short kids.

Nevertheless, at least at the high schools you could get some reading done: I always kept somewhere in the car an extra copy of my favorite book, Boswell's *Life of Johnson*, to bring with me to read during quieter periods or at least at lunch time.

One day I caught two rude bullyboys in the locker room (I had P.E.) who were trying to wrap the American flag like a diaper round the loins of an innocent nerd/sissy with a visage like one of those—I swear to God—gag nose-and-glasses dealies, one of those Grouchoesque or Woody Allenish disguises. I almost peed my pants laughing; I couldn't *help* it. I'm already delirious with wariness and wonderment when I'm subbing, and sometimes stuff like that just tickles my funny bone with a mega-sized feather duster and I bust up like mad. It's the worst when one of the full-timers catches me essentially aiding and abetting some juvie tomfoolery. I almost wanted to *help* them haze the poor Poindexter. Shoulder the creeps aside and go "Here, this is how it's done—I should know: it was done to *me* more than once."

This job has made me one sick fuck—don't think I don't know that.

I'm fucked up, for sure, but kids are more cruel than any innovative Turkish or Chinese dreamer-upper of torture devices. I will never forget Chip Dorset and Will Wallace, two of the hulking stars on my eighth grade B-ball team, those heroes of tallness and premature brawn and braceless teeth! Pretty observant were they, too! They noticed right away when my mom let me make the big transition from Y-fronts to boxers: a very big deal in a young boy's life. And Chip and Will celebrated along with me one afternoon after practice by lifting me up by the chones till my proud brand new plaid boxer underwear was torn to shreds and around my neck like a turtleneck, or a wimple, or a dickie.

What *guys!* Immense! Shall never forget them!

And here I am again—*in* junior high again in more than one way.

Think about the ambiguity.

I believe in God and all, I really do, and Jesus-Buddha-Krishna-Allah too, but sometimes I have to question the motivations of a Supreme Being who could make a) sharks; b) crocodiles; c) famines; d) plagues, herpes and the like; and e) thirteen- through eighteen-year-olds. What's up with that, Your Godness? What in your Glorious and Supreme Wisdom were you thinking? Jesus, sometimes I don't think You think at all. You really should pull Your head out of your Royal All-Powerful ass once in a while, Dear Our Father—I mean, You're supposed to be able to do anything, right? Be all All-Powerful and shit? Like turn ice cream back into snowflakes or bring me back the supergirl I lost in college? Tell the time on Jupiter at will and stand on Your Holy head for a zillion thousand trillion days? Hey, Lord! Is it all just one big joke to You? Are You just like those other gods, the ones who were cackling at me earlier? I certainly hope not; I hope You in Your Immense Immensity are better than that, I really fucking do. I hope you are. I pray about it, actually.

In class, then, any attempts on my part to *teach* anything, to *read from a text* and *illustrate with examples*, to *discuss* things seriously, and even *write a paragraph* or two about them, are greatly frowned upon.

Snarled upon, rather.

The texts have all mysteriously disappeared anyway. "We don't *got* no texts for this class, mister sir," say; or, "Well, we *had* some books but Randolph here [they point at a woefully shy sophomore or seventh-grader with pitted, piebald skin and a keg-like gut and Michelin-neck]—you ain't gonna believe this, mister, but Randolph, well, he done went and *ate* all the books! He went and-a ate 'em!" I swallow the same laugh that they bellow. They can be the funniest fucks on earth. They probably have to develop an excellent sense of humor, most of them, on account of all the inner city shit that swirls around them every ever-loving living day. I try not to look at the poor sap, poor Randolph, and take part in the ridicule party that's happening. If I do, I just know that I will picture him, Randolph or whoever, munching on a tasty copy of *The Diary of Anne Frank* or *The Scarlet Letter*, maybe licking his fingers and smacking his lips between chomps, and I will lose it and hugely and the kids will take even more advantage of me than the advantageous advantage they already do take. Daily.

And yet. And yet. Every so often I'll realize that my compassion and empathy and human goddam feeling has not been entirely sandpapered and turpentined by this job as, smiling to myself, I notice some sweet-cheeked angel-face with her brown black red blonde or blue-haired head bent over her pencil or pen and a sheet of ready paper and a happyish, determined look on her sweet visage as she tries, amidst the *Cirque du Soleil* of mischief she's in the midst of, to do some work, to get something academic done. I'll go over, all curiosity, all encouragement, with the best of intentions and even a touch of excitement, and bend my head over her desk—only to find she's drawing an angel being rogered by a demon with a wang like a pitchfork. Or she's sketched a crude caricature of *me*: all beak or with a superchin, with vestigial fangs and horns and tail and testicles for eyes and a hairy dick for a schnozz. At least she's drawn me riding on a cool motorcycle (but it's on fire, heading for a wall of brick, or for a forestation of dicks).

Invariably in the course of the day a kid will comment callously on my unkempt appearance (I never, band rehearsals or no, get enough sleep nor enough, as you've witnessed, time in the morning to wake/shake myself up). Executing a sort of St Vitus Dance as he or she does so, said imp will without compunction come up to my desk and say: "You sure are nappy, mister! A *nasty* ass sight! Don't your momma never iron your clothes? Did you go sleep in them shits last night? Look like. You shouldn't party so hearty, mister. You a bad one, I's can tell . . ."

Or he will coyly gauge my probably hung over state of mind and, putting his or her mossy teeth on glorious show, ask me if I am feeling okay, if I am sick or something on account of I look yellow or like "death's self."

They can verbally abuse me as much as they want. There's nothing I can do about it. However, if the offending kid in question is Armenian, I will answer in Spanish; if African-American, French; if Russian, in the voice of a deaf person; if Asian, with a very blank look; if Latino, with an exaggerated Indian accent, complete with lisp; if Caucasian, a sneer. Some of these little ghouls have zilch compunction, boy.

Yet none of this will assuage me.

And contrary to what you might think, given that I have told you many of the kids are big and angry and armed with something, I am not all that afraid of them. Not all that scared. I *should* be, I know, but I'm not. I even fight back a little bit sometimes. It all depends. Occasionally, however, the culprit in question will be six-five, two-sixty—an eighteen-year-old eighth-grader. Him (or her) I will not antagonize. Before him or her I will quail.

I mean, I'm not an *idiot*.

In the hallways and byways and corridors and playgrounds and on the way to the grownups' cafeteria, I will never forget to put on my Clark Kents: the likelihood of a finger in the eye from a jumping-jacking tyrohood is very great. The hot food they serve in the caff I would not throw to a starving hound. I eat my apple, purchase perhaps a lardy, pallidly underbaked biscuit and maybe some orange juice and try, as I sit at an, I hope, unoccupied table, to look as evil mean nasty surly sour offputting unfriendly and unapproachable as possible. It isn't difficult. I fairly dare the other subs and teachers and admin people to address me.

At times, however, they are unstoppable zombies. I try to be nice, I try to be sweet, but it's just too onerous a task. They just will not take a hint or a hike.

"Hey?" one (weak chin, strong breath) comes up and says. "Anyone sitting here? How's it going?"

"Fine. You know."

"Yeah, I hear ya. You a sub?"

"Uh-huh."

"Me too."

(Here I might gargle something in response, choking a bit on the biscuit or apple.)

"How long you been doing this?"

"Just started two months ago."

"Really? I am just coming back to it after a break for a while. After rehab, that is."

"Oh?"

"Yeah. Alcohol. Heroin. Sex. The hat trick, huh."

"Interesting. Listen: nice meeting you but I have to . . ."

"The only way, back in the day, I could really deal with the kids was to be strung out on smack."

"Wow," I manage.

"Yeah—it was getting pretty out of control. So, though: what else are you doing? Aside from subbing, I mean. You're an actor, right? I'm only saying that 'cause you look like a guy that's in my improv class. *Aren't* you? Aren't you an actor as well?"

(And here you can picture me going all shades of crimson and flinching and shaking my head 'cause I know that this guy's an actor himself and thus all he wants to talk about is him. Wasn't it D.W. Griffith or David O. Selznick or Yogi Berra who famously/wonderfully said "*An actor is a guy—you ain't talkin' about him, he ain't listenin'*?)

"No."

"Come on: I have seen ya somewhere. Haven't I seen you in some production or other?"

"I don't think so, mate. I have a strong, wholly irrational and quite healthy prejudice against actors, actually."

"Oh, me too! I do as well!"

"That's what all actors say."

"I have definitely seen you somewhere, though. You're in one of the classes on Fountain, I'll bet."

(I think it was Hitchcock who famously said—aside from the bit about them being "cattle"—that they should either be brilliant or just really stupid and malleable. Why do you imagine I am bringing this up right here? Maybe it was Blake Edwards. Can't remember. Brain *going* from dredging up this painful memory, I think.)

"No."

"I thought you really might be. I'm in theater myself. Exclusively. Want no part of the film thing. No, sir. I'm just subbing—you know—just till I get my . . . just to pay the bills. For now. *You* know."

"That's great. Hey, I have to . . ."

"You must be a mu*si*cian then!"

(My patience is now officially tried. And found guilty. Can't take this any more. Calls for drastic tactics. I might even have to excuse myself in order to get a drink of water from one of the decidedly unpotable water-spewing drinking fountains.)

"Musician?" I wonder aloud. "Nah. I do this 'cause I just love the kids, you know? I think teaching is just the noblest profession, you know? There's something about being around all these fresh minds, so eager to learn, that is such a *buzz*, you *know?*"

After an answer like that I'll surely be left alone. That fixes 'em. The other sub will look at me askance, like I am nosebleeding or gotta stigmata—like I am some kind of deluded, maniacal bonkersmeister. Then he'll mutter something and skim up his puke-green tray and port it far far away to the other side of the room.

Somehow, some way, I make it through the day. When the last bell rings at 3:10 (the last ten minutes go by far the slowest—for that's when you are most aware of time and how, if you are too aware of it, it seems to crawl like an wounded giant sloth), I scream past the kids in the halls and back to Administration in order to pick up an opalescent hours slip and my pale blue LA Unified I.D. My days as a prep school not exactly star but *participant* certainly come into play here as I hurdle, triple jump, high jump and one-hundred-yard dash my way to the parking lot. Then, semi-safely belted and locked into the good old Volvo, I try to make it out the gates before a galumphing cavalcade of urchins blocks my path. They are on their merry way to loiter somewhere where they can safely throw bricks or books through windows, take switchblades to trees or bus benches and spray cans to each other's faces, insufflate glue till they horf, or cadge a Forty from a trusty, drunken bum or grasping mercenary vagrant.

I know what you're thinking. You're thinking that surely I am being too illiberal and cynical. That there must be some youngsters who, after school, are going home to do homework or bake cookies for the poor, volunteer at an old folks' home, or shoot or weave innocuous baskets on church playgrounds.

Okay: maybe fifteen or twenty fill that bill. Twenty-some-odd tops—out of the close to one million seventh thru twelfth-graders in the greater LA area.

Happy now?

In a fury, in a frenzy, I motor down surface streets towards the freeway entrance. The bright yellow St Christopher that depends from my rear-view mirror swings wildly as I maneuver past bumps, earthquake cracks, and pits in the road large enough to conceal a minor dinosaur. When I get home (of course Jaz is still asleep—he doesn't get up till 5 p.m.) I put on some low, droney, comfortingly one-or-two chord-employing music like Spacemen 3 or Loop and begin *the drinking process*, pushing aside the veritable science project in the fridge in quest of beer. I must have a beer. I must.

I used to be the sort of person—even in college—who prided himself on never needing to have a drink: not when a friend died while on mushrooms in the Sierras (yes, a brown bear was involved) or when I didn't get in to Yale or Harvard grad schools (I should have at least applied), or when I was told I had advanced chlamydia or when Mary McNulty McCartney told me, two days after we split up after going out all of Senior year, that she was engaged to St John "Sinjin" Overstreet, the captain of the volleyball team and a guy who'd blackballed me from his frat (one I never even rushed 'cause I rushed zero frats, okay?). Drinking is/was recreational. Now it's mandatory. A required course. A prerequisite to getting over the day I've had and working up my nerve for the one to come. Drinking prevents me from thinking very murderous thoughts. From committing suicide or from something potentially worse than suicide: thinking about my life: its emptiness, its bathos, as, on a daily basis, it dawns on me that I have made a most untoward quote-unquote career choice.

I'm not talking about getting plastered—though that does happen, usually around Thursday or Friday (okay, Wednesday, and a lot); I'm talking a couple of beers. Talls. *Always* talls. And, if we have it, a shot or three of tequila. Then a margarita. And just one or two more before a couple of beers and half a pack of cigarettes.

But that's *it*. *Es todo*.

I'm kidding. Just having fun. Having a beer while I write this, too. Hope *you* are too, dear dear reader.

## psycho killer, qu'est-ce que c'est?

When the phone rang an hour or so after I'd gotten home of course I was hoping it was Jenny. I'd been thinking about her a lot, obviously, and I was looking very forward to talking to her again.

"Hello?"

"Buddy!"

It was Psycho, Jaz's and my psychotic friend—as you may have gleaned from his immemorial nickname.

"Hey! The Psychster! Haven't heard from you in a while. What's *up*, Psycho! Glad you rang. Whatcha been doing?"

Before I recount the rest of our doubtless fascinating conversation, let me tell you a little about ole Psych. A magna cum laude grad of Harvard (and later Ph.D. from Cal Tech), Psycho could potentially make much money in either of his chosen fields: thermonuclear dynamics and chemical *and* mechanical engineering. Yeah, he was kinda bright. But instead of going to work for the U.S. government or the Pentagon (same diff) he compromised the hell out of himself and got a kickback job inventing types of and running tests on types of mouthwash and toothpaste.

For testing toothpastes, mouthwashes, plaque-removers, flosses, choppers-whiteners and brighteners and various odd-shaped toothbrushes he was paid $95,000 a year, plus all the dental hygiene products and paraphernalia he wanted.

He was a couple of years younger than we were—twenty-four—and to think of his salary made starving non-students Jaz and me very very ill: as though we'd *chugged* half a bottle apiece (they came in one size—family size) of the cinnamon-flavored mouthrinse Psychster brought over *every time he came to visit*. Jaz started stopping him at the door and making him plump the dumb things on the lanai; our below-the-sink cupboard was groaning with the stuff. Jaz even in a fit of magnanimity and maybe *suggestion* gave Marie two bottles, but it turned out she drank them, thinking she'd been apportioned wine.

Psycho was one of those gregarious guys you can't remember how you met them. Jaz swore up and down we'd met him at a bar, which was probable. But I was convinced (sort of) that he'd been first encountered at some beach party, which was equally likely 'cause we went to a quantity of those. We puzzled ourselves over it all the time.

He, Psycho, had the wild-eyed look of someone who'd been beaten as a child. Actually, he had the wild-eyed look of someone who'd been *shot at* as a child, if you ask me. I could picture his dad standing him William Tell-style up against a tree and potting at him with Psycho's own Daisy BB gun. I don't know why, really: that's just how I pictured him—being plinked at.

Psycho liked to spend many of his piece-of-cake ducats on alcoholic beverages. He also liked to drive around in what he called the VRC ("Very Red Convertible"—a faggy Miata) and look for things that would be good to blow up. He had an absolutely unquenchable yen for blowing things up, a real lust for it. Even though we never actually saw him blow anything up, the way he talked about how beautiful it would be to explode, say, an armadillo or a medium-sized gas station or swimming pool, made us think his pyromaniacal desires were highly achievable.

Aside from digging fireworks displays of all flavors, darting around in the VRC, and laughing as he brought over untold quantities of unwanted mouthwash (one bottle every six months was enough), Psycho also loved to go out and look for girls, go bird-dogging.

You have no idea, no matter what rank of bird-dog you count among your horn-dog acquaintance, how much Psycho loved going out and looking for girls. The more he got shot down the more he wanted to get back on the pony, so to speak. No one could credit it.

"Buddy!" Psycho said. "Know what night it is?"

One thing I really liked about him was he didn't exactly waste your or his time with pleasantries or small talk. He got right down to it—whatever it was he wanted to get right down to.

"Uh, sure, Psycho."

"Monday night. Monday fuckin' *night*."

"Uh-huh."

"Do you know what kind of night Monday night is, Johnny? Any *idea?*"

You had to play dumb with him, let him get all wound up: "No, what?"

"Monday night, bud, is the perfect night to . . ."

But sometimes you couldn't resist: "Go out and look for girls?"

"What? Is that all you think I think about, bud? Is that all there is to me? Ah, I'm just kidding you, man. Of course I'm calling you up to see if you wanna go out bird-dogging! Of course that's what I'm seeing if you wanna do. Are you with me? Do you and I think alike or what? You are thinking exactly what I was thinking if you were thinking of going out and looking for *chicks* tonight, old sport. We have got to hit some bars tonight, man. Monday night is the *perfect* night to . . ."

"I can't, Psycho."

"What?! Why not?"

I told Psycho that, no, I could not go and look for girls.

*I would not go and look for girls.*

*I would not, could not go tonight.*

*I would not go—it was not right.*

*I could not go and look for girls.*

*I would not go and look for girls.*

*Girls with curls or girls without.*

*Girls all smiles or girls with pouts.*

*I would not go this Monday night.*

*Perhaps I would some other night.*

*Psycho, Psycho—yes, that's right.*

*I would not go tonight, tonight.*

*I would not feel that it was right.*

"That's cool," Psych said coolly. But I could tell he was way disappointed. I consoled him with the prospect of going some other time, this upcoming weekend maybe.

"Okay, then. All right. I will hold you to that, Johnny boy. I will call you at my convenience."

"Okay," I laughed and said goodbye.

During the spectacular riots in Los Angeles following the infamous Rodney King incident (ah, no *wonder* the kids spazzed so bad—it hadn't been that long since), Psycho, instead of cowering under a couch duck-and-covering in a closet like most white people, had on purpose driven round the worst-hit areas of the city (he'd followed the news on TV—like everyone else). Top down on the VRC, videotaping the most splendiferously smithereened and still-smouldering buildings and cars, the ones in brilliant flames or crackling mesmerizingly as any hearth—Psycho had born witness to some of the most colorful crimes-in-progress. Little old men hilariously Sherpa-ing new refrigerators, stoves, and freezers on their backs. Washers and dryers too. Vandals Molotov-cocktailing down the middle of major boulevards; a keystone cops of overturned cars and buses and people queuing up to take turns marauding high-dollar stereo stores and photography equipment outlets. He showed the footage to us afterwards like it was a prize home movie. You had to love Psycho. He must have figured that the rioting inhabitants of South Central Los Angeles would be too stunned at the sight of a bantam-sized overeducated white guy driving cackling like a sanatorium-escapee through the war zone to go and shoot at him. What a sight he must have been: chem-lab goggles on, Stewart tartan golf cap stuck on backwards-like, video camera humming, long crimson-and-white-striped scarf pennanting tremendously behind him, brilliant flashy polished sparkly über-teeth, hands-free steering wheel on account of he could easily drive with his knees, the VRC was so compactish.

He was out of his mind, Psycho.

You had to love him.

But that didn't mean you had to hang out with him drinking on a Monday night, a school night, on account of (as I told you) I had a two-day assignment at Arnold Jr. I was exhausted. I had to be up early again to face the monsters. They might be even worse on a Tuesday—who knew? There was just no telling.

And besides, I was thinking I would check in with Jenny. I hung up the phone and got ready to call her when the bell trilled again right away.

Psycho.

"Bud!"

"Hey up, Psycho—thought it might be you again."

"Buddy?"

"Yes?"

"Let me tell you something. Do you realize what weekend nights at bars are for? Amateurs, that's who. *Week*nights, bud—those are the nights you wanna go out on and get stupid and wake up the next day feeling horrible on—hopefully with someone naked and female. That's what weeknights are for. Whatdayasay?"

"What I already said, Psycho: no. Negative."

"Ah, Johnny, come on! Let's go get totaled! Let's go get in a wreck, okay? Come on, man."

"Too burnt."

"Lemme ask you something. Lemme ask you one thing. One fucking thing."

"Shoot."

"What is the first and foremost weeknight there is?"

"Too rhetorical."

"Monday, did you say? Monday night. Monday fucking night."

"And so?"

"That's tonight, buddy. Tonight."

"That's a total tautology, Dave."

(I only used his given name when I was about to be in high dudgeon with him—which didn't happen much, or at all, *really*, 'cause he amused me no end. But this was getting to be too much.)

"Of course I know that, but I really wanna go out and look for some trouble tonight, okay? It'll be pretty easy to find. You go out Monday night, you get a jump on all the other suckers who wait till, like, Wednesday to go out and look for chicks—don't you get what I'm saying here? What are you doing tonight anyway—watching television and masturbating?"

"You know I don't watch TV, Psychster."

"Ha! Then you admit you masturbate."

"Well of course, Psycho. Of course. I'm touching myself right now at the sound of your soft, purry East Coast voice. It just . . ."

"Cut that out, man! You know how fag stuff freaks me out! Stop it. Seriously, though: what are you going to do tonight instead of what you *should* be doing which is going out and looking for girls with me?"

"God, I don't know, Psych. Reading a little. Playing guitar. Calling this girl. Organizing some dinner . . ."

"Hold it right there!" he said. "Girl? What girl? Really? Who? Who is she?"

Psycho was really into girls in every way—not just going out and looking for them, but obsessing about them as well, thinking about, talking about, dreaming about, seeing them in magazines and on television, just about everything about them. He got mega-excited whenever they came up in conversation, and they tended to come up quite a bit.

"Just this girl I met," I sighed. "She's our drummer's roommate."

"Okay, okay . . . *And?* What's she look like? She any cute?"

"Yes, very, actually. Auburn hair. Nice face. Very cute, in fact."

"Really? Damn! She's pretty good-*look*ing, eh? And you're gonna call her up?"

"*Yes*, Psycho."

"Tonight?"

"*Yes*, Psycho! Now if you don't *mind* I gotta . . ."

"Does she have any friends? Any friends you can set your old pal Psycho up with?"

"What? Oh, I don't know. I just met her, all right? There might be some. I'm not sure. I sort of met one the other day. I don't know though; she just moved here not too long ago."

"What?! She's fully friendless or something?"

"Yeah."

"You're kidding me, right?"

"Yeah. Look, Dave: I don't know her very well. I just *met* her, okay? Like I *told* you. Like I said."

"Well, she's gotta have some friends, man. She must. She can't be just some pariah or something if she's any cute. She's *got* to have some friends—some *babe* friends. I mean, this is California. This is why I came *out* here, okay?"

"Her friends' name was Wendy . . . Sandy or something . . . I don't know, Psychster. Listen: I really need to . . ."

"Now we're getting somewhere! Here we go. What's the deal with this Sandy, then? Is she any cute at all? That's *definitely* the name a cute girl could have and everything, Sandy. Definitely."

I could picture him drooling. Rubbing his hands together. I could just see him licking his chops. It made me laugh to think of him that way, getting all revved up for someone he'd never even heard of before. I was, I dare say, very fond of Psycho—I got a very big kick out of him. But that didn't stop me from winding him up as much and as often as possible. I got an even bigger kick sometimes out of fucking with his head. He never let you get off the phone till *he* was going to get off the phone. Never.

"Yeah, they were out biking around Hancock Park when I met this

Sandy chick."

"On bikes?"

For a brilliant genius Psycho was pretty thick sometimes; I think it was just that he couldn't think straight when the thought of chicks popped into his superbrain.

"Uh-huh."

"Biking, eh?"

"I just said that, Dave. I just told you . . ."

"Man, I fucking love a chick on a bike, dude. With their long legs all pumping and stuff? I love that. Short bike shorts all hiked up and everything. *Man*, do I love that. Don't you just love that? God, I love that shit. What's she look like, the friend of this chick you're calling up, huh, Johnny? Just gimme a little description of her, is all."

"She looked like a troll, okay? Green hair. No teeth. Four foot five. Munchkin voice. One eye. Cyclopsy, in fact. *I* don't know, Psycho. Could you please . . ."

"Seriously, John. Don't fuck around here."

"Psycho, I honestly don't remember. I really like this Jenny girl. In fact she jammed with us the other . . ."

"Does this Sandy chick have a boyfriend?"

"Oh my God . . ."

"Find *out*, you fucker. I just know she's some little cutie and you're holding out on me, man. Some little *fox* with pert high breasts and a nice round . . ."

"No one says 'fox,' Psycho," I said wearily.

"What?! *I* do. "

"Okay, you do. I'll ask, okay? I really don't know this girl all that well, though. What am I gonna say: 'Hey, Jenny—does your friend have a boyfriend? Cause if not I'd like to set her up with my psycho friend Psycho?'"

"Yeah well maybe you better wait a bit on that," Psycho said after a bit of a pregnant pause.

"No kidding."

"Seriously, though. Find out about her friends," Psycho said; then, changing tack, he went: "Aw, forget it. Girls always think their friend is cute when they're really not. They always go: 'Oh you just *have* to meet *Kathy* (or whoever)—she's *so* pretty. I really wanna introduce you to her. She's adorable. She wants to meet you too!' and you show up and they're, like, a monster. Just a beast or something, I'm telling you."

"Why is that, anyway?" I laughed.

"I don't know. How should I know? You west coast fucks seem to think that . . ."

"Wait a minute, Psycho. Why are you dragging geography into the discussion here? I mean . . ."

"You west coast fucks don't have that problem nearly as much as we do back east. There are so many girls here, John. So many. I can't even believe it sometimes. Are you sure you don't wanna go out tonight a do some serious Monday night bird-dogging?"

"I told you . . ."

"Here's my theory. Ready? Chicks want their friends, no matter how I-wouldn't-fuck-her-with-*your*-dick ugly, to be considered cute 'cause if their friend is cute then they will be, like, Cindy Fucking Crawford or something."

"That's so cynical, though, Dave."

"Ya think?"

"For sure."

"Oh well: you gotta be somethin' these days, though, dontcha? And cynical's just as good as any ideology, as far as I can tell."

I smiled into the phone.

"So anyway," Psych went on; "this fabulous girl you're gonna call—what's her name anyway?"

"Jenny."

"Jenny, huh?"

"Uh, yeah," I said sort of warily.

You see, the thing with the Psychster was he had this thing where, when you were telling him about a girl you just met at a party or somewhere, well, he'd find out from you her whole name and they he'd find a way to tell you that he'd quote-unquote already slept with her. "Michelle McFarlane?" he'd say, all nonchalant and everything. "Did I hear you say 'Michelle McFarlane?' You're kidding, right? I know her. Jesus, *I* went out with Michelle McFarlane. I went out with *her*. Incredible in bed, actually. A total goer."

Then he'd laugh like the villain character in an old-timey radio play, deep and long and wickedly.

Of course then you'd tell him to cut it out, that no Michelle McFarlane type would ever even give him the time of day, and blah blah blah.

Then he'd shut up for a bit.

But you never knew, really. There was always some little lingering doubt that somehow, some way, he had known Michelle McFarlane or whoever. And maybe even got something quote-unquote off her. You never knew with Psycho.

"So here name's Jenny, yeah? Jenny what?" Psycho went on.

"Dave! I'm going now, okay? We're gonna wake up Jaz here."

"Well, this Jenny—if she doesn't have a last name or any *friends* she'd better have some *breasts*, okay? Are they pretty big or what? Pretty nice-sized?"

There was no getting him off the horn sometimes if you didn't just play along with him: "Yeah, okay. She has great tits."

"I knew it, man. I *knew* it. God, I love boobs. Some *big* old breasts. You know I do."

His big laugh honked over the line. I was laughing at him too. Some people, they have the sort of laugh that makes you laugh when you hear it. You're not laughing at anything that's happened or has been said; you're laughing at a laugh. The Scather was like that too. On the other hand, there's laughter killers too. I mean, you should hear the effect Walter's hee-hawing guffaws have on a roomful of roisterers: chilling.

"Yeah, well, I'm not one of your breast men, actually."

"Are you serious, John? You're not into them? God, I love big tits. Tremendously."

"Really?" I said sarcastically. "You do?"

"You have no idea. So: what about her face—tell me about that, then."

"I already told you, Psych-o. I gotta hang up now."

"And you're gonna call her right now, you say? You're calling her tonight?"

"Yes!"

"Fuck *that*, man. Fucking call her some other time. She'll appreciate it a lot more if you wait. Take my advice. A lot more. Girls hate it when you are, like, hounding them all the time. They do not like that shit at all. They hate it."

"Uh-huh."

"I'm serious, Johnny. I'm not fucking around here. Don't call her tonight. There's gotta be some mystery about it. Some suspense involved. You gotta James *Bond* her a little bit. You gotta make her *want* you, dude. So let's go out tonight and get in some trouble instead, okay? Let's just go have around *one* hundred drinks and that way you will be prevented from making a big mistake here!"

"Oh my God, Psycho, you are too insane," I laughed. "You ought to go into sales instead of research—you could make a mint. And besides, girls hate it if *you* are hounding them all the time. They like houndage from *me*."

"Funny. That's a laugh, Johnny. And speaking of making mints, I already do. So there. You know that. In fact, I'm buying tonight, so meet me at Casa Escobar in around twenty minutes. It's not like I'm proud of it or anything. I just majored—unlike you guys, you and Jaz—in the right major in college, that's all. I feel bad for you arty types, I really do."

"Thank you," I said. "On behalf of all of us, thank you."

"Aw, come on, John. You know I'm only putting you on. And that wasn't very nice to say girls don't want me to hound them, by the way."

"I'm only kidding you, Psycho. You do have a tendency to treat them like breasts-on-wheels, though. You must admit *that*."

"What?!" he said. "You don't think I treat chicks right? You don't think I treat them well? I do! I treat girls like fucking *queens*."

"*Dairy* Queens."

"Oh man. Fuck *you*."

"You *are* from Queens," I continued; I was cracking myself up now. "But that's about it."

"Hey, watch it, Johnny. I *am* from fuckin' Queens. I'm from the *streets*, all right? The goddam gutters. You got a problem with that?"

"It seems like you expect an answer here. What are you—a combo platter of Robert De Niro, Joe Pesci, Harvey Keitel, and Al Pacino all in one? You're from the Hamptons, Psycho. We know that. You went to Queens College when you were sixteen or something—before Harvard. You *told* us."

I was harshing on him a little much, I guess. Sometimes Psycho displayed his (hyper)sensitive side and you couldn't help being thrown off a bit. I could picture him patting down the light brown wisp of hair he, Baby Huey style, had left on top of his head and looking all perturbed—in a minor sort of way.

"I can't believe you said that."

He meant the bit about him and tits.

"All I'm saying is you might think about not fixating quite so much on a woman's . . ."

"Fixating?! Who's *fixating?*" he screeched, then got kinda quietish. "That is *so* not fair. And, well, okay, even if I do like breasts overmuch—and I'm not saying that's true 'cause I don't think you *can* like them too much!—it's probably on account of I'm a scientist and all. We *all* do. As a chemist, you're surrounded by tubes that remind you of boobs, dude, like, all day long! Just think how I'd be if I worked at a Silicon lab like my friend Nicholson does! I don't even want to go there!"

There was another long pause.

"That was so unfair, John."

"I know, Dave; don't get all offended. And don't worry: you'll grow up one day."

"Think so? I hope not. I'm having the time of my life in this town. I really am. You think so, really?"

"Nah," I said, "you'll never grow up, Psychster."

"Thanks, man. You had me worried for a bit there."

"Don't mention it," I said. "But you do realize you are completely psycho, don't you, Psycho? You do realize that."

"Well, of course," he said and I could tell he was smiling 'cause no one in the history of nicknames ever loved his nickname more than Psycho did—I mean, he had given it to himself. "Now, are you absolutely positive you . . ."

"Psych . . . "

"Okay. I mean, *I* took the early middle and late morning off today—plus most of the afternoon—just to get some good *day* drinking in here, you know? Day drinking seguing into night drinking. Is that ideal or what?"

"I'm sorry, man. I really can't. Why don't you call the Scather?"

"That's a great idea, man. Sterling! That guy loves to get chemical."

"Yeah, well, I think he's trying to cut down on chemicals right now."

"Fuck! This is no time to cut back on chemicality, brother. This is not the time for that at all. Hallo*ween*'s coming up soon. I just made some killer ecstasy in the lab last week. It's gonna be immense. I tried two hits over the weekend and wham! Really good stuff. *Really* good."

"Oh no."

"Oh yeah. Hey: what's Sterling's number, then?"

I gave it to him. I probably shouldn't have.

"Just don't give him any drugs, okay. He's really trying not to do any right now."

"Okay. Talk to you later, then. Anything going on for Halloween?"

"I don't know. Maybe Jaz does. I'm not too crazy about Halloween, anyway."

"Really? You're crazy. Halloween's the best."

"Not into it."

"I am. I'm going as a Psycho. I'm going as myself."

"That's great."

"I will call you . . ."

"At your convenience."

"Exactly."

At last, after this endless silliness, I got off the phone with him and called Jenny at work; I was going to try to catch her before she left. Got the number from Information. Punched it in.

# VERSE

## she said she said

Asleep in the light of the plum, vanilla, lavender and cedar-scented candle flicker, thick bottom lip limned with bits of spit and eyes strangely just a touch open, in a thin white cotton nightdress complete with Renaissance-y drawstrings across the chest, she looks like an angel. That's a total cliché, I totally know; but it's true, she does. She might as well have wings and a nimbus going, a gold harp propped up by the foot of the bed. I get up, rub sleep from sleepy eyes, yawn audibly but not too loudly, and pad to the upstairs bathroom for a long whizby (red wine, five glasses, 'cause Jenny doesn't drink beer). When I return, stealing back into bed, she stirs and pulls me in to kiss her lips. I draw a line through her just-moist hair and an "Mmm" from her larynx. Her mouth moves to my neck and she murmurs "Where'd you go?" and before I can answer she says "I want you inside me again. This sponge is okay for one more, I think." Parting her thighs with one knee I get her wet again with my right hand. It doesn't take much: a couple of gentle circles round her pubis, thumbstrokes to the right temple, fingers working the back of her neck, giving and receiving vigorous kisses both teasing and breath-snatching.

Here we go again, doing the push-ups of love.

Afterwards, exhaustedly we watch her curtains blossom and deflate in the middle-of-the-night breeze. There's a hint of rain in the scudding clouds parading past a well-ringed moon. And I for one am truly deeply madly happy.

Why, you might well ask? Jenny and I have had two blissed-out whirlwind weeks of the Deep & Meaningfuls, in capitals (conversations, that is). About past relationships (especially her most recent, one she'd had with a guy called David, a.k.a. "the David," who, after he'd broken up with her, ripped her heart apart, had been nice enough to drive her more than four hundred miles south so that she could get away from him); about Big Mistakes, Classical Music, Art History, the Cars We Used To Drive; Her Brother, My Brother; the Beatles; Our Parents; Foreign Countries; the Beatles; Embarrassing Moments; Jobs; Holidays; Roommates; College; the Beatles; Work; Philosophy and How Only Fools and Children Believe That Everything Happens for a Reason; Elementary School Triumphs and Catastrophes; and Favorite Foodstuffs.

Five dinners out; two made by me; one heavy period-piece drama, one weepy chick-flick (a PMS flick, Jenny termed it). One Francis Bacon retrospective at LACMA on splashy-rainy day sans umbrella. Seven rehearsals, four with the band, three with just me and her, in her room, working on songs, working like Puritans, singing like Baptists, well, maybe not *Baptists*, but some sect of the devoted and joyous. For the songs that poured out of me—three in one week—Jenny suggested chord alterations and elongated bridges that she'd then cut and reshape and shape again. Urged repetitions of choruses; encouraged me to write songs with only two chords. *Abhorred* a modulation—abominated waltz time (though a 6/8 dreamsong passed her melody test).

And nightly we'd swoon to cassette-recorded music on her toy boombox.

Furthermore it turns out she plays more than capable guitar and quickly takes all the lead parts. A mean guitar, in fact—at once aggressive (apologetically so, somehow) and brightly chiming, on account of she didn't know what she was doing. A classically-trained *punk* is what she was! Or post-punk, I should say, as none of our songs came with, as it were, safety-pin nose-rings or motorcycle jackets or spit and mosh pits. The chords she forms come weirdly. "What's this?" she'll wonder. "A 'D' chord." "And this?" "Good God, who knows?! But it sure is pretty and dissonant at the same time! Don't forget it, Jen!"

Her small hands round the guitar's neck find their uncertain, delightfully surprising way.

Like they find their way around *mine*.

She's beautiful and interesting and funny and nice. Talented and silly and well-bred and hardworking. Sexual in a shy way and naughty and smart. Tortured and melancholy and stubborn and stolid. Dowdy (almost) and doughty and quiet and sweaty (we *all* are in the practice sweatbox edifice shed—it's like a sauna in there, rain or shine) and industrious in a lazy sort of way. Laughs as she dances, and dance she does to any music, music that seems forever to be emanating from her, flowing through her, around her, within. A guy's guy's girl. Has to be—in *this* band. Responsible and self-sufficient and carrying an air of, as I told you at the outset, something ineffably, ineluctably sad. Something tragic she meets up with daily and greets with a brave smile, maybe—I don't know; she won't say yet what it is, and I know better already than to push her or she'll let herself, I reckon, be nudged right out of my life.

The first time we kissed was one week into it, this so-far miniature romantic marathon where we found ourselves, the second week, spending every night together, at her house, which makes more sense (plus I didn't think it was that great of an idea to introduce her too early to the squalor/austerity in which/with which Jaz and I lived). The kiss came late one night after rehearsal with Rob and Walt. I'd squired her downtown to her downtown office: she'd forgotten something one of the lawyers needed done the next day early—would find much trouble waiting if it wasn't taken care of. So we motored down to Grand and Third and down into the subterranean parking structure and up the way-up-there elevator, forty-seven flights, to the sterile/creepy football-field-sized office, eerily lit, threading through the labyrinth of desks and chairs and conference rooms to where her cubicle was. I'd maundered over to the window to gaze at the hypnotizing immensity of palpitating lights on the freeway, in the skyway (random choppers chopping the night), from the other highrises, the streetlamps and lights fuzzy mini-Novas far below. Turning round to have a looksee to see when she might be ready to go, I found her already there beside me. Said "Hey" in that thick voice you get when you know you're going to kiss someone. Her increasingly more lovely and incandescent face wasn't lifted cinematically to me—she wasn't looking, she told me later, for a quote-unquote magic moment—but she didn't resist when I gathered her to me and put my mouth on hers in a way that made me (I can only speak for me) feel all filled up and left empty at the same time.

And so surprised. A dulcet shock. A solid tingle.

Everything you'll ever have with someone in a first kiss.

And nothing is.

I'm not trying to be all profound.

It just *is*.

*

"Are you good?" I asked. "I am! That was wonderful."

"Yeah," she smiled. "I'm *fine*. Ha! Thank you."

"Look at the way the curtain's blowing."

"I like how heavy the night air is right now. And the clouds. They're beautiful."

"I know," I said. "So are you."

I got up and blew out the candles and we just lay there breathing till we drifted off as a late Indian summer sprinkling was just beginning, the soft tattoo of skywater coming down on the roof and the porch thatch just below us; then it really came down in great lusty drops and the last thing I remember thinking was . . . nothing.

*

In the morning, in the kitchen, before breakfast, with an explosion of rainwashed light coming through the yellowed window, Jenny said: "*You* were talking in your sleep last night. Do you know you do that?"

"Was I?"

"Oh yeah."

"What's that supposed to mean?" I laughed.

"Nothing."

"Uh-huh something. What did I say?"

"Oh, I dunno. Who's Heidi?"

"Oh my God!"

"Someone you used to date? What's so funny?"

"Heidi's an emu that lives next door to Jaz and me. I can't believe I didn't tell you that we live next door to an exotic, flightless, giant, quasi-prehistoric, freaky-looking bird."

"Oh sure, an emu."

"Don't believe me."

"I won't!"

"Come over tonight then and see! Or don't, then."

I went over and kissed her and she pretended to turn away but then at the last second before I could grab her she wiggled away and took up a spatula and made like she was fending me off. We danced around each other a little bit till I maneuvered over to her and snatched the offending (defending?) nasty plastic thing out of her hand. She gave out this Hayley Mills or Sandy Denny squeal and we kissed again. Then, on account of we both must have realized we were making too much noise goofing around, I went back to organizing breakfast. No one was up yet, despite the fact that it must have been nearly eleven. Mostly people at Walter and Nasty's slept in till thirteen o'clock or later: it was very much the party house, especially on weekends. The kitchen midden of six hundred roommates and their respective sleepovers was huge. There were stains the size of Asia Minor on the checkerboard floor, and implacably filthy dishes and indeterminate utensils in the sink, "flowers" of paper towels and napkins, milk cartons, defeated cereal boxes, cigarette-filled beer bottles, etc.

I cleaned some frying pans and plates and melted a square of butter in one of the aforementioned and pummeled some eggs real good. Raked cheese through a grater. Heaped salsa on one plate to have at the ready. Got mushrooms shriveling in another pan with garlic and more butter and steadied the woggling teakettle and poured a cup for both of us. "Borrowed" some new potatoes from someone and sautéed them with a pony onion and soft red pepper. Crossed my arms and watched my handiwork.

"Hey Jenny?"

"Hmm?"

"How come you didn't stop me from talking in my sleep?"

"I don't know. I was actually sort of asking you questions to keep it going."

"Vixen! What if I'd said something really incriminating—like 'Natasha's *so* sexy—I want her so *so* bad?"

Oh God: who padded into the kitchen just then? Guess.

"Hey you guys," Natasha said sleepily. "Is there any coffee?"

"Tea," Jenny said and held up her cup.

"Gulp," I said, but only to myself.

"Okay," Natasha said and padded back out.

The look Jen and I exchanged then was a look you probably know.

What we'll maybe never know is if she heard us—me—making sport of her.

Youch.

Then we gave out that nervous after-laugh of ostensible relief. But it wasn't very hearty or hardy, let me tell you.

"Anyway: do you know what you're wearing tonight—do you have a costume?"

"A witch," she said. "I'm going as a witch. I can't think of anything else, really."

"A nice witch?"

"Well, I could be a very bad witch."

"Oh," I mock-moaned, "don't go as a bad witch; if there is one thing I can't handle it's a bad bad witch!"

I folded the now-done omelette and set it down and seared it in half. Jenny declined toast so we went upstairs to eat in bed. Then, sated but famished for each other again, made love quite quietly—then, after anhelating together for a spell, went off again to sleep, dreamless, talk-free sleep.

*

"Jenny?" I said as we lay there listening to *Revolver* on her cassette deck next to the bed.

"Hmm?"

"Do you talk to him still?"

"Hmm?" she said again but she knew exactly who I meant. I didn't want to say his name.

I gave her a look like, "*You* know."

"David? No," she said.

"How come?"

"There's no point."

"What do you mean?"

"What do you mean, 'What do I mean?' There just isn't."

"Oh, I get it."

"Get what?"

"Never mind."

"Whatever," she said. "Can you throw me my robe, please? I need to . . . I feel like taking a shower."

I felt bad. This could be an incipient issue. Handle with care, I thought. This calls for non-Johnlike behavior. This calls for the suave/right think to do.

"I'll take one with you," I said as I held the ghost-white terrycloth robe she stretched herself into.

Foolish fool.

"That's okay—*really*. I need to be . . . I'll just be a minute, okay?"

The wash-off she took lasted three hours, it seemed. She was draining Lake Arrowhead. I could've finished several Russian novels, written six songs and learned Italian for Travelers, it seemed. She took a long fucking time in there.

*

When she came out and came in to her room, all hot and red, I pulled her to me by the robe's lapels and kissed her on presented cheek, tonguing aside wet strands of resplendent hair.

"I think if I lost you I would be so sad for so so long," I said.

"Oh John," she said and with a kiss not-brisk this time and on the mouth she melted into me.

## wham bam thank you ma'am

We had to get ready for the party. We were playing it. It was our first gig. We'd called all our friends. We'd warned Walter's neighbors. We were really nervous and excited—well, I was. We only had eight songs. We had new strings on the guitars and a set list all made out and rehearsed as best it could be. What we didn't have was a *name*.

"What?!" Psycho said when I called him to remind him that Walter and Nasty were throwing an immense Halloween party that we, the band without a name, were playing. "You guys don't have a name yet?! I'm going to a party where there's a band playing that doesn't even have a *name?!* I'm supposed to tell people I'm going to a party where the band playing is the fucking No Names? Not good, Johnny. You gotta get that straightened out. And of course I remembered the party! I wish I didn't have this good-a-memory, if you really wanna know. There are some things—like *last* night, for instance—that I would really like to forget!"

"Psychster, this is gonna be a great party," I said like someone trying to convince a little kid to eat something that didn't appear from inside a fast food bag. "Walter and Natasha do throw great parties."

"This is Halloween, my friend."

"I know that."

"This is a big night. This is *Psycho's* night, a night for *serious* wastedness and astronomical party downedness. This party *better* be good."

"It will."

"And you guys had better come up with a name by the time I get there, okay?"

"Don't worry. But we probably won't. Ha! Nothing seems the right thing. We have brainstormed on it and written down loads of names, boy. Trust me. And don't call me 'dude!' Or ever call California 'Cali!'"

"You want me to come up with a name for you guys?" he said, ignoring completely my little remonstration. "I can do it. I've heard you guys."

That was true; Psycho had come by with Sterling one time to hear us practice—ostensibly—but I think they, Psycho especially, but Sterling in a strictly musical way, were more interested in checking out Jenny. There wasn't really room for them in the practice shed so they had to stand outside and listen, then have a cigarette with us (Rob and me again, that is) and a chat with Jen and an uncomfortable laugh with Walter 'cause Sterling instantly disliked him and vice versa and Psycho rubbed Walter the wrong way in every way and vice versa there too.

Still, Psycho loved to be involved in things; he loved to be consulted. Anytime anyone had a science-related question or some totally obscure trivia like what you get in the *New York Times* crossword puzzle he was all *over* it, jumping up and down to share out information. If you ever had a problem or a dilemma he was all ears for sure. And he loved to come up with suggestions for any old thing. He was just like Sterling in that respect—he knew what he was talking about. Most of the time. And an opportunity to kibitz about a friend's art, even something as picayune as a band name, was right up his alley.

Within limits.

"You want me to come up with a band name?" Psycho went on.

"Why not? Sure. Allen Ginsberg named the Blake Babies 'the Blake Babies' (even though they both suck, if you ask me). And fucking William Burroughs named a whole genre heavy metal. You could be just like them, Psycho (though Burroughs is as overrated as they come)."

"*Your* band's name."

"Well, duh, Dave. I just said that. Suggest something—you know you love stuff like this."

"Come up with a name for you guys? Fuck *that!* If you guys aren't creative enough to come up with a viable name for your band, you aren't creative enough to *have* a band, man. You certainly aren't creative enough for a music fan such as myself to show up for your band, man. *You* better get a name, John."

"Okay, *man,*" I said. "We'll get right on it. Don't come, then, if you feel that way about it. We'll just have to Halloween without you!"

"Hey!" Psycho said. "I never said I wasn't coming! Even though there are lots of other parties old Psychster is invited to, believe me. One of my old Cal Tech cronies is throwing a shindig where he's gonna blow up with dynamite this little kids' playhouse that he turned into a haunted house. At the end of the night he's gonna blow it up."

"That's wonderful," I deadpanned.

"*Isn't* it?!" he said. "And what about *chicks?* You promised chicks galore, as I recall. You said Natasha has God's own amount of cutie gothic chick friends, right?"

"She does, actually. You just better hope they aren't *like* her."

"She's a fucking bitch, huh."

Dear dear Psycho.

"There are definitely going to be girls here, Psycho-my-chum. College girls. *Junior* college girls. Halloween's about how, with chicks, the shortest skirt wins, the most slutty outfit takes the cake, the most naughty . . ."

"I will be there at my convenience," Psycho said precipitately and hung up.

"Of course you will," I said to the dead phone in Jenny's room and put down the receiver.

*

There were at least thirty-six million hundred vampires and witches—and that was just in the living room and kitchen, I saw as I came downstairs in quest of alcoholic sustenance. Nearly every thoroughgoing goth-type friend of Walt and Nasty had the full-on Boris Karloff or Elvira thing going, with variations, of course. It looked like a movie set. Or a try-out for a movie set, rather. A Bauhaus or Sisters of Mercy video shoot. Jenny and I were laughing like mad about it till we kind of simultaneously came to the realization that this was our audience—and we, a chiming, catchy, guitar pop band with (when Jen played keys) a much more mellotronish,

60s kind of vibe than spooky spookiness, were *the* furthest thing from goth rock you could think of. Dark sometimes—yes. Droney—sure. Atmospheric—I hoped so. But there were way too many bouncy choruses juxtaposed with dissonant, one-note two-guitar attack passages (yeah, we liked Sonic Youth a lot and were doing our very best to disguise it, get rid of them as an influence) to please these people, for sure.

Uh-oh.

Hadn't thought of that.

Now why, it just occurred to me, wasn't Walter in a goth band where he belonged? That was his and Nastasha's music, after all. And their image and their predominant topic of conversation (unless it was their dog or Nasty's outfits or moods or migraines) and all the rest of it. Ah, that's why, I now realized: 'cause it doesn't really matter just so long as he's *in* a band. (Plus Walter had these secret pop penchants: he liked surf music, for crying out loud, the Everly Brothers and the Bee Gees. Bet none of his friends here knew *that!*)

What can you do? Drink, that's what you can do. And so we did. Rob and Jenny and I (well, mostly Rob and I—Jenny never really got more than a little tipsy, it seemed) were glugging glugs and wines and shots and bonging bongs and sharing spliffs and scarfing chips and salsa and guacamole and nuts and candy to offset all the alcohol.

The beer was flowing like, uh, wine. We were having a great pre-party party.

*They* were having a grand time too, Walt and Nasty's friends. Even the most humorless of them couldn't fail to note how absurd it was that there was so little variation (with exceptions, with exceptions) in costumery. Psycho came. the Scather too. He'd brought Sarah-Who-Hates-Me and an entourage. He never went anywhere major without a major, fawning entourage, Scather. It was like a cape he wore or something, these four or five people trailing behind him, clustering closer as he held forth, laughing like anything. He even referred to them, right in front of them, of course, as his quote-unquote *non*tourage.

And good/big news: Jaz brought a date! He was escorting this quite pretty (and pretty buxom—he'd better keep her away from Psycho, I reflected) Latina lawyer from the law firm he worked at. She did have a sidecar—a dull girl who looked like a much less attractive version of her—but Jaz acted like it was a date so good for him. The lawyer girl was called Claudia and I spent a little time chatting her up and she was really nice and super smart and funny. Sure enough, Psycho spotted her almost lickety-split and the whole time I was talking to Claudia Psycho was sort of hovering and I could tell he was riveted by her bust, boy. It was, I had to admit, really hard not to look at it—the sort of motif where it would be better somehow if you turned to the girl and just told her: "Look, I'm not even a boob guy but I gotta tell you straight up that our conversation will be greatly, um, augmented, er, enhanced I mean, if I just tell you right away that it's going from time to time to be hard for me to make eye contact while we are having this stimulating conversation on account of . . . *you* know." I've never said anything like that, though. Have you? Maybe I will one day—just to see how she reacts, my busty imaginary interlocutor. I should hope she'd laugh and look down and go: "So you *like* these, do you?" Then she'd be the sort of imaginary girl who has a real sense of humor, who's super fun to be with.

Rob brought Rhiannon, his tall and beautiful twin sister (actress alert!), who was really nice as well and fun and a lot like Rob—easygoing and unassuming; he also had in tow three guys he used to be in a cover band with who didn't dress up for Halloween (I was with them—even though I had a costume on, a witch one, with a witchy hat and a black graduation gown, I hated dressing up, and Halloween in general) but who were pretty cool, talking about the their good old bar band days doing three sets of shit like "My Sharona" and "I Got You" and "Sweet Jane," half of the Cars catalogue, all of *Candy O*, for sure, and loads of early Beatles and Stones, "Wipe Out!" It sounded . . . like a nightmare, actually. I couldn't imagine playing even one cover, let alone three whole sets of them. Rob's old bandmates were telling me how he used to be the first guy off stage and the last guy on, the last guy to the gig and the first packed up. Us smokers, boy—we're gonna take our time. And yours too. Plus they said that Rob got all the chicks. *All* the chicks. The *bass* player. They were teasing him pretty hard but you could tell he was loving it. (Rob was like the little kid in your childhood neighborhood who didn't care what kind of attention he got so long as he got attention. Every 'hood has one. ) I can only imagine the chicks, back in the big-hair post-disco 80s, that Rob must've pulled. Big blonde clouds of sticky hair teased out to tomorrow; tight, high rise "space pants"( as in "Are those space pants? Cause your ass is *out of this world!*"); blue eyeliner lavishly applied; and black leggings and headbands up the wazoo. As those guys were ribbing the hell out of him, all Rob kept saying was "Well, all's I'll say is, '83 was a really good year. A *really* good year. I lived right on the beach, went to the beach in the day, and played with these guys and drank all night and took home . . . yeah, '83 was a *good* year." I laughed at that.

The assorted roommates of Walter and Nasty besides Jenny (Les Paul-playing guitar-hero Jimmy Han, who was in this very successful hardcore cartoon band called the Holy Smokes; April somebody who never said boo; Michele C., a hairstylist for the movies and nice girl; and Linehan, a guy who was *never* home and who did nothing, it seemed, but work work work at a job he wouldn't tell you what it was—just like he wouldn't tell anybody his other name, if he even had one, or whether Linehan was his first or last name) were all there too, and a thousand-some-odd people we had no idea who they were. Jaz had invited a ton of other people (Walter said come one, come all) who might turn up later: you know: the types who barge in around three million o'clock when everyone is all slurrish and ready to go to sleep at last in order to wake up the next day for a nice vomit or with their head in a vice.

And speaking of vomit, this was one hell of a pre-party. People were already *ripped* and it wasn't even eight o'clock. Psycho, who'd announced that he'd been drinking since one that afternoon, had already yakked twice from a profuse infusion of Jägermeister shots and Jello shots. For a guy who was a science genius—not just supposed, either; he really was—he sure wasn't terrifically clever when it came to the chemistry of mixology. It was like he wasn't going to be content till he'd tossed his proverbial cookies. Like he hadn't had a good time till he could prove it with an unspeakable grandiloquent upchuck. I saw him in action. I didn't like what I saw but I saw it. He sort of zigzagged out to the backyard and went kind of ghost-white, all pale. Then a sweaty sort of scrap metal gray-green gray. Then blue. Then black, almost. I know you can't turn *black* unless you're Mick Jagger or Darryl Hall or someone but that's what it seemed like. Then, theatrically gripping the rotten railings of the wooden back porch like he was about to do some impromptu chin-ups, Psycho went kinda piqued and sallow, a candle tallow yellow. He was kind of heaving himself back and forth and back and forth like he was doing some Army exercise from WW1 or a little-known yoga move or a weird Icelandic sporting warm-up routine. Then, when he'd finished making a succession of outlandish barnyard-and-other animal kind of noises, a whole thesaurus of them (lowing, clucking, grunting, snorting; oinking, bleating, neighing, hissing; honking, cockadoodledo-ing, crowing; cawing, chirping, barking, bellowing), he waxed this bubblegum ice cream pink hue and started dry-heaving like mad.

He had an audience too: there must have been seven or eight people watching him by now.

Had he, without informing anyone, initiated a round of "Puke Off," a popular collegiate-type game where people drink to see who can throw up the fastest? Would he live? Would he survive? Would he pass out before it was even half-eight? This was a Guinness Book of barfing, a marathon barfathon. Was he going to be all right? Was he going to be okay? Were we going to end up on the six o'clock news like one of those frat houses in the deep south or at USC, weeping on national television over the untimely, tragic, drink-related death of our dear, overeducated, psychopathic pal?

After about nineteen dry heaves in a row (well, not "about"—*exactly* nineteen, on account of people callously started counting them, going "*Thir*teen! *Four*teen! *Fif*teen!" as Psych ralphed on), Psycho looked up, smiled his inimitable maniacal smile and waved the cheering/jeering gaggle off.

Which meant one thing: he was ready to rinse off and bounce back!

"Psych-o! Psych-o!" everyone, around *twenty* people now at least, was chanting; "Bounce *back*, bounce *back*, bounce *back!*" Bowie ("The Jean Genie") blared over the pair of outside Klipsches just then and Psycho cried out for another drink and another shot and the pre-party partiers went *mental*, cracking up in an almost synchronized way and slapping him on the back like they were in some sort of Off-Off-Broadway play or something, handing him towels and bottles of water: "The Psychster wants another shot!" "Psycho bounced back! He fully bounced! Do you believe that?!" "What a hero!" "What a legend!" "What a knucklehead!" "Psycho bounced *back!*"

"Psych, are you all right?!" I asked.

"Gosh," he said to the party at large: "I thought I was gonna be *sick* there for a second! Hahahahaha!"

And the biggest roar yet went up from everyone. People started dancing to Bowie's "Changes," which came on next, and they were clinking drinks and high-fiving people they didn't even know and digging one another's costumes and lighting each other's cigarettes and clapping one another on the back so hard that their beers and gin-and-tonics and vodka drinks jetted forth and then they went back inside for refills and refreshments.

This was going to be a great party. Psycho, what were you thinking?! You must be *psycho*, Psycho, you psycho! You must be in*sane!* What are you—crazy? Are you out of your *mind?* Everyone was rolling. Shaking their heads and smiling to themselves and tisk-tisking and clucking and hoisting their glasses. Even Psycho's hair, what was left of it, that is, looked heroic, the way it was sticking up through his goggles and making his head look like one of those helmets dashing cavalrymen wore in the Napoleonic Wars. What a guy! A guy crossing a Rubicon of his own making, no less.

The party, officially, had started.

Someone twisted a black baseball cap over the lab goggles that Psycho had on. It read "Drink.Drank.Drunk." Thereupon, he oafed past a Playboy Bunny, gooned by two sexy kittens, and blunderbussed all bandy-legged to the unsuspecting backyard keg (there was one inside as well, in the room off the kitchen). He playfully swatted the black tap hose out of the hand of a guy in a Celtics jersey and fizzed the nozzle straight into his muzzle. His antics were sort of anticlimactic after his quip about thinking he was gonna be sick for a second there.

Here's what everyone went as: The Scather went as himself. Like the guys in Rob's old cover band, he wasn't donning any costume. He wasn't about to assume a character; he *was* a character. Jenny went as the witch she'd said she was going to be—a "bad" one with tremendous cleavage and pixie dust and gelatin in her silken-gone-ropey cherry hair. Walt and Rob were witches too—that meant the whole band were witches—but Walt was one in drag, with prosthetic tits he kept plumping magisterially into people's drinks; he kept on throwing his head back and giving out that honking laugh every time he did it. He couldn't wait to get behind the drum kit, he said, so everyone could watch his witchy tits bounce as he played. Rob didn't really want to dress up but we'd convinced him at the last minute to put on at least a witch hat and, as with everything, he goodsported it and complied.

Nasty went as—what else?—a naughty French maid. Big surprise. You had to admit she looked pretty cute, though. Pretty sexy. But then you remembered her personality. Jaz went as a Dodger fan (don't strain yourself or anything, Jaz, I thought), and his "date" Claudia and her friend dressed up as sexy vegetables, a carrot and a broccoli respectively.

There was a bloody cowgirl and several angel-devils; there was an angel covered in whipped cream. One guy, with muttonchops out to tomorrow, raccoonish eyeliner, shirtless and completely bald, had these suspenders on and Doc Martens and green *speedos*—who *knew* who he was supposed to be? Sterling went up to him:

"Don't tell me—"an escapee from Lollapalooza?"

"Not!" the guy said.

Even Sterling didn't have a come-back for that. If you weren't around in the days when people started saying "Not!" a lot, well, you didn't miss much. After the five hundredth and twelveteenth time you heard it, it wasn't that amusing. I never got into it—*not!*

There was a Cindy Sherman-looking girl in frilly-frumpy baby bonnet and see-through robin's-egg-blue dress. She kept pulling a phallic-shaped pacifier in and out of her mouth. Someone told me it was filled with whiskey.

There was a walking penis, a Batman, an old man, a milkman (in short shorts, gay as all get-out); a walrus, a warren of Playboy Bunnies, an ambulant chandelier, two sets of Charlie's Angels, five or more pirates, one scary Bozo, one I Dream of Jeannie, one Gilligan, one Skipper (female), one Nixon, one Reagan, two Jackie Kennedys (who kept their distance from each other, I could tell, all night long). A Buddhist monk with painted-on third-degree burns; a Tin Man, a Tiny Tim, a Marilyn (male, of course), and a Jungle Jim (guy in trucker hat that said "Jim" and a leopard print caveman wrap). And loads of others: scarecrow, bellhop, devil, doctor, village idiot, jester, jughead, skinhead, blah blah blah.

There was a dude in a t-shirt that said "DUDE, SO THE FUCK WHAT IF I'M WASTED." There were two Druids with eyes like mottled clouds; I had no idea how they did that.

There was a guy who went as a giant mushroom. Psycho, of course, got a huge kick out of him. Several people were trying to get a huge kick into him on account of he kept grabbing people's drinks out of their hands and drinking them. He was with these two beautiful girls kitted out as fairies who just laughed and laughed at everything he did. The guy was around six foot twenty and burly as could be, so no one said boo to him. Not even one of the ghosts! Hahaha! (How silly. But then Halloween, if you ask me, is the silliest thing ever, anyway.) The fairies kept on pretending to take bits out of the mushroom guy; then they'd swoon and swan away like they were tripping. After around the twelfth time I saw them do it, it wasn't all that funny. There was this chick whose quote-unquote costume was that she was obsessed with Jim Morrison: she had her hair cut all shaggy like Morrison's and grayish black leather pants like Morrison, and a Doors t-shirt, and a thousand-yard stare like Morrison as well. She was standing talking in the kitchen to this twerp of a guy in a twerpy maroon and white striped turtleneck, twerpy stovepipe stonewashed jeans, twerpy zip-up Beatle boots and a supertwerpy bowl haircut that only an über-twerp would sport. What a fuckin' twerp! He had on these way passé deep blue, Roger McGuinn-issue granny glasses and he kept nattering on about Brian Wilson while the Morrison girl was abstractly discoursing on the Lizard King. They were both of them referring to their respective idols by their idols' first names—it was bugging the shit out of me but I couldn't for some reason walk away. Why is it senseless arguments at parties always seem to take place in the kitchen?

"What you don't get is that Jim always stood for revolution, okay?"

"What—by whipping out his *dick?* Some rebel. Ha! The Doors sucked. Suck. What a rock and roll *clown* Morrison was! Whereas Brian's teenage symphonies to God were . . ."

"Well, Jim *was* God, okay? So that means Brian Wilson was writing songs in praise of . . ."

"You're completely kidding right? The Beach Boys had no respect for . . ."

"You're crazy. The only *poet* was Jim. And then maybe Jimi. I bet you don't know any of his poems, you Beach Boys freak. When Jim wrote about his . . ."

"Ha! Brian Wilson's lyrics could kick . . ."

"Jim . . ."

"Brian . . ."

They were yammering fully contrapuntally now, Brianing and Jimming each other at increasing volumes.

"Brian *Jones*, maybe," the chick screeched worse than Courtney Love with a microphone in front of her. "*He* was a genius . . ."

"At being fucked-up, maybe. How can you compare Brian Jones to Brian . . ."

"Who *cares?* If you don't get the Doors I don't know why I'm even standing talk . . ."

"Oh, please."

"I mean, the first Doors album is . . ."

"You Doors freaks always fucking bring up the first Doors album, man. It never fails. There's no com*par*ison to *Pet Sounds*, okay? None. And *Smile*, if they ever release it . . ."

"Oh my *God*—you Beach Boys nuts are forever going on about . . ."

"Fuck you."

"I got one word for you Beach Boys retards, okay? Mike *Love!*"

And with that she stalked away in a major huff.

This Dracula came up to me as I was talking to Jenny, her bike-riding friend Sandy, and a couple of friendly-in-a-vacant-way friends of hers from work.

"Hey! John, right? You're in Walter's band, right? Someone told me you're a Sub? How's that, anyway? I'm Todd, a friend of Walter's."

"Hey, Todd," I said. The eyeliner he'd applied was running distractingly down his face and the dry ice in his cup was blowing into mine and his breath was spelling "halitosis" with every syllable, but I was determined to be nice to everyone that night: we were about to do our first gig; we were meant to start playing in about fifteen minutes; we didn't need anyone in the crowd against us; we needed sympathizers of any and every kind, even egregious ones who referred to us as members of *Walter's* band.

We were probably going to suck.

"*Are* you?" he said. "I ask because I was thinking of getting into it."

"Think again, Todd, my friend," I said. "Really."

I could tell that Jenny's and her friends were listening pretty intently—or about to. Girls who might become your girlfriend? Those girls' friends scrutinize you like anything—at first. They make up their minds, most of them do, right away so that they don't have to think about you much more after that. They need the space in their heads to be thinking about guys they are or are potentially dating; they don't need to waste a lot of space on you, one of their friends' paramours or prospects. Everyone knows *that*. I mean, *duh*.

"Really?" Todd said. "It's a drag, huh? Someone said it was kinda the perfect job for people who don't, uh, really want one, though."

This observation drew a little laugh from the girls. Who were now looking at me hard, it appeared, in order to see what I would say. One of the Jenny-friends was tall and sexy in a sort of sorority-girl way—pouty-lipped and slim except for she had sort of a rhombus-butt. The other one was pretty, I guess, but a bit dumpy—way too short for anyone except Psycho, maybe. No matter how attractive a girl is, she loves it when you go pontificating about education and stuff. They just lap it up when you go on and on about the fate of the children, the state of the nation, kidwise. We Are the World! Save the Whales! Heal the Bay! I'll Have the Fruit Plate! I Brake for Animals! I Brake for the Homeless! Neuter the Rapists! Rescue the Rabid Strays! Eat Your Vegetables! Eat Your Girlfriend! Pay Attention to What My Clitoris Is Trying to Tell You! Get over Him by Getting under Someone Hotter! Sis Boom *Bah!* Rah Rah *Rah!* (Not!)

I had two choices here: I could gallantly say how rewarding and purposeful and crucial such a job was and how important tending to the needs of the kids of tomorrow was—or I could tell the truth. Tell the impolitic truth and say how fucking much I fucking hated it.

Knowing me, as you must needs do by now, which answer do you think I went for?

"Oh," the cuter of the two friends of Jenny said when I had finished my phony spiel and sat back and basked in the glow of how giddily impressed they seemed to be by my unmitigated poppycock, "that is just so . . . so . . ."

"Hey!" Nastasha clacked dramatically up just then; "People are wondering if you guys are going to *play*, okay?! Get *up* there! Let's rock this shit *out*. Everyone's *waiting*. Like, come *on*."

"Where's Walt, then?" I sort of yelled—you had to as the party had hugeified by now.

"I don't know," Nastasha said without in the least trying to mask her burgeoning perturbation. "How should *I* know? Let's go! I mean, *fuck, man, I thought you guys wanted to do a* gig *here*."

"Couldn't you go look for him and I will tell Rob?" I said to Nastasha's back as she huffed haughtily away.

Nastasha gave me this look like she was about to have an extended turn of atrocious gas; Jenny was, it seemed, kind of still smirking at my glibly golden bullshit comments about subbing.

Jenny, turning elegantly, demurely, poised as could be to her friends, said: "Excuse me, you guys: I guess we need to get up there. John, make sure the guitars are still in tune, okay. I'll go find Rob."

"God, Nastasha chafes," I huffed. "Why can't she ever . . ."

"I know," Jenny said. "You don't need to say it."

"I'll locate Walter and tune up, then."

"Good," Jenny said.

I walked into the living room, looking for Walt; there, I ran into Jaz instead. He was on his own—no idea where Claudia and her friend were.

"Amazing party," he said and high-fived me. Then he tilted his head over to where Sterling was chatting with Sarah. "That the chick who . . ."

"Hates me? Said I was shallow? Uh-huh."

"My God—she looks just like Beatrice Dalle!"

The chick from *Betty Blue*.

"I told you!" I said.

"I never said that she couldn't conceivably look like the chick from that flick—I just said you shouldn't ever tell a girl who looks exactly like someone that she looks exactly like her."

"You're starting to sound like Psycho, Jaz," I said. "Wanna meet her? She's real sweet. She has the personality of an overtoasted marshmallow. A marshmallow toasted by a pyromaniac."

"You know me—I'll meet anyone."

"Maybe you can test out your own theory and tell her she looks like Audrey Hepburn."

"But she doesn't look at all like Audrey . . ."

"Never mind, Jaz."

"When are you guys going on?" he said and did some air guitar.

"Soon," I said. "Ten minutes."

"Excellent. I'll go find Claudia."

"She's cute," I said. "Very. I didn't know lawyers could have pink, punk rock hair."

"Oh, she just dyed it for Halloween."

"What's her last name?"

"Rodriguez. Claudia Montoya Josephine Benitez Von Dusseldorf Martinez Rodriguez."

I just stared.

"I know. I memorized it. I've gotten to know her pretty well the past few months."

"What a name, though—even Psycho can't psych you out on that one."

"Ha! Seriously. There's obviously a lot of downtime on the nightshift and Claudia, well, she obviously doesn't work graveyard like me but she stays late a lot of nights and sometimes she comes in to the proofreading room and we play cribbage and talk about books and movies and her crazy family—there's, like, six thousand of them, she said. She went to Berkeley on a soccer scholarship and majored in History like I did. Only: obviously *she* went to law school and I went to . . . the beach . . . to try to write. Haha! She's not like all the other lawyers—totally full of themselves and humorless except about how they screw people over all the time and make the big bucks."

"And just plain screw, too, huh? Berkeley, huh? Color me impressed."

"She's a great girl—in that great girl category, for sure," Jaz said; then, only half-kidding, added: "Keep away from her."

"She *is* fetching," I said.

"I'm serious."

"Okay, *okay*," I said. "I'm serious."

"Seriously!"

"Okay, okay. Only joking ya, Jaz."

"Good luck tonight, by the way," Jaz said.

"You, too," I said.

I went over to the "stage" area in Walt and Nasty's vast living room and got the two guitars out of their tweed cases and tuned them, then I went upstairs to Jenny's room to see if she was there, primping or something.

She was at her vanity, looking at herself and putting on fresh lipstick; she clocked me in the shimmering mirror:

"*You!*"

"What?!"

"You know."

"What?! What'd I do?"

"And right in front of me!"

I couldn't tell from her tone whether she was seriously miffed or just kidding around.

"Oh, that," I said sarcastically and rolled my eyes around nineteen times. "What are you talking about?"

"You were flirting—and so *hard* too—with Laura so bad! I can't *believe* you, John."

Laura was the prettier of her friends.

"That is so not true!"

"Whatever. You know you were. You can be so charming, such a big shot, make people feel like they are the center of the world or something, the way you . . ."

"You look great, by the way."

"As pretty as *Laura*?"

"Stop it, Jenny. I'm really sorry if it came across like that. I was just . . ."

"Oh, spare me, okay? It's not that big a deal."

Now was the time, I knew I knew I knew, to go over and take her in my about-to-be-guitaring arms and tell her how much I appreciated her and how beautiful she was and how sorry I was and did I mention how beautiful she looked tonight?

Did I do that?

You bet I did.

"I'm really looking forward to hearing you tonight, by the way. As well. Have a great gig tonight, okay?"

"You too," she laughed. But it wasn't a big one. "Let's go. Let's rock."

She let me kiss her on the cheek, as she got up from the stool in front of her vanity—but I didn't let her get quote-unquote away with that, so I turned her face to mine and brought it up from where it was down and not meeting mine and looked her very very straight in the eye and made her, kinda, kiss me meaningfully and all let's make up, and down we went to where Walt and Rob already were on stage in the living room.

## it takes a teenage riot

Here I am, lying in bed thinking—about last night, yes, but mostly I'm thinking how I wish I were very dead. My head! (Not so loud.) My head. (That's better.) I'm even thinking too loud. My head is like Sonic Youth jamming with two or three Sonic Youth tribute bands that are trying to out-Sonic each other. Out-Youth each other in terms of crazy feedback and loud loudness. I have to think more quietly. It hurts to think too much at all. What am I thinking? Why am I? I need to go back to sleep immediately: sleep this thing off, hope it's not one of those hangovers that gets even worse as the day goes on. Oh God: please don't let it be one of those encroachers. Don't let me have one of those, Lord Jesus. Dear God, I will never drink again—I *promise*. Never. The very thought of it appalls me, Dear Sweet Jesus. I'm giving it up for good, amen.

Never. Never again. Although I do need to drink water right now, need to rehydrate. If I don't miraculously make it to the loo to drink water my head will throb like this for all eternity. But I can't move, can't budge. Is that a full glass of water by Jenny's bed? Is that something I can drink? *Oh Jesus God it's a tumbler full of wine!* Yeck! I think I'm going to Psycho all over Jenny's Persian rug—the one she loves. She would kill me. I hope she does, actually. I hope someone does, someone comes along and puts me out of this misery. It'd be my pleasure—a pleasure to end all unpleasantnesses. I need *water*. And one hundred aspirins to wash it down with. Kill me. Or call me a doctor. Preferably Kevorkian. Please. I can't take this. It's absolutely awful. Completely unbearable. Can't handle it. What's that over there by the door on the floor on a plate? Oh my God it's a half-eaten sandwich. It looks disgusting. I hope I did not eat the eaten half of that. Those had better not be my toothmarks on that shit. It looks improbably gray and viscid and revolting, that *thing*. Look at the cheese sticking out of it like a jaundiced tongue!

"Jenny?" I said softly.

"Mmm?"

"Are you asleep?"

"Yeah."

"Oh," I moaned. "Sorry."

"That's okay. Are you okay?"

"No."

"That's good," she garbled and went back to sleep.

## yesterday I got so old

I got up and got some water. It was not very easy. Hercules himself, were he in the state I was in (and required to perform the extra credit/beyond the twelve or however many tasks he had) of levitating himself from his Herculean bed and getting himself a glass of Artesian water actually from Artesia or Thebes or one of those Greeky places might have gone: "Fuck—that's going to be a *tough* one, dude. Near-insurmountable." That's how bad it was.

From what I remember, last night's post-party-gig was like one of those desperate just-post-college binges where, in a lackwit attempt to prove you can still party like you did when you were a fucking sophomore, you wake up at quarter to seven the day after and realize:

a) That you are not at home, in your own bed.
b) That you are in an unfamiliar (yet oh-so-familiar) place.
c) That you must have slept with your head pointing towards China or the center of the earth or somewhere and that it would take a grad student in calculus to figure out what position your throbbing neck is currently stuck in.
d) That parked against your nose is (choose one or more):
    1. Someone's butt.
    2. An ashtray, very full.
    3. A bottle, empty, of unmitigated poisonousness.
    4. A linoleum floor—probably the kitchen floor.
    5. A pool of your own spewage.
    6. A pool of someone else's.
    7. A toilet.
    8. A tree.
    9. A car tire.
    10.

You begin to wish that:

a) someone would bring you a cocktail of aspirins and Alka Seltzer.
b) someone would bring you a loaded gun.
c) you would have harkened to the guy who warned you that the spliff you were unquestioningly honking on might make you

have an extremely-disadvantageous-to-you conversation with Satan.

d) you would not have slept through all of those beastly alcohol awareness lectures in high school.

What I remembered about the gig itself, our set, was this: just before we made it, Jenny and I, on to the stage where Rob and Walt were tuning up and tapping toms, respectively, I got waylaid by Psycho, who was deep in conference with the Scather and Jaz and this handsome guy with long ash blonde hair tied back in a very straight ponytail:

"Purple Violet Squish!" Sterling said.

"What?!" I said. "Hey, you guys!"

"*The* Purple Violet Squish!" Sterling repeated.

"What?!" I said. The crowd was really big now and everyone was crowding into the gargantuan living room, chattering excitedly, it seemed.

"That's what he's suggesting you guys call yourselves," Psycho explained, yelling right in my ear. "I told them you'd asked me to help you find a name!"

He turned back to Sterling: "What was the other one, Sterling, my good man?"

"Orbiting Wyoming!" he said. He did a little dance and, making a fist-microphone, said: "'Ladies and Gentlemen, Orbiting Wyoming!' Haha! I like the sound of that!"

"It's a little too weird, sister!" I told him.

"Weird Sisters!" Psycho suggested. "I got it! 'Weird Sisters!'"

"Yes!" Sterling said. "It would have to be 'The,' though: 'The Weird Sisters.'"

"The Weird Sisters," I said, trying it out trippingly on the tongue. "That's pretty cool."

"Shakespeare, wot," Jaz chimed in.

"*Very* cool," Sterling said, then added: "Oh! This is McLeary—how rude of me! McLeary—John."

"Nice to meet you," I said. "Friend of Sterling?"

"Yeah, brilliant," he said in a limeyish accent I couldn't place as he accepted a fresh beer from a Natalie Wood-looking girl dressed up as a farmer's daughter or a Dorothy—I couldn't tell.

"Cool," I said. "Did you guys get a chance to talk to Jenny some more?"

Jaz, Psycho and Sterling all nodded yeah and then Psycho said: "She has got some nice . . ."

"Well, we gotta play now," I interrupted him.

"Break one of your guitars on the last song, John," Psycho suggested. "Fully Pete Townshend it!"

"You break one, Psych," I said and everyone kind of chuckled as just then Claudia squeezed her way next to Jaz and hoisted a red cup my way as if to tell me to have a good gig.

"You guys better keep an eye on Dave," I said. "Don't let him near the equipment. He will break a guitar."

"Have a good show," Jaz said. "I'll watch Psycho. I'll keep an eye on him."

"You'd better keep a *hand* on him," the Scather said.

"Break a leg," McLeary said.

"Very funny," Psycho said. "Seriously, John: break a guitar. At least break some strings!"

"Oh that probably won't be a problem!"

"You'll be fine; you guys are great," Sterling said.

"Hey," I said, stage-whispering in Sterling's ear. "What's the deal? I thought you hated Brits."

"McLeary? McLeary's different. He's almost not even a Brit. He might be Irish, for all I know—I dunno. Tasmanian, or something. Doesn't matter. He's *awesome*; you'll see. He's like a nationality of one or something. *Love* McLeary."

"Just picture everyone naked," Psycho said.

"Something tells me, dear Psycho," the Scather said like he was in a smoking jacket, holding a highball, with a cigarette holder going, "that you already are doing that—to certain members of the throng."

"Fucking A, I am," Psycho laughed.

"You'll be fine," Jaz said. "You'll be all right.

But we were not all right. We were not fine. We played everything too fast, especially the really fast songs, and especially everything I started on guitar. A perfectly less-than-auspicious beginning was nicely counterbalanced by a muddled middle section of the set, capped off by an epically catastrophic cringe-and-wince-inducing crescendo ending. On the very first song we committed the cardinal rock sin: stopping, then starting again. We twanged changes, I bungled lyrics, I personally plucked at least fourteen wrong chords. Well, maybe not that many but when you blow two or three changes it seems like way more. I felt myself lift out of my body when I caught myself straying off key. The wrong kind of out-of-body musical experience, surely. It was a good thing many passages called for screaming instead of singing; I was doing a lot of that, anyway, internally, that is. Just shrieking. Help! I thought-screamed. Get me off this stage. The P.A. caterwaulingly fed back and cut out and you couldn't hear what you were singing half the time and you were sure you sounded just like that bootleg of Linda McCartney crooning almost Olympianly out-of-tune on "Hey Jude."

I am convinced that Rob played at least one song in the wrong key entirely. An improper if not unheard of key. The key of Z, like.

And don't even talk to me about Walter. Horrendous. Stupendously so. Sometimes his drumming was like someone dragging a heavy body down stairs of Mayan temple proportions.

But still: though the tempos sometimes sagged, he did some good fills and started many a song out with the right beat. That was something.

Maybe we hadn't been so atrocious. Jenny, for one thing, was amazing. There aren't words to describe how confident she was amidst the occasional mayhem. She chopsticked and plinked and laid down long lines on the synth passages, sang sweetly-beautifully (if tentatively at times on account of the P.A. problems); smiled charmingly at the crowd when the sauced applause got a little over the top (people, in party mode, did clap—and loudly—for us after every goddam song). When she switched to guitar she strummed steadily and with style the insistent, humming, simple Cure-like/Bunnymenish lines she'd mastered in practice. She looked so sexy with a Telecaster on! A *monster* of rockist beauty. Rocking elegantly back and forth (I mean, this girl was not going to *headbang*, for heaven's sake). Come to think of it, we'd played like we meant it; there were times when the songs sounded like they were meant to sound. There were moments of reallygoodness. There were moments of undeniable okayness. There were certainly moments when, looking up from looking at the frets on my guitar, I could tell that *people were into it*. Fancy that. *Wal-ter!* Walter's friends near the room off the kitchen were chanting. *Wal-ter*—you *rock!* You half-expected them to come carry him away on their shoulders, make a palanquin of their persons for him or something as he smiled his most imbecilic smile.

After we played the last song (no encore—those were for sell-out bands) some people even came up and asked if we had a tape.

Even Sarah-Who-Hated-Me, well, she didn't exactly smile or anything but she nodded as I passed her in the hallway, looking for the bathroom, and she didn't even point her nose too skyward.

The Scather said a couple of people had asked him if we had a record out.

"You're kidding!" I said. "I *wish!*"

"Not at all. You should go talk to McLeary now; he's a producer. I wasn't gonna tell you till you'd played; I thought it'd make you all rabbited out and nervous. He seemed into it. Really into it, actually. You should go talk to him."

"You're kidding," I said, more incredulous than anything that an actual record producer would be in the same room as me—let alone that he'd been impressed by us. I must have smiled with my eyes, then. Sterling could tell I was flattered.

"He's worked, in fact, with a number of those limpwristed English bands you like."

"You like them too, Sterl."

"Not as much as you do. You know I am all about New Zealand, baby. Go talk to McLeary."

"You aren't taking the piss here, are you?"

"Not at all. Let's see: I think he worked with the Jasmine Minks. The Perfect Disaster . . ."

"No way! I love the Perfect Disaster!"

"The Jesus and Mary Chain . . ."

"What?! You're definitely kidding me now!"

"Well, maybe not the Jesus and Mary Chain, but *someone* very like them. Someone on Creation. the House of Love, maybe. Or Biff Bang Pow. You should talk to McLeary."

"Sterling?"

"*Yes?*"

"I should go talk to McLeary."

I found McLeary a little while later, told him we were looking for someone to engineer and produce a record; I introduced him to Jenny, who, I could tell, was instantly charmed by his hushabye Irishish voice and warm-bright smile and just slightly fucked-up teeth. We traded phone numbers and agreed to have a chat next week. Then, in celebration of having made it through the trial-by-fire trial of our first gig, and having met a cool producer who was interested in us (maybe), and lived to tell the tale, I drank myself into a tizzy, smoked a pack and a half of Marlboros, and laughed off all the mistakes I/we'd made on stage . . . and incurred the 747 in my head that I was telling you about.

And that's all I remember about the first gig.

Except for one thing: as we got ready to start the first song, Psycho had come up to my microphone, grabbed it, and, in a real Ed Sullivan sort of voice, ululated:

"*Ladies and Gentlemen—the Weird Sisters!*"

## god save the queen

I sat up in Jenny's bed and tried my best to down the full glass of tap water. Downstairs the faint strains of a heated argument between—guess who?—Walter and Nastasha could now be heard. I got up and went out the door and down the hall and poked my head into the stairwell.

Shameless eavesdropper.

"I never said that!" I heard Walt say.

"Yes, you did!" Nasty protested, her voice all Nancy of *Sid and Nancy*.

"Baby, I . . ."

"I'm not your baby, Walter! Don't you 'baby' me, you fuck. You *fucker*. Don't even think about it. You did say it, and you know you fucking did, so fuck you, fuckface. You know you did!"

"Natasha . . ."

"What?!"

"Would you just listen to *reason* for a second? Could you just be *rationale?*"

Oh, that'll help, I thought. Plus he said "rationale." Poor Walter. Poor Walt in every way.

"Rational? *Reasonable?* I'll show you *rational*. I'll show you *reasonable!*"

And then I heard a cup or a plate or an espresso maker go crack! against the wall.

Time to go back to Jenny's room, get Jenny, climb out the window and shimmy down the side of the house and *outta there!* Is that what I did? Not a chance. It was one of those awful, awful things you can't tear yourself away from—I hated myself for it, but I found myself being, for the moment, like those people who slow down on the freeway when there's an accident, the rubberneckers, the utterly, egregiously voyeuristic. I *hated* those people, made myself never look at an accident, made a point of putting them down occasionally and in general whenever they came up in casual conversation. Now I *was* one of them.

Great. Just great.

"There's reason for you!" Natasha shrieked. "You want another reason, huh? *Want* one?!"

"Go right ahead."

"You asshole!" she yelled and another harder, heavier object went thump! then bang! then crinkle crinkle crinkle! against something. Maybe she'd picked up the stove or the fridge or something and hucked it at him.

"Nice going! I mean, so what if I said you were being 'little' about some things! So what! I mean . . ."

"So you admit it! I *knew* it! You *are* an asshole. And a sizeist too. What a fuckity *ass*hole you are. That does it—I'm moving out!"

"Natasha . . ."

"And don't try and stop me!"

"I wasn't!"

"You weren't going to try and *stop* me?! You fuckhole. And if you think I am kidding here . . ."

"Nashy . . ."

"You think you're so *big*. You think you're *so* cool. Big rock star after just one gig! 'Hi, I'm *Walt*er. I'm in a lame band with a lame *name*. Aren't I bitchin'? I'm the *dummer*. I play the *dums*. I . . .'"

"Shut up!"

"I hate you! I hate you, I hate you, I *hate* you!"

"Shut your fucking . . ."

"I can't even stand to . . ."

"Shut up, Natasha! Shut up or I'll . . ."

"Or you'll *what?* Hit me? With one of your dumsticks? Go ahead: why don't you just go ahead and hit me with a drumstick, Walter . . ."

"Oh my God."

And then she just screamed and you could hear footsteps and doors upstairs about to be opened.

I dashed back to Jenny's room.

"What's going on downstairs?" she said, lifting her pretty head from the pillow, her hair a rich red-brown meringue and rinsed with sunlight coming from the curtains. "I thought I heard shooting. I mean shouting . . ."

"It might as well have been gunshots."

"Walter and Natasha?"

"Of course."

"Terrific."

"Let's get out of here—go out to breakfast, unkay?"

"Unkay. Kiss me."

"Umm."

# CHORUS

## just like honey

An eternal internal summer. That's what breakfast, later that afternoon, that night and the next few weeks with Jenny turned out to be. A summer of love. Even though it was fall. You know what I mean. The weather turned yuck and rain raked the ground and silvered the emptyish streets and wind-harried trees for five days straight there. In or out of the rain, being with Jen felt like queuing up for a matinee showing of a fifties classic you were dying to see again on the big screen, and it's crispy cold and she's in her favorite pea coat and you're in your favorite duffle coat, the dark blue one that wants replacing soon, and there are bright wet red and yellow painted leaves on the ground (we have seasons here—they're just not that drastic/dramatic) and once you're inside the movie theatre you get the hot chocolate for her and popcorn for the two of you and it strikes you that you got too big a bag of it on account of you're in love and the cornucopian overabundance of absolutely everything is a major theme in your eudaemonistic existence, your happy happy life.

Then the quote-unquote love interest next to you laughs to find you have popcorn butter on your chin and there she is with a ready napkin and she napkins you off with a little laugh and you laugh too and some people behind you shush you and do you care?

You do not.

When the rainy spell stopped and the air was fresh for a day or two after, we went on bike rides up to Griffith Park and looked at the picnickers and the tall hills and shrubs and eerie-pretty trees so spindly and rain-wet and water green that they look almost black. And sat under them, with anoraks under us, gazing at the indefatigable California post-rain sky so impossibly blue and the sun a fuzzy gem and so low in the sky you felt like you could command it down to the palm of your hand and hold it like a coin.

It's not like I'm romanticizing here or anything! Ha! Could it really have been this good?

Yes.

Here at last was someone to talk to and play my songs for and more importantly play my songs *with* and let her shape them. Someone to kiss and hold and kid around with and stuff: someone to reassure and quell fears for and tell her how great she really truly was on a daily basis, yeah.

Someone to lie around with in a daydream and listen to *Psychocandy* and *Darklands*; *Pet Sounds* and *The Village Green Preservation Society*; *Brotherhood, Low Life*, and *Power, Corruption and Lies*; *The Piper at the Gates of Dawn*; *Crocodiles*, *Heaven Up Here*, and *Porcupine*; all of the Cure, William Shatner, and Sonic Youth. Cocteau Twins. the Buzzcocks, the Jazz Butcher, Soft Boys, the Shaggs. The Carpenters. Robyn Hitchcock. And everything the Beatles ever did—even the ludic Christmas interviews.

And what more? What more did we do? Erranding. Shopping. Even in *malls*. Thrifting through thrift stores. On a goddam spending spree. Of course the money spent wasn't mine. Any given pickpocket approaching me was bound for a fistful of lint, let me tell you. There were times I scoured couches (other people's—not Jaz's certainly) for small change. Jaz was in the same bad way I was—underpaid, overspent, reckless, hopeless, devil-may-care about it. Sometimes we played rock/paper/scissors to see who got a piece of frostbitten garlic bread wrapped in foil that was Robert Scott-ed at the back of the ice box.

But Jenny and me—there was no end to the things we bought together. She bought, that is. Matador style, I'd just let her pass me by in the checkout line. After you with the credit card, darling, ma sponsor, mon amour.

One time we went shopping in Hell itself. Hell being Guitar Center, the totally commercial supermarket of guitars on Sunset. A complete headache of a place, with seventy-two heshers—especially on the weekends—wheedling at full volume on preposterous pointy-headstock guitars; and fifteen sales geeks dog-piling on you soon as you walk through the door. It's awful. You need to keep your visits there to a minimum—just like real Hell, Hell itself.

Jenny was checking out some electrics—she needed one of her

own and didn't want to borrow my spare Telecaster any more. Maybe a Jazzmaster or a Mustang would suit her, fit fine in her beautiful hands. I was pockity-pocking away on a candy apple red Jaguar, sitting on a nice Fender Bassman reissue in attractive tweed (accompanied with an unattractive $799.00 price tag) when a guy in a vest and with a neck-warmer haircut (you know, a mullet, a business-in-the-front-party-in-the-back "do," *hockey* hair, the Tennessee Top Hat or Canadian Passport dealie, the Kentucky Waterfall, the *Scholong*—as in "Short/Long"—the Ape Drape, Pharaoh Hair-o) came over and burbled: "Hey, man, how's it going, bro?"

Incorrigible mercenary.

"Fine," I said [pause] "man."

"You looking to buy a guitar today?"

"No, an aeroplane, man."

"I'm sorry. I didn't hear you . . . It's loud in here today."

"I said 'This is insane—this guitar."

"Isn't it bitchin'?"

"Very. But no—I'm not buying a guitar today. *She* is."

Sales guy surveyed the sea of guitars and spotted Jen over in the Fender solid body room. I walked over with him.

"Basically," I said, "I think she's tryna decide between this four hundred dollar piece of junk I was playing and the three hundred dollar piece of junk she's playing right now."

"Well," the mullet man said, trying, obviously, to be a good sport about my less than subtle way of telling him that we weren't no novices here, "I can talk to my manager about working a deal with you guys if you are serious about buying . . ."

"'Today'," I said. "Go ahead and ask her."

He got a look on his face like "*Huh?*—the only chicks who work here are the greeters at the door, man. You can't miss them. You've probably seen them at their other jobs as strippers on the Strip."

I gave him my Ah-I'm-Just-Kidding-Ya look and off he went, flopping away like a busy bee in too-tight designer jeans and funky, rockerguy-issue/superdork vest. (I don't *trust* guys in vests—vests with no suit attached, at least. Just as I don't trust a guy with a baseball cap with no logo on it: I mean, get an affiliation already, okay? Pick a team, fer chrissakes. Guys in caps with no logo on them are, if you ask me, possible C.I.A. agents or F.B.I. fuckers—that's what *I* think, at least.

They gotta be hiding something behind the no-emblem thing. Got to be.)

"Well," I asked Jenny, "what do you think, Jen?"

"I like this black one better than the red one. This is a . . ."

"Telecaster—like my back-up one you've been playing. How does it feel?"

"Nice, I think," she said and bent her head to form one of her weird chords.

"Do you want to plug it in or something."

"That's okay."

"Do you want me to, um, negotiate with the sales fellow?"

"No," she said, "I can do it. He's probably going to think I'm just some stupid wannabe rock chick that he can take advantage of."

"Probably," I said. "Half-mast your top—okay? A couple of buttons at least! Put that cleavage to work here."

"John!" she laughed.

In the parking lot as we were loading her new axe into the trunk of my Volvo, Jenny threw her arms around my neck the way excited girls always excitedly do (it never gets old) and she kissed me for the sweetest, longest time as heshers, rockabillies, jazz-o's, drummers, Cobain clones (afghan sweater, bleached long mop-bob), Slashes (leather jacket, Charles II cut), Geddy Lee-wards leaners (not even gonna describe *them*), Robert Smithies (trench or greatcoat, spider "do"), Clashmeisters (Levi jacket with cut-off sleeves, greaser backcomb), indie kids (plaid shirts, bad skin, reverse mullet), little kids and their dads or mums oafed, strolled, strutted, loped or marched past.

She got the thing for $255 or something, *with* a *case* (which costs a store like that nothing, by the way—next time you buy a guitar at a megastore, remember that): a good deal. Jen knew how to negotiate, all right. You take a prodigy-type kid who doesn't come from money and earns her own—she knows how to spend it, and save it, and make the most of it. Ever known a child prodigy now grown up, reader? What weird lives they've lead—all the same, all different.

And speaking of weird, Jenny definitely liked the Weird Sisters as a name and the name stuck; in our rehearsals since the debut we'd come to rely on her more and more and more for musical guidance in assembling and re-assembling the songs: she was really integral now.

## we've only just begun

I don't mean to make you nauseous or anything but being with Jenny felt like going to watch a Technicolor sunset made by advanced smogginess and someone comes up and gives you a free box of the freshest sushi and a bottle of Japanese lager extra chilled. The kind of as it were *live dream* where you are forever beachily pulling each other towards each other in the cooling squeaking rain-hardened sand. It felt like a chilly blackberry midnight sky frosted with close stars of aqua blue and dazzling topaz. It felt like the first time you have a girl alone in college and a lascivious look glosses her sparkly eyes as she informs you that her roommate's gone for the long weekend. Her tongue lolls to one side of her mouth or she bites her lip *just so* and she turns her head one way then the other in order to pull off her tight white top and she's suddenly kneeling on her dorm room bed, then lying back on it expecting you to get her cute, short, university-acronym-stenciled shorts and no-nonsense but still quite sexy panties off with maximum collegiate efficiency and confidence. It felt like that. Or maybe the best analogy is, it's Christmas morning and your dad's just opened the door to the garage where there's a new green ten-speed Schwinn with North Road handlebars and a purple bow on it big as your head. It's a bike about which you've dreamed and dreamed, though your parents have spent the past two months saying: "Now, Junior, don't go getting your hopes up. We don't know if Santa Claus can afford to bring you a new bicycle this year. We'll just have to wait and see."

Junior. Remember Junior? The kid with the Sears catalogue? Junior's never known bliss like this, like what, latterly, Jenny and I have known—not even in high school has he. Of course not in high school! For high school is a spirit-dampening, spirit-trampling construct of loneliness, alienation, melancholia and bewilderment. Plus hormonal quiddities. It's not for nothing that American high schools are surrounded by chain-link fences, padlocked and ominous. Junior knows by now what metaphors are—and a chain-link fence is one: of that he's certain.

So are the school uniform metaphors: the itchy, drab gray, characterless slacks, blank white button-down Oxford shirts, boring blue blazers and choking red-and-blue striped rep tie for boys; the itchy drab gray or alternate itchy Stewart kilt regulated to three inches above the scraped or suntanned knee, imagination-dashing yet strangely titillating plain white blouses and dowdy rayon insignia-emblazoned blue cardies for the girls.

When we last met him, post-"the talk" with Junior Senior, Junior, inspired by all those LPs and 45s, has taken up the Folk Guitar. He's had fencing, drawing, French, painting, singing, horse riding (English *and* Western), tennis, ceramics, photography, golf, German, judo, moccasin making, calligraphy, piano, remote-control airplane flying, kite flying, chess, swimming, waterskiing, trumpet, drum, origami, Japanese (well, *one*), and skiing lessons, not forgetting Cub Scouts, Indian Guides, Webelos, Boy Scouts, science camp, summer camp, tennis camp, bible study summer camp, catechism camp, and creative writing camp.

But this—taking guitar lessons—is something he swears he's gonna stick with, follow through with, get real into. "I *promise*, Mom and Dad," Junior pleads. "This is something I really really really wanna do! Pretty please? Please? *Can* I?"

A super-pretty hippie chick's been engaged to tutor him in basic chords and keys. Her genuine middle-parted, board-straight, lemon-blonde Joni Mitchell-issue hair's a silken curtain and her smile's a living sunbeam; her color-flowing clothes, Junior notices, hang tight around the golden-tan top of her and loose around the bottom part of her and her sweet voice, like her sweeter face, is debatably Elizabethan and unquestionably spine-tinglingly beautiful; and Junior, ever the overeager student, learns guitar fast in order to impress her, or try to: in a mere month's time he knows seventeen chords and four strums and three intricate and two simple fingerpicking patterns. He's memorized three Beatles songs and even written one of his own. It's a simple I-IV-V that goes "Get ready to go—with the rise of the sun" *ad infinitum* and the chorus is "The sun, the sun, the sun." And that's all it is, but he plays it for her and she smiles her immeasurable smile and she says languidly-thoughtfully: "*Hey*, Junior. That's really good. Your first song—how great. I'm real proud of you." And he beams shyly back at her as she ruffles his short-back-and-sides. And the blush he blushes momentarily blots out some freckles.

His crush on her ("Debbie") is a singularly crushing thing until he learns she's quitting college and going off to India for six months to be with her *boyfriend*, a race car driver who's found a spiritual leader for the both of them called Sri Sri Swamikrishna Mahanrati "Bobo Baba" Hosenally Singh. Then it, his crush, is just a crushed thing. As a parting gift, she prints out "Both Sides Now" in her own handwriting (the "i's" of course dotted with little flowers) and gives him her personal copies of *The Piper at the Gates of Dawn* (she wrote her name on it in the upper left corner!) and *Safe as Milk*. She also hands Jr. a stick of cinnamon incense which he surreptitiously bungs in the trash can, thinking his mom and dad might think the stick is a stick of hallucinogenic hippie drugs.

Thanks, a *lot*, hippie chick! Give Junior a heartbreaking song to learn to play so that he can experience over and again his first very own heartbreak—courtesy of *you*, hippie chick. Way to go. How can you not know that he's fallen in hopeless junior high school love with you? How could you not? To crown all, give him records about which for years he'll think: "I can never do *any*thing like this! This is the most mind-blowingly intimidating music I have ever heard. I could never do anything like that! I'll never be a rock star—or even write *one* song as cool as this guy Pink, that guy Captain."

At their last session together Debbie tells Junior to look within himself for his *dharma*, to watch out for *kharma*, and that everything is *maya*. In fact, Maya's what she's changing her name to. But what Junior remembers most is that her wide-striped sun-dress, so sheer, clings to her throat-catchingly when she swirls to put her guitar in its case for the last time. He vaguely remembers her talking excitedly of Benares and New Delhi and Kashmir and Goa and Rishikesh and Bombay. But the diaphanous ass-shot is what he gets for the most part to remember her by. He will never forget her. And he doesn't. And he'll look up in his *World Book* the places she was meant to stop at and look at the pictures and picture her being there and regret jettisoning the incense; and he will have her name on his lips for months and months at night like a kind of prayer.

Wow.

But now, in the quote-unquote big time of prep school high school, the four *worst* years of your life, and in the wake of the pretty hippie chick's international/spiritual/boyfriendly defection, Junior's put playing music on hold in order to concentrate on playing serious sports. Or trying to, that is. His nice dreadnought guitar languishes in his bedroom closet. His folky songbooks (Dylan, Donovan, Doors) yellow on the bookshelf. The purple Nehru jacket he begged his mother like a fakir to buy for him (and that he wore all of twice) hangs forlornly in the back of the closet. *When the music's over*, as our old friend Jim moans on *Strange Days*, there are more pressing things to attend to, for playing sports is the way to get chicks, apparently. Junior can't fail to note the sun-lightened cinnamon-sugar ponytails of the always-smiling cheerleaders, songleaders, homecoming/prom queens and cutie-pie impressionable freshman girls bobbing alongside the guys on the football team of the mostly very preppy school he goes to after Cretin Vallley Junior.

Around the most choice, verdant part of the quad, the football team, their maiden minions, and certain sporto elites from other popular squads such as lacrosse or baseball (never wrestling—too queer and sweaty; never water polo—green-haired weirdos) clique together symbolically apart from the rest of the school. On occasion, at the lunch or snack break, said jocks will fill their empty milk cartons with drinking fountain water and, en masse, like a mini-legion from stories Junior's read in Greek and Roman mythology, catapult said water bombs towards an unsuspecting, timorous set of baloney-sandwich-munching non-sport kids. The chess club dweebs are the favored target. the athletes are, junior sees, perpetually intimidatingly insouciant; they and their smiles and high fives seem to own the school; and they experience an almost unreal elation in watching the chess club unfortunates holding their chessboards above their heads like shields ("scuta," Junior learns in Latin class) as the waxen milkwater projectiles rain right down on them. It is apparent that a few of the lacrosse stars and baseball big shots have been welcomed into the football clique solely on the merit of their strong and viciously accurate throwing arms, and they all dispute the mastery of who's nailed the most nerds each lunch.

Neither brawny, burly, beefy, brave, stupid, reckless, fast, violent or insane enough for football, Junior tries out for the volleyball and tennis teams—sports where the other side is on the other side of a net. a net that will ostensibly stop the opponent from hurting and thus humiliating him in front of the understandably far fewer ponytails that come to watch the matches in his fields. The nets are immaterial somewhat, however, in that, even though he makes both teams, Junior is a sempiternal scrub: he rides the pineski all year in junior varsity volleyball and holds on by his teenage fingernails to the last rung on the Tennis ladder. As the lowest of the low on a team that is ranked high in the Golden State, Junior is not permitted to travel with the tennis team; Coach "Chip" Von Chipp only lets him play home matches. Junior's usual opponents in said contests are hefty, incessantly sneezing allergy or asthma sufferers whose draconian parents have forced them to play sports—boys whose lackluster or effete strokes, as it were, would be more appropriate on butterfly-catching excursions to central Ecuador or in public swimming pools than on sun-kissed Southern California tennis courts. How, with all the sneezing and wheezing, they even keep hold of the handles of their respective Jack Kramer Pro Staffs and Björn Borg–endorsed Donnays is a total wonder.

There must be *some* sport Junior can adequately acquit himself at! There must be some field where he can pocket his little share of the glory, sew a letter on his sweater and have a shot at a ponytail! Track and field requires swiftness and/or strength and stamina: *disqualified*. As does cross-country: *pass*. The basketball coaches not only constantly Stanley Kowalski at the players, but also require them to get crew cuts and sign affidavits that they will not, under any circumstances, drink beer or bong, puff, toke or pipe the demon weed marijuana: *foul*. Forget *that*. Junior is convinced that the basketball coaches' rebarbative edicts may even be illegal. He's done some research. He hopes to become a lawyer someday, just like Junior Senior. In his requisite yearly interview with the school counselor Junior has waxed semi-eloquent about his barristerial aspirations. The counselor has, in a way, been very encouraging. She's told Junior that, judging from his junior high transcripts and current class performance (52 in Latin, 47 in Biology, 74 in Mythology, 86 in English, 34 in French, 75 in History, this term), his not exactly model Citizenship, and the sarcastic responses to the various Rorschach inkblots she keeps waving at him, he's definitely well on the way to becoming the sort of person who will spend a *lot* of time in court!

Re: basketball? Junior's pretty good at hoops, he can really shoot, but he has curiously deduced that adolescent hormones *need* a certain amount of beer and drugs in order to thrive, flourish and produce clear skin. For evidence, *just look* at the kids on the B-ball fifteen! Many of the poor players have archipelagos of maximum acne on their faces. And ponytails, Junior's pretty sure, do not find acne an attractant. Jr. imagines the basketballers' kit bags stuffed with bottles and bottles of puissant tetracycline along with their warm-up jackets and uniforms. Youch. No thanks. He'll look for another sport.

There's always the soccer team, but soccer, it seems, is exclusively for foreign exchange students and people of that ilk who don't mind the occasional cleat or toe in the shin: *punt*.

Golf? *Please*. You ride around in a cart, wear repellent plaid pants or pants with *pleats*, and hit a little ball towards a little hole—*and no one tries to stop you*. That, Junior epiphanies, is the definition of a sport: *someone has to try and* stop *you from doing something*. Golf, like bowling or quoits or something, is a *game*. The minute you get to run (and maybe scream) at Arnold Palmer or Jack Fucking Nicklas and try to knock his club out of his hand as he's putting? *Then* it's a sport, baby. Then it is, okay? Otherwise, it's as our other old friend Sam Johnson says "a good walk spoiled." Golf's for the last-picked for kickball, Junior thinks. The chess club has more *chutzpah*.

The rugby team is . . . ah, come on.

Lacrosse you have to have a hyphenated name or at least III ("the third") after it even to try out for—plus a personal chauffeur, an overweight trust fund, a mean streak a mile wide, and Lacoste shirts in every color (plus terrycloth): *nix*. Mrs. Junior's mom has gasped at the cost of the three Lacostes Junior's managed to get her to shell for. He can't possibly risk asking for two more—which would make one for each day of the after-school week. She's not taking him to Brooks for surrogate, alligator-free alligator shirts, either. She's put her foot down.

What about baseball? Baseball—there's a thought. Girls must like baseball players a *little* bit. At a San Francisco Giants vs. Los Angeles Dodgers game Junior Sr. took Jr. to just last summer there were nice-looking, always-smiling females almost everywhere you looked; and right before the seventh inning stretch he heard his father mutter "Goodness gracious!" at a filly with overinflated tetherballs for breasts who, whooping and waving her arms about like a madwoman or a politician on television, had jounced out onto the field and was attempting to catch a piggyback ride from the first baseman.

Baseball! Eureka! The national pastime. Although no nets are involved, and the other side is plentifully armed with potentially GBH-inflicting clubs of polished ash and hollow aluminum, a baseball diamond, Junior figures, is, barring the backstop, a wide open space and, if necessary, he can run. Furthermore, in Little League he was pretty good. A two-year all-star, in fact. He pitched without catastrophe. Fielded at third sack *sans erreur*. Didn't strike out too many times. And not once did he, jitterbugging beneath a high fly ball in the outfield, lose it in the supernova-ing sun or drop it with two out in the bottom of the ninth. Baseball. Yeah. Why not?

So, in his junior year Junior signs up, tries out, and garners a pat slot in the starting rotation. He wins two games, fanning a total of thirteen batters and allowing only three unearned runs and one earned one—a cheap shot inside-the-park home run. Junior's name appears in the school paper. Junior's *picture* appears in the school paper. (Ah but unfortunately it's not a picture of him on the mound or at bat; rather, he's in a shot of the football clique at lunch break, off to the side of course with gob hilariously agape as he bears open-mouthed witness to another round of milk carton bombardment. The picture's not part of some prep exposé; in fact, the caption under it reads "Seniors Have Some Fun at Lunch Break—*And* Keep Their Throwing Arms in Shape!")

Twice there's a "W" after Junior's name in the box scores of the seaside community's daily rag. On the field, in front of everyone, Coach Krunsch, the J.V. coach, slaps him on the back after Junior's second win. A notorious hard-nose with hard, dark blue eyes closer than were Karen and Richard Carpenter, beadier than Cher in her "Cherokee People" phase, and meaner-looking than cat shit (though you rarely see them on account of he rarely takes off his Ray Bans), Coach Krunsch has, to the best of the rest of the team's knowledge, never slapped *anyone* on the back. He has slapped players in the *face*, all right, but never on the back. Nope: this is a first. All right, Junior! The team gives him a cheer that goes "Yippipakaw! Yippipakaw!" and in unison and with alacrity showers him with sunflower seed shell cud and chewing tobacco juice.

Way to go, Junior! You've thrown a helluva coupla games.

In the locker room Thatcher, Slater, Chandler, Spencer and Gardner from the starting varsity football team, surprisingly, notice Jr. and tell him "Hey, nice going, buddy!" Then they frog-march him into the gymnasium bathroom and quote-unquote baptize him by shoving his head into an open toilet and flushing it archetypally thrice. *Rite de passage! Un, deux, trois*. Tell me acceptance to the key jock clique is not just around the corner! Maybe tomorrow at lunch Junior will even be invited inaugurally to milk-carton a docile circle of drooling handicappers! Wouldn't that be swell. Maybe he'll be called in to help "baptize" a few of the chess clubbers, some of whom are former friends. For a brief spell he actually attended a few meetings, though he never joined. Junior would feel real bad terrorizing kids he actually knew, kids he's traded horses and bishops and rooks with, but he's sure they'd understand. I mean, come on: tell me they wouldn't willingly trade places with him now that a few of the glorious sportos have certifiably acknowledged him. Tell me they wouldn't relish the opportunity to dunk their *own* heads in the locker room johns. With Thatcher, Slater, Gardner, et al. looking admiringly on. Come *on!*

And get this: he can't be certain (the babel of the halls between periods being what it is) but he thinks *one of the J.V. cheerleaders even said hello to him yesterday*. Although the Christian name she hailed him with—Tommy—is, alackaday, not his own, at least she spoke to him, at least she made a sound that was directed towards or at him. Frampton-comes-a-fucking-live! What a great spring this is gonna be! What a great school! How good life is. Who knows?—he might even get a date to the Spring Fling, or maybe, just maybe, the prom.

In Biology one Friday after the doll-faced, super-succulent cheerleader may have said hello to him, a *magnificently* bewitchingly princesslike girl in an incandescent lemon sweater (for casual Friday) *winked* at him! She winked! An apple-cheeked Snow White brunette with jewel-y blueberry eyes. Just the most torturously beautiful girl he's ever seen. In tight white pedal pushers and champagne dance shoes. What a honey. What a fox. There's no mistake this time: girls are starting to like him. This sporto thing is paying off. Chicks are digging his trip, man.

"Hey, Sanderson," Junior psssts to his lab partner, the starting first baseman on the J.V. team, "you're not going to be*lieve* this but Michelle MacGregor just winked at me!"

"What?! No way."

"She winked at me! Michelle MacGregor did."

"What?! Get *off*. I mean 'out.' She did not."

"Did so!"

"Did not," Sanderson definitively states, making a simply hideous face: "I just heard her ask Mr. Sell for a pass to the nurse. She said she bumped her eye on a microscope. So there."

"Oh," says Junior, all deflated, and goes back, with even less enthusiasm, to butchering a frog.

*

Near the end of the season Junior's team, the St Caulfied the Martyr Academy Mariners, is tied for first with their crosstown rival, the Millhouse School Blue Whalers. Coach Krunsch gives Junior the nod as the starting pitcher. He also gives Junior a ride home after practice one day in his sporty Porsche convertible, a hot red job that's chillingly fast, low to the ground, and seems to be mufflerless. Junior anticipates the high soprano engine exploding any moment. Accompanying them, sitting on Junior's lap in fact, is a foxy sophomore who keeps stats for the team and also, rumor has it, fucks Coach Krunsch.

For Coach Krunsch walks taller than John Wayne, is more tan than George Hamilton, and has teeth that sparkle harder than any set of dentures in an Ultrabrite commercial. Handsome, is he? Cut? With facial features more chiseled than any personage painted by Modigliani? You might say so. The fine skin at his jawline tightens in a New York instant. His slightly ski-jump nose is thin and perfect. His softly wavy wine-dark ex-Marine hair marinates in Brylcreem. Palpable muscles ripple every which way, pulsate, bulge, heave, and wave. Even Coach's *ears* signify *I can bench press three times my body weight.* In bun-tight blood-red lycra coaching shorts, gray workout St Caulfield Athletics tee, blinding white knee socks and flatulent black windbreaker he struts towards his classroom—U.S. History—where he not only advances the theory that American television lost the war in Vietnam (yes indeed he served there—two tours), but that the New Deal was a raw deal and that Kennedy (an obvious Commie Pinko) was, thankfully, ordered murdered by LBJ. The landing on the moon? A waste of time and money. The Holocaust? Dubious. Hiroshima? Human progress. The Great Depression? A scam. Prohibition? Another one.

Coach Krunsch is serious. Very serious. So serious that he doesn't even take off his trademark Ray-Bans during the jingoistic, super-tendentious films he shows his U.S. History class. There he stands at the back of the classroom, arms akimbo, palpating his super slender, very fit hips, ready to punch something or bark at it. Sometimes he's so serious he speaks entirely in capital letters. Perhaps as a stab at egalitarianism, perhaps ironically, he customarily refers to the students as *individuals*. Here he is addressing an ambitiously obese kid who just barely made the J.V. team as third string catcher: "Pendleton! *You're* a very *large* individual. Well, we're going to do something about THAT! [And here he had Pendleton up on a scale in the locker room and trembling.] You are approximately *one biscuit* away from TWO HUNDRED POUNDS, Pendleton! That is UNACCEPTABLE in a boy your goddam squat height! Perhaps we should have some of the huskier individuals on the football team see if they can BENCH PRESS *you!* WOULD YOU ENJOY THAT, PENDULOUS? *WOULD* YOU? NO? I DIDN'T THINK SO! PENDULOUS! GET BACK ON THAT TREADMILL AND SEE IF YOU CAN'T SHED AT LEAST ONE OF THOSE BREASTS YOU'RE SPROUTING! OF COURSE YOU *HAVE* NOTICED THAT YOU ARE GROWING SEVERAL BREASTS, HAVEN'T YOU, PENDLETON? I PERSONALLY HAVE SEEN YOU SHOWERING AFTER PRACTICE WITH A SHIRT ON. ARE YOU EMBARRASSED BY THEM, PENDLETON? *ARE* YOU? I IMAGINE IT *IS* EMBARRASSING FOR YOU, SON. I KNOW A COUPLE OF THE PITCHERS HAVE NOTICED THOSE BREASTS OF YOURS. IN FACT, SOME OF THEM ARE HAVING TROUBLE CONCENTRATING ON THE STRIKE ZONE ON ACCOUNT OF THEY ARE THINKING THAT THERE'S A *GIRL* SQUATTING BACK THERE IN THE CATCHER'S POSITION WHEN YOU ARE ON THE PRACTICE FIELD! NOW DROP AND GIVE ME FIFTY, YOU TWINKIE, BEFORE I HAVE YOU MEASURED FOR A BRA!"

"We need this upcoming game, Junior. We NEED it," Coach Krunsch opines, offering Junior a menthol Pall Mall while simultaneously downshifting into third round a hairpin turn, ramming in a tape of *The Best of Lionel Ritchie* and friskily tickling the left knee of the foxy sophomore. It seems Coach has as many arms and hands as a Hindu Love God. From where he sits, natch, Junior has a good shot at the girl's legs. My God, they're the color of perfectly toasted and buttered and honeyed Wonder Bread—creamy, lean, lithe, smooth; gorgeous, golden, delicious, flawless.

She's *so* beautiful.

Coach Krunsch, you are a lucky lucky man, thinks Jr. A pedophile of great moral turpitude, yes, but a fucking lucky one nevertheless. He's read *Lolita*, Junior has. He knows what's up. One thing Junior also knows is that the foxy sophomore's a shoe-in for the lead role in his masturbatory fantasies for the next two months at least. As soon as he gets home, in fact, he will beeline for the bathroom and ease profuse, approaching-sexual-peak sperm into the pearly sink. In order not to get an exceedingly ill-timed boner, what with the foxy sophomore sitting on his lap, Junior fills his mind with thoughts of, er, baseball . . . Yeah, baseball, that's it . . . ". . . the city playoffs, you know? Junior? JUNIOR? Are you *LISTENING*?"

"Huh?" Junior says, snapped out of his randy reverie. "Sorry? Sorry, Coach."

"I said 'The winner goes to the city playoffs.' And get this, Junior: *those* individuals get a steak dinner at the Kiwanis Club, then go to Disneyland for the day, then the next day see the California Angels vs. the New York Yankees. Don't smoke? Good. Good for you, Junior. So many of your classmates do, unfortunately. Nasty habit, smoking. Wish I could quit. Isn't that what I'm wishing all the time, Shelley?" the Coach says winkingly, like he's some sorta Jack Nicholson in the early scenes of *Cuckoo's Nest*. "A very bad habit. Like a lotta things. Ha! Anyway, we're counting on you, Junior. We need this win. WE GOTTA HAVE IT."

The day of the big game, Junior's very nervous, naturally. He's also utterly exhausted from choking the bishop an average of four and a half times a day, his eroto-ruminations of course trained on the foxy sophomore Shelley. His brain is damp pulp. His mind's a Scantron with all the bubbles blank. Shelley's legs *haunt* him. In his hormonally kinetic mind they follow him everywhere. They're private detectives; they're ghosts; they won't let him go, leave him alone. They're Sam Spade, Nancy Drew, the Hardy Boys and the apparitions in *The Turn of the Screw* and all of Edgar Allen Poe all rolled into one.

The pressure's on, the grandstand's packed, it's practically groaning like a freshman getting more lines in Latin for talking during prep. The bowed benches are rows of staggered canoes, ponytails and assorted sportos and civilians in mufti paddling all over the place, chattering like magpies. Teachers, reporters, younger siblings, alums, and community boosters. Some major league farm team scouts are even said to be about. Practically the entire school's there! The adjacent varsity stands are also overburdened with rubbernecking and simply necking spectators alike. People are starting to wander over from them on account of the senior team is winning by a score of 21-1 in the third inning, simply pasting St

Caul's oft-vilified crosstown rival. Junior heard a rumor that one of the stars on the varsity team ran out a shot to left by *running backwards to first*. Amazing, this sporto school. What *showmanship!* What, well, not *sportsmanship* but, um, tradition? Aplomb?

Fans fan out along the J.V. backstop, the far back of the third and first baselines. The snack bar's running out of hotdogs, popcorn, ice cream sandwiches, Red Vines, and Crackerjacks. Individual-size pepperoni pizzas are flying out of there like Frisbees. It's crazy.

Tall clouds merry far-awayly in the mid-spring, lightly smoggy tangerine and Prussian Blue sky, and a soft, tinselly light suffuses the longish grass of the outfield. It's a good day for baseball, as good old legendary Vin Scully might well say—very slight breeze, air dry and not overripe with pollen, lambent but not overweening sunshine. The infield grass blushes from the recent mowing it's had and the base-path dirt's been freshly sprinkled and looks a fine dark pink. Most importantly for Junior, the mound's had a meticulous manicure not too long ago. It's not too tall and not too short. There's a gopher hole-sized divot right in front of the right side of the rubber, but Junior's right toe knows its way around it; after all, it is his home field.

Post-warm-up pre-game pep talk: Coach offloads a concatenation of clichés as the players gather reverently round him, intermittently turning their heads in order to spit out sunflower seeds and hack garden-variety loogies, yawn or blow their noses using the quote-unquote Italian Handkerchief method of holding an index to one nostril and blowing out the other one: "Get out there and give a hundred and ten perCENT today, boys. Keep your HEAD in the GAME and your EYE on the BALL. We gotta play together as a TEAM! There's no 'I' in team, boys. There's 'meat' if you make an anagram out of it, but . . . Never mind! Let's be a MEAT out there, TEAM! You know what I MEAN. The best DEfense is a good OFFense. ALSO: the best *defense* is a good *defense*. So let's play DEFENSE out there, today, when we're on the field playing . . . defense. OKAY?! And when we are at BAT, well, we gotta step up to the PLATE! And play OFFENSE 'cause the best OFFENSE is . . . Look: let's play ALL NINE INNINGS today—go all *out* out there. Till the INDIVIDUALS on the opposing team ARE out! Junior's gonna help his own cause today and YOU GUYS are going to TOO. GOT it?! All right all right all RIGHT ! Let's get the JOB DONE and WIN one for, uh, the TEAM, okay?! *All right! Be the* MEAT *out there,* TEAM! WIN, WIN, WIN!"

"Yippipakaw! Go Mariners!" the team shouts in unison and the ump cries "Play *ball!*"

Getting an early read on said umpire's concept of a strike zone, Junior is pitching well. His arm's well-rested and loose and he mixes his "stuff"—fastballs low on the inside or high and just catching the outside corner; goofy, looping change-ups; unpredictable curveballs; and zany, trifling forkballs—like a champ. He even has an (albeit intermittently unintentional) knuckleball going. What's going on? Junior's thrown a great, almost out-of-his-head eight innings.

Top of the ninth, the score's 2-1, Mariners' favor. The visitors have only gotten three hits off him—a singing, meteoric double to right that results in their only run (Junior walked a man that inning who stole second). The first batter's crowding the plate; his bat makes little upside-down butter-churning motions. Junior winds up and throws low-and-away for ball one.

"Come on, Junior," Coach Krunsch yelps.

"Junior!" someone from the stands sharply barks. "Bear down, buddy!"

Anderson, who is playing first today in the stead of Sanderson, urges "Let's go, Junior. You can do it!"

(Sanderson, an explosive, irremediable vandal and prankster, has been suspended for painting all of the saddles in the school stables with turpentine, Ben Gay, and Cool Whip.)

Junior winds up, hurls the next pitch straight down the pipe.

"Stee-rike one!" the ump calls.

"Atta boy, Junior!" Junior Senior hand-megaphones from behind the backstop.

"Atta boy!" McHearson, the second baseman, calls out.

"Way to go, Junior!" Mrs. Junior's Mom hollers.

Junior palms the rosin bag, weighs it in his thoughtful hand. He's lookin' mighty fierce. His eyes narrow, go all aluminum-cool blue.

Everything's an intense phantasmagoria of suspense and tension.

*Calm down and breathe,* Junior counsels himself, virulently hucking the ball into his glove a couple of times and cursing under his breath, *calm fucking down.* He shakes off the catcher's next sign, shakes off the next one. He wants to throw his change-up. He's gonna catch this guy off guard. Hoodwink him. The catcher's Pendleton, by the by: the first and second string catchers are in the infirmary with food poisoning they got from eating the hall pudding that, as it turns out, wasn't all pudding.

"Hey, batter-batter," Junior's infielders chatter. Here's the wind-up and the pitch: the ball floats towards home; it's bigger than the Hindenberg; the batter's eyes go fucking popping; he takes a monstrous, Casey-at-the-Bat-sized cut: whiff! "Stee-rike two!" the ump pronounces . "Woo-hoo!" Shelley the foxy sophomore comments and claps her clipboard against her burnished, beautiful, white-shorted thighs.

Junior's sweating now, just dripping. Perspiration fairly rills down his jerseyed arms. The mound's a moat, almost. Any moment the ump's gonna row out to it and call him for throwing unintentional spitballs.

The next two balls Junior throws over the backstop, practically. 3 and 2. Coach Krunsch canters out to the mound.

"All right, Junior?"

"Yeah."

"You sure? You want me to pull you?"

"No, Coach."

"Okay, then. Let's get this next goddam individual OUT! Keep the ball low. Stop trying to AIM it, okay, Junior? Throw. Throw LOW. Bear down, rear back, and THROW! OKAY?!"

"Okay."

Junior looks up, looks down, looks up. Cleats the dirt. Nods. Krunsch pats him on the butt and trots back to the dugout. He's got Michaelson, a junkballing lefty, and Stevenson, a smoke-throwing righty, warming up in the bullpen. The crowd is going wild. Everyone's clapping and huffing and puffing and chattering. "Junior!" they encourage him. "Come on, Junior!"

"Hay *Shoon*ior!" the voice of one of the soccer-playing foreign exchange students unmistakably ululates. "You can doos it, Shoonior. I known you can! Dontchoo letsa them keek a homerun, Shoonior! Dontchoo *lets* them, my fren!"

Junior concentrates harder than ever, more than if he were taking his SAT's. Thinking hard about what Coach has told him, he throws low. Too low. The ball scuds into the dirt in front of Pendleton. If he were playing cricket, it would have been a perfect bowl. Unfortunately for Junior, this is America: we don't play cricket here, old bean. We don't *bowl*, old chap; we *pitch*. Ball four. Man on first, no outs. "Awwwwwww!" grouses the home crowd. "Fuck!" breathes Junior, sweeping up the rosin bag again and slamming it down just as rapidly. "Fuck!" Coach Krunsch goes. "God fucking dammit!" "God fucking *bless* it!" Bjornson, a born-again Christian bench-jockey seethes. "Fuck!" everyone else on the bench goes. "Fuck fuck fuck fuck fuck fuck fuck!" The foxy sophomore is shaking her foxy locks on her foxy head. "Fuck fuck fuck!" Junior, echoing his teammates, swears. The overexcited visiting team quacks like an overbooked barnyard. Out Krunsch comes again to the mound; his face is as red as his cap; the St C insignia on it's whiter than any scary-movie spectre. The Millhouse team's fans boo. The St Caul's fans razz them. The visitors blow raspberries back. Someone discuses a smoking tyro pepperoni pizza into the dugout of the visiting team. Their starting catcher catches it like a foul line drive and pops it, whole, into his mouth. He chews it, spits it back into his glove, kneads it into a quote-unquote fastfood-softball, then rifles it back towards the hometown stands. A Freshman in silver wire rims catches it with his chessboard. The St Caul's fans, with voices high and eminently taunting, jeer once more. One of the girls' soccer team angrily kicks an errant batting helmet high high above the head of the visitors' first base coach. It has all the force behind it, her kick, of a frustrated Catholic prep school girl in a very sexy kilt. It's exactly the sort of legendary sexually frustrated behavior that has lead Junior, raised Protestant, to beg his parents to send him to a private Catholic prep school. The helmet flips cinematically up and up into the air; Junior watches in utter fascination as it then bonks, plop!, backwards, right onto the first base coach's head. Reeling around trying to pull it off, the hapless coach wanders like a drunk onto the infield and bumps right into Anderson. Childishly, Anderson shoves him disgustedly and makes a mouth like Laura Dern in *Blue Velvet* (though it will be a few years before that fine film is made/released). Both benches empty. Suddenly everyone's got a war yell going. Even the benignant bat boys bomb in and start swinging, having unquivered Louisville Sluggers in pine and black, and gun-metal blue Thumpers. There's a brouhaha, a rhubarb, a gang-fight, a barney. A set-to, a what-for, a battle, a scrap. The Millhouse pitcher, a funny-toothed beanpole with a lazy left eye, bounds out to the mound and essays an uppercut to Junior's chin that misses badly. The guy's arms are so long that when he misses it seems more than likely that he'll punch *himself* out. What's this funny-toothed beanpole with the lazy left eye thinking? Jr. thinks. I didn't do anything to *him*. Of course,

I'm *going* to do something to him if he gets another turn at bat. What happened to my resolution exclusively to play sports with nets, anyway, huh?

In short order the umpire restores order. "Play ball!" he yodels. Sure, some punches got thrown, some pushes were pushed, but nobody's hurt, really; it's all been in good fun.

*Some fun*, Junior thinks, some *fun*.

The infielders tenderize their gloves with their fists. As a freak wind picks up, some darker, less tall clouds roll ominously in. The faithful leaves on the trees on the old St Caul's campus sigh and whimper and whimper and sigh in the breeze, auguring "the thrill of victory and the agony of defeat" like what Junior and every other American sports fan's heard about on ABC's *Wide World of Sports* for years and years and years.

There's a dull lull, the eeriest of silences. Everyone, it seems, notices it.

Then the J.V. cheerleaders start cheering:

*One potato, two potato, three potato, four*
*Let's go, team-o, dontcha let 'em score*
*Toy boat, toy boat, toy toy boat*
*Junior, dontcha be the goat!*

As the cheerleaders yell "Yeah! All right!, etc.," Junior, who's now rattled, nettled, spooked and shaken, *knows* he's going to be the goat. He can feel it. He can sense it. Thick whiskers are starting metaphorically to sprout from his chin. Any second a pair of horns is gonna punch through his cap. He takes it off, his cap, wipes his brow and kicks at the dirt at the edge of the mound. Sweet St Caulfield!—he's even stamping like a billy goat! This is appalling. When he tries to talk to the shortstop his voice sounds like a bleat. He's all bandy-legged and shit. He can easily picture himself chomping on a tin can or shoe. A baseball shoe, retired. Any minute someone's going to come along and transfer him to a prep school in the outer upper Andes. This is it. He's got to get the next batter out. He's got to.

The next batter is a monster-at-large, a cannon on the loose—the kid who ripped the shot past Henderson. He has a legless park bench for a bat, distracting acne, and a facial tic that's straight out of an Abnormal Psychology class instructional movie. The black eye he's received at who-knows-who's hands during the melee shines blackly, like he's Alex in *Clockwork Orange* or Rocky in *Rocky*. Holy Mary Jesus Christ Almighty. Junior puts on his most grim game-face and says a little prayer: "Dear Jesus God and Holy Holy Ghost, forgive me my sins and let me whiff this guy, O Lord. Please—if it be your mercy, Lord—let me. Just this once, Father. God grant me the strength to fan this batter, God, or at least to get him to ground out. In the name of the Virgin and all the Saints and especially St Caul we pray. Amen."

He pulls the bill of his cap so far down he might as well be an atavistic extra on the set of *The Treasure of the Sierra Madre*. On that mound now he's one mean *hombre*, a ballplaying *hidalgo*. The batter chokes up. Junior winds up. Throws a really fast fastball. The batter takes a cut so hard he spins round twice. "Stee-rike one!" ughs the ump. Junior's got him now; you can sniff the batter's fear. Reaching back and throwing all he's got into it, Junior blows another fastball the batter's way. The batter connects. The ball swans then arabesques up up up and out out out and swims away from the diving left fielder—*foul! It's a foul ball!* Whew. 0 and 2. All reet! Nervous applause tentatives in. Junior relaxes a bit; he gets his nerve back. The next pitch, an unbreaking curveball, the batter grounds hard to Robinson, the shortstop. 6-4-3! Robinson to Sorenson to Anderson! A beautiful textbook double play! Yes, yes, yes, *yes!* The hometown crowd is absolutely bonkers. The bullpen bench, Coach Krunsch, and the foxy sophomore are positively crackers. Two out. Two down. Two away. One to go. Let's get this next guy! All right all right all right! This guy can't hit. Hey batter! Hey batter-batter! The bench sounds like a convention of Jerry Lewises. The stands hubbub like a courtroom at a Hollywoodish murder trial. The cheerleaders come a-tumbling in mid-air, semaphoring madly. Romanian or Bulgarian trapeze artists have nothing on *them*. Well, almost nothing: it seems that one of the tumbling song-girls didn't *quite* round out a backflip and is being carried away on a stretcher, her tongue lizarding out of her mouth, her neck fully pretzeled. The crowd are now out of their heads, beside themselves; they barely even notice that the girl is turning ultraviolet purple. "*One* more *out!*" they mantra. "One *more!*"

Junior's pumped. He's no goat. He can do it. His mom just said so. "You can do it, Junior," he just heard her yell. "Come on, ya sonofabitch!"

*Sonofabitch?* thinks Junior. She's never even said "dang!" in front of him before. This is unbelievable. What's the matter with her? What has gotten into her? Alcohol. Alcohol, Junior thinks—that's what's gotten into her. My mom drinks. She *day* drinks, no less. Good God.

Junior looks over at the dugout. The bench has their rally caps on. With their red caps backwards they look like signal escapees from a snaggle-toothed chain gang from Devil's Island, French Guiana. *Papillon*, much? Junior muses. The cheerleaders cheer one last singular cheer:

*Hollywood, Westwood, Southern California—*
*This here cheer is here to warn ya*
*Pep squad butts and pep squad tits*
*Junior, Junior—this is* it!
*Yeah, team! Yeah, team!—watch that bunt!*
*Junior, you can lick some cunt*
*For the first time in your life*
*Fuck me like a drunk housewife*
*Strike him out and get this win*
*Then perhaps you'll get some trim*
*Jupiter, Mars and Holy Venus*
*You want me to suck your penis?*
*Aren't you tired of pulling it about?*
*Junior, Junior, get this OUT!*

Junior has struck this next guy out twice. No problem. Just get this last out and ready yourself to be orgulously carried from the glorious field on the victorious shoulders of your triumphant teammates, he tells himself. One more out. One more out. One more.

The sun's humming low in the sky now. The clouds look like they're puckering. Junior fingers the seams of the new rawhide the ump tosses out to him and throws a screwball for strike one. But then, on the very next pitch, the batter squares around and soft as kisses, bunts down the first baseline. Fielding! Yowsa! Junior forgot all about it. He hurriedly penguins towards the ball, picks it up with his bare right hand, does a little crow hop and *hurls it straight over the head of the first baseman*. Oh my God, he's forgotten that Anderson, Sanderson's backup, is shorter than the attention span of a kid on Ritalin. Shit! Fuck! The batter's numinous royal blue helmet rounds first and pop-up slides into second as the right fielder throws too late. "Oh, no!" the despairingly querulous home crowd goes; "Oh, *no!*"

Next up is the guy who lanced one to right for a double. Shoot! Junior, who has been well-coached by his ex-Little League coach father, decides to walk the batter in order to have a force-out at third. The inspissated visitors rooting section hisses as the batter takes first. Now it's two down, man on first and second. Junior's thinking he's going to wet his baseball pants. Ball one: low and inside. Ball two: high and away. Ball three: just missing the corner.

Pendleton wheeze-waddles out to the hill and plumps the ball into Junior's pancaked glove.

"All right, Junior?"

"What do *you* think, Pen?"

"Throw your slider."

"I don't have a slider."

"Oh."

Junior's eyes are goggling incredulousness now.

"Junior?"

"What?"

"Good thing I didn't have the pudding, huh?"

"Pen?"

"Yes, Junior?"

"Get back behind home plate."

"Okay, Junior."

Pendleton clink-clanks fatly back the regulation ninety feet and turns round and thumps his mitt. The batter's laughing. He's nearly cackling. Junior's starting to wish that he himself had had the pudding, had taken a bath in it or something. Oh, that's just nonsense. He can do it. He can get this guy out. He's not going to walk him. He's not.

He doesn't. What he does do is *bean* the batter with the very next pitch. Bases loaded! The tying run's at third. The go-ahead run's at second. Junior's in more trouble than when he accidentally started a major forest fire in the third grade by introducing in a game of make-believe a can of kerosene to a box of Strike Anywhere matches.

Before Coach Krunsch has a chance to sprint out to the mound and yank him Junior wings an ebullient fastball to the next batter. Déjà vu: it's another bunt! Again down the first baseline. His only hope is to throw to first. Déjà *vu:* Junior fires the ball even farther and harder over the head of the hopeless, hapless, horizontally-challenged Anderson. Two runs score. Three runs score.

Of course *now* Coach storms out to the mound and pulls him. "Nice going, LOSER!" he sneers and *orders Junior to run twelve laps around the field while the game is still going on*.

Crestfallen isn't the word for it as Junior dons his warm-up jacket and starts his laps. No Romantic poet in the history of English Lit has known dejection like this. Not even the ones who had to deal with coming down from laudanum and opium, having tertiary consumption, being perennially destitute, losing duels, dating crazy poetry groupies, or drowning in picturesque Italian lakes. No Ro-poet ever played prep school baseball. No Ro-poet had to deal with the vituperative likes of Coach Krunsch or a depressingly diminutive first baseman, either.

Oh, no, Junior lugubriously muses, it isn't Anderson's fault—it's mine.

This isn't a metaphor anymore—this is life.

A wiser and a better boy takes a shower in the St Caulfield locker room that day, a boy who was savvy enough to run two laps, say "fuck it," quit the J.V. team, and go home and dig out from the back of his closet his steel string dreadnought acoustic guitar and practice on it till his fingers fairly fucking bleed.

## who can know

Anyhow, loving Jenny (who has also started to practice guitar till her fingers fairly fucking bleed) felt like soundtracks played by Simon and Garfunkel and the Velvet Underground in their most dissonant phase simultaneously. It felt like new snow, like a schmaltzy waltz you can't resist. It felt like we were constantly half-asleep and flushed with post-coitus glows and in each other's arms and listening to Nick Drake pull his one-string lead on "The Thoughts of Mary Jane"—the lead that takes you to the stars. And I thought: *She's my very Mary Jane*.

# BRIDGE

## you're on top of the world

On the three or four days a week I was called in to substitute I had taken to cruising over to Jenny's right after school. She'd had a pocket-shreddingly sharp, lustrous gold key, banded with indigo rubber, made for me and I'd pad in and go upstairs to her too-warm room to read or nap or shift lyrics around in my chiaroscuro piebald Composition Notebooks till she got home from work. Then we'd make tea or love or both and then start working on our songs. Sometimes, humming to himself as he puttered round the kitchen, Walt would be home from the menswear shop he labored in, having a late lunch, or Nastasha would've called in sick to the boutique she worked at, and I'd get a little bit of a weird vibe from them but for the most part the house was so big and I was so quiet that I was convinced they didn't care, couldn't have cared less. It was stupid for me to go all the way back to Santa Monica, then turn around and in mass traffic come back to Midtown, on the nights the Weird Sisters had practice. I mean, Walter *was* my bandmate and all.

The week after Halloween, on the phone, McLeary had said he'd really liked what he'd heard at the party but wanted to come by rehearsal a few times in order to get a better idea of what we were trying to do as a band, and to give him a better clue as to what he'd like to do for us.

The first two times he turned up he didn't say much. Just mm'ed and said "That one's quite nice" or "Maybe if you went to the bridge where you put the third chorus" or "Would you be so kind as to try that one again?" Then he'd twiddle the knobs on the amps and things and smile his big wide smile and go "Kewl!" Once or twice he got on Walter's case—gently, though—about the tempos, which was good: Jenny, Rob, and I had often bellyached amongst ourselves about how certain songs would have a tendency to slow down and others get noticeably heavy in a way that was not good; and certain others would seem like Walt had chugged three Jolt Colas in the middle of them and was trying to get to the end of the song as fast as he could in order to go to the loo or something. Once, McLeary asked him if he knew Bun E. Carlos.

"Not personally," Walter quipped.

Too subtle, McLeary, I thought.

"He wants you to simplify the beat here, Walt," I said a little more condescendingly than I'd meant, risking it.

Okay, a *lot* more condescendingly.

Tactless boy.

"Why don't you *all* just jump down my throat here!" Walt complained. "What do you guys want from me, man? This is how I *drum*, okay? This is my *style* here!"

While Jen and Rob looked cluelessly at one another McLeary gazed at me with a sort of you-have-said-quite-enough-mate way and, lamb-like, I turned down my mouth neutrally and shrugged my shoulders apologetically and on we got with it. Ever the musical martinet, Jenny was driven, I knew, more crazy over Walt's erratic drums than she ever let on. But she was not only too nice to speak up, but also cognizant of the fact that he was her landlord, after all. *She* wasn't going to tell him his meter fucking sucked.

One rehearsal, while "Mac" was coaching Walter on making one of his tribal, tub-lugging patterns more simple and steady, and while Jenny was using the loo, Rob and I ducked outside for a huggermugger and a smoke:

"What do you think, John? Is McLeary into it, or what?"

"I think so. I like the way he's riding Walt about the tempos. That's a good sign, don't you think?"

"Yeah, well. Walt'll get it down . . . maybe."

"Hahaha."

"He has a studio in mind?"

"Some place in Hollywood that's cheap, I think—where the B-52s did something early on. I don't know. Them or someone else. Not sure. Maybe it was Talking Heads."

"A twenty-four track? I love the B-52s, don't you?"

"Yeah. But I hate the Talking Heads. Except for *More Buildings about Food and Songs* or whatever it's called."

"No kidding. A twenty-four-track studio, eh?"

"Very good enough."

"That is awesome. That's fucking awesome. I just hope we'll be . . ."

"Ready."

"Yeah. Yeah I really hope that."

## everybody wants to rule the world

McLeary, to give you a CAT scan of his personality and some of his attributes, was defensive, curmudgeonly, complainy, arrogant, a yeller, never wrong, sanctimonious and hectoring, a vegetarian, imperious, and almost deaf—well, a little hard of hearing, but maybe it was an affectation he affected when convenient. Yet he also was the following: hopeful, cheerful, charming, charismatic, obsessed with personal hygiene (especially tooth-brushing, on account of his teeth were as craggy and nodose as Stonehenge), majorly into the Beatles (almost as much as we were, Jenny and me), and outright hilarious.

After the fifth or sixth rehearsal with him we all went out to Swingers, the trendy diner on Beverly where I first took Jen. I was chomping down on an impossibly juicy cheeseburger, trying hard not to ogle the stunningly beautiful waitresses in their short dark pleated tennis skirts and swelled-to-bursting bowling blouses, when McLeary suddenly said: "Would you eat snake there, John?"

"Sorry?"

"Would you eat skunk?"

"What?!"

"Cat? Dog? Horse? Iguana? Porcupine? Would you eat *rat?* Would you eat a donkey if I put it on your plate? What about a bat?"

"Okay, McLeary? I think I get your point."

Rob, who'd ordered a chicken breast awash in cheesed cream and swaddled in bacon, was laughing: "I think he just *swallowed* your point, Mac! Haha! How's your sprouts and lentils, McLeary—pretty tasty?"

"Brilliant," McLeary bristled. "What of it?"

"Oh nothing," Rob said, taking a theatrical bit of his entrée and making a wow-that's-heavenly/delicious face.

"Janey mack!" McLeary said. "You Yanks! Disgustin'!"

"What exactly do you mean?" Walt, tearing into a smoking pork chop, asked.

"What do I mean? I'm telling ya, mate. The whole big wide wicky-wacky world could be fed twice over on the arable land they spoil raisin' cattle and kine! The amount of water it takes to produce one cow for the slaughterhouse, to produce one cow—that could be used to grow enough grain to feed five starvin' fookin' villages? Janey mack! That's a fookin' *fact*."

"Really?" I said.

"What is?" Walter said, looking up from his plate and around the table.

"Sure is," McLeary answered me. "You're a big reader 'n' all, are you not, Johnny boy? A right bookworm?"

"You might say so. Pass the ketsup, would you, please, Jen?"

"Fookin' hell," McLeary said. "I'll give yer somethin' to read, all right," McLeary spluttered. "Have you any idea how those animals you're eatin' are slaughtered?"

"Stop saying 'slaughtered,'" Rob joked.

"With big old American guns, maybe?" Walter snickered, and picked up the bottle of Heinz. "Do you say 'ketsup' or 'catsup'? I've always wondered which one sounded right or *was* . . ."

"Itsnottafuckinjoke!" McLeary squealed like he was really hurt.

"I'm sorry, but I don't see anything wrong with eating animals," Rob said. "I mean, a chicken, for instance? That's just a vegetable with legs, if you ask *me*."

"Jaysus!" McLeary said.

"You must be starvin', McLeary," Rob said, doing his best Ringo or Paul or George in *A Hard Day's Night*. He was really fond of McLeary; we all were. But Rob especially. He laughed at everything McLeary said, practically—got a terrific kick out of him. They'd become fast friends. We all had—to a degree. Well, almost. I mean, McLeary never said anything bad about anybody the whole time I knew him. He might object to something about you or your opinions or beliefs right to your face, but never behind your back. Never. Everyone was "brilliant"—as was everything.

Except of course meat-eating.

Turning conspiratorially to Jenny, McLeary said: "Jenny-my-dear, I don't see you eatin' any meat, now, do I now? There you are with a salad right enough. "

"Red meat's fattening," Jenny said.

"You people," McLeary sighed, then came on with a murderous look right at me. "There's an essay by Jeremy Rifkin called 'Anatomy of a Cheeseburger'—read it if you dare! It'll turn your stomach, it will. Turn it right over. Full stop."

"I'll read it," I said. "I'm open-minded."

"Tellin' ya," McLeary tisked.

"Jenny likes *meat*," Walter tittered. "Just not the kind they serve in a restaurant. She es*pecially* likes a hot beef injection! Hahaha! Don't you, Jenny!"

"Jesus, Walt," I said. "You're not well."

"Decidedly not," McLeary said. "Mental."

Jenny just laughed, as did Walt, that high, obnoxious predictable chortle I told you about. I do not think that I have described it nicely (as in fastidiously) enough. Were you here, I could certainly do it, "do" Walter's horrid, putrid cackle for you, so that you could know what it incontrovertibly was. But you're not. So: you know those phoney warm-ups carolers do when they're going "Ha-ha-ha-ha, he-he-he-he, ho-ho-ho-ho, fa-fa-fa-fa, te-he-he-he" and so forth? Well it was like that, only about an octave higher and like he was doing it *at* you or something. Like it was a sort of assault. Thing was, he had a pretty voice, a pretty singing voice—singing along to the songs, and especially bumptiously when a song came on the oldies radio station that he really liked, like "Little Deuce Coupe" or "I Heard It through the Grapevine." I lived in total mortal terror of the day he was going to ask me if he could sing at the live shows: if there is one thing I *really* can't stand, it's a singing drummer. Those are just the *worst*. Why? I don't know. Do you know why all the things that bug you bug you? Thought not. It just looks fuckin' stupid, is all. So dopey. Some guy back behind the kit who's supposed to be doing a job, okay? Who's supposed to be keeping all this rock and all this roll stuff together and he's looking up with a dumb look on his stupid face all happy and singing and shit? The worst. I got two words for ya: Phil Collins. Okay? Don Henley. Those idiots. Karen Carpenter. The guy from Kiss. You might say, though, "Hey, Beatle-guy—what about

Ringo, huh? You gonna include him in your little jingly jeremiad?"

You impertinent imp.

Of course I am going to exempt Ringo; he's a *Beatle*, okay? He can do no wrong. He's one of the gods.

"Not to change the subject, but how many songs are you thinking of recording, Mac?" Rob said.

"Sorry?" McLeary said.

"He asked how many songs are we going to track," I said.

"Oh. Ten, twelve, maybe. Dunno yet. Twelve for good measure."

"For a *demo?*" Walt said. "That many?"

"Demo?" McLeary said. "Who said any fuckin' t'ing about a bloody demo? I don't do demos."

"McLeary doesn't 'do' demos," I said with what I hoped was not too fulsome a smile (but that surely must have been); then I gave Walter a quote-unquote and-that's-certain sort of look.

"Too fucking right," McLeary said, draining another creamless cup of coffee and waiving the impossible waitress politely over: it was simply uncanny how servers of all sorts, dogs, pretty girls, policemen and—especially—women, meter maids, and bartenders catered almost instantly to McLeary on account of his accent and charm. "Records. A record is what we're making here. This is a record and a number one fuckin' record. If we're taking the time to book a twenty-four track, almost state-of-the-art studio—tiptop and all that—we might as well do it and do it right and proper. Right? You know that Tears for Fears song 'Everybody Wants to Rule the World'?"

"Yeah?" I said, with a little bit of an attitudinal "So what?" in my voice—more than I'd, as usual, intended.

"Well *I* wanna rule the world—don't *you?* Someone has to rule the pop world, might as well be me as the next fellow, right? Know what I'm sayin'?"

"There's just one thing I don't understand, Mac," Rob said.

"And what's that, Robert?"

"Every living motherfucking thing you just said."

We all started laughing affectionately and, utterly nonchalantly, McLeary pulled out from his cool corduroy-collared Levi jacket a thick red toothbrush (at first I thought it was a flashlight) and started jabbing it around in his mouth right there at the table. The sound of him brushing was more like someone taking a shower or something.

"Uh, McLeary," Rob said, trying not to crack up too much, his eyes fully twinkling, "just what do you think you're *do*ing?"

"Cleanin' the teeth. What's it look like?! Do *you* not clean your bleedin' teeth after meals?"

"Well, yeah," Rob said, "just not at the table, mate."

"Suit yourself," McLeary said.

Then he took a big crunch of a green onion stalk and chewed it up while he smiled at all of us.

"McLeary?" Rob said.

"Yes?"

"You are *way* too much."

McLeary gave Rob a look as blank as my bank account just then.

Unflappable bastard.

"The Scather told me that in London when you were producing and engineering there that your nickname was 'Right Here McLeary' on account of anytime there was a joint or hash pipe going you were all 'Right here! Right here!' Is that true?"

"*Could* be," McLeary said, but he couldn't hold his pokerish face much longer; so he added with a minatory chuckle: "Sterlin' said that, did he?"

"Uh-huh," I said.

"That's hilarious," Rob said.

"You guys are all out of your minds," Jenny said. "Truly crazy."

Walt was fidgeting; you could tell he was just waiting it out.

"Hey!" he said. "Check it out: about this, like, recording thing or whatever? I thought this was, like, just going to be a *demo* sort of so that we could get some club gigs or whatever. I mean, nobody told me it was going to be, like, a real *record* and—you know? No one said that. And exactly how much is this going to cost us, McLeary, anyway? I don't have a whole lot of spare . . ."

"It's only four days," I said.

"How are we going to make an *album*, an entire LP, in four days?" Rob said.

There was a pause of some suspense and everyone's attention was of course intensely trained on McLeary who was streaming sugar—I swear to God—for about seven straight seconds into his coffee cup.

"Easy. You'll see."

## white light goin' messin' up my mind

In the middle of rehearsal the next Wednesday night, McLeary stood beside me concentrating intensely on one of my candy-colored effects pedals , looking at it like it'd insulted him or something. It was a Boss Chorus pedal, an expensive turquoise job that my guitar sound like a chorale or guitars mixed with the Vienna Boys Choir or whatnot. He picked it up, cocked his head to one side as he scrutinized it, and flung it straight across the shed room; it made a dull deep thud against the orange-carpeted wall.

"Hey!" I screamed. "What are you *do*ing, McLeary? I just *bought* that!"

"Well, you shouldn't have," he said, too calmly, and went over and twiddled the P.A. knobs. "Useless, those things!"

"It is *now*," Rob said.

I went over and picked it up. It was fine.

"Why the fuck did you just do that?"

"Shite!" McLeary answered. "Flangers and chorus pedals. Delays digital and analog and fuckin' wah-wah pedals. Gizmos and gadgets! Pure jiggery-pokery. Utterly! How do you reckon your Velvet Underground made their statement on that album you love so much, John? Huh? Or 'And Your Bird Can Sing'? You want to make your mark by putting your amp on and turning it up to eleven—that's what you want, la. Simple as that. Put it on—turn it up. That's what's needed."

"Yeah, sure," I said, "but you didn't have to . . ."

"Bloody stupid, those things. Offensive. *Cheating*," McLeary said.

"Jeez," Rob said.

*

As I've told you, McLeary did a lot of yelling, just ranting. There he'd be, going on and on about the unmitigated importance of *something* or other (and of course your astonishing-to-him ignorance of it), just *barking*, and I might say:

"For fuck's sake, Mac. You don't have to *yell* here. I'm standing right here. Stop *yelling*."

"I'm not yellin'!" he'd yell; then, in a much softer, sweeter voice, as if to emphasize that he wasn't yelling, had never yelled in his life, didn't know the *meaning* of the word, he'd go: "All's I was tryin' ta say wus . . ."

It was his voice that got you. It wasn't really Irish, though it had that softness (when he wasn't barking, of course—as in barking mad, as in mental); it wasn't really Scottish, though it had a little brogue in it; it wasn't quite Englishy English, though it did sometimes seem as though he could easily be narrating one of them plummy Hallmark Hall of Fame shows or Masterpiece Theater or playing some butler on the BBC.

And it wasn't Welshish—not at all.

It was the sort of voice that sort of demanded that you take him very seriously—more seriously than the seriously that you already took him in the first place. When he talked to Jenny, making suggestions for alternate guitar lines and la-la-la's, some *tone painting* on the songs, some ideas for layering overdubs on lead guitar, it was like he was wooing her. You could tell he loved working with her. I mean, of course he loved working with her: she could do almost anything he asked her to—and she almost anticipated what he wanted anyway. Rob and I just got nods from him from time to time. The rest of the time he spent massaging as it were Jen's parts. And of course riding Walt about the tempos and the fills that didn't quite make it.

## there's a world where I can go

"Rolling?" Walter said.

We were all set up in the main room, Studio A, at Tantamount Studios, Hollywood, the mikes in place and on, headphones donned, coats doffed, instruments tuned (even the drums), facing each other, ready to go.

"It means the tape is rolling, Walt," I said.

"Oh," Walter said dully.

He clicked us off with his clickety sticks: one, two, three, four.

And we played the first song through.

"All right," McLeary said, more like he was ruminating than giving us the old thumbs up, when the sound of our throbbing, rumbling amps had decrescendoed. "Okay. Let's, um, just try that one again. One more time, please, everyone. With a *touch* more feel, if you don't mind, this time—all right, boys and girl? Brilliant."

"I thought that take was pretty good," Walt said and looked around at us all, one at a time, for some sort of confirmation, a modicum of approbation.

McLeary came to the very front of the control room and smiled his big wide smile at us through the glass: "One more time, please."

"But why?" Walt said. "I mean, as I said, I thought it was pretty good."

"Well, it wasn't," I said. "It was pretty wobbly, actually."

"We can definitely do it better," Jenny said.

"Let's just give it one more go," McLeary intercommed.

"Oh God—all right," Walt said, tapping his floor tom, jimmying the high hat, then leaning way back on his throne.

Rob's bass grumbled and I rang out a couple of nervous, determined chords. Jenny honked on the Rickenbacker (she thought it better than the Telecaster for this particular song) a pleasant little riff from the first chorus and we settled down to do another pass.

"You're doin' just fine, Walter-la," McLeary said. "Just peachy-creamy. Just give us another try-go, then."

And so we did try it again. And again. And again. Twelve hundred thirteen times. Well of course not that many but a billion times at least.

"Walter can't hack it," I said to McLeary as he and I stepped outside to gag a fag.

"Easy, John. He'll get it. He's got to."

"Sometimes I must admit I am a little leery of you, McLeary."

"Couldn't *count* the times I've heard that one, Johnny boy, if you know what I mean," Mac said and smiled his irresistible smile. "Let's get back in there and do this."

*

If you've ever been inside a near-state-of-the-art twenty-four-track studio, you'll know what I mean when I tell you it's completely bitchened: lights of many colors concertina from the mixing board console, boxes with knobs you have no idea what they do but they look super important are everywhere, and with all the electronic apparatus humming it's womb-warm and quite comforting. So much so that it's easy to get sleepy, despite your unalloyed excitement at being there, working there, making something out of nothing, rocking out. I think that's why lots of studios have a "tea boy" working there—an assistant engineer who's not so much responsible for things sonic as he is for things caffeineish. There's a washing machine-appearing kind of thing that has the two-inch tape reel spinning with these yellow boxes with needles dancing; and there's a rolling sort of R2-D2 little guy the engineer sits punching buttons on. A good, plush, firm couch, normally, and some swivel chairs for the producer and engineer and one or two of the band members. Red, black, blue and green chords spaghetti-ing from the outboard gear and two enormous overhead and two control desktop monitor speakers that make you think you've never heard something so clearly, so beautiful and angelic. We always called the big honking big ones the Ego Boosts. "Let's hear that again on the Ego Boosts," we'd say. "Just to make sure it's very good enough and stuff."

When we went back in, expecting to do take 37 of the first song, McLeary had us play one of our other numbers, a faster one this time, so as to loosen us up and make it fun and give the first song a rest.

"That was excellent!" McLeary said. "Really grand. Let's go on to the next one."

"Can we come in and hear it?" Walt whinged.

"No!" all of us said and laughed.

"Let's just keep rolling—now that we're on a roll," McLeary said. "All right, the Weird Sisters! I'm keeping that one—deffo!"

By just around after ten at night we'd managed to track six of the putative ten songs.

"Well," Walt said with an actorly yawn. "That's it for me. Gotta work in the morning."

"Um," I ummed, "I don't think we've quite finished what we need to finish tonight, Walt."

"McLeary!" Walt shouted. "I have to take off!"

McLeary came out from the control room and into the studio room and over to Walt and put his hand on Walt's back: "The thing is, Walter, John's bang on: we aren't quite done with what we need to get done tonight. Couldn't you just manage to . . ."

"Yeah, well, "Walt said prissily, "some of us have real jobs, okay?"

"Come on, Walter," I said.

"Yeah, well, check it out, like, I'm really sorry but it's, like, getting really late and I need to split."

There was a tremendously awkward pause. Then Jenny said: "Sterling!" and Sterling exploded through the double-doubled doors of the control room and out to where we were.

"Hey, Sterling!" I said, at once surprised and glad he hadn't brought a nontourage. "Glad you made it! Had no idea you were coming!"

"I was at this party, but there were too many *crashing* crashing bores, which is never really a problem unless they keep crashing into you, which they did to me. Which isn't very nice of them, but that's what they *do*, isn't it? So I left. I got a message that McLeary'd called me, invited me down. Positively, I thought—*sure* I'll come to the studio. I reckoned I'd come check on you guys, see how it was going. How's it going, kids? Kicking out the jams? Taking the Weird Sisters to the toppermost of the poppermost, are we, McLeary?"

Sterling seemed really jazzed, pumped, excited, *on*.

"Walt says he has to go, though," I tattled, as Sterling gave McLeary a Marlboro. "And we still have four songs to track! Who threw a party on a Wednesday night, anyway?"

"Really?" Sterling said, evading the superfluous question about the shindig. "You can't just do some overdubs and come back tomorrow and finish the drum tracks?"

"Yeah, well," Walt said, "I have to work in the morning. And are you guys sure you're supposed to be smoking in here? I mean . . ."

"Oh," Sterling said. "Speaking of working—can you work for me on Sunday, John? Remember how you owe me a favor from . . ."

"Not a problem, Sterl. Saturday's our last day in the studio anyway."

"Can I get you a coffee, Sterling?" McLeary said.

"Ha! No. No thanks," Sterling chuckled. "So what are you guys gonna do if he [indicating Walter] has to split?"

"McLeary?" Rob said.

"Sterling can drum," McLeary said.

"What?!" Rob said.

"He's good," McLeary said.

"No kidding," Rob said.

Jenny just stood there smiling.

"No way!" Walter said. "I don't know if I can let someone use . . . I mean, I have to pack up my drums and stuff now."

Churlish churl.

"What?!" I said.

"We'll pack them up for you," McLeary smiled.

"I just don't know if I feel all that comfortable . . ."

"Jesus, Walter," I said, "If you have to bail, bail. But if Sterling can cut the remaining tracks we ought to give him a shot. We have four more . . ."

"I know how many more, man," Walter said. "Hey! I don't mean to, like, be a dick or anything but . . ."

"You are being a dick, though," I said as neutrally as I could, notwithstanding my awareness that it's really hard to be Switzerland about it when you've just called someone you know and have to keep on you're-not-really-a-dick terms with—well, when you've essentially just called them a dick. You might as well just go right ahead and call them a *fucking* dick, at that point. They know you think they're one; they know they are being one; just call a spade a . . . dick.

"Just let Sterling do it, okay? He's not going to hurt your drumkit or anything. Come on, Walter," I pleaded.

What a *total* dick he was being. I mean, how dickish can you *get?*

"I can pack them up for you," Rob said reassuringly, like always, like he was looking after things and one was not to worry. "Wait, though: you're coming back tomorrow night, right?"

"The thing is," Walter exhaled, "I forgot to tell you guys that I can't make it tomorrow night. Nastasha got tickets to see the Beach Boys at the Universal Amphitheatre, so . . . um . . ."

"*The Beach Boys?*" I said. "You gotta be . . ."

"Natasha has had the tickets for forever, okay? So . . ."

"You're going to the *Beach* Boys instead of playing on your own . . ." I said incredulously. I was so stunned that I couldn't spit out anything more.

"*Any* road," McLeary said. Then he addressed Sterling: "Any chance you actually know these four songs they have left?"

"Sure," Sterling shrugged. "I mean, what are they? Which ones? I'll do them. Sure, I know 'em. I've heard them a few times, of course. Let me just run through them a couple of times and we'll see what happens. I'll have a bash—as you would say, McLeary. Hahaha! Why not?!"

"See you later, then, Walter," McLeary said.

"Later," Walter said to everyone and no one and picked up this black backpack he had and went out the door.

We worked through some songs with Sterling drumming. He kept the beat simple and steady and, miraculously, by six in the morning we had finished tracking the backing tracks—drums, bass, two guitars—for not just ten but *twelve* songs: an album.

Not without some quote-unquote help, however.

At about midnight, as we were listening to the second song Sterling had done, sitting around the console, differentiating between takes, trying to pick the better of the two, Sterling said: "I don't know about *you* people, but I could do with a little *bump*."

"Huh?" Rob said.

So that's why Sterling'd been so exceptionally garrulous, earlier! I thought.

"A bump?" Rob said.

"Speed," Sterling said, breaking out the biggest baggie of thick crystals the color of raw sugar I'd ever seen. "The White Lady. The Nasal Rocket. *Amphetamine*. Care to dive in, anyone?"

"Oh, no thanks," Jenny said.

Pure girl.

"I don't know, Sterl," I said.

"All right," Sterling sighed. "More for me and . . ."

"'Right Here McLeary'?" McLeary laughed. "Set us up there, then. Gi' us a line."

Sterling laid out then chopped up some lines on the back of Mac's clipboard; McLeary snorked up a fat rail.

Sterling then held it up to me like a salver, like he was a butler, a *drug* butler. Ha!

"Oh, all right," I said. "Just one. I'm getting kinda tired here."

"It's delicious," Sterling said. "Won't you have a sip?"

He said this to Rob who laughed his Rob-laugh and shrugged his shoulders and went ahead. Then I did one more and McLeary two and Sterling laid out two more for himself while Jenny went to make some coffee for herself—possibly so that she wouldn't have to watch. I wasn't sure but I don't think she was too into us doing speed. I'm pretty sure she would never have said anything—she wasn't censorious in the least; she really did, as a sort of honorary one-of-the-guys, roll with things—but I can't imagine she approved.

"Excellent!" Sterling said after he'd hoovered up the last line. "Now let's burn! The rest of the tracks shouldn't be a problem."

"Janey mack!" McLeary said. "That's quite good stuff."

"I'm flying," Rob said.

"I'm floating," I said.

"Hey, you guys," Jenny said, sipping from an oversize coffee cup with a silly ceramic flower protruding from it. "Ready?"

"Yes!" Sterling said. "That was special of Walter to let me play his drums, wasn't it."

Sarcastic bastard.

"He *is* special," I said.

"Let's track all the drums with Sterling drumming!" Rob said.

"Hey!" Sterling said: "I like this guy!"

"You guys," Jenny said.

"Oh come on, Jen," I said. "You know as well as the rest of us do that Walter's—what's the best word for it?—impossible."

"I know, I know. I just wish he wasn't so . . ."

"Lame?" Rob said.

Jenny just looked down and said: "Well, are we ready to keep going?"

"In every group," McLeary said, "there's someone lagging, pulling up the rear. No matter what it is—a band or a band of hunters and collectors; someone in Parliament or on a camp out—there's *some*one who is gonna be last: late, slow, stupid, out-of-it, and, likesay, halt. In a *band* band, it never fails that it's the drummer. Never fails. Never."

"We're going to have to kick him out, you realize, right?" I said to all.

"Drummers always get the old heave-ho," Rob said.

"Or they quit and join a band much bigger than yours," Sterling said.

"Too fuckin' true," McLeary said.

"Maybe he'll join the Beach Boys," Jenny quipped, and we all busted up.

After that, everything went sort of a million miles an hour and the next thing I knew I was loading all of our guitars into Jenny's car and the sky outside was all yellow, red, pink, and blue as the sun came up.

## silver threads and golden needles

Lest you go feeling all sorry for Walter, reader, who, as I imagine you've gathered, *is* going to get himself kicked out of the Weird Sisters, think of this: in three or four years' time he'll hardly even remember the name of the band he made half a record with. Hell, he'll probably hardly even remember that he used to play the drums. Let's face it: Walter is bourgeois as fuck. He's a whiner and not very bright, artistic, talented, or easy to hang out with. A conventional, narrow, clueless person—and not exactly a human metronome, either. In his defense I'd say it's a tough gig, being a drummer: no one respects your opinion on music, people make up jokes about you all the time, and your equipment is inordinately heavy and takes a lot of time to assemble and break down. It's like an erector set made of he-man barbells. Drums are really pretty when they're up on stage and spangley-sparkly, but it's a prodigious bitch to get them to that stage. Every time. Plus there's only around four or five real drummers in the whole wide world.

Ask Linda Ronstadt.

Linda Ronstadt famously said that if she ever found a drummer she could live with, in both senses of the term, marital and musical, she'd marry him.

Well she ain't married yet, is she? And she's around two thousand years old now, bless her socks and dimples. She ain't married yet.

What do you call someone who hangs around with musicians? (A drummer.)

How do you know when there's a drummer at the door? (The knock speeds up.)

What do you call a drummer without a girlfriend? (Homeless.)

What's the difference between a pizza and a drummer? (A pizza can feed a family of four.)

Most musicians' playing styles—their timing, inventiveness, taste, and individuality—are reflected, nay, determined by their personalities. "People play like they are," Jenny always said, and I concur. Your parts, and your performance of them, come from your parts, as it were.

Walter's corybantic flailings, for instance, must've stemmed from the fact that he's undisciplined, dorky, vain, impish, silly, trivial, boorish, lazy, and stolid. The way he plays is by turns stiff (never a good thing in rock and roll) and out of control—the sort of mad, bashing, Bamm-Bamm from *The Flintstones* kinda drumming that the patron saint of it, mad old Keith Moon, God rest his soul, might have admired; but had he atavistically caught one of our sets, even Keith might've pulled Walter aside and said: "Er, Walter, old top, I think you might be a mite over*doing* the old fill-up-every-space-with-a-fill there, old man."

Rob's occasional lack of ass and fumble-proneness on the bass comes doubtless from the fact that he's humble-to-a-fault and the whitest white guy in whiteland. Rob's chuffed to be in a band—any band—period. Rob's a good laugh but he's a bit uptight, despite his aw-shucks demeanor. It sure would help if he danced.

I'm not kidding. Sterling told me that in Milk Amplifier they'd audition bass players not by having them plug in and play but by making them dance to one of their practice tapes. Hahaha! Priceless. The best rug-cutter, Sterling swore, always ended up being the best bassist. Unfailingly.

Jenny's startling fluidity and astonishing inventiveness comes from, in part, the fact that she's been not just playing or studying music but living it from the time she could eat with a spoon. But it, her inimitable, wonderful style, is also evinced by her obvious intelligence, true humility, poise and self-consciousness (the good kind), plus discipline.

And the fact that I can play serviceable, if not pretty rocking, rhythm guitar stems from the fact that I am a kind of a steady worker, I suppose. I like to work. I really do. And by work I don't of course mean subbing but working on music, making something out of nothing, making (as pretentious as it sounds) art.

There's not much in life that's better, if you ask me, or more of an August buzz. If there is, I can't think of what it could be.

*

On Saturday morning, having spent another night at Jen's after being at the studio all day and practically all night, I woke up early but then went back to sleep. McLeary didn't want to start our last day in the studio till 1 p.m. because there was the possibility that we'd be there all night, mixing the record. At about noon I stumbled downstairs to the kitchen, fully groggy and ready for coffee. I could hear Jenny and Nastasha talking in there by the time I got down the stairs. I stopped before I turned the corner.

"So," Nasty was going, "you and John seem to be quite the item these days."

You could tell she was doing her level best not to sound too pissy—which of course made her sound all the more miffed.

Jenny didn't reply—or at least if she did I didn't catch what she said.

"You've been almost, like, inseparable."

"I suppose so," Jenny said.

"Although . . . I don't know . . ."

"What?"

"Nothing."

"What? Tell me."

"It's just that, well, it just doesn't seem like he's, well, like . . . a very good *catch*."

"He's a catch," Jenny said softly.

"*Jenny*," Nastasha said, "he's not even a good throw! I'm sorry to say it but that's just how I *feel*, okay? I mean, he doesn't really have a job and . . ."

"He has a job."

"And he just kind of waits around for you to come home like he's some kind of dog and he doesn't have much more ambition than to be in a band and . . . I don't know. I just don't know. I know it's none of my business but . . ."

*You're goddam right it's none of your fucking business*, I thought-screamed to myself. How much longer was I going to stand there? How much longer was Jenny?

"It's not like I have anything against him," Nasty went on. "It's just that he comes over here and, like I said, just waits around for you. Like some kind of pet. He's here by three-thirty or . . ."

""That's not fair," Jenny said.

"I just think you could do better, is all."

*Better?* I thought-screamed again. Better as in "You had better shut the fuck up right now, Nastasha!"

"I see why you might think that, Natasha," Jenny said after a sec or two had passed, "but I think he's wonderful, mostly. He has some amazing qualities, actually. And he's really dedicated to being an artist—and he works really hard at it. I admire that."

But you yourself said he wasn't your type!" Nasty said. "I distinctly remember you said that. I remember you saying . . ."

"Hey, you guys," I frothed, coming into the kitchen at last. I was doing my level best to mask how livid I was, and mortified. "Should I make some more coffee. I bought some Kenyan brand and brought it over, actually."

Incorrigible calculator.

"John!" Jenny said.

"See you later," Nastasha pointedly told Jenny and, slipping into the sandals that were on the floor next to her feet, walked out. "I have to meet Walter at Farmers Market. He said you guys didn't really need him at the studio anyway today. Bye."

"Bye," Jen said.

Nastasha turned at the end of the kitchen: "Oh, by the way: I got you guys a show at USC, I think. This daytime festival they're having. My brother's a DJ at the college radio station there and, like, involved in Student Events and stuff. I'm supposed to talk to him about it tomorrow maybe. I'll let you know."

"Oh, that's great, Nastasha," Jenny said.

"Yeah, thanks," I said in a blank manner.

"Have a nice chat with Nasty?" I said as I heard the door go boom.

"Not particularly," Jenny said.

"Yeah, I *guess*," I said, more peevishly than was, I knew, good for me, for us.

"What?!" Jenny said.

"Oh, nothing."

I walked over to the stove, toggled one of the knobs, sifted through the kitchen midden and plucked out a purple potholder, threw it Jenny's way.

"Here," I said, "*catch*."

"John . . ."

"I think I'll go home now. McLeary can mix the record by himself. He will want to mix it how he wants to, anyway. I'll see you later."

"John. We have to go to the studio. McLeary will want us there. "

I came out with it: "What were you *doing* listening to her spew that spew, anyway? I mean . . ."

"John, I . . . What were you doing, listening to us, I might ask?"

Had me there.

"You're too sensitive," she said. "Nastasha's an idiot. I mean . . ."

"I know that, but why didn't you . . ."

"Stick up for you? Is that it?"

"Well, of course."

"Do you think that if I had, it would have made any difference, John? Nastasha's gonna think what she thinks and say what she wants to say. People never change. They don't. They're just . . . relentlessly themselves. Whether I told her to shut up or agreed with her wholeheartedly or slapped her in the face? None of it would make a bit of difference."

"Yes it would," I protested.

"How?"

"It would have made a difference," I said, hanging fire, "to *me*."

"I don't want to have this fight," Jen said, raising her voice.

"Oh, like I do," I said. "You think this is my idea of a good time? A nice way to spend a Saturday morning? I'm going home. Tell McLeary to mix it how he wants to, okay?"

"John. Don't be like this. We have to be in the studio in an hour, okay? Come back upstairs. Just because I'm in love with you doesn't mean that . . ."

"You're what?"

"In love with you. You know I am."

"Why are you only telling me *now?*"

"I don't know!" Jen said. "Who knows how these things happen?"

"You're in love with me?"

"I told you I was."

I stepped over to her and took her around the waist: "I love you too, Jen. I really do."

"Will you just come back upstairs and get ready, then, please?"

And I nodded yes.

# INSTRUMENTAL INTERLUDE

## it's in the way she talks

I was having a bit of trouble unhooking the bra of Sarah-Who-Hates-Me.

"Here," she said and gingerly reached behind herself, wiggling out of the white, lightly-padded job that held her pert, perfect, pearish breasts. Then she pressed herself towards my parsed, parched, incredulous mouth.

This really happened. I'm not putting you on this time.

Here's how:

On the Sunday the Scather asked me to cover his shift at Finyl Vinyl, Sarah, in cowboy boots and short, tight, black skirt, the obligatory belly-button peepshow peeping from her shimmering, ice-blue top, open pea coat, black hair tinctured red as the light on the top of any ambulance, blew into the shop around quarter to five.

"Hey," I said.

Inveterate prevaricator.

"There's no Sterling today," I continued. "He asked me to work for him."

"Fuck," she said tersely and put a cigarette portentiously between her sexy teeth.

"What's the matter?" I asked as, lighting her cigarette for her, I noticed how her lush lips got all the more feathery-lined when she pursed them: she had a mouth that freighted your throat and groin with desire, I swear, and even without lipstick as they were now, her lips could never be described by anybody, even the most ungenerous rival or frenemy, as anything less than kissable.

She didn't thank me for the spark-up, natch. Nor did she put her hand up to cup mine the way girls with a more charming, elegant kind of sass did—an action you appreciated so much 'cause it hinted at or even heralded sometimes the possibility of greater closeness, even coitus; it was something you palpably missed when it was missing: it could really bug you, like seeing someone leave a public loo stall without washing their hands, or when you do something really nice for someone, something you didn't even *have* to do, and you've perhaps gone way out of your way, and they don't thank you or even look right at you. They just, like, *leave*.

People, boy. They can really zing you.

Exhaling a big nic hit Sarah said:

"Fuck and double fuck. My *car*. There's something fucked in the fucking fucker. And I don't know what it is. It's fucking fucked, is all I know."

"What exactly?"

"The fuck if I know."

I half expected her to stamp her foot right then like a little Alice.

"The goddam thing," she said, continuing, "won't start. That's all I know, okay? Jesus."

She treated me to a look with eyes like lapis lazuli that suggested *I go to all this trouble to give you this great big explanation and you don't say anything here? What the fuck's the matter with you? Thanks a fucking lot*.

I don't know: maybe it was the frequency and vigorousness with which she was employing my favorite word, and in such an inspiring and ferocious way—but in lieu of wondering why she seemed to hate me so much I was wondering what it would be like to sleep with her. With her thick, straight, black hair all piled-up and pinned and willowy wisps of it winding down her temples and Eiffel Tower cheekbones, she looked a lot like a red/black-haired version of that wowsome girl from the Sundays, Harriet Wheeler her name is, who I was obsessed with of late. Of course I declined to point out the resemblance to Sarah herself, having learned my lesson proverbial from the disastrous *Betty Blue* comparison.

Reaching for something to say, I told her I had jumper cables and that I could try to start her car for her as soon as the clerk for the next shift came in.

"Okay," she said and blew exasperated smoke, no kidding, nearly right in my face, just off to the side of it.

"Tim—the guy who comes in after Sterling's shift—is supposed to be here any minute. Can you wait?"

Now she gave me a look like *What the fuck else am I gonna do?*

"Do you have a cigarette I can bum?" I said.

"You just put one out that wasn't all-the-way smoked!"

Snarky twatling.

"Here," she said, "if you absolutely must. I only have ten left. Sterling told me you're a total mooch, smokewise."

"Oh, thanks," I laughed—or just managed to. "Do you want to hear something in particular?"

"The sound of my engine whirring."

"I meant a record," I said synthetically and looked at her somewhat askance. "I've been listening to the Velvets all day and I'm getting kind of sick of them—well, as sick as you can get, which isn't much. You like them, right? Figures you would. Anyway, there's only so many times I can hear "Femme Fatale," you know, in one day."

I couldn't believe it, but she was actually going to have a sort of conversation with me: "I know what you mean," she said. "But I don't come in here, into this shitbox, to listen to records. I have all of those at *home*."

"So you just come in to catch up with the Scather and have fun with the customers—at their expense, of course."

"Of course. He hates that name, by the way."

"No, he doesn't! He loves it."

"Hates it, basically," she said and looked around at the walls as though any moment they were going to close in on her. "I can't believe I used to work here. When is Malcolm [that was the owner] going to put up new posters? I'm dead sick of fucking looking at these ones, that's for sure."

"These," I sententiously said.

"What?"

"*These*. Not 'these ones.'"

"Whatever," she practically expectorated, but then tried it out on her lips: "These. You're right. God, I hate it if I fuck up grammatically."

"Grammatical-wise."

"Yes. Hey, are you taking the piss out of me?"

"I might be."

"Well, bully for you, John."

"What did you do to your hair? It's redder. More red. It's cool. Good move."

She got all Betty Davis on me: "I simply loathe personal comments of any kind, you know. But thank you."

"You're *thanking* me? Are you feeling okay, Sarah? Do you need an aspirin or something? A lie-down?"

"Very funny. When's that *guy* coming so you can help me so I can get outta here? What's-his-fuck? *Bobby*."

"Tim."

"I thought he was a fucking Bobby. He looks more like a Bobby than a Tim."

"Well, he's a fucking Tim," I said. "His name is fucking Tim. Speak of the devil, here he is now."

In came Tim: this hulking, smiling, irony-free rockabilly dandy with fully oiled pompadour, rolled-up Levis—a walking Elvis fetishist. You practically expected him to say "A-one and a-two and a-three and a-four" instead of "Hello." He could have gotten a job in Vegas easy. A cartoon of sorts, Tim. But a very nice guy.

"Hey, Tim," I said. "*Fucking* Tim, Sarah here was calling you."

"Hey, John. I like that, man. Fucking Tim, huh? I think I'll go by that from now on. People will be all: 'Where the hell is Fucking Tim?' and 'Here he is: here's Fucking Tim.' Cool. How was today? Any money left in the till? Hahaha! Just kidding you, man. Hahaha! 'Do you believe how drunk Fucking Tim was last night? Did you see how much he *drank?—gallons*, dude.' Hahaha! That's awesome."

"It was pretty slow," I said. "Maybe a hundred and fifty or something? Sold some Smiths and Dead Can Dance and—let's see—Ramones, Durutti Column and, as always . . ."

"Joy Division?"

"Good guess. No, um, Bauhaus. Guy bought the whole section. Anyway, I gotta split. Good to see you, Fucking Tim."

"Hahaha! You too, man. Take it easy, Sarah."

Sarah just gave him that chin upswoop motion that people who are too indescribably cool to speak to you give occasionally. They're not courageous enough to totally ignore you, so they do *that*.

"Later," I said. "Shall we?" I said to Sarah and she smiled at me—I swear—for the very first time.

# VERSE

## please please baby lemonade

In the blue gloom of the early evening, then, we walked to her car, a beat-up, Bloody Mary-colored MG Midget convertible with a tatty black top bleached to fuck and the aluminum protective strips boinging away from it, and the grill askew and paint all piebald and fading. Melrose was still humming with tourists and trendoids heading for the touristy, trendoid eateries and shops and bars. We passed some male models in sailorish attire and a couple of strutting Asian babes and a gaggle of punks who hadn't realized—like, *hello!*—that punk was over around, um, fifteen billion years ago.

Sarah got in and did the hood and I peered into it and in all my brilliant brilliance said: ""Won't start, huh?"

"Duh! What did I tell you?"

"Sarah?"

"Yeah?"

"You don't have to be such a megabitch all the time, you know. Take a day off once in a while! I'm *helping* you here."

"Okay. All right. I know."

"Then why are you?"

"What?"

"Such a bitch to me?"

"How should *I* know? I'm sorry, all right? Where's your car—I thought you said you had jumper cables?"

"I do. I'm getting them now. I just wanted to see . . . Okay, okay."

By way of quote-unquote answer she raised her fine nose. It was a good thing it was small and thin and aquiline, I thought: that way it's easier for her to look down it, at everyone and thing.

I cut down an alleyway and made for the Volvo. It wasn't far. I thought hard about just getting in it and motoring straight away from there and from Sarah-Who-Hated-Me. But no: there I went, revving around the corner, turning round again, and meeting Sarah's MG head-on. Got the cables out of the boot and tickled open the hood.

"Hurry up, please."

"What's the matter with you?!"

"I just want to . . ."

"No, you said 'please.'"

"Oh come off it, John. You think you're *so* clever."

"I *am* clever. That's why your best friend is *my* friend too. Where do you have to be, anyways?"

"Nowhere. Anywhere but here, okay?"

"All right, then. Don't rush me. Let's see . . ."

Throwing her nose once more towards the skies Sarah turned to a short-haired, short, zaftig, possibly lesbian woman with a sort of plumber's mien counterbalanced by a welder's butt who was passing by just then: "Excuse me, sir? Do you know what time it is, by any chance?"

In response the woman made a face like she'd just been punted in the gunt.

"Fuck you very much," Sarah carped at her as she walked quickly away. "Jeez, why are people such assholes, I always wonder. I mean, *really*."

"Um," I said, "maybe because they don't exactly relish being called 'Sir' if they're a *chick*."

But I had to laugh: "No wonder you get along with Sterling so well!"

"She was a man. She *was*. Her beard was thicker than yours."

"I simply loathe personal comments."

"Touché. But I hate mocking. I hate mocking of any sort."

"Would you be so kind as to get in and start your car?"

The swish of mad traffic being what it was (at night people in Los Angeles Mario Andretti around like you wouldn't believe; I think they do it because during the day they *can't* do it, on account of all the even-more traffic and congestion), I had been very cautious in clamping down the negative blacks first, then the positive reds.

As more cars rocked dangerously closely past, it was no go: her engine just made this scratchy-rackety sound over and over, then just tick

tick tick tocked lamely. I shouted at her to stop, then start again, which effectuated no change.

"Fuck," I said.

"Fuck," she said.

"That's a drag. Sorry."

"Telling me. Now what do I do?"

"I can give you a lift home—unless you live in the Valley or somewhere. Kidding. I'll take you wherever, all right? Hop in."

"The fuck I would live in the Valley."

"Didn't you grow up there—with Sterling?"

"That's exactly why. Let's go."

She got in and lit another smoke and puffed a puff thickly out and I had to ask her with a little cackle: "How come you hate me so much, anyway?"

"I don't hate you."

"Really."

"Really. I despise you, but I don't hate you. I don't hate anybody."

"Incorrigible haters always say that! But how come? What did I ever do to you or say to you? Seriously now."

"Um, you existed. I don't know. I just don't like you."

"It must just be sheer sexual frustration, plain and simple. The obverse of hate in its most textbook form. You're actually in *like* with me and your attempts to mask it as a sort of psychological *reaction formation* are utterly in vain. That's my theory, at least."

"Ha!" she said. Had she really wanted to nail me for all the bullshit I'd just shoveled her way she should've yawned. A yawn is sometimes a brilliant retort.

"Yeah, *well* . . ." I said, all blithe, my tone a trail of smug, fake self-aggrandizement."

"Fuck *you*," she said, sort of laughing. Sort of.

"O-kay!" I said, in faux response, in a punning way, to her faux quote-unquote suggestion.

"You *wish!*" she parried, and took a particularly rapacious puff on her butt.

We pulled up to her house/apartment on the corner of Curson and Willoughby and she said: "You want to come in and have a coffee? I have coffee. Espresso."

I was too stunned to speak.

"Do you or don't you?"

"Uh, sure," I said, baffled as all get-out. "Seriously?"

She tilted her head to one side and lifted her right shoulder slightly by way of assent.

She lived upstairs in an immaculately-kept one-bedroom, the top left part of a craftsmanny fourplex from the 1920s. Cherry hardwood floors. A dwarf sort of balcony. Diaphanous bluish curtains blowing from the windows when she opened them. Incense smell still lingering? Something like that, anyway. Computer. Cat. Cat smell. Smell of cat. Faint. Purple and white polka-dotted loveseat. Television, stereo. Wall of records. Posters of Patti Smith, Robert Smith, the Smiths. Japanese prints, a whorling lava lamp, a wrought iron sculpture of *something*.

*Hmm, that's weird*, I thought, *a nymphomaniac's place looks just like everybody else's place*.

The sunflower-faced, azure-eyed kitty cat dove under a florid armchair when I bent to pet it.

"Hates men," Sarah said.

"But of course," I said. "Mind if I use the bathroom?"

She shrugged and I found it down the hall. Above the john was an arched cubbyhole loaded with Jesus and Mary paraphernalia, glow-in-the-dark crucifixes, Mexican saint candles, a couple of hideous bleeding Jesuses of obvious Hispanic provenance, the thorns going in deep and good, the eyes huge and blinding white with brown irises. *Jesus*, I thought, and would ya just look at that Virgin Mary all covered with fake fur! I went back out and sat on the loveseat. Whereupon I heard the whirr and hiss and tinkle of her espresso maker in the kitchen going great guns.

About ten awkward silent minutes later she came out with a tray with two quaint pale blue-and-white Delft cups with raw sugar cubes and arty little coffee spoons with some sort of ancient Greek god faces on their hilts and some flesh-colored sugared biscuits and bits of dark chocolate and orange slices and one wedge of lemon on a plate. When she set it all down on the coffee table some chrysanthemums in a small clear fishbowl, some plump pinks and tarnished whites, bobbed; she rimmed each cup with lemon juice and rind and rigged the peels eighth-of-a-moonlike on the cups and handed me one and picked up the biscuit and chocolate plate and held it theatrically up to me.

And suddenly I realized what this bizarre bizarreness was all about: she was going to poison me.

Okay, okay, I reckoned—if she's really going to go through with this poisoning-me business, at least it won't taste bad: before I went writhing around on her shiny hardwood floor, clutching my turning-blue neck, spasming grandiloquently and reciting the major soliloquies from *Hamlet* and stuff, I would at least have a nice taste in my mouth as I died in mythopoeic, theatrical agony.

She took a couple of elegant dainty tentative sips and umm-ed and then, going "Oh!," jumped up and went back to the kitchen and brought back a milk-white bowl of what can only be described as voluptuous strawberries swimming in fresh pink cream.

The infamous strawberry that Tess gets fed in Polanski's *Tess* had nothing on these things, boy.

"Try one," Sarah commanded and, though I didn't as you might be wondering take it from her hand or anything, it was just the same as if I had—and it tasted insane.

Her insolent violet eyes (the irises rimmed—perfectly encircled—with harder, darker, deeper blue) regarded me as she held one of the plumper, more pickle-like and infinitely phallic fruits up to her kissyface lips and then took it in with a slow, cinematic, pucker-laugh.

Could this girl possibly be serious?

All the while holding my gaze unflinchingly.

My gaze? My God!

One thing I remember thinking right then—if thinking was even remotely what I was doing during all this—was *if she's such a nympho and all, she certainly won't mind if I try and kiss her*. She couldn't possibly mind; surely she expects it.

Yet what if she doesn't want me to? What if I am the one guy in the entire incomprehensible universe this nymphet doesn't want? The one guy ever she'd go "Um, that's not what I meant at all; that's not it at all" to? How humiliating would that be? That would be voluminously unhandlable. Shut down, turned down, deflected, denied and given the quote-unquote Heisman by a girl who'd be with practically anyone? No, thanks. I had to get out of there as soon as humanly possible. But how?

How indeed, I wondered, as large swathes and washes of lust thrilled through me. And I thought again of the gods above who continued to pour like so many dainty little pitchers of milk into innumerable *cafés au lait* their derision down on me. Remember them? And the faux 18th-century chocolate house way I had them speak as they bombastically made great sport of me subbing? Moreover, ever wondered what they're saying about *you*, wonderful , wondering reader? I pictured them caucusing as follows:

"Well, well, well! What have we *here*, my Lords? Another pricklish Predicament for our former Favorite? Note Ye how the Hook is stuck thick in his Cheek in the Wink and Blink of an Eye! What Chance hath he, Fate's Coxcomb that he be, against this *quite* fetching neo-goth Temptress, Wench, and Strumpet, however strident his Methods and Manners may be? None! No Chance at all, fellow Immortals! The front Door to her Flat, to him, may as well be right now made of Granite six Foot thick for all the Opening of it he'll ever get before she has him in her wanton Clutches—which, well Ye *and* he know, is precisely where he wishes to be! Ha-ha! What a Fool of Cupid and Venus combined! Any moment we'll see Evidence of the Fact that *Betrayal*, my Lords, is the only Theme when it cometh to Chicks and Dicks! Gaze on!

Snapping me out of this horrid reverie, Sarah got up and flew just then over to the LPs she'd massed against the wall and asked if there was anything I wanted to hear. I was about to tell her that I didn't care what she put on when she unjacketed Syd Barrett's *Barrett* and took it out of its paper sleeve and put it on her turntable. The needle dribbled onto the first cut and her speakers shrieked like a cat being stepped on by a lumbering giant. She put the arm back into the groove at the beginning and, turning round, poufed her hair out like Winona Ryder at the end of *Heathers* and made this face that seemed to lower her glittering eyes three inches and raise her eyebrows about the same. Oh my God, oh my God—she looks just like Syd! She's doing an imitation of the Pink Floyd madcap here—singing, pantomiming playing guitar, dancing around.

If you're surmising that right about then I was looking round for the *Candid Camera* camera you're absolutely right.

What oddness next? A belly dance? A breakdance that broke into a belly dance? A recitation, note perfect, of *Medea?* She sure did appear a Medusa—though an extremely attractive one. Would some kind of small, furry, teeth-baring jungle animal burst from one of the stereo speakers and affix its tusks to my unsuspecting neck? Would a rainbow of horrors emanate from behind the curtains?

"Wow, Sarah," I said as she laughed immoderately at her little masquerade—all the more so as she was trying not to crack up, and failing, "that's, um, pretty interesting, what you're doing. But now I'm wondering if you put acid in my coffee or something!"

"LSD or the other kind?" she cackled and crashed down right beside me—not exactly snuggling, but almost.

"Acid acid," I said. "I mean, I'm thinking I'm starting to see things. Was that you just imitating Syd Barrett?!"

"Of course!"

"Unreal. I'm starting to wonder things too."

"Oh? Like what?"

"Like what it would be like to kiss you."

She gave out a wee, derisive laugh: "Yeah?"

"Yes."

I could feel my voice going huskier and phonier by the second. Interesting: the sort of oozing folderol that you'd assume would never quote-unquote work on a hardcase like Sarah melted her like a popsicle on a sunny summer sidewalk:

"I think you're one of the prettiest girls I've ever seen."

"You're just saying that," she said and rolled her eyes.

"I'm not just saying that."

"You just did. I don't know. Thanks, I guess. But you have a girlfriend—that girl in your band."

"We're . . . She's . . ."

"It doesn't matter. Do you wanna sleep with me?"

Gulp.

"You know I do."

"Okay. Kiss me first."

Reader, I know what you're thinking: What about Jenny? What about *her?*

I'm glad someone was thinking of her 'cause God knows I wasn't. Or I was, but I wasn't. Sarah with her almost trenchant cheekbones was too sexy for me to include thinking about anything I was doing right then. I never had a chance.

"Here," she said [as I told you at the beginning of this scenario] as she helped herself out of her shimmering-sparkling shirt as I fumbled, as I also told you, with the bra I was having trouble unhooking. We kissed, long and deep, and she got up and straddled me and hiked up her skirt and got me out of my jeans and, wet as fuck, got me in her so fast my head spun. I had my grateful hands all over her heaving, much-larger-and-more-impressive-than-I'd-imagined breasts. Just spectacular tits, Sarah's—even for a non-boob guy like me.

That's what I'd say to all you fellow non-boob guys out there: you can be converted. You former ones know exactly what I'm talking about. Maybe you're just minding your own business, walking along in a city park, doing differential equations in your head or conjugating verbs in Sanskrit or thinking about what to fix for lunch—a salad or a sandwich—and along comes this pretty girl and she sits down on one of the benches and you do too and you strike up a conversation with her and she's really interesting and really tall and really funny and really smart and has such a nice face and you make a date with her and take her out and so it goes and so it goes and suddenly you're quote-unquote seeing her and there's just one thing: she has zero breasts. And all you can think of sometimes as you pass by girls with lovely bubbies—bigger, natch—is that you have *got* to get your hands on some bigger ones; it's crucial, and the Smiths' "Some Girls are Bigger than Others" is your personal soundtrack, and what you thought wasn't going to be an issue suddenly *is*, and she senses it, and she gets all pissed off at you and eventually breaks up with you, and now *you're* the boob 'cause you lost a great girl on a fucking technicality. And, contrary to what you might think, it's not that she's caught you staring at other girls' chests or cleavage or anything; it's that she caught you trying really really hard *not* to look. And she sees what's up. And she dumps you. That's how girls' minds work: they're always one intuitive step ahead of us—and don't you forget it.

Know what I'm saying? Again, one hopes not. One hopes this hasn't been/isn't in your personal realm of experience. Sincerely.

Now: re: the Sarah sitch: don't go thinking I'm some helpless, innocent victim here: I'm a guilty victim. Fucked and self-fucked.

So blah blah blah we started having sex. (You don't think I'm in some soft porn way going to give you a play-by-play, do you? But if you really wanna know, it wasn't that sexy-o'-sex, actually; it wasn't what you'd expect from a girl with a rep as a nymphomaniac.) And after a few still quite velvety minutes she slipped off and got down on all fours on the floor and told me she wanted me to take her from behind. The utter weirdness of the whole thing was starting to sink in like a shot-put in quicksand. We quote-unquote got down for a while (such a jejune and ugly phrase, to "get down" with someone) and then she slithered me out of her again and breathed out that she wanted me to come with her into the bedroom. My pants were accordioned around my ankles now as I sort of penguined along behind her.

"Sarah," I said as we got on the bed and I was in her again. "I don't think this is such a good idea."

I might as well have told her that some zombies from a cult were coming and that I had to go get ready for them.

"What?" she clucked optatively. "Of course it's a good idea. Don't you *dare* stop. I'm sopping wet!"

"I just don't think I should . . ."

She sat up abruptly.

"What's the matter? You don't want to?"

"Of course I do," I said, scrounging for something meaningful and appropriate and gentle to say. "I'm sorry. Sarah, I can't do this! You have no idea how attracted to you I am. It's just not cool for me to do this to Jenny, you know?"

"No, I *don't* know," she said.

I stood up and did up my pants: "I'd better go."

"Fine, then."

"I'm sorry but . . ."

"I said 'fine.' Good*bye!*"

*

On the remorseful drive home, with the radio on just barely, I wondered if I had really cheated? What were the technicalities? The parameters and definitions? What were the fucking facts?

Exhibit one: I had played tonsil hockey with Sarah. Full-rink. Exhibit two: I had placed my hands on her impossible breasts, moved them around, those hands, them breasts, and placed my mouth on them and tongued her ample nipples with ravenous, lapping, teeth-gritting, pleasurable, madman abandon. Exhibit three: I had placed penis A into vagina B. Okay. All right. But I had not squirted semen of any kind into said vagina. Seminal fluid in profuse abundance, maybe, but decidedly no semen. Surely that was significant, mitigating? Surely that counted for something. It had to. It must.

Did what I'd done with her constitute actual sexual congress and hence unalloyed cheating, or was this just a snafu, an understandable screw-up, a lapse, a mistake of the I'll-never-do-that-again variety?

Oh, who was I kidding?

Me, that's who.

One thing I knew about even then, in my callow post-youth, was the phenomenon that happens when someone who's just come in from the Land of the Emotionally Lost becomes absolutely *ace* at assessing other people's problems. Isn't that curious? Countless were the times when I'd realized that someone who was doling out brilliant advice, telling me *just* the thing to do about love or family or school or work problems, was only having all these incredible insights on account of he or she was way absconding from their own quandaries and imaginatively entering one's own. I could probably have gone around wowing all and sundry with my sagacity re love and other conundrums right about then. But what I really needed to do was *not* think, or at least think of something else, something other than the fact that I had really really really fucked up.

Think of something else, I thought. (Isn't that what our inrushing defense mechanisms always do—get our culpable minds off the subject?)

What, then?

The record. Oh yes, that. I popped in the mixes that McLeary'd made and brought by Finyl Vinyl just before Sarah turned up. What a curious combination of elation and mortification I felt when I thought of what my band had achieved—and what I'd just done with Sarah-Who-Hated-Me. My band had made a record. I had made a record. And, sure, you might be thinking, So what? Anyone can do that nowadays. Swing a dead cat and hit a zillion twenty-somethings in this neighborhood alone who've recorded an LP. So what?

And yet what we, the Weird Sisters, had made was, in all modesty, really pretty good. *I* thought so. But then I was pretty biased. Bands always think that. There's some band right now, as you're reading this, going "All right! *That* is a hit if I've ever heard one, man! We are awesome!" (Bands are stupid for themselves. Bands are stupid period. "Bands Are Stupid"—that's my one great t-shirt idea. Like it? Please don't steal it.) A hair band, a punk band, a *prog* band, a reggae band, a pop band, a death metal band, an indie rock band, a salsa band, a funk, a ska, a full-on mainstream unimaginative collective of guys rhyming the most clichéd rhymes you can think of, a grunge band, a Triple A bunch of guys with acoustic guitars and tacky three-part harmonies, somewhere they're patting themselves on the backs and clinking glasses and cashing big fat royalty checks in their minds and picking out the dream guitar they're gonna plump for or the supermodel du jour they're going to be quote-unquote nailing as soon as the record comes out and hits the charts and gets them on *Letterman* and an opening slot spot with Radiohead or the re-united Talking Heads and a talk with Todd Rundgren about the possibility of doing the next record.

Even if they're a walking/"rocking" musical atrocity.

When I pulled up behind my apartment I rewound the tape and, despite my utterly hallucinogenic exhaustion, for forty-three minutes and thirty-two seconds I listened to the record once again, top to bottom. And I thought that, with McLeary's invaluable help, and some from the Scather, I had led three people to create something out of nothing. We'd fashioned melodies, guitar screes, other interesting noises, bridges, choruses, beats, breaks and harmonies out of *nothing*. That was the weird thing. The songs I'd written and the ones I'd written with Jen now existed on a two-inch tape and they'd been mixed down to a quarter-inch tape and transferred to a little cassette tape; and one day, if we were lucky, they'd be used to make artifacts of vinyl and cassette that people might review, and listen to, and buy, and maybe really enjoy. I'd thought of myself as my ideal listener: I'd set out to make a record that I would want to listen to. And whether or not I'd succeeded in pleasing anyone else—well, that wasn't up to me anymore, was it? Someone like me might be consoled by music and lyrics that evoked concerns that people had every day. They might be reminded for two sides of an LP that someone else thought like they did—or differently. That words could be strung together in ways that seemed like nonsense but really weren't; that getting over lost love was one of the most poignantly significant, grown-up, and difficult things one could do; that psychedelic states of mind could be attained without substances—or with. It didn't matter that that's what nearly every non-political songwriter wrote about; it didn't matter at all. What we'd made was ours, a portrait of where we were at the time as a band. No huge deal on a worldwide scale, but something incomparably important to us. To me, solipsistic me.

That was surely something—to make something out of nothing. Wasn't it? Sure.

But then I started thinking about Jenny and what I'd just done and I started swirling really really bad.

Have you ever cheated on someone you loved, reader? I hope you haven't. Cause it *sucks*.

## i'm not the kind who likes to tell you

In the morning, another Monday, by 7:45 there was no call from downtown, so at 7:46 I took the initiative and rang the LA Unified Sub Pool switchboard myself to see if all the assignments had gone out, even the dreaded Junior High School ones. Nothing doing: the regular teachers, those fuckers, must be saving their sick days for the upcoming holidays. In a groggy muddle and sort of wall-bouncing I went out to the kitchen to burn some coffee. There was Jaz, up and at his computer, snapping some plutonium through the bong, laboring away on his screenplay, the pitter-patter of his typing aping the gentle plash of rainfall outside. I caught him looking in the computer screen when it went black and reflective to see if he'd lost any of his hairline but of course I didn't let on I'd seen him.

Jaz'd made java, so I helped myself to a dreggy cup and sat down on the living room lawn chair, hoping not to collect my thoughts. Because if I collected them, I'd think about the Sarah debacle and the financial repercussions of missing yet another day of being paid to screech at the youths of Los Angeles, America. Substituting's an all-round Catch-22: it's a piece of cake and yet it's an ultrabummer if there's no or scant work. It's great to have time off, but if there are too many days away and you're broke, totally tapped, and looking at eating ungarnished pasta till the end of the month, it isn't much fun. You can't really afford to do something cool with your down time, like go to the movies, or shop for records and books, or purchase a home visit from a couple of whipped-creamed strippers.

Just jesting about the strippers.

I didn't feel like doing anything, anyway, other than concentrating on freaking out about yesterday's contretemps. I didn't feel like reading, writing, playing guitar, or going out to a lonely, greasy, budget breakfast (at least, the kind I could then afford). What remained? Smoking a hundred cigarettes and staring at the ceiling from my futon? Holding my weary, cheating head in my weary, cheating hands? No: there had to be something more in life. There had to be.

"Hey, Jaz," I said, "wanna take a break and . . ."

"Play some Nerf ball? Absolutely."

Just as we were getting going with me pitching first like I liked to, the phone rang. It could be a late call for a late assignment—but what if it was Jenny? How was I going to stave off the unavoidable tone of guilt in my voice. Oh God. I had to pick up the receiver. Had to. I said hello and the Scather's voice blasted heartily out of it:

"Juan!"

"Sterling? What are you doing up so early?"

He just laughed; then said: "Hey! You've apparently done something with your life! Hahaha! Sarah told me you gave her a terrific ride home last night. Ride being the key word here. Thanks for working for me, nevertheless; I really appreciate it. And I'm sure you did! Hahaha!"

Gulp redux.

"Sterling," I said sternly, "we're about to play an important indoor baseball game here—can I call you back?"

"Of course. How do McLeary's mixes sound anyway . . . you naughty naughty thing?!"

"Great. Sterl. I gotta talk to you, but not right now, okay?"

"Okay. Good luck."

I was sure he wasn't talking about the contest between Jaz and me.

"Fuck!" I said as I put down the phone.

"What?" Jaz said.

"Sarah told Sterling that I kinda slept with her!"

"What?!" Jaz said. "The Sarah that hates you! *Betty Blue* Sarah?"

"Precisely."

"When? You're kidding, right?"

"I wish, Jaz."

Now *Jaz* was laughing.

"*Kinda?*"

"Technically. Theoretically."

Now he was really chuckling.

"Oh my God."

"I know. Better forget it for now."

"That's a policy I'd certainly advance right now. But, seriously, what are you gonna . . ."

"I have no idea. Let's just play right now, okay?"

I opened up with a screwball that Jaz took a walloping cut on and lanced against the right field wall—which we'd deemed "foul."

"Nice pitch," Jaz opined. "So are you going to tell Jenny?"

"I thought we weren't going to . . ."

"Oh you *know* we are!" he said. "This is a sort of moral forkball and you are batter up right now, my friend. You know there are only two ways to go with this one. Which way are you going to go?"

Winding up to throw the next pitch I said: "Well, if I tell her she . . . I can't tell her: I'll probably lose her—plus she'll . . ."

"Bail out of the band? Is that what you were gonna say?"

"*Kind* of."

"Yet if she finds out somehow and you didn't tell her . . ."

"I'm fucked."

"Exactly. What happened, if you don't mind my asking? If you don't mind a little vicarious . . ."

"Oh God," I said, and gave him the play-by-play that lead to the—I insisted—*half*-lay.

I threw a knuckleball that plummeted two feet before home plate (which was the cover of *Power, Corruption and Lies*—the record Jaz had put on to hit to).

Jaz bent down and hucked the Nerf back to me: "You confess, you'll be the caring, honest, respectful, sensitive, conscientious guy she got terribly hurt by, really appreciated *for* his honesty, and summarily dumped; you don't tell—you eat the guilt and remain paranoid, and if she finds out you'll be totally demonized and it's quite likely she'll never speak to you again . . . These are just theories, by the way. I could be wrong. Some people have really strong feelings about the ethics of this kind of thing. I don't, really, but I thought I'd chip in my two cents, you know? Fuck, John: what are you gonna do?"

"I have no idea. Maybe I should ask Heidi—*she'd* know."

Jaz's laugh was very halfhearted: "I mean, what *happened?* Normally, I'd be the first guy to congratulate you on getting more and on-the-side sex. I like Jenny and everything—she's a cool girl—but that Sarah chick? Aside from being too sexy for words, she just seems like very bad news."

"I know. I was totally wrong-footed. Wrong-footed totally. One minute she's explaining how she despises me, the next she's got me in her apartment having coffee and . . ."

I threw a total blimp at him and sat on his couch: I didn't feel like playing anymore.

"Bottom line: you should tell her."

"Jenny? You *think* so, really?"

"Oh, I don't know."

"You think I should tell Jenny."

"Who'd you think I meant—your mom?"

"Oh fuck off, Jaz."

"It's an all-round disastrophe. Or maybe not. Who knows?"

"A what?" I said.

"A disastrophe: a word I made up: a combination of catastrophe and disaster. Like it?"

"Oh, brilliant."

"Not to change the subject but did you bring home a tape of you guys's record? Play it for me. Should help take your mind off things."

"Okay," I said.

"Let's get high and listen to it. Do you want to chortle some pot?"

"No thanks, really."

"How about now?"

"Nah: I don't want to be high right now."

"Me either," Jaz said and reached for the bong on his desk and ripped a huge bong hit while I went to my room and got the tape and put it in the cassette player in the stereo.

"The way I see it," Jaz continued as pot smoke rolled from his exaggeratedly opened mouth, "the only solution to all these problems like our respective poverty and my chicklessness and your recent and quite frankly astonishing overabundance of chickage and these sad, underpaid and underachieving jobs we have is this: I am going to have to write a total blockbuster with a thousand explosions in it, make a trillion dollars and have the Laker Girls over for barbeques at my mansion in the Palisades. Just me, you, the Laker Girls, and a full-on rodeo of filet mignon, plus a keg of Cuervo Gold margaritas. That's my plan."

"That *sounds* like a plan."

"That's because it is."

"Hey, whatever happened with you and Claudia, that lawyer babe from work you brought to our gig?"

"Boyfriend."

"Oh no!"

"She told me after I dropped off her friend. Pretty bummed about it—even though, as I told you before, I don't get bummed."

"You're bummed, Jaz. Just admit it."

"Very. Anyway, she's a great girl, and as my friend Konigsberg always says 'Always keep the door open.'"

"Plus you have the Laker Girls to think of now—on top of your sell-out script."

"Absolutely. The record sounds great, by the way. The vocals are a little low but the guitars sound cool. Good singing by Jenny for sure. And you. And you know I like you guys' songs a lot. It reminds me sometimes of R.E.M."

"R.E.M.?! Kill me."

"Okay, okay: New Order, then. But more fuzzy and . . . and . . . and . . . distorted . . . and rockin'. Rockin' for sure."

"That's better. Just so it doesn't sound like the Church—we really've tried really hard to mask that influence. Plus the Sonic Youth thing."

"It's still there, though. You can hear. Just a tiny bit. It's not a bad thing. Sonic Youth you guys don't sound like at *all*. What are you gonna do—try to get a record deal? You guys definitely have a certain sound."

"We were thinking we'd just raise the money to put it out ourselves. Punk rock and all. Though we're not, of course, punk at all. Dunno yet. We have a band meeting on Wednesday to talk it out, figure it out. Not sure."

"That's good. Hey, do you remember that time we went to the basketball courts down by the beach and we brought a six-pack and there were these two little kids shooting around on the good hoop and I offered them a beer each if they'd trade us ends and they made a face like 'You're crazy!' and refused to move and there was this perfect pause and *you* said 'It's *Miller*'—holding up the Miller Lites for them to see?"

"Uh, seeing as that was only around a couple of months ago, yes I do remember that, yes."

"*That* was hilarious, is all I'm saying."

"You're just trying to cheer me up."

"How could I be?" Jaz laughed. "We were drinking Miller Lite. How cheering is that?"

"None. None cheering. We must've been desperate—and broke."

"How things change," Jaz said.

"Yeah, right. Do you remember the time when some kids were kicking a ball in the back alley and you were writing and I was—I don't know—reading or maybe trying to write some lyrics and it seemed like they'd been out there shouting for hours till you came into my room and leaned out the window and said . . ."

"'Hey! Can you guys scram? My wife and I are trying to have *sex* in here!' Yeah, I remember that on account it was only . . ."

"Two weeks or so ago."

"Right," Jaz said. "That was pretty funny too."

He tilted his head to listen a bit more carefully, it seemed, to the song that was on, one called "Your Mary Janes": "I just wish it was as raw as you guys live, though. Especially that song 'Tear the Sky'—you know that's my favorite."

"You're not just saying that 'cause we're roommates and friends?"

"No."

"You're sure?"

"No."

"Jaz?"

"Huh?"

"You're just about the fucking funniest guy I know and have ever known."

"I know," Jaz said.

*

I spent the rest of that rainy day in a bit of a daze, mooning around in my room and making feeble, foul-tempered attempts to concentrate on a new novel I was reading by a foul-tempered but hilarious guy called Martin Amis, picking up a guitar and putting it down after a few plinks and strums, taking around seven showers, going out in the rain to say hey to Heidi, going down to the newsstand to get the *Times* (which I read about fifteen words of) and a café latte. I had an aimless afternoon chat with Jenny at work that left me feeling even more guilty as she was so sweet and all. In the late late afternoon, as Jaz was getting up from the nap he took before he had to haul off downtown for work, I checked with him to see if he felt like calling in sick and hitting a budget/early bird movie with me. Like anyone who semi-hates his job and feels somewhat above it, he was tempted, but after a bit of deliberation he decided nah, he couldn't afford it.

I could relate to him: I too needed all the work I could get, especially if the Weird Sisters were going to have to come up with even more funds to put our record out. The amount of cake I was getting from subbing two, three, four if I was lucky days a week wasn't cutting it. I was starting to worry, to say the least. And the last thing I'd needed to do to my already complicated, penurious existence was complicate it further by going and putting my penis in someone.

Why had I done that?

*Why?*

# CHORUS

## 1, 2, 3, 4, 5

"*These* days," Rob was saying (somewhat uncharacteristically pompously, I thought), record companies are nothing more than glorified banks. Nothing more. It's just not how it used to be. It wasn't always like that, but that's just the way it is. Nowadays they're just a bunch of rip-offs."

"Pirates, basically," I said.

"Totally," Rob said.

Thus far, twenty or so minutes into our Wednesday night band meeting, Rob and I had been doing almost all the talking.

"They are total shysters," Rob said and tilted way back on one of the high-backed teak chairs at Walter and Nastasha's enormous dining room table.

"Totally," I said.

"Completely," Rob said.

Walt set his hand in front of him at the table, then folded them like he was praying or something: "I dunno," he said. He passed a quivering hand through his already-slicked-back hair. "I don't see why we shouldn't send out a *few* tapes before we go committing ourselves to spending . . ."

"*Fuck* labels, though," Rob urged. "Forget 'em. We should stick to our initial plan of putting this out on our own label—get some reviews and college radio—and then see if any labels bite. That's what we should do. I thought that's what we'd agreed on."

"Yeah but if . . ." Walt started to say.

"Rob's right," I said. "Punk rock!"

"Absolutely," Rob said. "The punk aesthetic all the way."

"Yeah, well, check it out," Walt said, squirming further, "this is not a punk rock band. Not at all. This project is not punk by *any* stretch, okay? I've *been* in punk bands, man. I've played in *dozens* of punk bands, so don't go telling me that . . ."

"No one's saying we are punk rock, Walt," I said, "I mean . . ."

"Rob was in a fucking *cover* band, and neither you nor Jenny have ever even *been* in a band before, so . . ."

"Hey: I've been in some original bands too!" Rob said.

"You guys are missing the point," I said. "Rob was talking about an aesthetic, an ideal—not the music. And this isn't a quote-unquote *project*, okay?"

"Okay, okay," Walt backed off.

"I hate that term," Jenny said.

"Obviously I do too," I said.

"Yeah, man," Rob said, "get real."

I'd never seen him be more assertive, ever. Normally he just went along with whatever, whenever, and let Walter do the advanced kvetching, whinging, pissing, and moaning—throwing all the wrenches into the works himself. It was really strange to hear him having all these *opinions* on and ideas about things.

"I *am* getting real, Rob," Walt said, much more calm now. "Like, fully real, okay? I just don't know about having to shell out—what?—another two hundred and fifty bucks on top of the two-fifty I shelled for the recording? I mean, we use *my* practice space—you guys don't pay a penny for that, you know. I mean . . ."

"What's *that* got to do with it?" I said.

"I just don't think it would hurt us to send some tapes out and wait a bit and see if we get any, like, bites," Walter said.

"We don't want any bites right now," Rob said. "They can bite *off*."

"Bite me," I said.

"Bite my left one," Jenny said.

"Bite my *arse*," Rob said, imitating McLeary who was sitting next to him.

"Bite *me* arse," McLeary corrected him.

"*Me* arse," Rob laughed.

"Bite my cunt!" Jenny said, and we all looked at her, kinda stunned, then started busting up utterly, just losing it.

"*Jenny!*" Walter said. "You are taking this one-of-the-guys thing a little too far, young lady."

"No kidding," I said. "Wow. Very naughty."

Jenny was blushing of course and covering her capacious mouth with her hand but you could tell she was loving it; she really was one-of-the-guys material all the way—and all the more so since we'd made the record and really bonded and jelled as a band. Even with Walter bailing and Sterling having to finish his tracks for him.

"You total whore!" Rob joked.

"Okay, okay—that's enough," I said. "Let's get serious, okay?"

But that just made everyone laugh even harder.

After a little spell of calm we all started laughing again till Walter said: "Let's get serious here!"

"I've never been more serious," Rob said. "We don't want to play the game of prostrating ourselves in front of a flipping record company so that they can put a seal of approval on what we do or whatever."

"I under*stand* that," Walt said. "But if some label was cool . . ."

"But none of them are, don't you see?" Rob said. "Right, McLeary?"

McLeary just shrugged.

"That's what we've just been saying for the past half hour," I said.

"But how do you know?" Walt sensibly said. "How do you know that until you try them?"

"They *just* aren't," Rob said. "Every time a label talked to one of my other bands—original bands, okay?—we got screwed over. Every time. Led on and stuff. They're useless."

"Was that 'cause you were in a band called the Uselessnesses?" I joked.

"That was just a joke band," Rob said.

"Oh," I said. "Jenny—what do you think?"

We all turned to look her way.

"Whatever we decide on. If it means coming up with some more money to put out the record on vinyl and cassette, that's okay with me. That's what we talked about, right? Let's just get the ball rolling, I think? Not make such a huge issue out of it. I don't mind giving the band some money—even a little extra, 'cause I might make a bit more than you guys do? We should be able to come up with a thousand dollars, right? We should be able to come up with that."

"It's more like two thousand," I said. "Fifteen hundred, maybe."

"Oh, great," Walter said.

Rob and I, whose financial situations were nearly identical in being the most dire, most woeful and panic-ridden come the end of the month, tentatively nodded at one another. How, at this point, either of us was going to be able to come up with our share of the couple grand was anybody's guess. We'd all chipped in two-fifty for the recording, and Jenny had paid McLeary four hundred out of her own pocket—a hundred bucks a day: we were supposed to pay her back with gig money—supposing there was any, or that we got any paying gigs, other than the one that Nasty had supposedly snagged for us at USC. I was thinking I could sell my Telecaster now that Jen had one of her own; it would kill me to part with it, but *c'est la guerre*, you know? I had no idea what Rob might do: his car, a crumpled ancient coughing black smoke-billowing rusted unregistered cop-magnet Honda Civic barely got him to his new job as a telephone solicitor for a medical company.

"I can see what Walter's saying," Jenny went on. "It isn't just a small bit of money. It's a lot. It's an expenditure and everything, for sure. I don't like parting with money—I know you guys don't, either. But we might make some of it back, you know, by doing as many shows as we can and selling some to Arons and the Record Trader, Moby Disc and Canterbury's. Pooh-Bah's in Pasadena'll buy some too."

"Sterling surely can unload some at Finyl Vinyl!" I said.

"Exactly," Jenny said. "Like this upcoming gig we have at SC: that'd be perfect!"

"Except we won't have records by then, though," Walt said.

"That's true," Jenny agreed, "but this record deserves to get out there—I'm really proud of what we, and McLeary, have done, you know? It's a really nice LP. I don't know about you guys but I have listened to it a bunch of times. Not too many, you know—I don't want to be vain or self-obsessed or anything. I'm really proud of it. I don't say that all the time about the stuff I do, you realize. Nothing's ever good enough *most* of the time, I think."

There were times when I looked at her—she must have seen it in my eyes—with such admiration. And I also thought: I don't even know this person. This person is an utter mystery to me. She's so articulate and professional-sounding and she carries herself terribly well and with such confidence. Not all the time, but most of it. See how she held her shoulders square and looked everyone right in the eye when she spoke and voiced her concerns in a kind of detached but engaged way? How wonderful. What's she doing in an indie band anyway? With the likes of me? She really belongs in a super successful band that's flying all round the world every minute of the day—or maybe directing a boardroom meeting downtown, I don't know. I can't figure her out sometimes. And furthermore, what am I gonna do about, um, my transgression. That's the real question, isn't it?

I was thinking all this when I turned and said: "What do *you* think, McLeary? You haven't said much tonight."

We all turned his way now. We'd invited him—and gladly—to sit in on our meeting, as he was now almost a part of the band, the fifth Beatle and all (yeah, right); we'd bonded with him so tight and had such a good time with him in the studio (there was nary an outburst like the ones I told you he'd perpetrate sometimes at our practices) that we wanted him there. I was really keen to hear what he might have to say, but at the same time I was thinking how this meeting was getting us nowhere, and that we had to get rid of Walter anyway, and that we should just order a pizza and drink a few twelvers and get some wine for Jen and just get, as McLeary would say, legless.

"I dunno," McLeary said in his most utmost mellifluous voice, very serious, though, very knitted of brow. "Seems like some label should have an interest in having a number one record on their catalogue. Could do to give a bell to a couple of companies, you know? See where they're at. Ring them up and tell them you have the finished masters—that is, if we master it ourselves. Tell them they can put them out. Brilliant. That sort of thing, you know? Or you could do it yourselves. Fine. Good plan. Brilliant too. Management, though. That's the ticket. That's the key, if you know what I'm saying. You need representation. A sound manager. Find one of *them*."

Adorable innocent.

As if it were that easy!

McLeary, who was usually as you've seen beyond unflappable, seemed a bit uneasy, perhaps realizing that what he'd said was mere well-wishing in a wishing well, got up from the table and asked Walter if he could put on some music, some XTC or something, and Walt said it was okay.

"Okay, that helped!" Rob scoffed, but not severely. "I have an idea, though, you guys: I think what we should do is what a lot of English bands do initially which is release an EP—a small run of copies—which will be cheaper (as far as mastering goes but not manufacturing) and then when we put it out and it hopefully gets some attention we can say we have a full LP or two more EPs ready to go. You know, in case someone wants to put them out."

"I thought you said we weren't going for labels," Walter, calling Rob out, objected. "You just totally, like, contradicted yourself, Robert!"

"Maybe!" Rob smiled. "What about the EP idea, though—it's certainly cheaper."

We all looked at each other with sort-of looks of assent and agreement and Rob yelled over to McLeary who was by the stereo in the living room, hunched over Walter and Nasty's record collection: "Hey, McLeary, what about just making an EP out of it first?!"

"But it's an album!" McLeary countered.

"Yes, we know—'And a number one fookin' album,'" Rob mildly mocked.

"Fuckin' hell, it is," McLeary said.

Had you asked McLeary why he was a producer he'd probably tell you something naïve-ish like "'Cause I loike producing records"; he really was completely clueless about how the quote-unquote industry worked. He did have a point about management, though; I had always heard from my more veteran musician friends like Sterling that record labels took you way more seriously when you had an intermediary, when they didn't have to deal with *you*.

"Let's do it as an EP then! Rob's right. Let's just do it—okay?" I said more loudly than I realized at first.

"Do what?" Nastasha, who had just walked through the door as McLeary dropped the needle on track three, side one of *English Settlement*; her hookerish heels clacked irksomely across the hardwood floor. "Do what, you guys? What's going on? What are you guys shouting about? What's happening?"

Meddlesome munchkin.

"Nothing," I said.

"Hi, baby," Walter said and got up and kissed her pertly presented cheek.

She gave me a look as she did so, like "Yeah, right—don't patronize me, okay?"

"Seriously, how come you guys are arguing?"

"We're not. Just having a band meeting," I smiled.

"Oh I see—I'd better get lost then, huh? Even though I'm the one who got you guys this gig at SC!" Nastasha peevishly said.

"I thought your brother got it for us," I said.

Foolish fool.

"What's going on with that, by the way, Nastasha? That's really great news, by the way," Rob said, in a Hail Mary attempt to swat the air ball of tension that'd just been thrown up.

Nastasha just glared.

"Easy, baby," Walter said. "How was work?"

She didn't, of course, answer him. Instead she said: "I'm just sick and tired of the rest of them pushing you around, Walter. How much longer are you gonna . . ."

"They're not pushing me anywhere, honey."

"Oh, no? Oh, *no?*"

"No."

"*No?*"

"No.

"*No?*"

"*No! I said 'no!'*"

"I think I'll just pop out for some more smokes," McLeary said.

"No one's pushing anyone," I said.

"Yeah, right," Nastasha said. "Oh, sure. Listen, John—you think you're so cool. You think you fucking *live* here. You think you can just come over any time you like and just hang out like you just, like, *live* here! Just hang around and wait around for Jenny. [There was a very na-na-na-na-nah-na quality to her voice just then.] Well, let me tell you something: this is *my* house. My and Walter's house, and you just, like . . ."

"Take it easy, Natasha," Walter said. "Jeez Louise! There's no need to come un*bolted* or anything . . ."

"For me to come *what?!*"

"What's your *trip?*" I said, getting pretty worked up despite myself. My voice, I could tell, was acetone, daggers, nightshade, dueling flame-throwers, when it should have been kittens, sugar-frosted cornflakes, peppermint ice cream, cunnilingus. "When did I *even* . . ."

"My *what?!*" Nastasha fumed. "You guys can all just fuck off—*you* especially."

Of course the "you" meant *me*.

What was I doing/saying anyway? Wow. Was I quite insane or something to be addressing such a firebrand in this way, or what? I was way out of line. Still, she was way out of hand. Way.

"Walter! Are you coming now, or what?" Nastasha shrilled and went into her and Walter's room, just off the living room, and slammed the door as hard as she Lilliputianly could.

"Wow," Rob said.

"What a total . . ." I started to say but Jenny put her hand out on mine to stop me.

Walter gave me a look I couldn't exactly interpret—part remonstrance, part commiserative—and said: "Well, good meeting, then! I guess that's it for the meeting. You guys can go ahead and order a pizza if you want, but, um, I had better go see if I can calm her down. I may not come out alive, you guys."

You had to hand it to his henpecked ass—he did have a pretty okay sense of humor sometimes. He said all this in an almost little kid-like voice, one he affected almost always after one of Nasty's rage-outs.

"Find out all the details about the SC gig, okay?" Rob said. "Good night. I think we're gonna just split."

Rob wasn't even nonplussed: he'd known Walter and Nastasha for a long, long time; a scene like this was nothing.

"I think you hurt her feelings," Jenny said softly. "Sometimes I think you don't realize . . ."

"No, don't go, you guys," Walter said. "Just order a pizza, okay? I'll be out in a little bit."

"I didn't mean to," I said, turning to Jen. "Honest."

"Of course you didn't, mate," McLeary said; he'd never made his escape.

Rob and I exchanged looks.

"Try not to *hold back* or anything, next time, John," Rob sarked.

## melt the guns and never more desire them

We got an extra XL pizza (veggie, or McLeary'd have freaked—though Rob lobbied successfully for pepperoni on a quarter of it), and some beers and a bottle of red wine and everyone kind of drifted away around the house, taking plates of slices with them: Rob and McLeary to the couches to listen to another side of Andy Partridge and company (eventually they just shut it down and zoned out on the telly); Jenny to the kitchen to sit by herself then do to some presumably therapeutic washing-up; and me out to the front porch to have a look at the stars and ruminate while ruminating about the last slice—the one that no one ever takes. I hadn't eaten anything all day. I had a post-prandial smoke and a gander at the pretty-in-the-streetlamp-light, mulchly-wet-from-the-recent-rain streets; and after around fifteen more minutes thought I should maybe say goodbye and go home. Tonight would be a good night for that. When I came back in, Walt was sitting there with Rob and Mac, explaining the set-up for the gig. I could hear Nastasha in the kitchen with Jen; I wasn't going anywhere near there. I wasn't about to go a-sinking my plate in the sink just then. I was setting it down on the coffee table when in came Nasty. She didn't seem to notice me or anyone; she just sort of broomsticked past and went into her and Walt's room once again, this time quietly, not slamming the door or anything. Jenny came out of the kitchen shortly after, head down, eyes averted, and in a kind of rush, I thought, to skimble-skamble upstairs.

"What's going on?" Rob said, momentarily tearing his eyes away from the television where someone in a beyond-ludicrous sitcom was prancing around with a Ganesh-head on their head till they fell off a pier, backwards. Rob was such the television addict kid. But even the most far-gone couch potato would've noticed that something was wrong wrong wrong in that household. McLeary noticed it; he got up abruptly and said he'd see the lot of us later. Rob followed closely behind him, saying goodbye as he was already out the door.

"I'll get the info on the SC thing from you tomorrow, okay, Rob?" I shouted to him and went upstairs. There was a muffled, kind of pained sound just then from Walter and Nasty's room.

Jenny's door was closed of course so I rapped gently and said "Jenny, are you in there? Can I talk to you for a sec?" and shouldered it open.

"Jenny?"

But she didn't answer. She was lying kinda fetal, her face averted.

"Jenny, are you sleeping?"

"No," she sniffled.

"What's the matter?"

The tears came in a gush now.

"Nastasha . . . just . . . she just told me . . . she told me that instead of saying you can't come over for anytime except on rehearsals . . . you have to . . . I mean, I . . ."

"Slow down. You're not making sense, sweetheart."

"She told me I have to move out. She and Walter decided . . .

"What?! You are *kidding* me!"

"No. She means it. Two weeks."

"That's insane!"

"It's their prerogative, I guess. It's their house."

"Two weeks, though? That's not legal. They have to give you a month at least. I can't believe how uncool they are—of course Nastasha especially. What an unbelieveable . . ."

"It's okay. I was thinking of getting my own place, anyway."

I took her in my arms and kissed her numerous times on her face and head and she sobbed a little more—a lot more, if you really wanna know—and I told her she could come stay with Jaz and me for as long as she liked: Jaz wouldn't mind.

"Are you sure?" she said.

"Of course. *You* will mind, on account of it's a dump-of-dumps, but Jaz won't mind at all. He sleeps almost all day, anyway, and you know he works the graveyard. Plus, you know—he thinks you're great. He really likes you."

"I like him too; he's funny."

I got her a tissue from the box of it on the nightstand.

"Thank you. I don't wanna be an imposition and all of that," Jenny said.

"Give me a break, Jen. It'll be fun. Imposition? What are you—crazy?"

I had her laughing a little now.

"That fucking bitch," I went on. "She is really unbelievable. What a fucking . . . Look, you are not to worry about this right now. Just come and stay with me, okay? I want you to. And what was Walter's whole bit about backing out of putting the record out. I mean . . . he's just such a cretin."

"He's been pretty sweet to me while I've stayed here, though."

"Oh, I know. That's true. He can't stand up to her, is all. I've never seen a guy so . . . Let's kick him out right now! We were going to, anyway, right? Kick him out and get Sterling to drum for the SC gig."

"Natasha would just cancel it if Walter wasn't in the band anymore."

"Oh. You're right. She probably would. Anyway, let's get out of here; let's go to my house right now, okay?"

"Okay. John?"

"What, honey?"

"It seemed like you wanted to tell me something. Talk about something?"

"Why do you say that?"

"I don't know."

"Look, Jen: you are the best thing that has ever happened to me, okay? I really mean it. Do you realize that?"

"Yeah," she said, kind of little-girlishly.

"Get your things for a few days at least and let's go. Let's get out of here and go to Santa Monica."

I felt so in love with her right then. She was such an amazing girl. It didn't hurt that the more I was with her, the more beautiful she seemed to me. And she was quite beautiful. I mean, all of my friends basically wanted to sleep with her. You could totally tell. That's how you measure whether a girl's cute or not—whether all your friends want to fuck her.

That and what she looks like when her hair is wet.

Jen was getting some of her stuff together in her overnight bag while I was resisting the temptation to keep on going on and on about Walter's "project" comment and how lame he and Nasty were and how stupid it was that they'd take their animosity towards me out on Jenny when the phone rang and Jenny gave me a look like "Should I answer it?" and I just shrugged so she went over and picked it up:

"Hello?" she said. "Yes? Oh, hi. Wow. I thought I'd . . . Listen, is there a number where I can call you back tomorrow? . . . Let me get a pen . . .

Okay. You know. Fine . . . Good . . . Thank you—you do too . . . Oh, yeah? When? . . . Uh-huh . . . Playing in an alternative band, actually . . . Yes, very . . . Listen: I have to call you back? What's the number? . . . Okay, I got it . . . Really?! . . . Sure. Okay, I'll call you . . . Bye."

I didn't ask who it was but I was probably wearing the question on my face or something. Jen had to have sensed it. Her eyes went kind of saucerish.

"That was David," she said.

"Your old boyfriend David? 'The' David?"

"Uh-huh. So weird."

"Oh?"

"He says he's coming down to LA."

"Really?" I said, quite nonchalantly and all—which almost always means nervously: when you're trying to act all unconcerned, that is.

"This weekend."

"Oh."

After a longish pause Jenny said quietly that she wondered what he wanted.

"Yeah, I *won*der," I said.

"What's that supposed to mean?"

"Nothing. So are you going to see him?"

"I don't know."

"You don't know?"

"No. Would that be . . . Is that going to be a problem, then? I mean . . ."

"Of course not," I snorted. "Why should it?"

"I don't have to, I suppose."

"Uh-huh."

"John, why are you being so . . ."

"So what?"

"Nothing," she sighed. "Maybe I'll just tell him to come to the SC gig."

Some more time went by—but not much.

"Are you . . . Would you be okay with that?"

"Sure. Fine. Why wouldn't I be?"

"No reason. I'm almost ready. A few more minutes. Can you just grab my sweater?"

"Okay. You'll take your car too?"

"Of course. Listen . . ."

"It's fine," I said. "Invite him if you want. I don't mind—really."

"Really?"

"Really.

## no more teachers' dirty looks

In the morning the telephone tintinabulated at 6:45 with my new assignment: an indefinite stint with a Senior Honors English class at one of the less war zone-like high schools. Wow! Bowl me over with a feather! For $156.42 a day I would actually maybe get to talk about something substantial. A substantial sub! (Possibly—you never knew.) I would get to teach something, help some kids who actually wanted help. What a concept. Plus I would most likely not have any chewing gum, pens, pencils, erasers, crayons, Walkmans, spitballs, chalkboards, fire extinguishers, hunting knives or desks thrown my way on a daily, nay hourly, basis. And when I wanted to kick back and read a novel or the paper, I could just give the kids an easy reading or essay assignment and trust they would do them, those tasks, with minimum clamor. I could give them Poe, or Langston Hughe,s or Gregory Corso's "Marriage," or some Emily Fucking Dickinson! It might even be, I dare say, *meaningful*. A chance for me too—to take a break from hating kids and my job and my humdrum-other-than-the-band existence.

Jenny'd left before six even in order to get downtown before the traffic hit so I shared my nascent high with Heidi: "Hi there, Heidi!" I said as I passed her yard on the way to my car, but she, as usual, just stared and thrust her head forward a couple of times, then bobbed away with her big butt high in the air—it wasn't likely she had an use for the likes of me, as I didn't have anything to feed her, which made sense as I had no idea what a domesticated emu fed on, not a clue. And thank God there was no Marie to be seen; I had a weird and totally irrational superstition about seeing Marie first thing in the morning. The way her beetling brows could kind of fixate you and freak you out. That and the queer, elf voice she used when muttering to herself and when talking to the flowers. I knew it was nonsense—thinking that whenever I ran into her on the way to my car to go sub things would go wrong that day—but hey, when are stupid superstitions *ever* rational?

I got in the old Volvo and started her up, and just as she ignited the Alice Cooper classic came on, which was weird 'cause they normally only played that song, even on lame-o FM LA radio, in June; I switched it off so that I could be with my thoughts and enjoy the fact that I would, as a result of this windfall work-wise, be flush for a little while, but that didn't last long 'cause as I was pulling up to the school forty minutes later I thought of Jen and me and my transgression again and the mood was spoiled to hell.

I had been thinking anyway, before the David's phone call, that, strangely, Jenny was becoming somewhat disenchanted with our relationship anyway. It didn't really have anything to do with the fact that he'd contacted her—but it was an odd coincidence. Something was really bothering her. Beyond getting (and mostly on my account) kicked out of her place—a place she, despite the tumult of it, seemed to really like. Something was bugging her, but fucking hell if I could say what it was. I'm just a *guy*. What would I know about what a woman's feeling, thinking, doing, going through most of the time? I didn't think she suspected I had, um, done something (nice euphemism, huh?) with another girl. But something was definitely quote-unquote off with her. Do *you* have any tidbits, insights, notions, suggestions you'd care to relay? I'd sure like to hear 'em. I"d welcome them and warmly. I mean, what do I know? What does any guy? Zero, that's what. Zilcheroo.

The school I got assigned to, William Westmoreland Senior High, is this ornate, gorgeous edifice with hefty, elaborate iron gates and red brick walls, well-preserved and sculpted lions roaring from atop plinths on its front lawn, and impressive colonnades all over the shop. One half-expected chandeliers in the classrooms and jellied candies on immaculate doilies at the Admin counter, trumpets and escutcheons in the hallways. Of course there weren't any such things, but there was a bunch of people in front of the parking lot gates holding up inexpertly magic-markered placards in the blustery but super clear air.

Oh-oh, I thought: something's brewing, and it's not beer.

Protesters? Protesters! Are they protesting *me*, I narcissistically wondered for a sec, the District's most sour, refractory—narcoleptic, even—sub? Had some previous school called to warn this new school that LAUSD's honorary imaginary Worst Attitude Award winner was on his unmerry way there? Were these picketers trying to bar my way? Physically? With calligraphically challenged signs, no less? This does not look promising, I remember thinking. Not at all.

But no: it's not me; it's not me at all! It's the teachers! A teachers strike! Now I'm a *scab!* And I didn't even know it! Great. Here I am, innocently or maybe partly innocently on my way just to do my job and do it, for once, with a little bit of enthusiasm, into-it-ness, and a somewhat better demeanor, and I'm crossing a goddam picket line! Fuck it. Fuck it out the window, as McLeary often said. Sub/scab? What's the difference? A vowel and a consonant, that's what, that's all.

One striking teacher (a tall fellow with a walrus sort of mustache that went out in, oh, 1970, or perhaps *1870*), gave me a profoundly filthy look as I emerged from my car and loped towards the building's entrance. Then I thought I heard a woman's voice utter an absolutely unfucking-printable series of astonishingly accurate expletives. This was ominous, dangerous, even. Maybe tomorrow, I reckoned, I'll park the old Volver blocks and blocks away and hop the fence somewhere—if I make it to tomorrow. The haphazard gauntlet they'd set up outside looked pretty severe, though. My immediate plan was to try to look as unteacherly as possible, which, as you know well by now, wasn't normally a problem for me. My hair was tousled like the leaves of a pineapple crushed by a speeding jeep, and I had a cigarette butt depending blue-collarly from my fully frowning mouth. I hadn't shaved or showered or had enough coffee yet to appear more with-it than your average lobotomized personage. Maybe they'll think I'm only one of the substitute *janitors*; maybe they'll think that. I don't think they thought that, though. Perhaps the fact that I yelled out "Hey, you guys? Is this the substitute teachers' parking lot?!" as I made it to the side door was a sort of dead giveaway. I don't know.

Impudent prankster.

(Of course I yelped no such thing: what do you take me for—a death-wish artist of the first water? I simply pushed through the door, smiling inside, but not very widely. And of course the fact that I had on a black cardie for the changing weather, sunny-crisp but colder, a regulation teacherly blue button-down Oxford, and Gap-issue baggy khakis, plus the Chuck Taylors and the Kurt Rambis glasses, not forgetting the well-thumbed copy of Boswell's *Life of Johnson* I brought to read during downtime, marked me out as nothing but a sub—maybe one who was just coming in from a nap in the gutter, but a sub just the same.)

The first person I encountered in the halls was a tall kid in an Alice Cooper t-shirt with a tequila sunrise-colored pair of trousers and a knock-wurstish sort of nose bonering from out his bowlish, black Ramones kind of hair-do.

"Hey there—would you be so kind as to tell me where the front office is, please?" I said.

"I'm lookin' for it myself," he said.

"Oh."

"It must be ovah dis way," he said as we went out another door and into a sort of lushish patio, past some towering jacarandas, their purple petals dandruffed all over the cement floor. "You a sub ta-day?"

The guy had the most monotone voice you've ever heard. East Coast sounding, sorta.

"Yeah, I am," I said.

"Me too."

Startled, I gave him a look like "What?!"

He just chuckled, very briefly. Sort of a one-breath kind of laugh.

"Yeah, I know. Ya thought I was a student. I'm an undercover school cop most the time—over at Gilmore June-yah, mostly. Don't tell anyone or I'll haveta kill ya. Just kidding. They called me in today to sub, though, on account of I have a credential and all that. Looks like we got ourselves a situation here today, huh?"

"No kidding," I said. "The teachers at the gate looked more vicious than any kid I've met yet."

"Fuckin' A," the undercover guy said.

"You don't look much older than sixteen!" I told him. "Twenty at the *most*."

"I got DGD as a child. Dorian Gray Disease, man," he said. "Ha! Some people stop growin'—I stopped *age-in*'. It's weird, all right."

"But how come you told me you were an undercover cop? Isn't that kind of not what an undercover cop is supposed to do?"

"Ah, I'm not an undercover cop," the guy said. "I've just been subbin' too long, is all. My imagination goes kinda . . . gets kinda outta control, you know? I make shit up. I got MSU disease too. Make Shit Up disease."

"Wow," I said. "You definitely had me going. How long have you subbed for, if you don't mind my asking?"

"Why should I mind? Thirteen years, man. Thirteen. This has *got* ta be last year I do dis shit, though. Got ta be."

"And when did you start to *lose* it? I'm not meaning to offend you: it's just . . ."

"Oh, no worries, man," the guy said. "It must've been around tree years into it, though. Either dat, or I've *always* been a lil' crazy."

He made an abrupt, very Jack Nicholson sort of face and I laughed.

"My advice?" he continued, deadpan as all get-out.

"Get out of it as fast as I can?"

"Bingo. Have a good day, man," he said banally. "Have fun while ya can. And *mucho suerte* getting' out of dis joint when da bell for whom da bell tolls tolls for *thee*, too, man."

"Thanks," I said, shaking my head at him and giving him my most understanding smile, even though he'd said "man" around thirteen hundred times and was probably higher than Jaz and me put together at our most baked. "You, too."

We went past this palm tree like a thistle in the sky and towards the most solid-looking and monstrously impressive building. I remembered someone saying something about Westmoreland being one of the most-used schools in Hollywood—for sets and all. Made sense.

The commotion at Administration was very Barnum & Bailey indeed but it didn't take too long for me to get a roll sheet and the classroom number and teacher's note. The bell had shrilled for first period. I caught a glimpse of my zany former interlocutor going in the opposite direction. He was *hopscotching* down the hall. What a way to start the day. I mean my own. But his too—why not? What a nut. What an utter nut. I hoped for his and for some kids' sakes that he wasn't meant to sub for Biology or Chemistry—classrooms where things might go *kaboom* and dramatically. When I found my class there was someone—a sweet-faced Asian woman in a billowing bright yellow dress—supervising, sitting at the teacher's desk and calling roll.

"Oh!" she said as I came in. "You must be the substitute?"

"I'm the substitute," I said and waved hello to the very bored-looking class. "Me substitute, you class," I said, holding up my hand like a Native American going "How!" God, did I do stupid stuff sometimes when I was nervous. The class gave me a look blank as any frat-boy's physics quiz. "You guys probably thought I was a new student, though, huh? Or someone who was wandering aimlessly around and thought 'Hey! I think I'll re-enroll in high school."

Two or three kids courtesy-laughed at that one.

"Oh, funny!" the Asian lady said, seemingly sincere. She pointed at the roll sheet to show me where she'd left off, asked me my name, and told the class not to give me too terribly hard a time, especially, she said, as I seem like such a quote-unquote nice gentleman, and witty too.

"Yes, Mrs. Hamamura," a couple of wise guys chanted in chorus.

Mrs. Hamamura gave them an affectionately remonstrating look as she swish-trundled out of the room.

"Okay, all right—Honors English!" I announced as I sat down and set my protection-specs down carefully on the teacher's desk. "Let's see who's here! Gonzalez?"

"Here."

"Hansen?"

"Present."

"Hernandez?"

No answer.

"Hernandez?" I quizzed again, and, looking up to see if someone was just raising his hand I saw out of the corner of my eye a kid in the very back sort of half-stand, then cant, motioning somewhat animatedly towards me, like he was demonstrating a hip new dance move of much aggressiveness, sort of; then I clocked a small green round projectile of some sort hurtling fuzzily and rapidly towards me.

Towards my eye, actually.

My left eye, to be exact.

Before I had time to put my hand up like a ping-pong paddle, duck beneath the desk, turn the proverbial other cheek, or think to myself "Think fast, you fool—a kid has just thrown a superball at you!," I saw the thing bounce once—then pain seared through me like a pipe-cleaner going down a greased drain, starting, of course, in the immediate locus of my eyeball, then shooting through what seemed every single nerve in my body. It was like razors. It was like scissors. Like the worst hangover ever descending on you Thor-like and instanter. The kind of lowdown dirty nasty sneaky relentless headache you might get if you went on a three-day bender with low-grade white tequila and no chasers of any kind.

Not of any kind.

*Shit fuck shit fuck piss fuck goddammit!* I thought.

"Shit fuck shit fuck piss fuck goddammit!" I said and loudly. I mean, the thing stung.

My self-control defenestrated. Underfuckingstandably! Straight out the window. Where else would it go? When you've just had a hard, cold, round, dense, presumably grimy from kids' hands, rubber object barked with über-velocity against one of your peepers? Duh. Dizzy, was I? Stunned and blinking? Crying? I could easily picture myself like one of those cartoon characters who's been bonked on the head with something *steel* or something and little pink stars and green moons start orbiting crazily above him.

"Fuck fuck fuck fuck fuck," I yammered. "Who *threw* that?! I want to know right now which one of you fucking fuckers fucking hucked that thing!"

With both hands making a sort of makeshift hand-patch, a kind of manual pirate patch, over the just-hit eye I looked around the room with the unpegged one. Why oh why had I taken off my specs just then?! What little devil'd made me do it? I took my hands away to see if I could see. I could, but super fuzzily. And I was still in abject agony.

"Whover, I mean 'Whoever,' did that—why'd you *do* that? " I shouted, staring at the hazy space in front of me and rubbing and rubbing my eyelid. "I didn't do anything to you, did I? No, I did not. I was going to be *completely* cool with you guys till the strike ended, okay? Cool completely. Seriously: why did you? God*damm*it! I mean, what *for?*"

A girl with a very porcine face (it seemed, though it could be that my vision was distorted and make faces seem House of Funnish or something) and thickly gelled hair above a too-big-for-her black mohair jumper pointed and said: "He did it, mister. Heem."

"Listen, Heem," I said in the general direction of where she indicated, "come up here right now! Are you the one who threw it?"

"No," one of three boys said softly.

"No?"

"No."

"No?"

"My name is not 'Heem,' mister," the one boy said.

"He totally threw it!" the girl who'd fingered him said. "I totally seen him!"

"'Saw' him," I said.

"Whatevers," the girl said.

"Not 'whatevers,' I said: 'whatever.' This is fucking *Honors* English?"

I got a nice respectably hearty laugh out of them on that one.

"What's your name, then?" I asked the kid. "Heem? It is Heem, isn't it? Heem, huh? Well, Heem, you have a hideous name and a hideous habit of throwing superballs into the eyes of harmless subs, don't you, Heem?"

If there's one thing you can count on it's that people—whether or not they are horrid little junior superball-throwers of much malicious devilry—don't like being called funny names that aren't their name.

"I dint throw it," the kid said.

"He's lying," a white girl said.

"I saw him!" another girl's voice urged. "His name is Miguel."

"Miguel?" I said.

"Yes," the kid said and looked away.

"How come you threw that? Tell me!"

"I don't know, mister," he said with a really pitiful intonation in his voice. "I sorry."

"It hurt—and it's 'I'm sorry,' okay?"

"Okay. I sorry. I dint mean to!"

"You dint mean to what?"

"Hitchu in the eye, mister."

I could tell he was really scared—you would be too—but I was still more pissed than he was frightened: bet you anything.

"What were you tryna do, then—peg me in the *balls* or something?" I said and the class exploded like a game show or comedy gig audience on high sucrose.

"Pinche cabron chingaso burro!" I added and they all just rocked with mirth.

The poor kid just looked away and gave out a sort of sob, ducking, you might say, the barrage of Spanish profanity I'd just lobbed at him. My Spanish is pretty good, actually. Well, my cuss-Spanish, anyway. My eye wasn't throbbing so so badly now, though I could tell it was going to look like someone had grafted a blackened cantaloupe onto my cheekbone. Regaining a touch of composure and trying to have a modicum of a sense of humor about the whole thing I said: "Well, anyway, Miguel—good shot."

There was some residual tittering.

"You *diablo!*" I said after it had abated.

There was a fire-bright red and heavily thumb-and-fingerprinted telephone on the wall—for Emergencies only. Almost every classroom in the greater LA Unified School District has them (except in the most vandalized areas of the city). I picked up the receiver and got Administration and in a ferociously calm voice told the woman on the other end of the line what had happened.

"We'll send someone right down," the woman said.

Twenty minutes later, almost at the end of the period, a Birkenstock-issue, be-bearded and ursine sort of fellow in a plaid button-down and Sansabelt pants turned up with one of the school police, a whey-faced runt who looked like someone'd stuffed an overstuffed armchair down the back of his police pants. They took Miguel outside and indicated I was to follow and asked me if I cared to press criminal charges against the student Miguel Hernandez and I was all: "For what—assault with a deadly *ball?*"

In my most banally urbane voice.

You could tell the counselor was trying not to laugh but the cop got even more serious and said it was up to me, that I could file a report and everything and press charges.

"Forget it," I said. "But I want to see a goddam doctor right away, goddammit—if I can see one, if you know what I mean."

"Okay-okay," the counselor concurred and then the school cop took the kid away and the counselor ushered me over to the school nurse's office.

## wear your love like heaven

The school nurse, as far as I could tell, was this total and complete fox, a really sexy woman who didn't appear to be much older than me, with vast brown eyes and gingery hair and a sexy smile. Boy, was she pretty.

She couldn't see me right away so I stayed in the little waiting area and listened to that song that goes "Wear your love like, wear your love like, wear your love like heaven," by some groovy sixties artist I couldn't remember but that was maddeningly familiar: the kind of song you'll wake up at four in the morning going "Donovan!" or something. I was kind of getting in a bit of a wax on account of my eye was starting to smart and twitch and blink and water and stuff again—plus the fact that I couldn't see the pretty nurse so very well, of course.

Ineluctable bird-dog.

But I could see when she said hello and bid me take a seat that she had really nice legs—simply spectacular. You would've noticed them too. Even if you were a non-lesbian *chick*. Even if you were the kind of chick (I hope you aren't) who gives other chicks absolutely no credit looks-wise whatsoever. You know: the kind of super hypercritical, uptight, dried-up, bitter hater who looks at someone like someone straight out of the Victoria's Secret catalogue and goes: "I think her nose is kinda *pointy*" or "I bet she *smells* bad" or "Everyone thinks she's just so pretty, but *I* don't—I don't *at all*."

As if that settles it.

Anyway, and such a pretty face on her, this nurse. Just wow. You couldn't help but remark how lovely a woman she was. I bet kids were Cary Grant-ing headaches, stomachaches, cramps, and major head-wounds all the time just to get a gander at her, I'm telling you.

The nurse came back after a couple of more soft songs on the radio came over and, after I told her what happened, held one of those brown and red rubbery pointy doctor lights up to my eye and told me to look up, look down, look left, look right. Then she said I could put my glasses back on which I had in my hand.

"I think it's going to be all right, as far as I can see. I'm going to get you an ice pack."

"Thank you," I said. "I thought for a second there you said 'icepick."

"Ha!" she laughed. "I'm going to be right back, okay? And I wonder if now would be an all-right-time to ask you if you wouldn't mind making a report to our Principal directly? He likes to keep in the loop on these sorts of things—mishaps and accidents and, um, unruly behavior, you know—as often as humanly possible. Even at a good school like Westmoreland we have . . . well, I'll just say *in*cidents, more than you can imagine."

"I'd certainly like to make a report to a doctor," I said. "I'm trying not to freak out here."

"Of course," she breathed. "I'm in the midst of making arrangements for that. I'll just be a moment, okay?"

She put down the clipboard she'd had going and went out of the waiting area and came back with this bright blue ice-thingy and had me hold it to my eye. Then she went away again and when she came back she told me she'd made an appointment for me to go downtown to USC Medical; there was an ophthalmology lab there and she said I could see an eye specialist right away, as soon as I could get there. She reassured me that there would be no damage, permanently or internally, as far as she could tell, to my eye. If I could manage to drive there, they would see me straightaway.

"But please," she went on, "please won't you, just before you go, go in to the principal's office and talk to him for five or so minutes? I've just been on the phone to him—they're going to sign you out and give him your blue card and your full hours for the day: you can pick up your card in his office, all right? Of course, what with the strike and everything, he's dealing with a lot right now, but if you would be so kind as to . . ."

"You're sure I am okay to drive?" I said. "I mean, I hope I can see okay enough to make it there. I don't mind having full vision and everything when I'm driving, you know."

"I'm sure you'll drive just fine," she noted with a restrained, it seemed, sort of smile.

"Don't you think I should just go straight over to SC?"

"It won't take half a minute," she said. "You can take the ice pack with you."

"But honestly . . ."

"Please?"

"Oh, all right," I said.

I don't know if you've noticed but it's kind of hard to turn down a request, almost any request, from a very handsome woman. She could have asked me to run a marathon backwards, wash and wax her car with a fabric sample, pick up her dry-cleaning, and bounce a fresh superball into my okay eye right then and I'd have considered it. That's how stupid I get in the face(s) of girls like that. Boy, am I stupid. Most guys are as well. Did it ever occur to you that the word "infatuated" has the same root as "fatuous"? So when you're infatuated with someone, what you're really saying is, "You make me *stupid*; you turn me into a bona fide *id*iot, you do." It's a real compliment, I'm telling you.

She pointed me down the corridor, with its chiaroscuro tiles and glittering auburn wood walls and flaming red fluorescent lamp lights, and I thanked her and she wished me luck.

As she was on around nine lines at once, the lights on her phone blinking like strobe lights, the principal's secretary semaphored me in one-handedly and sort of grimaced a wan, sorry smile; his door was open, the principal's. I had the pack over my eye still; I must've looked pretty funny but my eye was starting to pulsate a bit again and my vision was prisming too. I went in and sat down without being asked to; the principal had his back to me; he was on the phone. When he turned round and stuck out his hand I could just make out that he had very dark blue close-set eyes and a tanner-than-tan tan; a great suit and a mile-wide smile.

"Well," he said, "that was some welcome to Westmoreland. Nice to meet you—but not of course under the present circumstances—the strike included."

He shook my hand like he was trying to pull it off. His voice was hoarse as hell: I imagine he'd been, as principal during an angry, bitter strike, getting it from all angles: politicians, newspaper people, bloody TV people, the teachers' union, the teachers themselves, the thirteen or fourteen quote-unquote concerned parents in all of LA, the safety people, other administrators, the lay busybodies in the community who watched the local news, the kids in their excited-for-some-kind-of-dramatic-confrontation state—everybody.

"Thanks, I guess," I said. "Everything's a blur in more ways than one right now. I told the school policeman what happened so if I could just go ahead and go downtown to . . ."

"Of course, of course," the Principal said as his phone set up its rail once more, "Why don't you go ahead and tell me what happened, though, son? Damn this darn laryngitis I've got going—worst time to get a bad cold. Hold on."

He put the caller on hold and I took my cue to start in on all that had happened. He nodded along to my every sentence and when I finished the last of what I had to say he told me this: "That's awful—and I mean that. My profoundest apologies, really. The individual you indicated we've had numerous problems with undoubtedly—despite the fact of his

Honor Student status and what-all. Let's have a look at your eye if you don't mind my asking you to let that ice pack down for a sec."

I showed him and he said "Oh!" to himself "Here!" to me and gave me my blue District card with my time slip filled out for the full day.

"Looks quite red, yep. Pretty red. Let me see. I've been apprised we've made some arrangements for you to hobble on down to USC," he said and gave me a fulsome smile that flashed around an hundred and seven teeth, quite white; so bright, in fact, that I had to shield my good eye, practically. I closed both; opened them again as the telephone ratcheted afresh and joltingly loudly.

I had a sort of madeleine-in-the-teacup moment as I started thinking this: this guy looks *really* familiar: those eyes; those teeth; that tan; that voice that I can just barely remember and, paradoxically, could never forget; that *word: individual.* My God: don't I *know* this guy? Don't I know him? Wasn't he a baseball coach at my prep school, St. Caul? Wasn't he? Wasn't he *my* baseball coach oh it must be twelve or thirteen years now ago. This is too unreal.

"I'm Jack Krunsch, by the way," he said, freaking me out even more by taking a pair of Ray-Bans out from his drawer and drifting towards me to pump my hand encore. "Terribly rude of me not to have introduced myself at the outset here, but of course I hope you'll forgive me, given the circumstances—which previously have been alluded to before. Nice to meet you."

"Nice to meet you as well," I said incredulously but my voice was like someone trying while choking on a piece of cactus to finish a Proustian sentence they'd got near the end of (but couldn't for the life of them let go of, as it were). This was the guy who'd tortured me and everybody else he could find lying around. This was none other than Coach Krunsch—yes, *that* Coach Krunsch, the one you've heard so much about.

(Reader, are you sitting down? You're not reading standing up like some medieval monk in a fucking scriptorium, are you? Good. The reason I ask is because I suppose now is methinks a good time to tell you that—*voilà—I* am Junior! Junior's me! That anecdotal alter ego guy—that was yours untruly all along.

But you already reckoned that, huh? You already had that sorted, didn't you? Pages ago, you did. Good, reader. Good job reading.

Big revelation.)

Any old way, here's what happened next: Principal Krunsch (the very thought of it!) kept saying my name over and over, around twenty-seven times at least and then opined that he could easily be mistaken but he thought that he thought he knew someone, a certain individual, by that name when he was for a short time an instructor at a sunny prep school by the sea.

"No kidding," I said.

"You wouldn't have attended a Catholic prep school by the beach up central California way, by any chance?" he said.

Squinting away at him I gave him a look like (or so I surmised) "Are you completely out of your mind?" and he got my drift and apologized and said it was his mistake but he couldn't help but think I looked a bit like, he obsequiously-unctuously said, this terrifically courageous kid who pitched for him when he used to coach baseball.

"Huh," I said. "Well, Coach, I think I ought to get going."

"Of course, of course," he nodded as the telephone of course sounded once more (he'd been ignoring it). "Shelley said the arrangements are all made and you can waltz right in to the eye ward."

I gave him, gratis, another, more blank look this time.

"The school nurse you just saw," he said.

Shelley! Oh my stars—the foxy sophomore! That was *her*? Wow. Whose long brown legs had haunted me so? No wonder she'd looked so familiar somehow. Blown away wasn't the phrase for it.

"Just a moment, John," he said and picked up the fire-alarming telephone: "Yes? . . . Yes, he's right here . . . Oh? . . . He did? . . . Thank you, Ms. Hamamura . . . That's what the students said? . . . Okay, I'll investigate it. Certainly . . . Thank you, Ms. Hamamura . . ."

Then, in a sort of slow slow motion, he hung up the phone: "Well, there's a bit of a problem here, son."

"Oh?"

"Quite a problem. The Miguel Hernandez individual in question appears to have alleged that during the incident, again alleged, you used profanity—profuse profanity, I might add, notwithstanding its status as foreign language speech and whatnot—in handling the situation aforesaid. It's been, the profanity cussing, corroborated by some of the other individuals in the class as well and, well . . ."

Gulp.

"I'm sorry to have to tell you this but I am sorry to have to inform you that a letter is going to have to be written into your file , that's going in your file, rather, re: the extreme use by you of profane language in handling the situation with your eyeball having allegedly had a superball thrown into it."

"Allegedly, a superball?"

"Well, the supposed superball has not, in fact, materialized, I've been informed here now."

"Supposed?!"

"I'm just concerned that the letter may have some repercussions as to your status authority wise currently as a substitute in the District. Serious repercussions. That sort of language and behavior, despite its bespeaking your bilingual abilities and all of that, is grounds for dismissal, son. Termination, perhaps. It might be considered a legit form of child abuse, sorry to say. We'll have to query the Miguel anent whether he or his parents or guardian are now—I know it sounds kind of bad—going to press charges against the school, with you of course being an employee of us, or maybe firee, depending how your hearing, if they give you one, that is (they don't always do) goes."

"You are fucking *kid*ding me," I said.

"Now, see, right there . . ."

"The kid threw a superball right into my eye, Mr. Principal," I scoff-moaned. "Come *on*, man."

"I'm sorry."

I just stood there cyclopsly staring at him.

Unflappable bureaucrat.

"Hmm," I mmm'ed at last.

"Is that all you have to say? Nothing to say in your defense, son?"

"No," I said. "Write up whatever you want."

"Now, listen here . . ."

"I might write a little letter of my own, actually, Coach," I countered, though I could scarcely believe what I was about to say. "I might have to inform the District about a certain coach I had who, speaking of child abuse, not only repeatedly humiliated a bunch of underage ballplayers, but was also sleeping with a fifteen-year-old sophomore while he was a teacher at a certain central seaside California prep school!"

"JUNIOR?!" he thinly yelped and affably laughed, "Is that *you?!* I *thought* that was you! Hell! How the hell haveya been, buddy? Good to see you! You were quite the fireballer, if I recall correctly, and I do—an excellent ballplayer, you were."

"Is that how you remember it? I seem to recall one game when . . ."

"Sure, sure, son! Of course that's how I remember you: you threw a helluva coupla good games back then. A *hell*uva coupla."

"And some good times too, huh, Coach?"

"Why of course, of course. Good times indeedly. Now, you scurry on over to USC, all right? We wouldn't want you to miss the appointment Miss . . . Shelley the school nurse has . . ."

"And I take it," I said like a snooty personage choosing from among different types of caviar, "that you won't be putting any sort of letters in any sort of file that is mine, that is?"

"No letter. All clear. Take care. Watch yourself with the strikers out there, all right?"

"Thanks, Coach," I said and just-audibly laughed it all off. My eye was even starting to feel normal.

Shelley was coming out of her office as I reached the double-doors that opened towards the teachers' parking lot.

"Hey!" I said.

"Oh, hi," said she. "How did it go?"

"Does he still drive a red Porsche?"

She gave me a real puzzled look.

"Krunsch," I added. "*Coach* Krunsch."

"Oh my God! I thought you looked familiar! You used to go by . . ."

"Junior."

"Oh my God! How are you—other than blinded, partially?"

You had to admit she was pretty funny.

"Fine. Good. I have an indie rock band. I just do this in order to . . . Aw, how boring. Listen: I used to have such a crush on you, you know."

I don't think I, at this point, gave a flying what I said to anyone at all.

"Really?"

"Absolutely. You're not still going out with . . ."

Golly did she ever goggle at me then.

"You're not still with . . ." I lamely rephrased it.

"Jack? How'd you know we . . .?"

"The whole school knew—basically."

She made a sort of scrunchy face, but she wasn't too distressed, it seemed. Changing tack, she asked: "Hey, if you had such a big crush on me then, why didn't you ever ask me out on a date? How come you never asked me?"

"How *come?*" I said, more than astonished.

"Yeah."

"You were dating a *teacher*, Shelley! And furthermore, you had to have been the most intimidatingly beautiful girl in a school *filled* with intimidatingly beautiful girls. Plus . . ."

"You should've asked anyway," she sort of giggled. "I'd've gone."

"What?!" I said, then joked: "This is the worst day of my life!"

She chuckled at that one and so did I; you've gotta admit she was pretty cool.

"Well," she said, "it was nice seeing you again. You really ought to get going and have them check you out, okay? And don't catch any more superballs in the eye, all right?"

"Sure," I said.

"Stop by if you sub here again, okay?"

"I get the feeling I'm not going to be doing much subbing for a while," I said.

"I wouldn't blame you," she said and held out a delicate, care-taking hand. "Take care of yourself, Junior."

## rock the casbah

The Clash was all the rage still on the radio but I turned the song off as I drove through the gates where the striking teachers were still milling around. I don't know what possessed me but as I made it to the street I rolled down the passenger's side window of the Volvo and told one guy—a guy with a droopy, Ilie Nastase kind of mustache who seemed to be in a singularly bad mood—that I'd just come from Krunsch's office and that he'd expressly instructed me to say that he'd like to see ALL STRIKING TEACHERS IN HIS OFFICE AS SOON AS POSSIBLE!

"What?!" a woman standing next to him whose placard read "Edcation for the Children" (no, I didn't make that up) said.

"That's what he said," I shrugged and she shouted "Who *are* you?" and I yelled "Joe—Joe Strummer!" as I motored away.

In the rearview mirror I could see her mouthing "JoJo Stammer?"; then I saw a group of protestors sort of get into a scrum/huddle; then I clocked them starting towards Administration, leaning forward, looking anxious, looking angry.

*

After the doctor—an intern waif of Indian or Burmese extraction with big black bags under her dour, doleful eyes—confirmed that there was indeed no internal damage to my eye, I called Jenny at work from a payphone on campus and told her what happened. She reminded me we had rehearsal that night, and of course asked me a thousand times if I was all right, going to be all right, etc.; then, as it was very hard for her to talk at work, she said she'd better hang up, but that we could go have dinner together before rehearsal and "Oh, one more thing: Nastasha called me this morning to apologize for being so harsh. She told me she was really sorry she lost it like that."

"Unbelievable," I said. "So: you don't have to move out, then?"

"Well," Jenny said, "she didn't mention anything like that."

"Oh."

"She did say we were all set for the gig this weekend and that—oh, yeah, I can't believe I didn't tell you this right away—the college radio station at USC has been playing our tape!"

"You're kidding!"

"Seriously! Her brother—Tad—is a DJ there and well as you know he's the one who set up the show for us and he said they have been getting a few calls about it already. The gig's this carnival or something and they want us to come by the station for an interview before we play."

"That's terrific!" I said. "Great."

"And also Natasha said that Tad said someone from a label called when our song was on to ask who we were."

"You're kidding me now, for sure!" I said. "It was probably Psycho or Sterling pranking."

"Nope. It was some guy called Chalet, they said."

"*Bob* Chalet?" I said. "There's a guy called Bob Chalet who does A&R at Independent Records, I think."

"Bob or Rob or Todd—I don't know. One of those. You know I don't pay attention to all of that. Label stuff. Signed or dropped? Signed or dropped? It's all so silly to me somehow. But that *is* pretty cool, isn't it? Listen, darling: I really need to get off the line now—my boss is any minute going to be giving me looks. Go home and get some sleep, okay?"

"Okay," I said. "I love you."

"Oh, I love you too, John," she said really quietly and hung up. "Bye-bye now."

"Bye-bye."

I made it home and as I came through the door the telephone trilled and I thought it might be Jen calling to see if I made it home okay (even though I felt fine now) or to tell me she was going to have to work late and would just meet me at Walter's for practice.

Nope. Sterling.

"Juan!" he hailed. "Or should I say *Don* Juan! Haha!"

Oh, Jesus.

I quickly shifted the subject and told him what had happened at school.

"That is so awesome," he said.

I asked him what he had been doing, aside from making constant trouble as a full-time trouble-maker, and he said "Heroin" in his most matter-of-fact voice. He was always joshing about using heroin—a drug I just knew he'd never tried and never would. I knew why he did it: it was funny, first of all, and it made his amphetamine intake look not so bad. I told him about the Jenny sitch and how she was going to have to move and what a bitch Nastasha was and of course he sided with me as always and he suggested maybe that he and Jenny could get a place together and I said "I think not!" and then he got a bit miffed and told me "I'll *step* on you!" (this classic Scather line he had) and he laughed but I didn't, that's for sure, 'cause I knew well the sort of impish mischief he could quite easily get up to at the drop of a hat.

He could easily end up, as a funny-to-him sort of joke, telling Jenny everything Sarah-Who-Hated-Me had ostensibly told him about our, um, encounter. He had no compunction about stuff like that. The weird thing was, in the most sincerely sincere way, he could listen to you for hours on end about some emotional/relationship problem you were having and give you the most comforting advice. He could pull the proverbial rug out from under your feet, all right, but then he'd wrap you up in it like it was the softest downy down comforter.

Unalleviated weird-o.

I proceeded to tell him about the gig at SC on Saturday and how much I'd have loved it if he were drumming instead of Walter. That seemed to placate him for a bit. Sterling was the sort of person who loved, as I might have mentioned, to be needed—even more than Psycho and the way *he* loved being consulted. It was just like Sterling to get off on getting loads of attention for *not* doing anything with his immense artistic talent: people were always coming up to him at Finyl Vinyl and elsewhere in order to go "Oh my *God*, Sterling—you're so *talented*, you're *such* a good songwriter, your voice is so *beautiful*, *you* have such a *gift* . . . why don't you get *out there* again?! It would just be so a*maz*ing if you made another *record* and still gigged and we could come *see* you, Sterling. *Please* do music again, Sterling, please, please, *please!*" He loved that shit. He got swarmed and lovebombed more by having quote-unquote retired early than if he'd kept at it like the rest of us and kept on doing little gigs and getting reviews from guys who printed fanzines at Kinko's and distributed them out of their parents' basements and stuff. It made him laugh to think he was more popular for quitting than if he got to open for the Rolling Fucking Stones, it really did amuse the hell out of him. It was just like with the speed thing: you always got the sense that he thrived more on having a reputation for being a big old speedfreak than he actually enjoyed being high as heck. I mean, he couldn't possibly have taken the amount of drugs he'd implied he had; all the models, rock stars, club owners, cops, and strippers in Hollywood couldn't have taken them.

"Listen, Sterling," I have to get ready for rehearsal tonight. See you Saturday at the university, then?"

"With bells on!" he said and hung up.

The phone went once more.

"Juan!"

"Hey."

"I'll bring Sarah!"

"Oh, God!"

"Hahaha!" he bellowed and hung up once again.

# OUTRO

## let me take you down

The quad at USC had all kinds of colorful booths and tents set up in it, and the largest stage I'd ever seen up close, the stacks of speakers towering thirty feet at least. Roadies and grips and lighting and sound guys scurried around the stanchions, plugging in generators and patching cables, securing lights to scaffolding and shouting things to each other in he-man and she-lady. The main sound man—this guy Jean-Michel with a mass of jouncing dreadlocks and an attitude big as the U-Hauls lined up behind the scarlet-and-gold band huts—was barking away at one of the stagehands. Walter and Rob were up on stage, soundchecking the back line, getting it together, four hours to go till the show, and McLeary was standing by the Jean-Michel guy, helping out on the soundboard, waiting for Rob and Walt to get their sounds right and balanced so that he could then EQ the drums and get the bass amp good and low and clear and rumbling and gutsy as soon as possible. It was ten in the morning and we were about to soundcheck for a show that, it was said by the excited promoters we met at every corner, it seemed, going to be attended by more than a thousand people. We were meant to be on at two, do a forty-five minute set; I had time to be a nervous wreck, if I wanted to.

It was a big gig. A bigger big gig than the big gig I'd imagined it to be.

On a patch of grass right near the dark bronze immemorial statue of Tommy Trojan, Jenny and I were tuning our guitars and having complimentary coffee. The odd collegiate jogger locomoted by, and there were co-eds on rollerblades gliding down the cement parts of the walkways. Beautiful flowerbeds whorled with red and yellow flowers, the school's colors, and hillocks of long, sparkly, sun-swathed lawn flowed up to buildings of undeniable beauty and inspiring majesty and there were foaming fountains in the distance that might have jumped straight out of any painting by Canaletto. Couples in baggy khakis sauntered around, looking very Returning Alumni while food service workers ran around and guys in little white utility vehicles got stuff ready and rigged things up. I kept pushing out of my mind the thought that Sterling was going to make good on his threat to bring Sarah. A guy—I knew he had to be an SC student on account of the fact that he had a backpack boiling over with books, plus an SC cap on backwards—came right up to Jenny and me and asked if we were one of the bands and Jen politely told him yeah. Then he asked what kind of stuff we did, and Jenny said it was heavy metal mariachi in a jazz sort of style, and he laughed and I laughed and she said she was kidding and that it was indie rock a bit like the Cure and the Beatles too, and the guy said "Cool!" and that he'd come and check out our set, man, after he did a couple of hours in the library, and we said "Cool" back to him and he split. But what I could really twig from the little encounter was that the guy was checking Jenny out, and who could blame him? Then it crossed my mind that the David was probably going to be there for the gig, though I hadn't asked Jen about it since the phone call—it would've been gauche and a totally insecure move on my part and besides, who was I to get all huffy-jealous when I'd done what I'd done with Sarah and everything was still sitting like a sumo on my conscience—a sumo who'd just had his second lunch.

Then I got distracted musing over lyrics to the song we were meant to open up with, a faster number called "Your Mary Janes" on which Jenny and I dueted all the way through; I was also thinking about how crazy it was going to be to be playing a gig that was only our second gig in front of a thousand people, nine hundred and eighty or so of whom were fully unacquainted with our music.

Scary, dude.

"Were you actually conversing with that person?" The familiar voice of the Scather rocked me out of my worrisome reveries and I looked up to see him standing there, smiling broadly.

"Sterling!" Jenny said.

"Chiquita *muy* bonita!" he said and sort of picked her up from where she was sitting stretching out the strings on her Telecaster and he gave her a big fat kiss on the lips and she squealed and he got down on his knees and started serenading her and then he got up again and kissed her once more even more ostentatiously on the cheek like Italians or people in musicals do; then he theatrically grabbed her butt, playfully but not in any sort of threateningly sexual way or anything (Sterling often did that to the women in his nontourage—we were all of us used to it), and all three of us laughed. I was really happy to see him; we needed all the support of course we could get. I was super chuffed, moreover, to see him flying solo: no Sarah.

And you know why.

Sterling was quizzing Jenny about the whole gossipy, incredible eviction thing when Tad, Nastasha's brother the DJ, ambled up all friendly and smiley and introduced himself and asked us if we needed anything. Then he said if we were all cool he'd take us over to KRAD, the college radio station that broadcast all the way to the dorms (he laughed), for the interview and lunch buffet.

Awesome!

McLeary and Jean-Michel were ready for us on stage now so we grabbed our guitars and chords and effects pedals (the ones that'd survived McLeary's berserkers) and went up the little side-stage stairs and plugged in and got sounds and levels. We ran through half a song till Jean-Michel stopped us and told us to turn down, down, down—the stage volume of both guitars amps was too much. I could tell McLeary didn't like that—you know he liked it, us, loud, loud, loud, but it was the dreadlocked guy's gig and what can you do? We did part of another song—a keyboard one—and everything seemed all right up there, vocals clear, and the rhythm section well audible and I risked asking Jean-Michel for a little more volume in Jen's vocal mike mix and he freaked.

"I'll just turn down the drums, then," Walter quote-unquote quipped and got no laugh whatsoever.

"We'll be fine," Rob said.

We pushed our stuff to the back of the stage and Tad came up and asked us if we were all set.

"For what?" Walter asked.

"The interview," Tad said. "Natasha didn't tell you?"

"I totally forgot!" Walter said. "I gotta go pick her up right now. Drag. She doesn't drive, you know."

Up came Sterling just then and he told us the soundcheck sounded good and he said hello to Rob and Walt and Walt said, sort of in a voice

I had not heard before, that Sterling could go and do the interview.

I couldn't tell whether or not he was being sarcastic. Poor Walt.

Oh, what did it matter?

"Sterling?" I said.

"I'll go with you guys [and here he nodded Walt's way], but I'm not doing the interview—no thanks. I was supposed to wait by the sound board for Sarah but . . . she'll be okay, I guess. Maybe McLeary can entertain her."

"Who's Sarah?" Jenny said.

*

At the radio station they had set up some mikes and headphones in the control room; they played two cuts from our tape and asked us all the stupid questions bands get asked on college radio; then they played another song of ours and we signed some of the posters the student activities people had made for the show. There wasn't any lunch buffet.

"No lunch buffet?" Rob said.

He was really into lunch buffets. The funny thing was he said it on the air. It was like a motif of his. In fact he answered "lunch buffet" to a couple of the questions about our influences and our plans for the record and what he'd thought about working with a semi-quasi-famous indie rock producer like McLeary.

"So," the on-air DJ said as he wrapped up the interview, "what are you guys thinking of calling this new LP?"

"*Lunch Buffet!*" Jenny joked.

"Yeah," Rob said. "*Lunch Buffet* was what *I* was thinking it was going to be called all along!"

*

Back at the quad there were scores of people starting to gather, eating shish kabobs (I bought Rob two) and hamburgers from paper plates, drinking beers or lemonades, and having sno-cones or cotton candy. On stage the first band had revved up, a drum-circle sort of outfit of be-bearded burnouts and a chick dancer with a sort of *I Dream of Jeannie* get-up prancing all around. Just awful. Jenny and I got some food and bevvies and found a shady/grassy spot pretty away from the stage and the band, and as we were eating I saw Psycho walking along with Claudia,

Jaz's lawyer friend, and two girls I didn't recognize. Then Nicholson, a scientist friend of Psycho's who wanted to but couldn't make the Halloween gig, came over with some of his buds. Then Walter and Nastasha and two other couples—friends of theirs. Then Jaz. Then Sterling and, yes, Sarah. Then McLeary and Rob.

Everyone. It was like a symphony of supporters—the end of the piece where everything comes together for a mad crescendo, a big payoff. Except of course for the fact that one of the notes, as it were, was, um, maieutic.

Apropos of that, reader, can you imagine how anxious it made me to see Sarah standing next to Jenny now. And can you imagine my roiling emotions roiling even more so when Jen, around ten minutes later, went tripping-bouncing over to a tall blonde guy who sauntered up and she hugged him so hard with a big fat hug I thought *I* would expire from it.

The David.

Who else?

Instead of waiting around to be introduced to Jen's former lover, her beau/stud of yore, I slipped away and went to the SC bookstore. I figured I'd hightail it straight to the self-help section, do some research on my possible future as a broken person, browse around till it was time for the Weird Sisters to go on.

*

At fifteen to two I went back to where the stage was. Now there were hundreds and hundreds of people in front of it, grooving along to the band right before us, something called Dick and the Fucks. They had just ended their last song and were just starting to fuck their equipment off the stage for us to get up there. We got all our stuff in place, and the guitars retuned, and riffed a bit and Walter smacked the drums to check the sound and I went "One, two, three, four!" and we started playing!

Unfortunately, however, I was playing one song and Jenny was of course playing it too but Walt and Rob were on a completely different song altogether.

Fuck!

One of the cardinal rules of rock is that you never ever stop playing in the middle of a song once you've started it—no matter what—and we didn't. What miraculously happened was, after all the cacophony of the mis-start that somehow we made even more of an off-key clamor out of it and the crowd thought it was intentional, like an *avant garde* sort of overture or something, and we landed on the first bar of the right first song ("Your Mary Janes," like I told you), and unreally the sound must've sounded even cooler to the punters 'cause they set up quite a roar and started cheering and woo-wooing like anything. Maybe we were being mocked, I thought for a second, but after the applause died down I realized the clapping was respectful and eager somehow and we were not sucking, not in the slightest, and we certainly weren't being made gross fun of. We made it through (with all four of us starting and stopping on the same beat!) six more songs and then McLeary's lilting voice came through the monitors to inform us that we had one more song to go before our set was up and even though it wasn't on the set list I shouted "'The King of Good Intentions'"—this two-chord drone that ended pretty frenziedly and that would be good, I now realized, to cap the set off with on account of it sounded like an encore but really wasn't. (One of the *other* cardinal rules of rock is "Always leave them wanting more"; I mean, so many bands, you see them rushing like soldiers going over the top in the Great War to get back on stage and do an encore when there's, like, three people clapping and two of them are kinda clapping 'cause the sucky band's sucky set is fucking *over*. Bands are desperate like that—they really are.)

The words to the song were, basically, pretty basic:

*I am the king of good intentions.*
*I am the king of good intentions.*
*I am the king of good intentions.*
*I am the king of good intentions.*

I sang them over and over, emphasizing a different word in each line, with varying intensity, till the drone got faster and faster and we broke into this jam that vamped and vamped until it sounded like a 747 taking off backwards. Very stadium rock—early Pink Floyd, you might say. Spacey and entrancing if it worked—overblown and self-indulgent if it didn't.

You can guess which option we were hoping for.

Somehow the song worked, I guess, 'cause people clapped and clapped as we hit the last note and waved ourselves off stage. Maybe they were applauding be*cause* we were exiting the stage! But no. Never fear. There were, I could see, too many happy faces for that to be the case. Psycho, for instance. Somehow he'd managed to get back stage; he had, I noticed, his infamous video camera; he was clumping me exuberantly on the back.

"Buddy!" he said. "That was *rad*ical! I got it all on video!"

"Brilliant!" I said. "Thank you!"

"I loved it! Everyone did!"

"That's fantastic."

"I will get you the footage . . ."

"At your convenience?"

"Precisely," he said and smiled his psycho smile.

Sterling and Sarah were talking to Jenny and some other people, I noticed as I put down my guitar. Jaz and Claudia were there, in conference with Nastasha and McLeary who was smiling so widely and proudly that I was more than touched. I helped Rob and Walt get the rest of our gear off stage and just as I put down the last amp this guy with wild, curly hair and John Lennonish National Health glasses and a toothy sort of smile came up and sycophantically shook my hand and said:

"Bob—Bob Chalet. Are you John? I loved your stuff, man."

"Thank you," I said, trying to be all cool (and failing, for sure).

"Do you think I could get a copy of your tape—I know you have one 'cause I heard it a couple of times on the radio here? I'm leaving Independent and starting a label of my own, man—really exciting. It's gonna be called Playing Records—get it? And I am wondering if you guys . . ."

I have to admit that I didn't really hear the rest of the stuff Bob Chalet was spewing 'cause I was alarmed rather to see, over my left shoulder, Jenny gabbing animatedly with Sarah-Who-Hated-Me. Or rather, and potentially even more perilous, Sarah jawing away like mad with a furious, fucked look on her face.

Before I could go over and maybe intercede, the David character, all teeth, approached and stuck out his hand in a "Hi, I just thought I would formally introduce myself before I proceed to try without sneaking around or anything to get my old girlfriend back and thus in the process unfortunately for you taking away from you your current girlfriend, thank you very much!" sort of way. At least that's how I perceived it. Without even saying "Excuse me one moment" or "Just a second, chum" or "Later, guy," I extricated myself from the situation and, almost taking the David's hand with me, started towards Sarah and Jenny just as Sarah was taking herself off somewhere, quickly. The next band, a very loud group with many horns, launched into their first song just then, an appalling cover of "Strawberry Fields Forever." "Let me take you down!" the band's bad singer was quote-unquote singing. "Let me take you *down!*"

How ironic is that? I thought as swam through the backstage throng and made it over to Jen.

"*Jenny, I . . .*" I started to say to her sad, beautiful face, but then the horrid band on stage crescendoed again and my words blurred in the clear, cacophonous air.

# ACKNOWLEDGMENTS

The author would like to thank Steve Connell for his unparalleled editorial affability; Bill, Mark, and Chandler Fredrick for their inimitable senses of humor and unflagging support; Steven Schayer, my brilliant friend and band mate, for doing the lovely cover drawing; Kesha Rose, Rachel Gutek and Luann Williams for things too many to enumerate here.

CPSIA information can be obtained at www.ICGtesting.com
Printed in the USA
LVOW120206100413

328247LV00001B/1/P